The Mine

The Mine

Northwest Passage Series

Book One

JOHN A. HELDT

ISBN-13: 9781731142412

Edited by Aaron Yost and Amy Heldt

Cover art by Podium Publishing

Novels by John A. Heldt:

Northwest Passage Series: The Mine, The Journey, The Show, The Fire, The Mirror. American Journey Series: September Sky, Mercer Street, Indiana Belle, Class of '59, Hannah's Moon. Carson Chronicles Series: River Rising, The Memory Tree, Indian Paintbrush.

Follow John A. Heldt at johnheldt.blogspot.com

To Cheryl

CONTENTS

CONTENTS (CONT.)

ACKNOWLEDGMENTS

A novel, like many worthwhile pursuits, is a team project, and this work is no exception. Many thanks go to Cheryl Heldt, Jon Johnson, and Diana Zimmerman for proofing the manuscript in its formative stages; to Amy Heldt for enriching the final draft in countless ways; and to Aaron Yost for providing the critical eye of a professional editor. I am also grateful to Podium Publishing for producing *The Mine's* creative cover and to several organizations for providing research assistance, including the Army Historical Foundation, Clatsop County Historical Society, National Park Service, Oregon Historical Society, Seattle Public Library, Selective Service System, and Washington State Library.

1: JOEL

Helena, Montana – Monday, May 29, 2000

Joel eyed the remains and laughed at the animal that had caused the carnage. The carnivore had done damage, serious damage, to the thing that covered most of his plate. But even serious damage was not a mortal blow – not to a 24-ounce porterhouse. They would have to leave it behind. Doggie bags didn't cut it on ten-hour drives home.

"I told you to ask our waitress," Joel said. "This is Montana. Things are big here – and different. They probably have a steer in the kitchen."

"I believe it," Adam said, staring at his steak with eyes smaller than his stomach. "It says on the menu they serve only free-range beef."

"There you go."

Joel stirred his iced tea. He had played it safe with a pasty, a meat-and-potato pie popular with Welsh and Cornish immigrants who had worked in Montana's hard-rock mines in the early 1900s. If it was good enough for them – and the flirtatious redheaded waitress who had recommended it – then it was good enough for Joel Smith. He liked trying new things, which is why he had overruled his fast-food-loving best friend in favor of a restaurant listed among the state's must-do culinary experiences.

The Canary's décor stood out as well. The diner was an eclectic shrine to every era since the Roaring Twenties. The thirty-foot bar, with its Formica countertop, glass-block trim, steel cabinets, floor-mounted stools, and black-and-white checkered floor, gave the joint a solid art-deco foundation. An antique brass cash register stood proudly beside a modern, functional cousin. Hardwood booths, upholstered in shiny red leather, lined the opposing wall and neatly framed everything from classic movie posters and college pennants to signed photographs of Harry Truman, Gary Cooper, and Evel Knievel.

Joel turned away from his half-finished lunch and watched a man put a nickel in an original Wurlitzer Peacock jukebox. The record player occupied prime real estate near the entrance, not far from the establishment's signature neon display. The Canary, the sign insisted, had served Montana's finest meals since 1925. The only conspicuous sops to the present were ceiling-mounted, 24-inch, flat-screen televisions at each end of the bar. Even fans of nostalgia needed ESPN.

"They don't make places like this anymore," Joel said.

"No. They don't," Adam said. "Maybe Marlon Brando will bring us dessert."

He took off his sunglasses and cleared a space around his plate.

"Damn, this is a big steak!"

"Quit bitching and eat," Joel said.

Joel glanced at the "Yellowstone" keychain next to his paper napkin. The embossed leather curio was one of several souvenirs he had purchased on the last-minute trip to Wyoming. Joel and Adam, college students from Seattle, had decided to clear their heads three weeks before graduation by hiking and biking America's oldest national park.

"Did you have fun this weekend?" Joel asked.

"You know I did," Adam said. "But next time, let's bring Rachel and Jana. We'll have more fun."

"I thought you and Rachel were done."

"We were – or at least I thought we were. She's been really nice to me lately. That's why I was reluctant to leave Seattle. I'm afraid this trip will be a momentum breaker."

"Get serious," Joel said. "A few days won't break anything."

"That's easy for you to say," Adam said.

"I'll tell you what. I'll say you stared down a grizzly or freed Bambi from barbed wire. She'll sleep with you all summer. Now finish up. I want to see more of Montana."

Joel silently conceded Adam's point. They would have had more fun with the girls. For that reason alone, Joel had considered inviting them. But he didn't want to send the wrong message. After dating Jana Lamoreaux off and on for two years, he wanted a break. Not that there was anything wrong with her. Hell no. Kind, funny, girl-next-door pretty, and bound for Stanford Law, Jana was as good as they got. But Joel didn't love her, at least not enough to make a serious commitment. She deserved honesty, if not someone better.

A different distraction snapped Joel back to the here and now. His twentyish waitress sauntered down the long bar, wiping messy spots en route with the grace of a dancer. She wore a pink pinstriped uniform and a spotted white apron. Neither did much to hide curves that could kill. She had topped off Joel's bottomless iced tea four times in thirty minutes and was now back for his plate. Once again, she appeared to be in no hurry.

"Will that be all today?" she asked.

"For me? Yes," Joel said. "For the velociraptor? Maybe not."

The waitress laughed and then smiled at Adam.

"Do you want a box for that?"

"No, thanks," Adam said with food in his mouth.

Joel handed the server a credit card. He noted the name "Sarah" on a tag pinned to her outfit and visually accompanied her to the register.

"I think she likes you. I'm pretty sure I saw some wink action," Joel said. He turned to face Adam. "It makes sense too. What woman wouldn't want a lean, mean, red-meat-eating machine who mumbles and grunts?"

"Shut the hell up, Smith. You picked this place, remember?"

"I'd come here again too. Now hurry up."

Joel watched a large family slide into the booth behind him and then glanced at the television screen above Adam's head. The TV was set to a cable news channel.

"Hey, check it out," Joel said as he pointed to the screen. "I read about this."

"Read about what?" Adam asked.

Joel started to answer but stopped when Sarah the waitress returned to Carnivore Central. When she gave him a credit-card receipt, he signed it, added a generous tip, and then offered the slip back to her.

"Here you go," Joel said.

Joel tightened his hold on the receipt when Sarah attempted to pull it from his fingers. Two smiles passed before he loosened his grip. Within seconds, the server's face turned the color of her curly, pony-tailed hair.

"Thanks," Sarah said. She gazed at Joel with playful green eyes. "You have a great day."

"You too," Joel said. He put his wallet in his pocket. "Say, uh, Sarah, before you go, can you turn up the sound on the TV? I'd like to hear this story."

"Sure," Sarah said. She grabbed a small remote from under the counter, adjusted the volume, and handed the device to Joel. "You can leave it here when you're done."

Sarah walked back to the register, glanced once more at the big tipper, and then directed her full attention to a heavy-set woman with questions about pies.

Joel increased the volume, eyed the screen, and listened to the news anchor.

"Astronomers are calling this the most significant planetary conjunction in almost sixty years. For twenty-four hours, beginning about noon Eastern Daylight Time, six planets from our solar system will fall into a rough alignment with the sun. Here's more on this from our science editor . . ."

Another family moved into a nearby booth, creating additional background noise. Joel picked up the remote and pressed the top audio button until he detected a hard stare from a burly, middle-aged man sitting at Adam's right. He pressed the bottom button.

"At that point, Mercury, Venus, Earth, Mars, Jupiter, and Saturn, in addition to our own moon, will be more or less positioned in a line with the sun."

The man, still glaring, got off his stool and walked toward the restroom.

"For millennia such alignments have spawned dire predictions of global calamities, but experts insist that the distance to the planets is too great for their gravity or magnetic fields to have a discernible effect on the Earth."

Joel hit the mute button and gently placed the remote on the counter. He watched a crowd form in the diner's tiny, gum-machine-lined lobby as Smiling Sarah, sans smile, barked an order to the cooks. The Canary's lunch rush was on.

"Come on," Joel said. "Let's go."

Adam did not respond. He instead continued his mission. Fork in hand, he hoisted the last piece of steak and studied it like a rare gem.

"Wow," Adam said with Ben Stein enthusiasm. "Six planets."

He finished his meal.

"I hope nothing weird happens today."

2: JOEL

Lewis and Clark County, Montana

Twenty minutes, seven stoplights, and ten miles after Adam Levy popped a half-dozen antacid tablets outside of the diner, Joel found open road. U.S. Route 12 spanned 2,483 miles from Aberdeen, Washington, to Detroit. For most Americans along that stretch, the highway was no more than an afterthought co-signed with Interstates 90 and 94. But for motorists in Helena, Montana, it was a big deal. It was the only way out of Dodge going east or west. Joel aimed his red 1998 Toyota RAV4 west, toward the Continental Divide, and repositioned his trim, six-foot frame in a bucket seat. On each side of the four-lane highway, flat fields of wheatgrass gave way to brown hills and green mountains. New homes stood between tracts of ponderosa pine.

"Put on some tunes," Joel said.

"What do you want?" Adam asked.

"I want *road* music. Pick something classic."

Adam opened a zippered fabric case, examined its contents, and pulled out a CD by R.E.M. He eased the CD into a slot in the dash, closed the case, and resumed staring at a wallet photo of a long-haired brunette.

In seconds, "It's the End of the World as We Know It (And I Feel Fine)" blared through six speakers and reminded Joel that he had failed to turn in his ten-page term paper on Jurassic ecosystems. But he didn't care. Even a severely docked grade wouldn't cost him his degree in geology. He reached across the console and turned up the volume.

"Good song," Joel said. "Well done, Jeeves!"

Joel shifted gears and accelerated. He loved driving his nimble sport utility vehicle, whether he was tearing up Forest Service roads, negotiating Seattle's freeway traffic, or passing annoyingly slow trucks, like the eighteen-wheeler that had drifted into his lane and was currently impeding his progress. He pointed to a sticker on the back of the rig.

"You see that, Adam? Our good buddy wants to know how he's driving. Call that number and tell him. Tell him I think he's having a bad clutch day."

"Joel?"

"Yeah?"

"Montana has a speed limit now. Ninety is no longer 'reasonable and prudent.'"

"It doesn't matter," Joel said as he peered into the distance. He tapped the brakes and looked at Adam. "There's construction ahead."

Joel slowed down when he saw a row of cones. He followed the truck into the right lane and rolled to a stop near a rural intersection, where a sweaty, expressionless woman held a stop sign. He turned off the ignition.

A minute later, a second road maintenance crewman, a husky gent wearing an orange hardhat, a matching vest, and a Grover Cleveland mustache, approached the Toyota. He reached the RAV4 just as Joel rolled down his window.

"It'll be about twenty minutes, guys," the crewman said. "You just missed the pilot car."

Adam slumped in his seat.

"No problem," Joel said.

Joel scanned his surroundings. To his left he saw a long gravel driveway that led to a ranch-style home nestled in a grove of pine trees. To his right he saw what a sign called Gold Mine Road, a paved local route that extended north into the hills. He spoke to the crewman just as he started toward the next car.

"Excuse me, sir," Joel said. Grover Cleveland turned his head. "Is there really a gold mine up there?"

"There is. But it's an abandoned mine. It went out of business a hundred years ago."

"I see. Can we drive around the construction on that road?"

"You can," the crewman said. "But unless you have an hour to kill and four tires to trash, you probably shouldn't. The road turns to crap a few miles up."

"Thanks."

Joel pondered his options as the man walked away. Then he turned on the ignition, shifted into first gear, and pulled out of what was now a quarter-mile-long line in the westbound lanes. He proceeded slowly along the highway's paved shoulder to the intersection and turned right.

"What are you doing?" Adam asked.

Joel smiled.

"I'm putting spice in your life."

3: JOEL AND ADAM

The crewman hadn't sugarcoated a thing. Gold Mine Road became Minefield Lane barely five miles from the highway. The pavement turned to gravel and dirt, shoulders disappeared, and ripples, rocks, and potholes showed up with increasing regularity. Spacious houses dotted the landscape every few hundred yards.

"Now *this* is something," Joel said. He laughed. "It's not every day you see million-dollar houses on a hundred-dollar road."

He slowed down to make a close inspection of a massive log mansion to his right. A well-manicured lawn ringed the two-story structure and three outbuildings. In the distance, a freight train, loaded with coal, sluggishly worked its way northwestward.

Joel started to pick up the pace until he noticed a fork in the road. The main route continued at right and displayed no signs of attitude improvement. The smaller, rougher goat trail at left veered westward and upward into a narrow gulch. When he reached the fork, Joel hit the brakes and brought his SUV to a stop. It was decision time.

"Thank you for that interesting tour of the outback," Adam said. "But I believe this is where we turn around and rejoin the wonderful world of asphalt."

For nearly a minute Joel stared blankly out the front window and lightly tapped the steering wheel. He turned down the volume of the car stereo.

"You're right," Joel said. He looked out the rear window and carefully adjusted his sun visor. "Hold on. There's not a lot of room here for a one-eighty."

As Joel maneuvered back and forth on the stretch's lone wide spot, at the junction of the roads, he noticed a small sign partially obscured by a bush. Weathered and worn, the three-foot guidepost practically begged for a fresh coat of enamel. Its four-letter message, however, was as crisp and clear as the day it had been painted. The sign read: MINE.

Joel smiled.

"No!" Adam protested.

"It'll just take a minute. We've come this far. Why not check it out?"

"I want to be in Seattle before the next millennium, that's why."

"Fifteen minutes," Joel said. "That's all I ask. Come on. Mines are geologic laboratories. Where's your intellectual curiosity?"

Adam slammed his fist against the door.

"It's back at the Canary, with my sunglasses. Damn it! Those glasses cost a hundred bucks. This day keeps getting better," Adam said. He lowered his head for a moment and then turned to face the driver. "OK. You have fifteen minutes – not a second more. I want to go back for the shades."

* * * * *

The drive to the mine itself took fifteen minutes. Joel left his Mario Andretti side behind and apparently took the crewman's words to heart. He navigated the twisty, rocky, mile-long road like a cruise ship captain sailing through a narrow, shoal-riddled strait.

Adam couldn't believe he had allowed himself to be talked into even leaving the highway. They had a long drive home. They didn't have time for a field trip. Yet here they were, driving up a mountain road in God Knows Where, Montana.

Joel had often talked Adam into things he didn't want to do. It had been that way since the two had raided Tina Torricelli's summer slumber party in the seventh grade. Adam didn't think any less of his friend because of his reckless nature. Like most who knew Joel Smith, he genuinely liked and admired the free spirit.

There was, frankly, a lot to like and admire. Intelligent, charismatic, athletic, and handsome, with thick, dark-brown hair, chiseled features, and a boyish grin that drew frequent comparisons to Tom Cruise and Keanu Reeves, Joel stood out in every crowd. He had an encyclopedic mind, the curiosity of an inventor, and the judgment and discipline of a three-year-old. He frequently coaxed friends into behaving in ways that would make their mothers blush and occasionally had fun at their expense. But he was also unsparingly generous with his time and money, whether helping someone solve a serious problem, picking up tabs, or hiring strippers for those extra-special birthdays.

Joel was predictably popular with the ladies. Though Jana Lamoreaux had cornered the market for two years, she was hardly the only one to shower him with attention. Adam knew damn well that the waitress in Helena had had her eyes on Joel – *wink action, my ass* – but he enjoyed playing along. That was part of the fun of running in Joel's pack. Life was a game to Mr. Smith, and he didn't care if others won.

18

Adam was less enthusiastic about Joel's latest adventure. He wanted to retrieve his sunglasses and hurry home, where the resplendent Rachel Jakubowski hopefully awaited. A thorough examination of Montana's gold-mining past could wait for another day – like, say, one in 2050.

Joel, however, had a different agenda. When the two friends finally reached the mine, he parked the SUV and quickly jumped out. He had found his toy for the day, and no one was going to take it away.

4: ADAM

The goat trail had widened into a relatively flat, peanut-shaped clearing about half the size of a football field. Junipers and Douglas firs formed a protective barrier on three sides. Numerous tire ruts marked much of the open space, suggesting that the property had enjoyed a second life as a parking lot for outdoorsmen.

On the far side, three badly weathered wooden buildings and a boarded black hole defaced what topographical maps called Colter Mountain. The tallest building, an enclosed, silo-like structure, rose eighty feet and leaned five precarious degrees off its vertical axis. Gravity and the elements had rendered it a bowling pin for the next earthquake.

High above, the spring sun shined brightly. Absent most of the day, it grudgingly emerged from cotton-ball clouds to provide modest warmth. Adam could not believe that any place in the lower forty-eight states could be this cool on the cusp of summer. He stepped out of the car, walked past the Tower of Pisa to a large boulder near the entrance of the mine, and watched his friend make full use of his boy brain.

Joel got right to work. Rechargeable flashlight in hand, he climbed a short incline to the main attraction, stopping only to remove a prickly weed that clung to his jeans. When he arrived, he ran his fingers along thick gray beams that framed the entrance, paused for a moment, and frowned, as if realizing that breaching the mine might involve more thought and effort than a chip shot from a bunker. A patchwork of unpainted boards and posts covered ninety-five percent of the opening.

Adam knew it was only a matter of time before Joel attempted to reduce that percentage, so he put his hands behind his head, reclined on the boulder, and settled in for the long haul. He had seen this sort of thing before.

"Joel?"

"Yeah?"

"I have a question."

"Shoot," Joel said.

"How is your English progressing?"

"What?"

"Well, I was just wondering what part of KEEP OUT and NO TRESPASSING and DANGER you don't understand."

Joel let go of a loose board and looked back at Adam. He smiled, formed a pistol with his right hand, pointed it at his questioner, and fired with his thumb.

"Good one. I'll be sure to write that down," Joel said. He returned to the board. "I think I can work this free. Why don't you give me a hand?"

"No, thanks. I'd rather watch you get splinters," Adam said. He sat up. "Come on, Joel. It's been more than fifteen minutes. Let's go. We still have to go back to the diner."

"We will. I promise. But first I want to check this out."

Joel stepped away from the entrance, scanned his surroundings, and then started down the path. He appeared defeated, not inspired.

"Finally!" Adam muttered to himself.

But before Adam could lift his sore butt off the boulder, Joel picked up a chunk of limestone the size of a cantaloupe and marched back up the hill. Twice he dropped the rock, barely missing his light-duty hiking boots. Twice he wiped debris from his hands, picked up the object, and continued his ascent. When he reached the top, he put the chunk on the ground and brushed himself off. He turned toward Adam and grinned.

"You didn't think I was going to give up that easily, did you?"

Joel hoisted the rock high above his head and sent it crashing through the boards. He kicked and yanked the remaining wreckage from its moorings, tossed it aside, and stared at his creation: a two-foot gap that now allowed easy passage. Joel retrieved his flashlight, flicked the switch, and directed a beam into the abyss.

"Looks inviting to me!"

"It's a good thing Montana doesn't have laws against trespassing and vandalism," Adam said. "The sheriff might even give you points for persistence. Now, let's go."

"In a minute. I just want a look."

"What do you think you're going to find in there? Carmen Electra? Come on. I'm serious. We have a long drive."

Joel faced his friend. He held up his right hand and extended every finger.

"That's all I ask. Five minutes. I'm curious, OK? I've never been in a gold mine and want to take a peek."

Adam's hard stare crystallized.

"All right," Joel said. He glanced at his watch. "It's eleven twenty-five now. At eleven thirty we leave. Fair?"

21

Adam jumped off the boulder, held up his cell phone, and pointed to its screen.

"Eleven thirty."

"I promise," Joel said with a smile. "And look at the up side. If I find a gold nugget, the next hundred drinks are on me!"

Joel wiped the grimy lens of the flashlight with his grunge band sweatshirt, kicked a baseball-size rock away from the narrow opening, and adjusted his first impulse buy, a felt cattleman crease cowboy hat he had picked up in Butte. It was not a hard hat, but he did not seem to care. He entered the mine and disappeared.

5: JOEL

The dust hit Joel hard as he stepped into the adit. It was industrial strength, the kind that sent asthmatics like Adam on benders and made even the hardiest breathers pine for a respirator. It filled a facility that practically begged for an OSHA inspection.

The adit, a slightly elevated passage leading into the mine, was also dark. Pre-Edison dark. Stub-your-toe-in-the-middle-of-the-night-and-cuss-three-times dark.

Joel mentally saluted the poor souls who had once made a living crawling into this hole. He wondered how much gold had been pulled from the mountain.

The tunnel's first hundred yards revealed solid construction. Thick crossbeams and smaller wooden strips that ran along the walls and ceiling appeared sturdy, if predictably worn. Steel rails broke up a dirt floor and guided the way inward. To the right, a smaller, less-structured passage led to points unknown. Otherwise, the mine was remarkably unremarkable. The last people to move through this place did not leave souvenirs behind.

Joel pushed forward. With each step, he thought of gold and glory. But he also thought of the running clock, the drive home, and Adam's wraparound sunglasses. Had Smiling Sarah put them in a lost-and-found drawer? Would she demand a phone number for their ransom? Or were they now the property of the pimple-faced boy who had claimed Adam's barstool as the college students had exited the diner?

As Joel pressed deeper into the mine, he experienced the kind of solitude generally reserved for solo jogs, beach walks, and bike rides. It had probably been a very long time since anyone had wandered through the bowels of this mountain – maybe decades.

Yet Joel was not alone. Brown bats hung from the ceiling in clusters, while rats scurried across the floor like they had places to go and rodents to see. The mammals did not appear frightened or agitated but did seem eager to see the trespasser leave.

Joel was about to do just that when he saw a narrow passage on his left. He aimed his flashlight at the door-sized gap in the wall but found he did not need the light. A bright phosphorescent glow lit up the opening and much of the space beyond.

Joel knew that gypsum, calcite, and zircon, among other minerals, could emit light when exposed to ultraviolet radiation, but he had never seen or heard about anything like this. The blue light flickered wildly and covered nearly the entire cell, which measured roughly fifteen feet by forty. Only the back wall lacked significant illumination.

Driven by renewed curiosity, Joel entered the chamber. He ducked under a low beam, walked about twenty feet, and turned to face a particularly bright spot on the nearest wall. He placed a hand to the rock, half expecting his digits to burn on contact or pass through a membrane. They did neither. The hard, smooth surface was cool to the touch.

Joel examined the opposite wall and found the same. He could see no reason why a solid rock cavity, deep in a mountain, would put on the airs of a discotheque. What was this stuff? Sapphire? Uranium? Kryptonite? It had to be valuable. The mine was amazing.

I picked the wrong term paper topic.

He took a few tentative steps toward the darker rear of the room but saw nothing more of interest. The walls here were just as glossy and sheer but less illuminative.

A distinctive noise punctuated the silence. Joel froze. He had heard the sound before – on television, in movies, and at the zoo. But he had never heard it in the wild and certainly never in a place like this. He heard it again. Any doubt about its source disappeared.

He peered at the back wall and saw a poorly defined form move closer. Joel stepped back and lifted his flashlight. He stared at his cellmate. His cellmate stared back. Fat, brown, ugly, and four feet long, it appeared none too happy to share Studio 54 with a college senior. It was a *Crotalus viridis*, or badass prairie rattlesnake.

At first the snake appeared to give its human intruder a break. It retreated into a tight coil, hissed, and stuck out its tongue. Twice!

Joel got the hint and began to retreat. Even King Solomon's mine was not worth a trip to the hospital. Shining his light directly at the serpent, he took a few deliberate steps toward the main tunnel and freedom. With fifteen feet to go, his confidence grew. Then he backed squarely into a pie-shaped depression, lost his balance, and hit the floor. The flashlight broke free and rolled toward the reptile.

The snake darted out of its coil and slithered closer. Leaving the lamp behind, Joel shot up, turned around, and raced toward the exit. He saw a sliver of reflected light that had found its way into the primary passage. He did not see the low-hanging beam, which popped his forehead like a Louisville Slugger.

The impact triggered stars and ringing but strangely no pain. For a few seconds, Joel felt nearly euphoric. He lifted his head and smiled. Then flashes of blue yielded to waves of black as the ground came up to meet him.

6: JOEL

When Joel came to, the snake was gone. He checked for bite marks, saw none, and slowly rose from the gritty floor. His head hurt. His whole body hurt. But mostly his ego hurt. Wandering into this dark, dusty den of killer reptiles was not the smartest thing he had done in twenty-two years. Once again, Adam's judgment had trumped his own.

Then he remembered the room, the one glowing at his back. It was still there, still real, still enchanting. The questions about its astonishing features came flooding back.

Joel looked forward to explaining his discovery to Adam and others. Leaving his flashlight to the snake, he stepped into the main tunnel and walked as quickly as he could toward a dot of daylight two hundred yards away.

When he reached the mine's entrance, he noticed that the boards he had labored so mightily to remove were gone. The rails at his feet appeared slightly less worn, as did the beams overhead. He stepped into bright sunshine and took a breath of fresh air.

Joel embraced the day. Just getting into open space, free of crazy creatures and stifling particulates, improved his disposition. But as he slowly walked to the parking lot, his mood began to change.

Adam was gone. So was the car. And surroundings that seemed familiar to him minutes earlier suddenly seemed foreign. Three buildings still guarded the entrance but looked less weathered. The one Joel had deemed structurally unsafe appeared upright and sturdy, even inviting. Unbroken panes filled every window. No persons, places, or things occupied the clearing, save a badly rusted, tire-free Model A Ford with a half-dozen bullet holes on the passenger side door.

So Bonnie and Clyde liked mines.

Joel grabbed his cell phone and dialed Adam but got no ring. Where was he? Had he returned to Helena for the glasses? Joel looked at his watch.

Both hands pointed due north. Thirty minutes late. Not good. Still, Adam could have left a message.

Rather than sit and wait and get angry, Joel proceeded down the goat trail, which looked wider, flatter, and smoother than the one he had climbed in his SUV. Perhaps he could get a signal on Gold Mine Road or at least find someone who would let him borrow a landline telephone. Anything beat doing nothing.

Twenty-five minutes later, Joel arrived at an intersection that looked very little like the one that had prompted his day-changing side trip. The mine sign was there but not the bush that had obscured it. Gold Mine Road was not Minefield Lane but rather a well-groomed, unpaved route that one might find in a national park. Trees that had formed a grove at the junction of the roads seemed smaller and less imposing.

But most alarming was the crystal-clear status of the log-and-stone estate that had once stood less than a football field away. It was gone.

There were no mansions, no outbuildings, and no impressive lawns. Not even a mailbox or driveway to hint at human habitation. What was once the most impressive property in greater Helena, Montana, was now a relatively flat field of bunch grass, half-buried boulders, and maturing junipers.

Joel tried again to reach Adam. No ring. No bars. No luck. He turned south, toward Old Sol, and started down Gold Mine Road with the hope he would find Highway 12 and not the Twilight Zone.

7: JOEL

Gold Mine Road did more than make a lasting second impression. It began to resemble a reasonably fine wine, improving as it progressed. Rocky dirt turned to less rocky dirt and then to mixed dirt and gravel. There was ample room for vehicles to pass.

Joel spotted three houses on the north, or mountainous, side of the road but none he had seen before. They were modest cabins, not full-sized homes and certainly not the ostentatious digs from earlier in the day. Nothing on this stretch of road looked familiar. He approached each of the simple wooden structures but found all devoid of life. Only one, in fact, showed signs of recent occupation. On a freshly painted picnic table behind the third cabin, an empty soda bottle shared space with a half-eaten sandwich.

The man without a plan continued his journey down the rural route. But with each step, he thought less about finding a way out of his unsettling predicament than about finding a satisfyingly creative way to strangle Adam Levy. They had a lot to discuss.

Twenty minutes later he heard and then saw a southbound vehicle work its way toward him. It traveled fast – Joel Smith fast – and kicked up a fair amount of dust and debris as it rounded a corner and entered a straight quarter-mile stretch at Joel's back. Within seconds it veered from the center of the road to the far right and slowed to a stop.

Joel stepped onto the wide grassy shoulder of the northbound lane and turned to face the shiny black car – a mint-condition Depression-era coupe – and the first person he had seen since leaving the mine. A well-dressed middle-aged man rolled down his window and stuck out his head and left arm.

"Need a ride?" he asked.

"I do."

"Where are you headed?"

"Helena," Joel said. *If it still exists.*

The man swung his arm upward and tapped twice on the top of his automobile.

"Well, get on in," he said. "I'm going there now."

Joel walked tentatively around the front of the car, never taking his eyes off the driver. When he reached the passenger side, he paused for a few seconds, glanced at the seemingly endless road ahead, and opened the door. The man looked at him curiously, like a souvenir in a gift shop, and then directed his attention forward. He shifted into gear and stepped on the pedal.

"I'm Sam, by the way. Sam Stewart."

"Joel Smith."

The two shook hands.

"Make yourself comfortable."

Joel did just that. He settled into a polished leather bench seat, extended his legs, and cracked his window an inch before giving the car a more thorough inspection. It was at once old and new, an early 1940s Buick that looked and smelled like it had just come off a showroom floor. Joel looked for obvious signs of restoration but found none. Even the horn-ringed steering wheel and Damascened chrome panel, with driver-side gauges and a glove box-mounted clock, screamed original equipment.

The driver, too, was something of a throwback. Fortyish, with a gentle face, short sandy hair, and a medium build, he wore a crisp white dress shirt, gray slacks, and brown wing-tip shoes. He was Bing Crosby on the Road to Helena. A gray flannel jacket and a matching brimmed felt hat rested in the middle of the front seat. *Is that a fedora?* The man appeared fidgety after a minute of silence.

"Not from around here, are you?"

"No. I'm on my way back to Seattle from Yellowstone. I came with a friend. We were checking out that old mine, but now I can't seem to find him. I think he drove my car to Helena to get some sunglasses."

"Hmmm. Some friend. That mine's been abandoned for years, and most of the folks with cabins won't show for another week. I came out only to look in on my place. We've had some break-ins lately. You're lucky I saw you."

"Yeah. Lucky."

"What kind of car was your friend driving?"

"A RAV4. Bright red. Toyota. You couldn't possibly miss it."

"A red what?"

"Toyota."

"Never heard of it. I sell Buicks myself."

"So this is . . ."

"Brand spanking new. Bought it just last week. You like it? I wanted to wait for the forty-twos this fall, but the little lady insisted on buying now. You know how that is," Sam said with a wink.

Joel took a deep breath and resumed staring out the front window.

Forty-twos?

Sam tapped the brakes as he approached a major intersection. He turned east but not onto Highway 12. U.S. Route 10 North now served Helena.

The speed limit was fifty miles per hour. In a field to the south, a billboard that had once touted George W. Bush for president now pushed a rural electric cooperative. But road signs were small potatoes compared to the landscape. Barren fields had replaced the homes and businesses lining the highway. No road crews regulated the approach to the pass and every vehicle that drove by in the westbound lane bore a striking resemblance to those manufactured in the twenties and thirties.

Joel closed his eyes and leaned back in his seat. This had to be a dream, or a bad interaction between his meat pie and iced tea. There had to be a plausible explanation. So Joel Smith, man of science, reviewed the data. Adam was AWOL, whole buildings had disappeared, and a crooner was driving him to yesteryear in a brand-new antique. What could possibly be wrong with that?

Sam adjusted an air vent and glanced at Joel, whose face had become pasty white.

"Are you all right?"

"My stomach's a little queasy, that's all," Joel said. "I'll be fine."

If this is a prank, Adam, this is choice.

"I assume you know where we're headed."

Joel perked up. He had all but tuned out his new acquaintance.

"I'm sorry. I need to get to the Canary. Do you know where that is?"

"I sure do. I eat lunch there at least twice a week."

8: JOEL

Helena, Montana

The drive through Helena proper did nothing to help Joel's stomach. The Gilded Age mansions he had passed on the way out were still there. So were the parks. But the fast food restaurants, convenience stores, and modern stoplights had taken a powder.

Joel observed people on the street. They too provided no comfort. Men in suits and hats walked beside women in dresses and hats – hats with brims and nets and flowers, not logos of grunge bands or baseball teams or even tractor manufacturers. Central Casting could not have outfitted the city any better. Only two young men, standing on a street corner in work shirts and dungarees, looked remotely contemporary.

Sam, thankfully, kept any questions he had to himself. He did not ask about Joel's Candy in Chains sweatshirt or why a tourist from Seattle was investigating an abandoned mine far off the beaten path. He limited his comments to observations about the weather and the impact of the economy on new car sales.

He turned onto Main Street, or Last Chance Gulch, as it was signed a few hours earlier, and pulled into a metered parking space in front of the Canary. The diner, tucked between a bar and a smoke shop in a three-story granite building that occupied half a block, did not have a neon sign. Nor did it boast a flashy red awning. But it was the same place and appeared just as busy as the one that had provided Joel his last meal.

Joel opened the door and stepped out of the Buick.

"Thanks for the ride."

"Any time," Sam said.

He pulled away from the curb, slowed down long enough to watch Joel's next move through his passenger-side mirror, and then drove out of sight.

Joel gracefully dodged two preschool-aged boys running down the sidewalk and entered the Canary for the second time that day. The interior looked much the same. The jukebox and not-so-antique cash register assumed their usual places and the bar, stools, and booths appeared completely unchanged. No televisions hung from the ceiling, of course, and a Frowning Frida had replaced Smiling Sarah. The thirtyish waitress warmed up as she approached the new customer.

"Will it just be one today?"

"Actually, I'm looking for a friend." Joel removed his hat. "He's my age, a little shorter, with curly black hair, and wearing a Red Sox jersey. He left his sunglasses here this morning. Have you seen him?"

"Can't say I have, hon. But it's been busy. Let me ask Esther. She's working the other tables."

Frida flipped the top sheet of her order pad and walked through an open door into the restaurant's kitchen. The sound and smell of sizzling beef filled the lobby.

Joel again took stock of the diner. More than thirty people filled the joint, occupying most of its booths and stools. Business conversations dominated, though the party closest to him, two women dressed for a Bible study, buzzed endlessly about a neighbor girl who had "gotten into trouble." Joel thought about Marty McFly, the likelihood that this was all a nightmare, and turning that rattlesnake into sushi.

Frida rushed out of the kitchen, dividing her attention between the customer who wanted information and a customer who probably wanted a hamburger. She approached the one with the dimples and shook her head.

"No one has seen him," Frida said. "And we'd remember if we had. Almost all of our patrons are regulars. Sorry."

"No problem. Thanks for checking it out."

Joel stepped aside as an elderly couple opened the bell-rigged door and walked to the register. He couldn't imagine the last time this place had needed a jingle to alert staff to new business.

At the far end of the bar, a tall man sporting a Stetson and a bolo tie put a newspaper and two dollars between an empty plate and a coffee cup. He grabbed his jacket and walked briskly toward the exit.

Joel looked at the newspaper and groaned. He had procrastinated long enough. He walked slowly to the unoccupied stool, braced himself for the inevitable, and picked up the paper. The headlines and the old-style layout on the front page fanned his fears before the date at the top confirmed them. It was May 29, 1941.

He put down the paper, nodded to Frida as he worked his way down the counter, and excused himself through a throng that filled the lobby. One of the church ladies gawked at him, turned away, and quietly asked her friend about Candy in Chains.

Be glad I left Barenaked Ladies at home.

On his way out, Joel stopped by gumball row, wondered how often the diner had filled the machines in fifty-nine years, and held the front door for a weary mother pushing an unusually large carriage. She smiled, said thanks, and plowed her way in.

Joel stood in the middle of the sidewalk and stared blankly at a grocery store across the street. It advertised bread for eight cents a loaf and milk for thirty-four cents a gallon. A pickup truck honked as it passed, snapping him out of his daze. He peered down the street in both directions and decided to head south, toward the downtown core. He entered his strange new world with angst, disbelief, and wonder.

9: JOEL

Thursday, May 29, 1941

The monetary crisis of 1941 hit hard and fast. Ten minutes after leaving the Canary, Joel discovered that stores on Main Street did not accept credit cards. They did not exist in prewar America. Two Sacagawea dollars clinking in his pocket were similarly useless, as was a checking account opened in 1996.

Joel *did* have two late eighties Washington quarters that depicted the same mug as those minted in the thirties and forties. He hoped to use them at a place that wasn't fussy about dates or keen on reporting counterfeiters to local authorities.

Joel paid particular attention to clothing stores. He wanted to replace his distracting attire with something more suitable. Elderly shoppers passing his way glared and shook their heads. Young women looked at him, too, though their stares were softer and longer. The time traveler found it nearly impossible to blend in.

As he wandered through the city, Joel noticed how little it had changed. Except for a pedestrian mall on the south end of Last Chance Gulch, Helena of 1941 looked a lot like Helena of 2000. Unlike other upstart communities, it had not rushed to replace bricks and mortar with concrete and steel. Romanesque office buildings and Victorian homes blended nicely with a Gothic cathedral and Moorish Revival civic center.

Under different circumstances, Joel might have taken some time to check them out. But he had more pressing matters to attend to, like solving his cash crisis, finding shelter, and figuring out how he had traveled fifty-nine years in less than fifty-nine minutes.

The mine was the obvious answer. Before Joel had wandered into the dusty pit and its supernatural wonder room, he could make sense of his situation. He had cell phone coverage, plastic accepted in two hundred countries, and reason to believe he would spend his salad days in the twenty-first century. Now he faced uncertainty.

Joel vowed to find his way back to 2000 as soon as he found money. He needed cash for cab fare, if nothing else. He doubted he could hitch a ride to the mine and wasn't particularly enthusiastic about walking several miles along rural roads.

He pulled out his wallet and gave it a final inspection. No tightly folded bills clung to his expired ski pass, student ID, or driver's license. His Ken Griffey Jr. rookie card, buried beneath two layers of leather, might be worth a lot some day but not this day.

Joel put the billfold away and walked to a small park next to a grade school, where a recess was under way. He sat at a poorly painted picnic table and observed the students, who were in full recreation mode. He tried to remember the last time he had swung on monkey bars, jumped through a rope, or ridden a merry-go-round.

Joel watched closely as two brawny boys escorted a porky peer to an isolated spot near a chain-link fence that divided the school property from the park. He sat up when the boys tried to extort lunch money from their classmate.

"Hey, you two," Joel shouted. "Leave him alone, or I'll beat the crap out of you!"

The bullies glanced at Joel, looked at each other, and opted to take his advice. They left their target with his nickels and dimes. The two walked toward a large brick building, along with dozens of other students, when a loud bell sounded.

The fat boy did the same but not before acknowledging a random act of kindness. He walked up to the fence, mouthed a "thank you" to Joel, and slowly left the scene.

No problem, kid.

Joel smiled, plopped on top of the picnic table, and stretched out like he was testing a mattress. He closed his eyes and tried to grasp the insanity of it all.

* * * * *

When Joel awoke, he stared at his watch and realized two things. The first was that he had slept three hours – too long to return to the mine that day. The second was that he had the means to finance his hopefully short stay in the past.

He jumped off the table, scanned the neighborhood, and walked toward a residence two doors down, where a lean, muscular young man with tattooed arms sat in a driveway littered with motorcycle parts. Joel approached him cautiously.

Attired in a grease-stained undershirt, patched blue jeans, and steel-toe boots, the man scowled at Joel like a southerner greeting a carpetbagger. He softened a bit as the visitor stepped onto the driveway.

"I like your shirt," Muscles said. "You get kicked out of school or something?"

"No," Joel replied with a nervous laugh. "But I can always try."

Muscles smirked and returned to his work, allowing Joel to relax. Whatever the price of interrupting this guy, it wouldn't be a wrench in the eye or a mandatory gang initiation.

Joel started to ask a question but stopped when he took a closer look at the man's late 1930s motorcycle. The streamlined bike had large skirted fenders and an engine that appeared to be inverted by design.

"Is that an Indian?" Joel asked.

"It ain't a Schwinn, Chief," Muscles replied. He glanced at his questioner. "What's the matter? Never seen a Four?"

"Oh, I have. I saw one last year," Joel said. *I saw it at the Smithsonian.* "I've never seen one with the motor upside down though."

"Pretty wild, isn't it? It's the only one in town," Muscles said. He grinned. "My ladies love it. It turns them to butter."

Joel shuddered as he pictured the biker turning his ladies to butter. He could conjure up at least a thousand more pleasing images.

He began to state his business but held up when Muscles caught his finger on a spoke and swore. Once again, Joel saw a DO NOT DISTURB sign on the man's face.

A moment later, Muscles sifted through the parts around him, dropped his head, and muttered more obscenities. He jumped to his feet and stepped toward his garage. When he retrieved a small shiny cylinder that had rolled up against the door, he sighed.

"There you are," Muscles said. "I thought I'd lost you."

The man returned to his station, wiped a brow, and attached the missing part. Smiling again, he picked up a wrench and tightened another loose end. He looked at Joel.

"So what can I do for you, Mr. Candy in Chains?"

Joel checked the vicinity for eavesdroppers and then slowly returned to Muscles.

"You can point me in the right direction," Joel said. "I need to unload some goods."

10: JOEL

Rick's Racket was no sporting goods outlet – or at least not the kind Joel had patronized in Seattle. The secondary store offered sportsmen nothing more than shoddy baseball mitts, bamboo fishing rods, and badly strung tennis rackets.

That was OK. Joel didn't want a tennis racket. He wanted cash. He needed only a few seconds to see that Muscles had sent him to the right joint.

"You want to pawn a watch? Then that's the place to go."

Joel had wasted little time acting on the tip. He had thanked his new friend for the information and headed directly to Rick's, located a dozen blocks north of his favorite diner in an edgy part of town. When he entered the shop, no one greeted him, save a three-foot-high lawn jockey standing on a display table just inside the door.

He walked along the perimeter of the store, passing shelves and glass cases filled with radios, guns, coins, musical instruments, and antiques. Six watches gleamed brightly in a small jewelry case near the cash register. None came close to matching the feature-rich dive watch strapped to his wrist.

Joel started to wonder if he was the only one in the store when he received his answer. He turned his head as he heard a gravelly voice.

"Can I help you?"

A stout, balding man of fifty emerged from a back room carrying a large cardboard box. He placed the box next to the register, removed a smoldering cigar from his mouth, and rested it on a stained metal tray.

"I'd like to sell a watch," Joel said.

"Let's see it," the man replied.

Joel unfastened his timepiece and handed it to the clerk, who was almost certainly the proprietor himself. He bore a strong resemblance to the man painted on a sign in front of the store. "Rick" pulled a pair of reading glasses from his shirt pocket, slipped them on, and gave the watch a thorough inspection.

"Looks expensive," Rick said. "What did you do? Bop someone on the head?"

Joel chuckled.

"No. It's mine. I got it for my birthday."

"So why do you want to sell it?" Rick asked.

Because I'm stuck in 1941, you dope, and hotels don't take baseball cards as payment.

"Well, truth is, I'm in a spot right now and need some cash."

Rick held the watch up to a bright overhead light and then put it next to his ear. A moment later, he returned it to Joel.

"I'll give you ten bucks."

"You're kidding," Joel said. "It's worth ten times that."

"Look, kid. That watch is hotter than two strippers on a griddle."

"But it's shock-resistant!"

"I don't care if it bakes a cake," Rick said. "Ten bucks."

Joel did the math. Even ten dollars in 1941 would probably buy a night in a hotel, a decent meal, and a cab ride. He handed over the watch.

"I like the name of your business," Joel said. "It fits."

Rick pulled two five-dollar bills from the cash register drawer and pushed them across the counter. He shook his head and picked up his stubby cigar.

"There you go," Rick said. "Now get out of here."

Joel did just that. He grabbed the bills, barreled out the front door, and made a beeline toward a budget hotel he had seen earlier in the day. The four-dollar rooms it had advertised were still four dollars and not subject to arbitrary pricing.

Later that night, he ate a ham sandwich and two apples he had purchased at a deli and crawled into a single bed that took up nearly half of his modestly appointed cell. He stared at the water-stained ceiling and once again tried to make sense of his predicament as X-rated sounds emanated from an adjacent room.

Joel thought about his family, Adam, and Jana and wondered if he would ever see them again. Part of him still clung to the possibility that this was all a dream. He liked the idea of waking up in a flophouse and finding four bars on his cell phone.

If it was not a dream, he would do what he had to do to set things right. He would take a taxi to the mine in the morning, find the fluorescent chamber, and try to travel forward in time the way he went back. It was a good plan, he thought. It was also his only plan. He went to sleep that night and dreamed of plans that worked.

11: JOEL

Friday, May 30, 1941

Joel slept until eleven. Despite the noise next door, a lumpy mattress, and two sirens in the middle of the night, he slept soundly. Helena may not have been as quiet as the country, but it was a vast improvement over Seattle's bustling university district.

He slipped on his hooded sweatshirt and jeans and walked to the hotel's front desk, where he asked for breakfast guidance. The clerk suggested a nearby greasy spoon that offered bacon, eggs, toast, and coffee for fifty cents.

Joel took the tip and his five spendable dollars and hit the streets. When he finished the surprisingly filling meal, he left three contemporary quarters near his plate, bolted out the door, and headed south along Main Street, where he found more flags on poles than shoppers on sidewalks.

The reason soon became clear. America celebrated Memorial Day on May 30 in 1941 and not the last Monday in May. Most stores and offices had closed.

Joel did, however, find a taxicab. Thirty minutes after leaving the restaurant, he spotted a yellow 1938 DeSoto parked in front of the Mother Lode, Helena's seven-story hotel to the stars. He opened the rear driver-side door and entered the vehicle.

A thin forty-something man in a leather jacket and a worn chauffeur cap lowered a newspaper. He looked over his shoulder at his new passenger.

"Where to, buddy?" the driver asked.

"That depends," Joel said. He pulled his liquid assets from a pocket. "Will four bucks get me to the abandoned mine off Gold Mine Road."

"Sure. But why go there? Are you running from your old lady?"

Joel liked this guy. He could keep up with Adam in a World Series of Wit.

"No," Joel said. "I just want to check the place out. I have nothing better to do today."

The cabbie smiled as he pulled away from the curb.

"All right, kid. I'll get you there."

12: JOEL

Lewis and Clark County, Montana

Joel's second trip out of Helena, Montana, went much faster than the first. With few lights, fewer cars, and no road construction to impede their progress, he and his hired hand reached Gold Mine Road in fifteen minutes. Pete, the full-time driver and part-time wit, grimaced as he turned off a freshly paved Highway 10 onto a dirt-and-gravel local route that put a little extra wear on his well-maintained work vehicle. He caught Joel's eyes in the rear-view mirror and gave him a look that said, "Do you really want to do this?"

Joel kept his thoughts to himself and stared out a side window at the scenery to the east. A freight train of at least eighty cars worked its way through tall grass and pine trees toward the mountains ahead. It appeared to slow with each passing minute.

"Where do trains go from here?" Joel asked.

"The eastbound go to Fargo, Saint Paul, and Chicago. I know because I used to operate switches in Billings," Pete said. He looked at Joel and then pointed a finger at a window. "But that one's headed to Missoula and Spokane – and from there to Portland or Seattle. Why do you ask?"

"Just curious."

Joel resumed watching the train's progress. A jaywalker went faster.

"Why does it move so slowly? There's nothing out here but acreage."

"The pass," Pete said. "The train has to get over Mullan Pass. It gets real curvy ahead and you don't go through that driving like Casey Jones."

Ten minutes later the DeSoto reached the peanut-shaped clearing and Colter Mine. Joel stepped out of the cab, stretched his legs, and quickly scanned the site.

The place looked exactly as he had left it. No boards covered the entrance, the buildings appeared undisturbed, and Bonnie and Clyde had not retrieved their Ford.

Joel walked back to the taxi and handed Pete four one-dollar bills.

"Here you go. Thanks for the ride."

"You want me to hang around a few minutes? It's a long way to town."

Joel pondered the offer but rejected it. Pete had a living to make and it would be unfair to keep him waiting. The trip through the mine might take some time, particularly without a flashlight. The significance of that blunder had hit Joel on the drive up.

"No. Go ahead and take off. I'll be a while. But thanks anyway."

"OK," the driver said. "It's your call. Have a barrel of fun, kid."

Pete performed a U-turn, glanced at his customer as he passed through the lot, and then found the goat trail. A cloud of dust followed the DeSoto down the mountain.

Joel walked to the mine entrance and peered into the adit. He cleared a sheet of cobwebs and noticed that local electricians had not installed halogen lights in his absence. But the sunlight that spilled through the opening penetrated at least fifty yards, and Joel knew he could follow the rails, if necessary, to reach his destination. He also knew how far he had to go. That would be important if he had to crawl his way there.

His primary concern was bumping into that badass rattler's forebears. Snakes belonged on jagged rocks in Arizona, not unlighted gold mines in Montana.

Joel wiped a few sticky strands from his arm and brushed dirt off his shirt. He longed for clean clothes. But mostly he longed for something familiar.

He looked back toward the sun. It burned as brightly as before, albeit from a different position in the sky. It was a bit later in the day – maybe one o'clock – but still comfortably warm. The tops of nearby trees swayed under the pressure of a gentle breeze.

Joel smiled as he thought of Adam's whiny protests.

You were right, buddy. I should have listened. But have I got a story for you.

He entered the mine and said goodbye to the Fabulous Forties.

13: JOEL

Joel had no difficulty navigating the first hundred yards. Aided by sunlight, he easily reached the side passage and a fractured beam that marked the halfway point to Studio 54. He tried to better gauge his progress by counting each tentative step. But it wasn't long before increasing darkness left him wistful for a flashlight.

When it became difficult to advance even a few feet without tripping, he drifted to the left side of the main tunnel and maintained steady contact with the uneven dirt wall. He knew the next opening would lead to the illuminated chamber and hopefully his portal to the future. The wall became his anchor.

Joel nonetheless remained uneasy about touching things in the dark. He admitted he would rather watch a ten-day *Barney & Friends* marathon than place a hand on a rabid bat. He heard wings flap more than once as he blindly worked his way through the long, narrow space.

Joel let his mind drift to better times ahead. Once out of the mine, he would find a swimming pool, shave, don fresh clothes, and order a beer, though not necessarily in that order. He looked forward to seeing familiar places, visiting friends, and graduating.

As the minutes passed, however, Joel went from optimistic to concerned. Two hundred steps into the adit, he still could not see the magic chamber's signature glow. Had he misjudged the distance? Was the room on the other side?

Then, just that quickly, Joel found the void. Though he could see precious little with a pinprick of sunlight at his back, he knew that the gap was the one he had sought.

Joel ran his hands along the low-hanging beam, making a mental note of its location, and entered the room. He listened for snakes, bats, and rats but heard nothing. The mine's indigenous species apparently had moved to greener pastures. That much was good. He walked along the perimeter of the chamber and found the walls as cold and smooth as he had remembered. That too was good. But the rock surfaces emitted no light, blue or otherwise. That probably was not good.

Joel began to question his phosphorescent-cell-as-time-portal theory. Had the room been nothing more than a dream? Was all this a nightmare without end?

He exited the chamber, remembering to duck his head, and stopped on a broken rail. He considered plunging deeper into the mine in hopes of finding another magic room but opted against it. The tunnel was dark and getting darker. No need to add injury to insult.

Joel leaned against a thick post and tried to sort it all out. He had expected to find more in this otherwise insignificant hole and now operated without a plan. For the first time in a long time, answers eluded him.

Joel commenced a slow, sorry walk toward the entrance. But on the way, he pondered another possibility – one that made all the sense in the world. Perhaps the magic room wasn't magic at all. Perhaps its luminescence was natural and fleeting and played no role in sending him to the past. Maybe the mine itself was the portal. Joel regained his lost optimism and picked up his step.

14: JOEL

The new theory succumbed to successive blows. When Joel reached the entrance, he saw no boards. When he stepped out of the mine, he saw a rusted, bullet-riddled coupe and three sturdy buildings with unbroken windows. When he approached Gold Mine Road, he saw a late thirties pickup kick up a cloud of dust as it sped toward town. No log-and-stone mansion beckoned at the intersection. Trees, meadows, and roads remained unchanged.

Joel had not cried since a beloved grandmother died in 1995, but he felt like crying now. He was without hope and ideas, a modern man mired in a not-so-modern time. He tried to maintain a tenuous hold on what was left of his sanity.

He sat on a large boulder near the Mine guidepost and tried to think of what he had missed. He thought of the snake, Adam's sunglasses, Grover Cleveland, even an under-the-table carpentry job he had done for a neighbor in August. Had God punished him for cheating on his taxes? It was only six hundred dollars. Then he recalled his lunch at the Canary and the cable news piece about a planetary alignment. The incident had coincided with his trip to the mine. There had to be a connection.

Joel replayed the story in his mind. Alignments were rare but not unprecedented. Nor were they the flashiest of celestial events. He remembered Hale-Bopp. The comet had lit up night skies for weeks in 1997. But it had not empowered abandoned mines or hurtled college students back in time, at least none that he knew. There had to be more. He got up and paced in a circle before the truth hit him like a low-hanging beam.

"For twenty-four hours, beginning about noon Eastern Daylight Time, six planets from our solar system will fall into a rough alignment with the sun."

Twenty-four hours. Noon Eastern. Ten Mountain. It couldn't be that simple, but it probably was. When Joel first visited Colter Mine, the time portal had just opened. When he went back, it had just closed.

He returned to the boulder, sat down, and put a hand to his forehead. As blunders went, this topped the charts. Joel couldn't believe his luck, or the injustice of it all. A good night's sleep, a decent breakfast, and a leisurely stroll through Helena, Montana, had cost him his world.

15: JOEL

Joel mourned his loss for five minutes. Never a fan of pity parties, he quickly accepted his predicament as permanent and regrouped. He did not know what he would do or where he would go, but he would not dwell on things he could not change.

He headed south on Gold Mine Road, toward the highway, and tried to figure out his next move. He had just twenty-five spendable cents and the shirt on his back. But he also had marketable skills and a gift that defied valuation: knowledge of things to come.

Because he had expected to return to 2000, Joel had not given much thought to using that knowledge. He had focused mostly on getting back home. But now that he was stuck in 1941, he gave the matter its due. And given the gravity of the times, there was much to consider.

With the possible exception of the Japanese high command, Joel alone knew that war was coming to the United States. He knew that thousands of quiet American towns like Helena would soon send their boys to fight in places like Guadalcanal, Anzio, and Omaha Beach. He knew that goods and services would be rationed for years and that wondrous technological and medical advancements were on their way. He knew that Whirlaway was about to win the Triple Crown and that Joe DiMaggio and Ted Williams were headed for banner seasons.

This knowledge could be both a blessing and a curse, he concluded. He could enrich himself and benefit others. Or he could muck things up for multitudes.

Joel remembered "A Sound of Thunder," a short story he had read in high school. In the work by Ray Bradbury, a twenty-first-century hunter, traveling back in time to kill a *Tyrannosaurus rex,* had subtly but profoundly changed the future by literally leaving his footprint on the past. Joel knew he could make a similar mess just as easily. For that reason alone, he would have to weigh every word and action carefully.

On the afternoon of May 30, 1941, however, Joel had more pressing concerns. He needed food in his belly and a roof over his head. He needed identification, a job, and direction. All the knowledge in the world would not be worth a hill of beans if he had to dive in dumpsters and sleep in cardboard boxes.

A mile into his journey, Joel stopped, rested a moment on a stump, and gazed at the valley below, where a freight train slogged its way west toward the Continental Divide. He admired the iron horse, a triumph of engineering, and wished he had even a fraction of its drive.

With nothing better to do, Joel left the road and walked to a stretch of tracks in a clearing a hundred yards away. Even from a distance, he could hear the dull, steady drum of steel on steel. As the train began its eight-mile push to the pass, Joel peered down the tracks and saw the locomotive spew a black funnel toward the sky. He laughed at the sight.

Steam!

When the train drew closer, Joel saw something else – people. Dozens of men and boys rode the rails. Many sat atop flatcars. Others occupied the roofs or interiors of boxcars. Most had hardened faces and wore ragged clothes. Several stared blankly at Joel. Some issued glares. But a few smiled and waved, including a leprechaun of a man who shouted from a flatcar.

"Hey, Johnny! Headed our way?"

Several men laughed.

Joel shook his head at the notion of going *their* way. But the more he pondered the matter, the more he questioned the wisdom of returning to Helena. The town meant nothing to him. He could go anywhere. There was no reason he could not go to Missoula, Spokane, or Portland.

Or Seattle.

He found that idea comforting. Seattle would not be anything like the city he left, of course, but it was still home. Maybe a trip west was just what he needed. If he had to make his way in 1941, he might as well do it in a familiar place.

Joel studied the slow-moving train and more dirty faces as the last ten cars approached. A skinny teenager, clad in overalls and a gray beret, looked at Joel and pointed to an apparently unoccupied boxcar. Just that quickly, the unthinkable became thinkable.

Oh, what the hell.

Joel stepped closer to the tracks and started jogging toward the open car. His jog soon turned into a sprint. He saw a ladder but wasn't sure he could reach it. As he followed the train through the stretch, he looked ahead and saw a problem. The smooth, flat shoulder dropped off sharply as the tracks approached a narrow, rocky canyon.

Joel slowed down as his legs began to tire. Catching even a slow train was proving to be a difficult task. He considered waiting for another train to come along when he saw a large, scruffy man stick his head through the door of the boxcar.

The man dropped his cigarette, stomped it out, and motioned to Joel to pick up the pace. He pointed to the back of the car.

"You can make it," Scruffy said. "Just aim high on the ladder."

Joel regretted canceling his fitness club membership in March. He looked at the man, the uneven railroad ties, and the jagged rocks ahead. This would be close.

With one final burst, Joel sprinted toward the ladder and threw himself at forged steel. Hands, feet, face, and body smashed into unforgiving rungs. Joel felt pain shoot down his spine. But he managed to hold on and quickly pulled himself out of harm's way.

"Take that, Spider-Man!" Joel shouted.

He smiled at the man in the open door. The man smiled back.

"Not bad," Scruffy said. He chuckled. "Welcome aboard, cowboy."

16: GRACE

Grace couldn't decide what she liked more – the room, the table, or the view. Even from the fifth floor, she could see most of the waterfront and Elliott Bay. In the distance, an orange-red sun began to slide behind the snow-capped Olympics.

Slender white candles, spring flowers, Waterford glasses, and origami napkins on bone china plates sat atop a linen-covered table. Forks outnumbered spoons three to two.

A few feet away, a white-jacketed waiter offered a man in a tux and a woman in a silk dress two bowls of lemon sorbet to cleanse their palates. He returned minutes later, to Grace's table, with two menus and a bottle wrapped in cloth.

"Good evening. My name is Gerard, and I'll be your server tonight." Tall, slender, and burdened with a wire-thin mustache, he spoke with a haughty continental accent that was probably honed in Tacoma and not Toulouse. "Could I interest either of you in a glass of wine? This is our most recent acquisition, a 1921 Bordeaux."

Gerard looked at each of the customers. When he didn't get an answer to his question, he focused on the patron who looked younger than the wine.

"Madam?"

Grace, suddenly pale, froze. She didn't know how to proceed.

"I suppose," Grace said. "Was 1921 a good year?"

Gerard let his eyes wander as he kept a firm rein on a tight smile. He looked again at Grace and provided more information.

"It was the best, madam."

Grace appealed to the man holding her hands.

"It's your night, baby," Paul said. "Get what you want."

"All right then," Grace said cheerfully. "I'll have some!"

"And you, sir?"

"Make it a double," Paul replied. He patted his wallet. "Ah, hell, leave the bottle."

The waiter poured two glasses, placed the bottle on the table, and disappeared. Grace looked over her shoulder and then at her date.

"I thought he was going to ask for identification," Grace whispered. She smiled and took a sip of the sweet red wine. "I wonder why he didn't."

"It must have been the uniform," Paul said. He chuckled. "I'm sure he figured there wasn't a chance in hell a Navy officer would corrupt a minor in a place like this."

Grace smiled warmly and put her hands on her hips.

"Your *'minor'* is almost a major."

"Oh, yes. I haven't forgotten."

"You're not upset, are you?" Grace asked.

"Upset that your friends get you on your twenty-first birthday? No. I know how important those things are. Besides, I don't think I could compete with the sisterhood."

Grace laughed.

"You're probably right about that."

Grace gazed at her dinner partner. She liked what she saw. Slender and sturdy at five-ten, Paul McEwan resembled a young Spencer Tracy. He had thick reddish-brown hair, hazel eyes, and a sprinkling of freckles on a boyish face.

"You look handsome in that uniform," Grace said. "You should wear it more often."

"I plan to."

"When do you start your assignment?"

"Right after graduation. I leave for Boston on the fifteenth."

With superior test scores and specialized training as a cadet, Paul had qualified to study at the new Navy Supply Corps School, located at the Harvard Business School. He would train to become an expert in supply, logistics, and combat support.

Grace shook her head and smiled.

"You'll be a Navy officer *and* a Harvard man. That's almost too much to bear."

Grace sipped more wine and thought wistfully of her parents. If they could see her now, they would surely send her to bed without supper. Alcohol had not been a staple in the many homes of Protestant missionaries William and Lucille Vandenberg.

Bill and Lucy would be strongly opposed to Grace's plans to go bar hopping with her Kappa Delta Alpha sisters in two days. They would be disappointed in her judgment. But they would be fiercely proud of their only child and the woman she had become.

They would like Paul too.

Paul and Grace had met at a Christmas party and dated for five months. He was a senior on the dean's list, a member of Zeta Alpha Rho fraternity, and a participant in the university's prestigious Naval ROTC program. He planned to make a career in the U.S. Navy. She was a junior who wanted to teach English and literature.

Grace played with the short string of pearls around her neck. The necklace was a gift from a doting aunt, as was the shimmering purple swing dress she had worn for the occasion. The outfit complemented gentle curves, milky skin, and platinum locks that came from God and not a bottle.

The petite honors student did not go out often and generally preferred a quiet evening with a book to the chaos of parties and dances. But the sorority had brought her out of a shell. So had her man in uniform. He rarely let her stay home on a Saturday night.

Paul was as dashing as ever but also fidgety. From the moment they had arrived at the restaurant, he had appeared distracted. He tapped his fingers on a glass of water.

"Is something wrong?" Grace asked.

"No," Paul said. He offered a nervous smile. "I just have a lot on my mind."

Gerard stopped at their table and took their orders. Grace requested halibut. Paul selected the New York steak and asked that it be "accessorized."

Grace beamed. She loved the way he phrased things, just as she loved how he pampered her. She looked forward to getting to know him better over the next year and seeing whether they had enough in common to form a lasting relationship.

When the waiter returned with their meals, Paul turned a pasty white. He pushed back his chair and straightened his jacket.

"Your halibut, madam," Gerard said. "Your steak, sir."

Grace assessed her meal and stuck a fork in the fish. She began to thank the server when she noticed that many eyes had drifted to her table. Grace glanced again at Paul. He had already dropped to a knee.

Gerard handed Paul a small velvet box.

"Your accessory, sir."

"Thank you," Paul said.

He looked up at Grace, opened the box, and offered it with both hands.

"I know we've known each other only a few months, but it seems like years. Every day I've spent with you has been an adventure," Paul said. He took a breath. "You've made me happy, Grace, *very* happy, and I want to return the favor. I want to buy you a house and support your dreams and give you the life you deserve. I want to do all this and more because I love you. I love you with my whole heart. Will you marry me?"

Grace felt her stomach drop. She stared blankly for several seconds before putting her fork on the table. She looked at the waiter. He offered only a noncommittal smirk, as if to suggest that Paul's proposal was probably better than the catch of the day.

Grace then consulted the curious masses. A plump, middle-aged man holding a martini and a cigarette grinned and shook his head. His plump, middle-aged wife scowled at him and gently nodded at Grace. A thinner, younger woman held up both thumbs.

"Do it, honey."

Blood rushed to Grace's cheeks as she turned to face Paul, who seemed unfazed by all the attention. He continued to gaze at her with soft eyes.

"There's no hurry, sweetheart," Paul said. "I know this is kind of sudden. But I had to tell you where I stood before I left town. I don't want to lose you."

Grace took the box from Paul and removed the ring inside. The half-carat diamond solitaire was no dime-store trinket. It practically lit up the room. Grace shuddered to think what it had cost. She feared that Paul had cleaned out his savings account.

She glanced again at the smarmy server, who remained on the fence, and the fat lady, who crossed fingers on both hands. Nearly a dozen others smiled and waited.

Grace looked at her suitor.

"You're right. This *is* sudden," she said with a sigh. "But that's OK."

Grace took one last peek at the white gold ring, which she held gingerly between her thumb and finger. When she returned her eyes to Paul, nearby conversations ceased.

"You're a good man, Paul. I know this means a lot."

Grace put the ring where she thought it belonged, snapped the box shut, and pushed the package away. The fat lady fainted, and the thin woman gasped.

"I love you too. My answer is yes."

17: JOEL

Spokane, Washington

Mr. Smith went to Washington, but his whistle-stop tour hit the skids in Spokane. Several bulls, or railroad police, cleared out the boxcars when the train rolled to a stop. They arrested those too slow to sprint across the sprawling Great Northern rail yards to the relative safety of the rough-and-tumble Hillyard neighborhood.

Joel spent the last day of May learning the ins and outs of hobo life. Scruffy, who went by the name of Hobart Katzenberger, taught him how to get a meal in a restaurant by offering to work for food and then waiting for guilt-ridden patrons to pick up the tab.

Charlie, the five-foot-two leprechaun, directed Joel to a nearby machinist shop that people could enter on evenings and weekends through unlocked windows. Once inside, the homeless and jobless could access modern restrooms and large washbasins. Never one to squander resources, Joel made use of both.

"Do you guys ever stay in one place?" Joel asked.

"I do when I can," Scruffy said in the gravelly voice of a longtime smoker. "But regular work is hard to find. You know that."

Scruffy and Charlie looked at Joel and smiled. Both had commented on his unusual shirt, but neither had asked how he had obtained it. They no doubt figured he had stolen it or found it in the garbage and seemed willing to let the matter drop.

Joel was fine with that. He did not want to discuss his attire or anything that might draw unwanted attention. He did not want to answer *questions*.

Joel didn't mind asking them though. So off and on, he did just that. He asked his new friends how they made it through each day, where they grew up, and how they had come to be transients. In the process, he learned a lot.

Scruffy, forty going on eighty, said he had once cut logs in Wisconsin. When his mill closed, he sold his car, packed his bags, and headed for the Pacific Northwest. He had bounced from one timber town to another for more than five years.

Charles Prescott was in a tougher spot. He had lost a Chicago factory job and his wife on the same day in 1938. Delores Prescott left her husband on his thirtieth birthday and took up with his sister. Charlie hopped a train when the bills piled up.

Joel listened to the stories with great interest. As the day wore on, though, he focused more on other things. More than anything else, he wanted to know how he could board a westbound train in Spokane without running into railroad security.

* * * * *

Joel got an answer around ten thirty the next morning when Charlie guided him to a grassy field north of the rail yards. Though they moved slowly and quietly to avoid detection, they probably could have announced their arrival. The bulls, Charlie insisted, rarely ventured far beyond the yards.

The two men waited thirty minutes before they saw a long freight train pull slowly out of its berth a half-mile away. When the locomotive approached the field, Charlie handed Joel a business card. Faded and worn, it bore the name of a Seattle company.

"Check that place out, if you get the chance, and ask for Brutus. He sometimes hires nobodies to move boxes around," Charlie said. He laughed. "Good luck."

"You're not coming?" Joel asked.

The small man shook his head.

"Not this time," Charlie said. He looked toward town as church bells rang in the distance. "I have better prospects here and want to play them out."

"Thanks for your help. Here are some shekels for your trouble," Joel said. He handed Charlie his last usable quarter and the two from the eighties. "Just be careful where you spend them."

Joel walked toward the train and pondered his second joyride. With several open boxcars, the still-slow-moving choo-choo was a target-rich environment.

Joel selected a car near the caboose and started walking with the train. As he picked up his pace, he glanced back at his companion.

Charlie stood where Joel had left him. He held a coin in each of his widely separated hands, chuckled, and smiled, as if to ask, "What are these?"

Joel laughed, waved, and returned to the train, which had increased its velocity. He ran beside a boxcar, noted the location of its ladder, and let it drift away. He kept a steady pace as the target car approached. Shiny, brown, and new, it appeared unoccupied.

Joel calibrated his steps as his moment finally came. He moved toward the car's ladder, eyed the middle rungs, and leaped. He landed squarely, safely, and painlessly.

As the train steamed through an intersection with a rural road, a well-dressed couple in a convertible honked and waved. Joel tipped his hat.

He climbed a few rungs and stared at the scene ahead. Pine trees, small houses, and narrow roads broke up gentle fields of yellow grass.

Joel visualized the arid landscapes of eastern Washington, the majestic Cascades, and home. This was not how he had planned to spend Memorial Day weekend – in *any* year – but it definitely beat cramming for finals.

18: JOEL

Seattle, Washington — Monday, June 2, 1941

Joel's joyride ended just after sunrise on Monday, when the Glacial Express rolled into the rail yard south of King Street Station. Because of a mudslide-caused delay near Wenatchee, the train did not cross the mountains until after dark. He spent most of the night shivering between two wooden crates.

When the train finally came to a stop, Joel wasted no time getting out. He had spent the better part of a day rattling around in an unoccupied boxcar and simply wanted to put his feet on solid ground. No bulls awaited him. No one awaited him. Why would they? He was a vagrant from another time and, to be honest, another place.

The city looked a lot like Seattle but very little like his hometown. No Columbia Center soared over a bevy of new skyscrapers, no partially completed football stadium abutted the train station, and no Space Needle loomed in the distance. The Century 21 World's Fair was twenty-one years away. Joel eyed the forty-two-story Smith Tower to the north. Completed in 1914, it was again the tallest building in the West.

Tired, sore, and hungry, Joel wanted to rent a cheap room, like the one in Helena, and sleep for a week. But he realized that was not an option for a scraggly young man with little more than two useless dollars and a Ken Griffey trading card to his name. He needed a job — or at least an honest bookie. He tried to remember when Belmont held its Stakes. He wanted to bet on Whirlaway. But even that required cash.

So he wandered down to Pike Place Market, in hopes of finding a way to get it. Farmers, fishermen, and merchants peddled their wares on the waterfront, as they had done for decades and would do for decades more. But when Joel learned that none had work to offer, he kept on walking. Seeing and smelling fresh seafood and produce was more than he could bear on an empty stomach.

From the market, he cut east and south to Madison Street and walked four miles toward his old neighborhood in Madison Park. He talked to several merchants along the way but got the same story. No jobs. Even businessmen with Help Wanted signs in their windows told him to come back in a week. Some said he did not have the right skills. Joel suspected he did not have the right shirt and shave.

He loved the irony. He had four years of college, technical knowledge from far into the future, and fluency in French and Spanish. But on June 2, 1941, Joel Smith, wearing a cowboy hat, a Candy in Chains sweatshirt, and a four-day beard, couldn't get a job sweeping floors in a city of four hundred thousand.

For the most part, Joel took the rejections in stride. He knew he couldn't solve all of his problems in twenty-four hours and knew that the day was still young. He thought of the business card in his wallet and his potential date with Brutus. Joel smiled.

Brutus. What parents would do that?

Joel's plight improved at noon when he walked into a grocery store on Capitol Hill. The place didn't have jobs, but it did have food, including a few boxes of fruits and vegetables that a teenage boy in a stained apron carried to a garbage bin in back.

"Are you really going to throw that out?" Joel asked.

"I sure am."

"Why?"

"Because they're old and starting to get mushy," the boy said. "They won't sell."

"Do you mind if I help myself?"

"Take all you want. The bananas are still pretty good."

Joel did not wait for a review of the apples, grapes, and plums. He tore into the boxes and ate until he could eat no more. He knew he would pay for eating raw fruit, and nothing but raw fruit, on an empty tank, but he did not care. He needed sustenance and he needed it now.

When he finished his feast, Joel resumed his journey. He noted the rails in the road and sighed. He had hoped to hop a trolley that ran the length of East Madison Street but learned that he had arrived too late. The city had terminated the service in 1940.

Two hours later Joel made his way to a house on Thirty-Eighth Avenue, a home twice named among Madison Park's finest by a Seattle historical society. With shuttered, multi-paned windows, two chimneys, gables, three dormers, and a front door framed by two columns and an arch, the redbrick mansion was a tribute to colonial Georgian style.

Joel pondered ringing the bell just to see who answered. He knew his parents had purchased the place in 1980 from a family that had resided there for three generations, but he knew nothing about them or how they had managed the property.

He knew he would not find a redwood deck and heated swimming pool in back or a Lexus in the detached garage, but he was pleasantly surprised to see a vegetable garden on the treeless south side of the house. He had spent some quality time there as a young child, harvesting his mother's crops whenever hunger called.

A few blocks away Joel found his alma mater, a four-story brownstone edifice that towered above neighboring homes. He had attended Westlake High for four years and made the most of every minute, lettering in football and baseball, serving as class president, and dating three-quarters of the varsity cheer squad as a *junior*. He had also started the school's first history club.

Joel had loved history since watching President Reagan commemorate the fortieth anniversary of the D-day invasion. Only six at the time, he stood mesmerized before the television. When Reagan spoke, he spoke to him. When he honored the ancient heroes assembled in Normandy, he honored Grandpa Smith, who had stormed Utah Beach with the Fourth Infantry Division. Patrick Smith died the next year.

His reverence for the past, and his grandparents' generation in particular, extended to entertainment. He loved movies like *Casablanca*, *It's a Wonderful Life*, and *The Grapes of Wrath*; syndicated sitcoms like *Happy Days* and *Leave it to Beaver*; recordings by Frank Sinatra, Elvis, and Buddy Holly; and even broadcasts of old-time radio shows featuring Burns and Allen, Abbott and Costello, and Jack Benny. His mother had once told him he had been born fifty years past his time. When he heard Big Band music blaring out an open window of a nearby house, he laughed.

Thanks, Mom.

Joel had wanted to major in history at the university, but his father would have none of it. To Commander Francis H. Smith, U.S. Navy (Retired), college was a place to learn a vocation, not expand your mind. Unless Joel planned to take a history degree to law school, he would have to find another discipline or fund his education. So he majored in his second love – rocks – and minored in his first.

The salutatorian of the Class of 1996 gazed at his school from across the street as a bell rang. Dozens of boys in slacks and button-down shirts and girls in knee-length skirts, ankle socks, and saddle shoes began spilling out the doors. Many wore smiles.

Joel put a hand to his chin. He tried to remember the names on an oak-and-brass plaque by the main office, names of graduates killed in various American conflicts. Life was about to change in a big way for the Class of 1941. He wished them the best. As he left the intersection of Memory Lane and Thirty-Eighth Avenue, Joel thought about the decisions he had made and the decisions still to come. Neither gave him comfort.

* * * * *

By the time Joel reached Pennington Storage and Distribution, he was spent. He had walked eight miles on one meal and not slept in thirty-six hours.

Bags the size of quarters hung below his weary eyes. To say he looked like hell was to slight hell. Joel didn't care. He had come to see Brutus, not a beauty queen.

Joel caught the beefy, fortyish owner at five after five, just as he locked his office and headed toward his car. He introduced himself and dropped the name of Charles Prescott.

"I remember him," Brutus said. "He was a short little prick."

"Charlie said you sometimes hire nobodies to move boxes around," Joel said. "He used those exact words."

"That sounds like something he would say," Brutus said with a laugh. "I'd like to help you, but I can't. Business is down, way down, and I don't expect it to pick up for weeks."

Joel frowned and glanced at the late afternoon sky. He would soon have more important things to think about than business cycles and iffy job prospects. He thanked Brutus, did a one-eighty, and started to walk away.

"Say, kid, where are you spending the night?" Brutus asked.

Joel turned around.

"I don't know. I just got into town."

"I thought so," Brutus said. He scribbled something on the back of a business card and handed it to Joel. "Call this place. It's a mission in the U-District. They'll put you up tonight and feed you in the morning. If you still need a job next month, come back. I might have something by then."

"OK."

Joel shook the owner's hand and once again took his leave. He didn't get far before he heard an observation about his attire.

"By the way, I like your shirt," Brutus said. "I guess I shouldn't ask about it."

Joel turned around and smiled.

"You're right. You shouldn't," he said. "Take care."

Joel noted the address on the card and made a beeline for the Montlake Bridge. He counted his blessings. If nothing else, he would sleep in a bed that wasn't rolling on rails.

19: GINNY AND GRACE

The troops assembled at six. Armed with lipstick, cash, and pin-curl permanents, the Twenty-First Birthday Brigade of Kappa Delta Alpha set out to shake things up on a Monday night. Or at least order a few decadent desserts to go with legal cocktails.

Ginny Gillette, the officer in charge, had asked a dozen coeds to meet at Harlan's Hideaway, located just outside the dry zone on University Way Northeast – or what locals called the Ave. Thanks to a series of legislative acts, the sale of alcoholic beverages was prohibited within a mile of the campus.

The law was little more than an annoyance to most students, including the ones Ginny had summoned to celebrate a milestone birthday. All twelve answered the call, though most seemed more interested in eating and talking than drinking the night away.

The participants had two objectives. They wanted to nudge a beloved but reclusive sorority sister out of her comfort zone and unwind one last time before jumping headfirst into dead week, the stressful stretch that preceded their final examinations.

"I feel guilty," Ginny said to Grace Vandenberg as she put down a menu. "If I had known that Paul was going to put a rock on your finger, I would have called this off – or at least rescheduled it. You should be with him tonight."

"Don't be silly," Grace said. "How often do any of us get together like this?"

"At least once a week," Linda McEwan replied.

Several girls giggled. Grace turned red.

"I guess I *have* spent too much time at the library."

"And with that handsome man of yours," Katie said.

Katherine Kobayashi, the outlier of the group, worked beside Grace three days a week in the rare books section of the university library. The second-generation Japanese American had not joined Kappa Delta Alpha.

Nisei did not join traditional sororities. But Katie had been welcomed with open arms into Grace's tight circle of friends.

The women had most of the dark, pub-like establishment to themselves. Four men in zoot suits at a nearby table cast leering glances from time to time but otherwise minded their own business. Most students hit the books – not the bars – the week before finals, so Harlan's, a popular haunt, was unusually quiet.

"So when's the date?" Linda asked. She turned to the guest of honor. "Big brother hasn't provided details."

"We haven't set a date," Grace said. "Paul wants me to finish school before we get married. I imagine the wedding will be next summer."

Grace smiled at Linda and grabbed her hand.

"Just think. We're going to be sisters-in-law."

"I'm looking forward to that," Linda said.

Linda lifted her Sidecar and clinked Grace's wine glass. She had ordered two of the brandy concoctions and appeared ready for a third. She started to raise her hand when the waiter approached the gathering but lowered it when no one else followed her lead.

Linda didn't like to drink heavily among people who didn't do the same. Only Ginny, Grace, Phyllis, Betty, and Rose had requested something stronger than iced tea. Four others had asked for lemon water. Lemon water!

"I'm so happy for you," Katie said to Grace.

"I am too. We all are," Ginny chimed in. The queen bee looked down the long table, counted the number of adult beverages, and frowned. She tapped her martini glass with a fork. "I must say I'm a bit disappointed, ladies. This is supposed to be a party. So let me get it going. The next round is on me!"

The sisters cheered.

Ginny stood up, lifted her glass, and smiled at Grace.

"Here's a toast to the birthday girl and the *blushing* bride to be!"

* * * * *

The festivities ended at nine, after two girls left for the library and Linda left for the ladies' room. She gave back to Harlan's on three separate occasions.

Grace provided comfort each time, helping Linda to a sink to wash her face and then to a glass of water to wash her throat. At the end of round three, Grace wiped a bit of celebration from the hem of her white cotton dress.

"Some birthday," Linda said. "I'm sorry."

"It's all right," Grace said in a forgiving voice. "Someone always gets sick at these things, and I'm glad it wasn't me."

The friends laughed.

The Birthday Brigade decided early on to stay at Harlan's rather than hop from bar to bar. The coeds agreed that they had all that they needed in the Hideaway and that Monday night of dead week was no time to seek additional distractions – like men.

Grace could not have asked for a better party, given the circumstances. She could not have asked for better friends. All had set aside their studies and other priorities to help her celebrate a big day.

A short while later, the women pushed out the door and began their long walk to the sorority. As they did, the sun set, the sky darkened, and a gentle breeze blew in from the sound. Some of the ladies buttoned their sweaters, but no one complained.

Grace embraced the crisp air. She loved this time of year, when Seattle's dreary wet season gave way to the best summer weather in North America.

Grace pondered her plans for the coming season, her final year of college, and her future with Paul. Oh, how he had surprised her Saturday night! Oh, how she had surprised herself by accepting his offer. Grace had dated only five men in her life, but she didn't need to date any more to know she had met Mr. Right.

Ten minutes into the walk, Grace and Linda fell behind the pack and found themselves stranded when the others crossed the Ave at East Forty-Seventh Street. As she waited for a caravan of cars to pass, Grace glanced at a young man in a dirty sweatshirt and a cowboy hat. He stretched out on a nearby bench and stared into space.

Grace paused to assess the man and noticed that he was uncommonly handsome, in spite of, or maybe because of, thick brown stubble that covered much of his face. When he turned to see Grace, he locked onto her crystal blue eyes and offered a long, weary smile. She responded in kind. He did not appear to be a student or one of the many transients who passed through the university district but rather something else.

Grace peered across the street and saw activity on the other side. Katie, Betty, and Rose motioned for her to cross. As the traffic cleared, Grace looked back at the man and gently waved a slender hand. He sat up straight and touched the brim of his hat.

Grace and Linda crossed the street. When they finally rejoined the group, Grace sought the group's leader. She found her smiling and laughing near the front of the pack.

"What did you do?" Ginny asked. "Stop to check the white sales?"

"No," Grace said matter-of-factly. "I just took a moment to look at that cowboy, the one on the bench. He looked very sad."

"Well, I'm sure he'll find his horse. Now, come, let's go."

Grace put an arm around Linda and gave Katie her purse. In the distance, dozens of moviegoers filed out of the Phoenician as impatient drivers in slow-moving cars revved their engines and honked their horns. The Ave was coming to life.

As she started down Forty-Seventh Street, Grace glanced back at the bench. It was empty. No one loitered nearby, and no one walked down the street. Satisfied that her cowboy had found his horse, she turned to join her friends and thought of other things.

20: JOEL

Joel thought about mattresses as he walked north on the Ave. He thought about the queen-size box spring he had in his apartment, the waterbed he'd had growing up, and the king-size memory-foam special in his parents' bedroom. He even thought about flimsy bunk-bed pads, the kind Saint Xavier's Mission had but couldn't offer when it told him there was no more room in the inn.

The pampered youngest son of Frank and Cynthia Smith couldn't remember the last time fatigue and hunger had gripped him like this. He gained new respect for those who spent each day walking the streets.

Joel also thought about the blonde. Who was she? And why had she stared at him? Was Joel Smith, world traveler, gold-card member, and former all-state linebacker, now an object of pity? He didn't think so. He saw empathy in those incredible eyes, not contempt. Still, he wondered.

As Joel proceeded down the busy arterial, he passed a few familiar sights. Some things had not visibly changed in fifty-nine years, such as two brownstone apartment buildings, a Mission Revival grade school in the Heights, and three taverns with colorful names. He stood before one, the Mad Dog, and considered his options.

The Mad Dog didn't have memory-foam mattresses for weary time travelers. But it did have a long sidewalk bench. Joel sat down on one end and extended his legs toward the other. He pondered walking to a nearby park but decided to stay put. The bench was hard but relatively comfortable. If necessary, he could make it his bed for the night.

He closed his eyes and thought of pleasant things – his mother's chicken cacciatore, the hot tub at home, Jana in a string bikini, Maui, and the blonde. He could still picture her face.

Miss Denmark has nothing on you.

Joel was about to drift off when a party of three crashed through the tavern door. Two men about his age escorted another to the other side of the Ave, where a narrow, unlighted alley between a redbrick law office and a used bookstore allowed for private conversations. An American flag flew in front of the office.

A moment later, one man spoke and another responded. Tension filled the air.

"I believe the sum was twenty dollars."

"And I said I'd have it by Wednesday."

"You said that a week ago. Let's see your wallet."

Silence passed for a second and then another. Pleased that the misunderstanding across the street had been resolved to the satisfaction of all parties, Joel again settled into the bench and let fatigue take its course. He visualized Kapalua and another epic dispute. In this clash, Jana and Smiling Sarah fought over his beach towel. Blondie from Forty-Seventh Street, whistle in mouth, mediated the spat, which had gone into overtime. The bliss ended all too soon.

"That isn't going to do it. You owe us twenty, not ten."

"It's all I have. I'll give you the rest later. I promise."

"That's not good enough."

Joel hated the dull sound of fists hitting bellies. He hated that total strangers had interrupted his best daydream in weeks. Most of all, he hated that he would have to jump into the fray or tune out a nasty assault. Violence, he reasoned, belonged on football fields and in boxing rings, not dark alleys in Seattle, Washington. He jumped off the bench, donned his hat, and walked slowly across the Ave.

"OK, gentlemen, break it up."

The bill collectors, in sleeveless shirts and cuffed denim, turned toward Joel. So did their better-dressed debtor, who bled from both sides of his mouth.

"Well, take a look," the larger aggressor said. "It's John Wayne."

With pompadour hair, low bushy eyebrows, and a six-inch scar that ran across his chin, he was all set for Halloween and not one to talk. He laughed, sneered at Joel, and resumed his business, lifting the ragdoll to his feet before knocking him down.

"I said break it up."

Mr. Congeniality kicked his prostrate victim in the side for good measure, then spun around and briskly walked up to Joel. With twenty pounds on the peacemaker, he got right in his face.

"And what are you going to do if I don't?"

"I'm going to run your ass up that flagpole and then do your mother."

The bully nixed the small talk. He crouched, shifted his weight to his back foot, and threw a clenched fist at Joel's face. The right hook grazed an ear. When he reloaded and fired again, Joel caught his wrist, twisted his arm behind his back, and shoved him face first into an overflowing garbage can. The metal lid rolled into the street.

The man got up slowly and brushed coffee grounds off his shirt. He lowered his shoulders, snarled, and charged with the fury of a wounded bull. Once again, Joel was ready. He stepped to one side, tripped the lout to the pavement, and jumped on his back. He grabbed a handful of hair and slammed his face into the ground.

"Do you give, or do we discuss your sister too?"

"I give."

Joel lifted the trash – the one with two legs – and kicked it hard to the curb. The man struggled to his feet, looked around, and appealed for help but found none. His scrawny sidekick had already taken the wallet and bolted. Stunned, humbled, and furious, the ruffian glared at Joel, extended the middle finger of his undamaged hand, and retreated north. It was over that fast.

Sirens pierced the still air, sending Joel's stomach to his toes. Though Joel found the idea of a stay at the Iron Bars Bed and Breakfast surprisingly appealing, he decided that he didn't need more drama in his day. He could picture the interview with Seattle's finest.

"And your date of birth, Mr. Smith?"

"Why, that would be June 7, 1978, Officer. The day the Sonics blew the Finals."

The sirens passed, bringing palpable relief. Then Joel looked at the man he had saved and wondered if he should call someone. The man needed a helping hand, if not a doctor. Blood flowed from his mouth as he sat up and clutched his head.

Joel looked for something to wipe the blood. He walked up and down the alley and even searched the garbage can. He drew the line at two oily rags.

"Stay put," Joel said. "I'll be right back."

A few minutes later Joel returned with a handful of toilet paper. He saw that the victim was still a little shaky but alert and on his feet.

"Here," Joel said. "Take this."

He gave the paper to the man.

"Thanks."

The man wiped his mouth, ran a finger along his lower lip, and tucked in his blue button-down shirt. Blood had dripped on the collar and a pocket.

"Don't thank me," Joel said. "Thank the next guy to use the restroom in the Mad Dog. I took all the paper in the stall."

"That's funny," the man said. He dabbed a corner of his mouth and looked at Joel. "Thanks also for running those guys off. I didn't think they would get rough."

"Don't mention it. Besides, I didn't have a choice," Joel said. He smiled. "You guys interrupted my beauty sleep."

"Well, thanks anyway. I'm Tom Carter, by the way."

"Joel Smith."

The two shook hands, drifted over to the concrete steps of the law office, and sat down. Before either could say another word, four talkative men exited the Mad Dog and walked across the street. One stared at Joel and shouted "Where's the party, cowboy?" before joining the others in a 1939 Packard sedan parked in front of the bookstore. They spun away from the curb and drove out of sight.

Tom tilted his head and looked at Joel with puffy eyes.

"I like your duds."

"You and half the planet," Joel said. He stood up, walked to the street to pick up the garbage can lid, and placed it on the can before returning to the steps. "So what was this all about? Did you lose a bet?"

"Two, actually."

Joel laughed.

"I would have paid them off," Tom said. "I never welsh on bets. But I didn't have the money just yet."

Joel studied his new acquaintance. Two inches shorter and a few pounds heavier, he was a nice-looking guy with a baby face, a strong jaw, and short, light-brown hair that was parted to the side. Unlike the two thugs, he also sounded educated.

"Are you a student?" Joel asked.

"I am, though not for much longer. I graduate in two weeks. I came out here to shoot some pool and clear my head. I studied all weekend," Tom said. He brushed dirt off his pants. "How about you? Are *you* a student?"

The question caught Joel off guard. Several people had asked about his attire, but no one had asked who he was, what he was, or where he came from. The truth wouldn't cut it. Though he looked – and probably smelled – like a wild man from Borneo, he needed a story that was a bit more credible.

"No. I'm a visitor of sorts," Joel said. "I just got off a train from Montana. I came here looking for work."

Tom squinted and stared at the man who had saved him from a savage beating. His rescuer wore a stained sweatshirt, a scraggly beard, and the aroma of unwashed skin.

"You didn't hop a train, did you?"

"I did," Joel said.

Both men laughed.

"That explains a lot," Tom said. He sniffed the air. "When was the last time you had a bath?"

Does a sponge bath in Spokane count?

"It's been a while," Joel said. "Is it that bad? I lost my sense of smell yesterday."

"You're a riot. You remind me of my girlfriend."

Tom tucked the bathroom tissue in a pocket and stood up. He waited for Joel to get to his feet and then looked at him again.

"Say, guy, do you have a place to stay?" Tom asked.

Joel pointed to the bench in front of the Mad Dog.

"My castle."

"I figured as much," Tom said. He smiled and draped an arm over Joel's shoulders. "Let's do something about that."

21: JOEL

S o *you're* the young fellow who slept in my trailer last night."

"I am," Joel said to a barrel-chested bulldog of a man.

The man rubbed his chin, studied Joel for a few seconds, and then walked across the well-furnished living room of his university district home. He offered Joel a hand.

"I'm Mel Carter."

"Joel Smith."

"Well, take a seat, Mr. Smith. We have a lot to talk about."

Joel walked around a walnut coffee table and sat down on a plush silk brocade couch. On the other side of the room, Mel and Tom Carter, father and son, claimed matching upholstered recliners. A mahogany console radio stood between them.

"I'll be straight with you, Joel. It's not every day we take in a stray off the streets and welcome him into our home, but then not every day is like yesterday," Mel said. "Tom told me about your little adventure. I'm grateful for what you did for my son."

"Thank you," Joel said.

Joel let out a sigh. He had dreaded this meeting, mostly because he did not know what to expect. But now that he had some measure of Melvin Carter, owner and operator of Carter's Furniture and Appliance, he could relax. He could see that Mel was a reasonable man. A good day was about to get better.

The day, ironically, had started on a bed on wheels, albeit one more comfortable than a rolling boxcar. Joel had slept soundly in an immaculate Airstream trailer, parked in a dirt driveway behind the Carters' three-bedroom Cape Cod house.

When he got up, Joel grabbed a shirt, some underwear, and a razor provided by Tom and made use of a downstairs bathroom and a round porcelain-tub washing machine that looked a lot like R2-D2. By the time Sandra Carter came home at noon from a pinochle game, Joel was a new man. Tom introduced his mother to a clean-cut friend, not a mysterious drifter who, hours earlier, had roamed the streets with a hairy face.

"Tom tells me you're from Montana," Mel said.

The statement brought Joel out of a daze. He tried to remember what he had told Tom the previous night, when he went from Joel Smith, time traveler, to Joel Smith, job-seeking cowboy from Big Sky Country. It was time to play the part.

"I am. I'm from Helena," Joel said. At least that much was true. "My family is into ranching."

Joel remembered Walter Scott's quip about tangled webs and deceit.

Mel gazed at Joel.

"Ranching, huh?"

Tom smiled and nodded. No scrutiny would come from his corner.

"So why does a Montana rancher hop a train to Seattle?" Mel asked.

"Well, sir, truth be told, the ranching hasn't been so good lately," Joel said. "Beef is in a free fall. Chicken is cutting into the market."

"Chicken?"

"It's sad but true. Consumers are on a white-meat kick, and our operation hasn't been able to adjust. I couldn't make it in a chicken world, so I hit the road in search of something better."

Mel smiled, shook his head, and looked at his guest as if trying to decide whether he was a serial liar or a marketing genius. He shifted in his chair and adjusted a pair of black suspenders that cut into a white short-sleeved shirt. A pack of cigarettes bulged from one pocket.

"What kind of work are you looking for?" Mel asked.

"I'm not looking for anything in particular," Joel said. "I just want an opportunity to prove myself and work my way up."

"Have you ever sold anything?"

I once sold Adam on protein shakes.

"I haven't, sir, but I'm willing to try."

Mel glanced at Tom, as if seeking some sort of guidance, and then at the mystery man. He frowned, rubbed his hands together, and leaned forward in his chair.

"I'll tell you what, Joel. If you mean what you say, I'll give you a chance to prove yourself. I run a home furnishings store just off campus. Come with me in the morning. I'll put you to work. If you can sell more than toasters in two weeks, I'll make the job permanent."

As Joel pondered a reply, a pretty, browned-haired girl, no more than eighteen, stepped into the room. She glanced at the visitor, blushed, and then addressed the oldest male in attendance.

"Supper's ready, Daddy."

71

Brenda Carter took her leave but sneaked one more peek at Joel as she ambled across the dark oak floor. Rounding an arched entrance that led to a hallway, she stopped, popped her head back in the room, and looked at her brother.

"Oh, Tom, I almost forgot," Brenda said.

"Forgot what?" Tom asked.

"Ginny's here."

22: JOEL

Sandra Carter knew fried chicken, the bane of the beef industry. She also knew gravy, biscuits, and corn on the cob.

Joel smiled to himself as he took stock of the food on the large, rectangular table, which occupied a fair portion of a well-lighted dining room. The fat grams alone could kill a herd of elephants. But he wasted no time digging in. Twenty-four hours earlier rotting fruit had looked like a feast. Now, he had meat and carbohydrates – and company.

Mel and Sandy took up most of Joel's time, asking questions about Montana, his family, and ranch life. Joel surprised himself by handling each query with aplomb. In his new, tightly written biography, he was not a free-spirited geology student who lived in an apartment complex ten blocks away but rather a restless rancher's son seeking something bigger and better in the big city.

He sensed from the start that Mel didn't buy his BS, or at least all of it. But he didn't sweat it. Joel suspected the boss would render his verdict after seeing how well he worked and played with others at Carter's Furniture and Appliance.

Sandy, a slender woman with a pleasant face, oval eyes, and steam-curled locks, was similarly accommodating. She asked Joel what his parents thought of his gallivanting, asked if he had a girl back home, and said he looked nice in Tom's green shirt. Brenda rolled her eyes at the first question, sighed at Joel's reply to the second, and nodded in agreement with the compliment but did not say a word.

Tom said only a few. Apparently grateful to be eating dinner at home and not in a hospital, he kept mostly to himself. He had told his family how two men had taken his wallet and tried to beat him to a pulp but not why. He seemed pleased that the questions around the table had been directed at someone else.

Joel did not need long to figure out the Carters of 4125 Baltic Avenue. They were good people. He appreciated their kindness and hospitality.

He had more difficulty assaying their other guest. Ginny, Tom's girlfriend of two months, spoke often about articles she had written for the student newspaper and about plans to move out of her sorority and into an off-campus house with three of her friends. But she left the questioning of the Montana man to others. Until dessert, that is.

"Have you lived on a ranch all your life, Joel?"

"I have. Why do you ask?"

"Oh, I was just curious how you managed to keep such soft, clean hands," Ginny said, sticking forks into two objects.

"I'm a firm believer in soap, ma'am."

Tom smirked and leaned toward his new friend.

"You weren't yesterday," he whispered.

Joel smiled at the observation and wondered if anyone at the table could read lips.

Ginny looked at Joel. She seemed as interested as ever.

"You're a charmer, Mr. Smith. And *ma'am*? Wherever did you find him, Tom?"

"In front of the Mad Dog."

Ginny laughed.

"I see I have two comedians. I may have to keep both of you."

"Would you care for more cake, Joel?" Sandy asked.

"No, thank you," Joel said.

"You're very articulate," Ginny said. "I like that. It's the mark of an educated man. Why is an intelligent-sounding person like you not attending college?"

"I never had the money," Joel replied. *My parents spent it on a condo.* "I value education as much as anyone, but I'm kind of a self-learner."

"I see," Ginny said. "And what do you hope to learn here in Seattle?"

"Armchairs, sofas, maybe toasters."

Laughter filled the room.

"Dad gave Joel a job at the store," Tom said. "He's going to try his hand at sales."

"Well, I hope you succeed and stay for a while," Ginny said with a warm smile. "You've made quite an impression on Tom. Any friend of his is a friend of mine."

A moment later Joel finished his coffee and put his cup on a saucer. Sandra got up and started pulling dinnerware off the cloth-covered table. No one rushed to assist her.

"Would you like some help with the dishes, Mrs. Carter?" Joel asked.

The matron of the house stopped in her tracks and smiled at her husband.

"I like this boy!" She grabbed two more plates and then looked at her questioner. "Thank you for offering, but I think I can manage with a little help from Brenda."

The teen frowned.

"Can't I stay?"

"No," Sandra said. "Leave your brother to his friends."

"I think that's my cue, too," Mel said. "I'll go check on the trailer. If you are going to stay here, Joel, we might as well make you comfortable."

"I appreciate that, sir," Joel said, thankful that he had left Candy in Chains in the laundry room and not the Airstream.

23: JOEL

Joel felt the weight of her stare but did not know what to make of it. For more than ten minutes Ginny looked at him like she was evaluating a member of a long-lost tribe.

She certainly was qualified to do so. As the women's page editor of the student daily and a stringer who often covered university events for the *Seattle Sun*, she was a trained observer of the human race.

"I hope you took no offense to my questions at dinner," Ginny said.

"None at all," Joel replied from Mel's throne in the living room. "I expected questions. I just popped into your lives. Of course you're curious."

Tom sat on the couch, next to Ginny, and read Tuesday's edition of the *Barker*, the university's student newspaper. He appeared to tune out everything else, including the woman who had brought the paper directly from the newsroom.

Ginny was not easy to tune out. Tall and lithe, with penetrating brown eyes, long dark hair, and a diamond-shaped face, she commanded attention. Colleagues and friends compared her often – and favorably – to Katharine Hepburn. Outspoken, brusque, and sharp-witted, she held her own even in the toughest assemblies of accomplished men. But those closest to her found her more endearing than intimidating. She placed a hand on Tom's knee and looked at each of her comedians.

"So how did you boys spend the day?"

"I took him to my classes," Tom said, still reading the paper. "I think he got more out of them than I did."

Joel nodded.

"Somehow I don't find that surprising," Ginny said. "Are you ready for your finals, Tom? You don't want to flunk a class on the eve of graduation."

"I studied all weekend, sweetie. I'm fine," Tom said. He flipped back to the front page. "I see they ran your feature on poverty in the U-District."

Joel grinned at Ginny.

Too bad I wasn't around for your interviews.

"I lobbied for weeks to get that in. My editors thought it was too controversial," Ginny said with a laugh. "Journalism is *supposed* to be controversial."

Joel looked at Ginny with newfound respect. She was a committed professional and a trailblazer who was years ahead of her time.

"So are you originally from Seattle, Ginny?" Joel asked.

"Oh, heavens, no. I'm from Forest Grove, Oregon. It's just west of Portland," Ginny said. She took a sip of coffee. "My family owns a chain of newspapers there. I came up here to make my mark on this glorious city."

Joel turned pale, slouched in his chair, and closed his eyes for a few seconds as he processed the information. Pulling himself together, he took a breath, sat up straight, and leaned forward with an extended hand.

"Can I see that article, Tom?"

"Sure."

Tom got up, stepped around a long coffee table, and handed Joel a folded paper. Joel flipped it open and scanned the front page until he found the feature story. He went straight to the byline.

"It says here you're Virginia Gillette," Joel said. He looked at the reporter in the room. "Why don't you go by Ginny?"

"Because Virginia sounds more professional," Ginny replied. "Journalism is a male domain, Joel. Women have to work twice as hard to get half the credit. They also have to be mindful of the images they project."

"I see."

"Ginny is the name my sister gave me. Virginia is the one I put on paper."

Ginny took another sip and smiled sweetly at her friend.

"But you can call me anything you want."

Joel sighed.

How about Grandma?

24: JOEL

Friday, June 6, 1941

The customer was not pleased. Sitting on a corner of a full-sized bed, the woman of thirty folded her arms and tapped her toes. Wearing a floral print sundress, wide brimmed hat, and a scowl the size of Texas, she threw daggers with her eyes at the cow monopolizing the salesman.

Joel sensed trouble even before Old Bessie decided on a nightstand. Carter's was unusually busy, even for a Friday afternoon, and the sales staff of three was stretched thin trying to cover a showroom of ten thousand square feet. When the fat woman left to find her husband, Joel drifted over to the dark-haired diva.

"I'm sorry for the wait, ma'am," Joel said. "It's been kind of hectic."

"That's quite all right," she said. She stood up and put the strap of her purse over a shoulder. "I know that sales bring everyone out of their shacks."

"What can I do for you today? Are you looking for a bedroom addition?"

The woman smiled thinly as blood rushed to her face. But the color quickly passed. She glanced down at the mattress and ran a hand across one of its seams in a swirling motion, then redirected her well-appointed sea green eyes to the hired help.

"As a matter of fact, I am. But I'm rather picky about my bedroom additions," she said, raising an eyebrow. "What can you tell me about this mattress?"

"It's our very best, ma'am," Joel said. He placed a hand on the cushion and slapped it twice. "It features hundreds of coil springs – all encased, of course – and an upholstered foundation. This particular model also has ventilators."

"Ventilators?"

"Oh, yes, ma'am. Ventilators. They're here on the side. Every time you depress the mattress, the ventilators breathe in stale, dirty air and expel fresh, clean air. So you get a good night's rest *and* help the environment."

"Fascinating." The customer got off the mattress, dragged her unadorned left hand across the fascinating product, and walked to another a few feet away. "And this one?"

"It's even better."

"Even better than your very best?"

"Absolutely," Joel said. He rushed over to the far side of the second bed, leaned over, and pressed down hard on the product several times with both hands. "This mattress has twice as many coils as the first. It's firm, very firm. It holds up well."

"That's good. I like things that hold up, Mr. . . . ."

"Smith. Joel Smith."

"You're very knowledgeable, Mr. Smith. My name is Doris. Doris Delamarter."

"It's nice to meet you," Joel said.

Doris sat down on the edge of the mattress.

"You're new here, aren't you?"

"I am. I started on Wednesday."

"I thought so," Doris said. "I haven't seen you before. Are you from Seattle? It's not every day that someone calls me 'ma'am,' much less a handsome young man like yourself."

"I'm not from Seattle," Joel said. "I just moved here from Montana."

"Montana? How interesting. What brings you out here?"

The chance to sell cots to cougars.

"Opportunity, ma'am. There's not a whole lot where I come from."

Doris kicked off her sandals, slithered to the center of the mattress, and rolled to one side. She propped her head up with one arm and petted the upholstery with the other.

"And have you found the opportunities you're looking for?"

"I believe I have," Joel said. He smiled and adjusted his tie. "The mattresses are really moving today."

"So it seems," Doris said. She slowly got off the bed, slinked over to Joel, and moved her face close to his. "And how much does this 'better than your best' mattress with ventilators and coils cost?"

"Forty dollars."

"Does that include delivery?"

"Indeed, it does," Joel said.

"Do *you* deliver the merchandise – or does someone else?"

"Others deliver the goods, but I make certain they get there. If you purchase this mattress today, I'll ensure you *get it* tonight. In fact, I'll guarantee it."

The customer smiled and blushed again as her flirtatious wheels rolled to a stop. Doris Delamarter had met her match.

"Then in that case, Mr. Smith, you have a sale."

"Thank you, ma'am. You won't be disappointed. I'll ring you up now."

* * * * *

Moments later Joel rolled up the sleeves of his borrowed dress shirt, leaned on a post near the dining room sets, and wiped his brow. Despite three consecutive nights of restful sleep, he was beat. He stared blankly at a section of sofas, chairs, and end tables until he heard raucous laughter from behind. He turned around and saw a familiar face.

"I like things that hold up? Bedroom additions? Good grief! We're going to have to get security for you. I'm surprised she didn't jump in your lap," Tom said as he caught his breath. He smiled, shook his head, and put a hand on Joel's shoulder. "That was the best show I've seen in months. Cary Grant couldn't have finished like that."

"You heard us?"

"I heard every word. I stood on the other side of the divider," Tom said. He walked across the hardwood floor to a dining table and pushed a few chairs into their places. "You got the sale though. That's more than the rest of us can say. Doris comes in here at least twice a month to bounce on the beds but never buys anything."

"Yeah, she was a bit over the top," Joel said with a laugh.

"So how's it going?" Tom asked. He swept the showroom with his eyes and saw several customers exit the store. A wall clock above the front doors read five to five. "Dad says you're doing well and starting to get the hang of the job."

"I am. I think I've finally figured it out. Customers don't want mattresses and couches. They want attention. Give them plenty of that and they'll buy a swamp."

Tom laughed.

"You're getting it."

"Why are you here?" Joel asked. "I thought you had a class today."

"I did. I just got out of it."

"Are you done with classes?"

"I'm done with classes," Tom said. "I still have four finals next week, but that's it. Then I'm done with college."

The comment hit Joel with surprising impact. He had forgotten about his previous life and what he'd be doing right now had he listened to Adam. He'd be preparing for his own finals, mailing resumes, and mapping out a career. He had already landed one interview –with an oil company – on June 12.

Maybe I'll show up when I'm eighty-one.

"Are you 'done' here too?" Joel asked.

"No. Not yet," Tom said. "I plan to peddle furniture at least until Ginny graduates next June and then take a look around."

"What does your dad want you to do?"

"He wants me to stay here permanently, of course, and eventually run the place, but I'm not sure *I* want to do that. At the very least, I want to keep my options open."

"That's smart. You'll have a business degree and experience when Ginny gets out. You can go places with that," Joel said. "If I were you, though, I wouldn't write off the store just yet. Your dad's sitting on a gold mine. Two hundred people came in today and at least a third of them bought something."

"I know. It's that way most days. That's why I'm in no hurry to leave. I want to take some time to think about what I could do here before venturing into the world."

Joel glanced toward the front of the store and saw Mel remove sale signs from windows as a clerk directed a patron to a door. A few feet away, an old man examined a floor lamp, turned it on and off, and headed for the exit. Lights flickered in the distance.

"It looks like the store is shutting down," Joel said. "I should get back to work."

Tom nodded.

"Yeah. You probably should," Tom said. "I'd stick around if I didn't have to get ready for a date. I'm taking Ginny to a show tonight. We're taking a break from the books."

"Have fun," Joel said.

"I'm sure we will. See you later."

Tom started for the door but stopped after two steps. He turned around slowly.

"Just out of curiosity, what are you doing tomorrow?" Tom asked. "The weather's supposed to be great."

"I have nothing planned, except to eat, sleep, and turn twenty-two."

"*Tomorrow* is your birthday? Oh, Lord, that's perfect!" Tom said. He rubbed his chin. "Do you like boats?"

"I do," Joel said.

Tom smiled.

"Then be ready at ten, my friend. The lake awaits."

25: JOEL

Saturday, June 7, 1941

Joel was no stranger to fine watercraft. His seaman father had taken him sailing to the San Juans several weekends a year in his gadget-rich twenty-five-foot sloop. But even that seemed to pale to the toy Tom Carter took out of Portage Bay.

The mint-condition 1935 Gar Wood Runabout sported a varnished mahogany hull, chrome fittings, leather seats, and a peppy Chrysler six-cylinder, 135-horsepower engine. At twenty-two feet, the inboard was small enough to maneuver through tight spots and large enough to blow away half the boats on Lake Washington.

Joel had seen pictures of wooden classics numerous times in boating magazines. But on his twenty-second birthday, he got to pilot one for the better part of an afternoon.

"Thanks for inviting me out here," Joel said as he powered the craft into open water near the southern tip of Mercer Island. "This is the most fun I've had in a long time."

"Don't mention it. Besides, it's your birthday. You're supposed to have fun."

"Thanks for the other stuff too." Joel throttled down and turned to face his friend. "You didn't have to take me in and your dad didn't have to give me a job. I might still be walking the streets looking for work had you not given me a break."

"I seem to recall that you rescued me first," Tom said, laughing. "Either way, it's no big deal. We're happy to have you. Dad thinks you're the best salesman on the planet, Mom wants to adopt you, and Brenda wants to bear your children. That's what I call a productive week."

Twenty minutes later Joel brought the vessel to a stop and dropped anchor off the west side of the island. In the distance, streams of automobiles crossed the eleven-month-old Lake Washington floating bridge. A second, more northerly span, connecting Seattle with its eastside suburbs, would not be built for another twenty-two years.

Joel climbed out of the deep cockpit and plopped onto the enclosed midsection of the speedboat, where he took off a gray sweatshirt, stretched out on one of Sandy Carter's guest towels, and welcomed his daily dose of Vitamin D. With the mercury mired in the high sixties, the mid-afternoon sun was a welcome sight.

"Tom, do you mind if I ask you a personal question?"

"No. What do you want to know?"

"How serious are you and Ginny?"

"Why? Do you want to date her?" ·

"Oh, no. It's nothing like that. Not that there's anything wrong with her. She's quite a woman. It's just that you two seem like kind of an odd couple."

Tom sighed, relieved that Seattle's most eligible bachelor did not have his sights on his girl. Sitting on a newly upholstered seat in back, he put his hands behind his head.

"We *are* an odd couple," Tom said. "I know as much about journalism as she does about business, and our personalities are polar opposites. About the only things we have in common are martinis, baseball, and this boat. But we get along great."

"Do you see yourselves getting married?"

"Who knows? Right now, I can't see myself growing up."

Joel laughed.

"Seriously, I don't know. We'll see how things look in a year. She might run off with her editor, or I might have two dames on each arm. Now, wouldn't that be a sight?"

Joel smiled and tried to think of other things. But getting close to Tom had made that difficult. Since meeting his once and future grandmother, he had obsessed over a bit of family trivia his mother had shared when he was seventeen, information that meant little in 1995 but meant a whole lot more today.

Virginia Gillette's first fiancé had died in World War II.

Joel could not help but ponder the possibilities should that fiancé turn out to be Tom Carter. If he saved Tom's life by steering him away from the Army, or even the war itself, he might meddle with his own existence. If Grandma Ginny does not meet and marry Grandpa Joe, there is no daughter Cindy or grandson Joel. Would he vanish into thin air like Marty McFly? Or continue on his merry way in a parallel universe? Joel knew now why people passed up philosophy classes. This stuff could fry your circuits. The grandfather paradox took on new relevance.

Ginny Jorgenson's grandson found another story line far more comforting. Maybe Tom was not the one. Maybe his new friend was just a brief, colorful chapter in the life of a remarkable, strong-willed, and stridently independent woman.

Joel gave the matter a little more thought and then cast it aside like an undersized sockeye. There was no point fretting over a boyfriend of two months or predicaments that may or may not be dire. He rolled onto his stomach, repositioned borrowed shorts that were a tad too loose, and let the fire in the sky do its work.

The world was becoming a complicated place. But on his twenty-second birthday, Joel Smith of Seattle reduced it to a nap.

26: TOM AND JOEL

Saturday, June 14, 1941

Thomas Alvin Carter's graduation party was two parts wedding reception and one part ticker-tape parade, with a dash of polka hall. When guests arrived, they walked past purple balloons attached to hedges and a "Congratulations, Tom!" banner that stretched fifteen feet. When they entered the large lawn in back, they navigated a maze of ten cloth-covered tables, wet bars, barbecue grills, and food stations.

A suitcase-sized cake competed with pagoda-style candle lanterns and a happy guy named Dick who played requests on a squeezebox. Sandra Carter, it seemed, knew more than fried chicken.

"You never cease to amaze, Mom," the graduate said.

"Thank you, honey, but the accordion was your father's idea. You know he can't host a party without putting his stamp on something."

On the other side of the yard, Melvin Carter rushed to a smoky grill temporarily managed by his twenty-year-old nephew, Lawrence, while his teenage niece, Lauren, and Brenda Carter guided guests to their tables. To the west, a setting sun illuminated similar outdoor parties in the university district as a slight breeze kept mosquitoes at bay.

"It's perfect," Tom said. He kissed his mom on the head and surveyed the celebration in his honor. More than sixty relatives, friends, schoolmates, and business associates had already streamed through the door. "Where's Joel? The store closed two hours ago."

"He was here," Sandy replied. "He got all cleaned up and everything, but then he left. Your father paid him yesterday. Maybe he went to the store. I really don't know."

"That's OK. I'm sure I'll see him later. I have a lot of other people to greet. It looks like Dad invited half the city."

"He did," Sandy said. "He's very proud of you, and so am I. Go enjoy your party."

* * * * *

Joel had not exercised this kind of time management since he had organized Adam's twenty-first birthday party at the Strip 'n' Whip eight months earlier.

After selling a washing machine at closing time to a woman who wanted to know if R2-D2 removed berry stains, he raced to the Airstream, showered, and donned some fancy, time-appropriate duds he had picked up on Friday. From there he walked to a nearby drugstore and purchased a greeting card and a current copy of the *Seattle Sun*. He returned to the Carters in time to find Tom delivering a pitcher of beer to Ginny and two others gathered around a picnic table covered with a checked tablecloth.

Tom smiled as he walked toward Joel and a buffet table loaded with burgers, hot dogs, chicken breasts, salads, corncobs, desserts, and Sandra Carter's famous biscuits. He laughed when he arrived.

"Where did you steal those?" Tom asked.

"I didn't steal them," Joel said. "I bought them. I got paid yesterday. Remember?"

Joel had upgraded his attire. Wearing a red pinstriped shirt, orange tie, gray vest, matching cuffed wide-legged trousers, and two-tone Oxfords, he looked like a man trying to bridge two decades on a salesman's salary and a college student's imagination. No more cowboy hats and Candy in Chains for him.

"It's not the most coordinated outfit I've seen today, but you look sharp," Tom said. "You're going to turn some heads tonight, buddy. Let me get you a drink."

"You can in a minute. First, let me give you something," Joel said. He reached in a vest pocket, pulled out an envelope containing a card, and handed it to Tom. "Congratulations."

"Thanks. But you shouldn't waste money on me. I have everything I need — maybe even new wheels. I suspect that the new Plymouth convertible parked behind the trailer has my name on it — and all because I didn't flunk out of school."

Brenda Carter approached stealthily from the side in bare feet, slowing to a stop to study Joel's revamped duds. She wore a pink cotton dress and a mischievous grin.

"You look nice, Joel. Can I get you anything?" Brenda asked.

"No, thank you," Joel said. "You look nice, too, Brenda — *very* nice."

"Thanks."

Brenda blushed and dawdled for a few seconds before skipping off to the kitchen to help her mother and her cousin.

86

Joel couldn't help but smile at all the attention she had thrown his way. She would need lion tamers to keep the men away when she went to UCLA in the fall. But for now, he was her sun and her moon – the unattainable cowboy with a knack for selling sofas and assembling creative outfits off of discount store racks.

Tom opened the card and laughed at the message. When he returned the card to the envelope, he noticed a slip of paper inside. It was the clipping of a newspaper article. The headline read: CONN, LOUIS SET FOR TITLE SCRAP.

"What's this?" Tom asked. "Did you buy tickets or something? This fight is in New York. Please tell me you didn't blow your first check on a fight we can't see."

"I didn't," Joel said. He smiled and put his hand on Tom's shoulder. "I just wanted to do something for the man who has everything."

"Well, I appreciate you keeping me informed. But I knew about the fight. Half the world knows about it. I plan on listening to it after work on Wednesday."

"I was counting on that. Do you know a crowded drinking establishment that will carry the broadcast, round by round?"

"As a matter of fact, I do. But let's talk about that later," Tom said. "Right now, you need to get a drink and mingle. There are people you have to meet."

27: JOEL

Tom and Joel swaggered across the lawn like Napoleon and his aide-de-camp inspecting the grounds at Versailles. When they approached the picnic table, they found Virginia Gillette puffing on a cigarette, holding a lager, and ruling her roost of three. She brightened at the sight of her male caller and his colorfully attired companion.

"Now you're what I call a sharp-dressed man," Ginny said. "How are you, Joel?"

"I couldn't be better," Joel replied. "I feel like a bee's knees."

Ginny and the others laughed uproariously, sending Joel into an unexpected retreat. He had wanted to practice his forties slang all week but now wondered whether he had botched his first test by saying something that probably meant, "I feel constipated." He gritted his teeth, stepped back, and sought a quick exit.

"That's good to hear," Ginny said. "Perhaps you can buzz for us later."

The girls giggled.

Tom smiled but did not pile on. He appeared focused on something else. He stepped behind his girlfriend, snared a pickle off her plate, and nodded, as if to suggest that marinated cucumbers were the bee's knees. When he finished chewing, he turned to the other young women at the table. Both looked past Tom to his sidekick.

"Ladies, this is Joel Smith. He just moved to the area and has been living with us the past few days." He put a hand on Joel's shoulder and slapped it twice. "Joel, this is Linda McEwan and Katie Kobayashi. Both are seniors at the university and will be sharing a house with Ginny this year. In fact, I think they move in tomorrow."

"Monday," Ginny said. "We can't move in until Monday."

"I stand corrected."

The women stood up and took turns greeting the late arrival.

"It's nice to meet you," Linda said, painting her target with luminous green eyes. She placed a highball glass on the table, next to a full beer and an empty bottle, and extended her right hand. "Ginny told us a lot about you. I see it's all true."

"I'll take that as a compliment," Joel said, with a nervous laugh. "She didn't tell me a thing about you, though. Had I known she had such ravishing roommates, I wouldn't have spent so much time hanging around this lug."

The girls smiled and turned toward Ginny.

"Where did you find this guy?" Linda asked. "I'm ready to take him home!"

"Tom can fill you in on that," Ginny said. She grinned and took a puff. "You may not want to know."

Joel glared at Grandma for a few seconds before casting more sweetness and light on her court. He would have to exercise caution around Virginia Gillette. Skeptical, dogged, and inquisitive, she was no doubt on to him.

Perhaps sensing an opportunity, maybe her only opportunity, to step out of the shadows, the quiet member of the trio leaned toward Joel and offered a hand.

"I'm Katie, by the way, in case you haven't figured it out."

"Hi, Katie."

Joel noted the mirthful eyes of the friendly Japanese girl in the lavender sundress. Gentle and benign, they contrasted sharply with the more covetous peepers of the curvy, freckled redhead at Ginny's side. Wearing a crisp white blouse and floral skirt, Linda McEwan was Smiling Sarah's more assertive and no doubt lethal twin.

"Ginny says you're from Montana," Linda said, eyes still locked and loaded.

"Yes, ma'am," Joel said. "I'm from Helena, the state capital."

"He's also a rancher," Ginny added with a wink.

"A rancher? Oh, my!" Linda said. "Where's your cowboy hat, cowboy?"

"It's in the trailer," Joel answered.

"Why don't you get it? I want to see how it looks on you."

"Maybe later. It's resting now."

And riding shotgun with Candy in Chains.

Linda switched from her gin fizz to her draft beer as if they were the same drink, never taking her eyes off Thomas Carter's newest pal. After two disastrous relationships in as many years, she appeared ready to test the third-time-is-a-charm theory.

"So what brings you out here?"

"Economic opportunity. Tom's father has been kind enough to employ me at his furniture store, and I have to admit it beats roping steers."

Ginny took another puff and flashed Joel a smile that said, "You're good but not that good."

"I'll bet it does," Linda said. "I haven't been in Carter's in a long time. I may have to stop by and buy a lamp or something."

"You do that. I'll give you all the help I can."

"I'd like that."

Tom plucked another pickle from Ginny's plate.

"Ginny, Linda, and their other housemate are members of the same sorority. They are Kappa to the core," Tom said. He examined his nearly empty schooner of beer and turned to Ginny. "Where is Grace, anyway? I know she was invited."

"She's running a bit late. She and Paul went to an ROTC function on campus after the commencement ceremony. He graduated too, you know."

"How could I not? He rubbed his grades in my face all week. I haven't seen him since Thursday, though."

"Well, maybe you should do some catching up. There they are now."

"I think I will, Virginia," Tom said, returning a warm glance from his girl.

Joel tuned out the exchange. Locked in a staring contest with Freckles, he debated whether to sit down and grab one of her pickles or roam some more and visit with others. Focused exclusively on pleasing the Carters, making money, and settling into his new environment, he had thought precious little about dating. But after five minutes with Linda McEwan, he thought a lot more. She had most definitely rolled out the carpet.

Mr. Available decided to stay. He could not think of a better way to spend the evening than in the company of these three. But just as he started to slide onto the bench opposite Linda, his social butterfly buddy unwittingly took his options off the table.

"Sorry to run, but we have rounds to make," Tom said. He tapped Joel on the arm and pivoted him toward the back of the two-story house, where Brenda and Lauren guided late-arriving guests to food, drink, and tables. "We'll see you girls later."

Joel smiled at Katie, who waved, and Ginny, who raised her glass, before taking one last look at Linda. Riding along on three drinks, she twirled her locks around a finger and blew him a kiss. She was an open book, for sure. But even open books were often good reads. Maybe it was time for Seattle's newest faux cowboy to get back in the saddle.

"Ladies, it's been a pleasure," Joel said.

28: GRACE AND JOEL

When Grace entered Mel Carter's castle on Baltic Avenue, she went directly past Go and straight for the booze. Though she had been a connoisseur of red wine for only fourteen days, she knew it was just the thing for a tired body. Three receptions, one commencement, and a ten-block walk in broken pumps had left her ready for some vino and a good night's sleep.

"Thanks," Grace said as she took a glass from Paul.

Wearing a green-and-white gingham dress, Grace stood next to her graduate on a flagstone patio that extended fifteen feet from the back of the house. She took a sip and turned outward to face dozens of diners.

"There are a lot of people here. Do you see Ginny?"

"No," Paul said. "But I see the guest of honor."

Grace turned her head and saw a man in a pressed white shirt and pleated slacks walk quickly across the freshly mowed lawn. The "guest of honor" wore a broad smile.

Paul removed his arm from Grace's back and stepped forward.

"There you are," Paul said. The uniformed officer shook Tom Carter's hand and gave him a bear hug. "Congrats, you dog. Did you ever think we'd make it?"

"You? No," Tom said. "Me? I never had a doubt."

Paul laughed.

"That's my man – always the joker."

Tom swigged the remainder of his lager and turned his glass over, shaking the last few drops on the dark flat rocks. When he looked up, he saw a pout and put it out.

"Hi-de-ho to you, too, gorgeous," Tom said. He threw his arms around Grace. "You look better every time I see you. I hope Navy Boy is keeping you under lock and key."

"He is," Grace said with a giggle. "Congratulations, Tom. This is quite a party."

"Yes, it is. At least half of these people are customers though. You know my dad. He never misses a chance to mix business with pleasure," Tom said. He looked at Paul and Grace and then at a loaded buffet table a few feet away. "Have you two eaten tonight? If not, dig in. There's plenty of grub, and I know we can't eat it all."

"We had some food at our last reception, but I might try some of those desserts," Grace said. "You can never have enough cheesecake."

"Then have at it," Tom said. "Before you go, though, I want you to meet a new friend of mine."

Tom stepped on a metal folding chair and scanned the premises twice before spotting his buddy. He shouted and motioned to a man filling an empty glass from the keg.

"Hey, Joel! Come over here," Tom said. "You're not finished meeting and greeting."

"Joel" waved back, blew foam off his beer, and proceeded toward the patio, stopping only to say a few words to Mel and Sandy. He straightened his citrus-colored tie ás he approached Tom, Paul, and Grace.

Grace felt her stomach flutter as the well-dressed man – a man she recognized – slowly came into focus. An interesting day just got more interesting.

"Paul and Grace, this is Joel Smith," Tom said. "He's been staying with us and working at the store for almost a couple of weeks now. He's from Helena, Montana."

Paul extended a hand.

"It's a pleasure to meet you, Joel. I'm Paul McEwan – and this is my fiancée, Grace Vandenberg."

* * * * *

"The pleasure is mine," Joel said as he shook two hands.

The perfunctory exercise turned into something less routine when Joel zeroed in on the second party. He answered a knowing smile and a lingering stare with a knowing smile and a lingering stare.

The Instant Recognition Society is called to order.

"Montana, huh? You're a long way from home," Paul said.

The comment brought Joel out of a pleasant daze.

"I am," Joel said.

"So how do you like the big city?"

"I like it a lot."

Joel did, too. Of course, he also liked it when he could attend eight Seahawks games a year, get a latte to go, and catch direct flights to Kona.

"That's great," Paul said. "Seattle's a fine town. I'm sure you'll do well here."

92

"I'm sure I will."

"Paul and I were roommates our freshman year in the dorms and our sophomore year in the fraternity," Tom said as he jumped back into the conversation. "We're both in Zeta Alpha Rho."

Joel smiled.

What a coincidence. So am I. Shall we all do the secret handshake?

"It sounds like you two had some good times in school," Joel said.

"We did," Tom said with a grin. "We had a lot of good times."

Joel glanced at Paul. He expected to see a similar expression but saw a serious stare instead. Paul appeared to be checking out the man who had given his intended a conspicuously familiar greeting. Joel couldn't blame him. If he had a fiancée like Grace Vandenberg, he wouldn't want to share her either.

"Don't believe this guy for a minute," Paul said. "Tom thinks *everything* is a good time."

Joel noted the friendly voice. He had apparently passed Paul's threat assessment.

"So I've learned," Joel said.

Paul turned to face Tom.

"Speaking of good times, where were you last night? We missed you."

"Ginny and I went to a movie," Tom said. "I knew my folks were planning a circus tonight and wanted to enjoy at least *one* quiet evening this weekend."

Tom looked at Joel and brought him up to speed.

"Paul went to a stag party last night," Tom said. "One of our fraternity brothers who graduated last year is getting married next week."

"I see," Joel said.

Tom shifted back to Paul.

"How did it go?"

Paul grinned.

"You mean you didn't hear about Graham?" Paul asked.

"No," Tom said. "What happened?"

Paul glanced at Grace, hesitated, and then turned back to Tom.

"This may be a good time to get a refill," Paul said. He looked at Grace. "Do you mind, sweetheart?"

"Not at all," Grace said. "I'll try to entertain Mr. Smith while you're away."

"Thanks. We won't be gone long," Paul said. He smiled at Tom and extended an arm. "After you, sir."

When Paul and Tom drifted out of voice range, Grace eyed the freshly shaved and nicely attired specimen in front of her. He was an improvement over the first incarnation.

"I've seen you before," Grace said. "You're the cowboy."

And you're the Vision of Forty-Seventh Street.

"At your service," Joel said.

"You're not really a cowboy, are you?"

"No, ma'am. I'm not," Joel said. He smiled. "But I have learned how to manage herds at the furniture store. We put up a sale sign and the cattle fall into line."

Grace laughed.

"You're funny."

Joel brightened at the sight of her mesmerizing smile. It could launch a thousand ships – and maybe a few aircraft. He could see why the ensign had not even waited to graduate before popping the question.

"I love your accent," Joel said. "It sounds vaguely British. Are you a royal subject?"

"No," Grace said. "I'm as American as you are, but I was raised overseas. The accent is a hand-me-down from my English mother. I'm not really fond of it. It makes me stand out."

"That's exactly why you should keep it. It's almost lyrical."

"Thank you."

Joel sipped his beer and then caught another glimpse of the annoying rock on her finger. It was just his luck that she was taken.

"Congratulations on your engagement," Joel said. "When's the big date?"

"Paul and I haven't set one yet. He's headed off to his first assignment next week."

"Have you known each other long?"

"I guess that depends on your definition of 'long,'" Grace said. "We've known each other only a few months. He proposed two weeks ago."

"He's a lucky man – a very lucky man," Joel said.

* * * * *

Grace glanced past Joel to the bar and saw Paul and Tom share a hearty laugh. At first she had wanted Paul to hurry back and save her from this unexpected distraction, but now she wanted him to stay put. For the first time since blatantly violating Washington's statute on underage drinking, she succumbed to guilt.

"So tell me, Joel Smith of Helena, Montana, what were you doing sitting on a street bench at nine o'clock at night looking like something the cat dragged in?"

"I was resting," Joel said.

"Resting?" Grace asked. "Resting from what?"

"I was resting from a bumpy, twenty-four-hour ride in a freezing boxcar, eight miles of walking, several job rejections, and a day on the streets eating rotten produce."

Grace blushed.

"I'm sorry."

"Don't be," Joel said. "My story is only half as bad as it sounds."

"Are you doing all right?"

"I am now. The Carters are looking after me. They're great people."

"They are," Grace said.

Before Grace could get in another word, Paul and Tom returned. Arm in arm, they held their sides and tried to contain growing laughter.

"If it weren't for his old man, he'd still be in jail. Talk about a wedding gift!" Paul said. He let go of Tom and looked at Grace. "I'm sorry, honey. We're just being boys."

"I understand," Grace said.

Paul walked up to Grace, pulled her close with one arm, and kissed her on the cheek.

"*This* is why I love this girl."

Grace glanced at Joel and saw that his smile was gone. He stared into space.

"We should go, Paul."

"Now?"

"Yes. I'm tired."

"But we haven't even said hi to Ginny," Paul said. "She's sitting at the picnic table with Linda and Katie. It'll just take a minute."

"No. Let's go," Grace said. "I'll see them all tomorrow."

"OK then. We're off. But at least let me get rid of your glass."

"All right."

"Sorry to drink and run, old pal, but Grace is right," Paul said. "We've had a long day. Let's do this again when I get back in August."

"Count on it," Tom said.

Paul shook Tom's hand and then looked at the Montanan.

"It was nice meeting you, Joel."

"You too."

Paul took Grace's empty wine glass and walked halfway across the yard to a table of dirty dinnerware, where Brenda and Lauren tried to get a jump on the massive cleanup. He waved to three familiar coeds, grabbed a brownie off a tray, and headed back.

When Grace saw Paul draw near, she clutched her purse and gave Tom a hug. She greatly admired the carefree young man who had made her best friend so happy.

"Bye, Tom. Congratulations, again. You should be proud."

"Thanks, Grace. Thanks for coming."

As Grace stepped away from Tom, she threw her eyes at Joel. His beautiful smile was back. But it was sad and wistful, not flirtatious or cocky. It was the smile from Forty-Seventh Street and not one she needed to see tonight. She offered her hand.

"You're an interesting man, Mr. Smith. Perhaps we'll meet again."

"That would be nice," Joel said as he took the hand. "Take care."

Exhausted, anxious, and more than a little distracted, Grace rejoined the man she had promised to marry and headed into the night.

29: GINNY

Monday, June 16, 1941

The nondescript rambler on the corner of Klickitat Avenue and East Fifty-Sixth Street was no Carter Castle. Peeling gray paint greeted its occupants on the outside, while peeling white paint did the same inside. Two closets lacked doors and a window in back required hydraulic equipment to open. But the place had four bedrooms, a spacious kitchen, and a large cedar deck. At forty dollars a month, it was a steal for three cash-strapped coeds and their old-money ringleader – even on a twelve-month lease.

"Who is he, really?" Linda asked, as she helped Ginny push a wool-covered club sofa against a living room wall. Tom had purchased the repossessed piece for a song and given it to the girls as a moving-in present. "Not that I'm complaining or anything."

"Tom thinks he really is from Montana, but he's not sure he buys the rancher bit," Ginny said. "Nor do I. Joel has smoother hands than I do and better diction."

"I noticed that too. He looks more like a banker's son than a rancher's son. Maybe he's an heir to an oil fortune who's lost his way," Linda said with a sly grin.

"Somehow I doubt it. I know the rich, dear, and they don't typically ride the rails in empty boxcars."

Moments later Katie and Grace, in shorts and sweatshirts, stumbled through the front door with a large cardboard box. They deposited it next to the sofa and took a seat.

"Make yourselves comfortable, ladies," Ginny said. "Would you like a pedicure before we bring in the other boxes? Or perhaps some wine to take the edge off your labor?"

Grace laughed.

"I'd like both, please. My feet are still sore from Saturday."

Katie reached into a pocket and pulled out a pack of smokes.

"Here are your cigarettes, Ginny. I found them in one of the boxes, next to your face cream."

"Thank you, Katie."

Ginny sat on a stool, struck a match, and found tobacco tranquility. She stared at Grace and Katie, who had kicked off their shoes, lifted their feet from the hardwood floor, and settled into the ends of the couch like cats curling up for an afternoon nap.

"Well, what do you girls think of our glorious abode?" Ginny asked.

"I like it," Katie said.

"Me too," Grace added. "I'm not sure I care for the leaky faucet in the bathroom, but I do like my bedroom. Are you sure you don't want to move downstairs, Linda? I'll let you have the room if you want it."

"No. I'm fine." Attired in denim overalls and down on her knees, Linda retrieved essential cosmetics from a hastily stuffed box of toiletries, knickknacks, and other small belongings. "I saw a big spider in your room this morning and one is enough for me."

Ginny scanned her surroundings for a makeshift ashtray and found one in a porcelain coffee mug sitting on a windowsill. She took a puff and glanced at the occupants of the sofa.

"Linda and I were just talking about Joel Smith. What do you two think of our mystery man? Katie? You didn't make much noise Saturday."

"That's because Linda made enough for a marching band," Katie said.

"Yes, she did. She was a one-woman percussion section," Ginny said, drawing a smile from Linda. "But what do you think of Joel?"

"I like him. He is much different than most boys at school – more polite, better looking, better smelling!" Katie said. "He needs a wardrobe consultant though. In his case, the clothes don't make the man."

Grace and Linda laughed.

"What about you, Cinderella?" Ginny asked, turning to Grace. "I saw you talk to him for a few minutes – more than a few minutes, actually. What were your impressions?"

"I thought he was nice."

"Just *nice*?" Linda asked. "Good Lord, Grace. Just because you're engaged doesn't mean you have to check your opinions at the door. I know you have more to say."

"Very well," Grace said. She looked at her interrogator thoughtfully and spoke in the measured cadence of a first-year foreign-language instructor. "I thought he was pleasant and articulate and intelligent and refreshingly well-mannered."

"You're impossible!" Linda said.

"He does have a nice smile."

Katie giggled and nudged her couch-mate with a foot. Grace smiled and answered with a kick of her own. Linda shook her head and rolled her eyes.

"Don't mind Linda," Ginny said. "She's already voted five times on the matter."

More laughter.

Ginny's wide grin grew wider. She loved these moments. They were why she had moved into a dilapidated house with three disparate personalities rather than ride out her final year in a sterile sorority or live alone in a lavishly appointed apartment.

Yes, they were talking about men, the insipid topic *du jour* of college women from coast to coast. But they were doing so in a way that brought out their delightful differences. When Ginny saw Grace's carefree smile, she could not help but think of the timid, grief-stricken creature she had roomed with her freshman year. She looked forward to discussions that drew her sheltered friend even further out of her shell.

Linda continued her assault of the box, throwing what she needed now in a paper bag and what she might need later into a smaller box. When she found a photographic reminder of Disastrous Relationship Number One, she smiled, tore it up, and continued on her way.

"You three can tease me all you want. As long as I get to see him again, I frankly don't care," Linda said. "Just promise me you won't let him get away, Ginny. The next time you and Tom go out, it's a double date. OK?"

"I promise. But it may be a while. Tom is going salmon fishing this weekend and he's taking the boy wonder with him. Next week they may go on safari. Who knows?"

Ginny snuffed out her stub, stood up, and tiptoed around a minefield of cleaning supplies, half-opened boxes, and assorted junk Linda had scattered across the floor. She picked up a pair of striped boxer shorts, stuck between the pages of one of the redhead's textbooks, and held them up.

"I won't even ask," Ginny said, drawing out each word.

The cats on the couch purred.

After flipping the underwear to its apparent custodian, Ginny pushed several boxes to the wall, making a path as she went, and strutted into the kitchen. She returned a moment later with a broom, a dustpan, and resolve.

"It's time to get busy, girls. Let's make this house a home."

30: JOEL

Wednesday, June 18, 1941

Typically quiet on Wednesdays, the Mad Dog barked up a storm on June 18. By six thirty, every booth, barstool, and pool table had an occupant, and every occupant had something to say. Some rehashed their workdays or summer session classes but most vigorously debated whether a scrawny upstart from Pittsburgh could beat the legendary heavyweight champion of the world. Two waist-high console radios, one borrowed for the evening, occupied strategic positions in the public area of the campus watering hole, while two tabletop models sat at opposite ends of a twenty-five-foot bar. Set to the same station, the four radios pushed sports commentary out of high-fidelity speakers.

Joel Smith and Tom Carter, ties loosened and sleeves rolled, settled into a booth near the borrowed console and studied dinner menus. The junior salesman pulled out a wad of bills and placed them on the table.

"Tonight's on me," Joel said. He hoisted a draft beer and smiled at his friend. "I figure it's the least I can do for all that you and your family have done for me."

"Thanks. But like I said the other day, it's no big deal. Don't waste money on me. If you're going to blow your paycheck, do it on a dame," Tom said. "I'm not going to kiss you good night for a hamburger."

Joel laughed.

"Well, in that case, pay for your own dinner!"

Tom grinned and looked around the tavern. At least twenty people had passed through the door since the salesmen had claimed the last available booth. Most crowded around the bar and asked if the fight had started.

"So are you going to tell me what this is really all about? You have something up your sleeve. I can feel it."

"I do," Joel said. "But just be patient and enjoy yourself. I guarantee you are going to have fun tonight."

"Whatever you say, sport. You're the man with the plan."

After the waitress took his order, Joel glanced at a table on the far side of the dim, smoky room and noticed two men in uniform join two others in civilian garb. The pair in street clothes teased their friends about their private stripes but in a manner that was unquestionably respectful.

"Do you ever think about the war?" Joel asked.

"I think about it all the time. Don't you?"

"No. Not really."

"You should. Things are getting pretty hot in Europe. I don't see how we stay of out it," Tom said. "Hell, two hundred students here just took their draft physicals and some hadn't even graduated. You don't make people do that unless you think they'll be needed, and needed soon."

"Aren't you still covered by a deferment?"

"Not anymore. My 1-D became a 1-A on Saturday. I'm fair game now." Tom sipped his beer and gazed at the bar. Even standing room was in short supply. "You are too, I imagine. You're not even in school. The Army would love a strapping lad like you."

"Yeah," Joel agreed. "I guess they would."

If they knew I existed.

Joel purged the awkward, unpleasant topic from his mind and eyed the waitress as she fiddled with the volume control of a console radio ten feet away. He found it difficult to hear the broadcast through the sound of patrons laughing, greeting, and talking. But he knew from modulations in the announcer's staccato voice that the opening bell was near. He smiled at Tom, picked up a twenty-dollar bill, and slid out of their booth.

"What are you doing, Joel?"

"I'm getting the party started."

Joel straightened his tie and walked toward a nearby table. Once there, he grabbed an unoccupied chair and waited for the noise to subside. When it did, he stood on the chair and introduced himself to eighty strangers with a two-fingered whistle.

"Good evening, folks. My name is Joel Smith. I don't know much about boxing, but my friend Andy Jackson does," he shouted as he waved the bill high over his head. "And Andy Jackson says Conn goes five. Do I have any takers?"

* * * * *

Joel got his takers, four in all. The two privates and their civilian buddies threw in five bucks apiece.

They talked the party closest to Joel and Tom into switching tables to better keep an eye on the clown with the whistle and the twenty dollars he had put into play. The foursome, however, spent less time watching Joel

101

than taunting him in the first two rounds, as Joe Louis, winner of his last twenty-five fights and forty-nine of fifty as a professional, dominated Billy Conn with a series of hard rights to the body.

"You want to pay now or pay later, big mouth?" a wiry private named Ricky said. "Nobody goes five rounds with the Brown Bomber."

Joel ignored the rabble at the table and several others who passed by to gauge the mood of the big bettors. He finished his second beer and smiled at his fellow diner.

"Having a good time?"

"I'd be having a better time if I didn't think you were risking a week's pay just to impress me. You don't owe me a thing, Joel. This is reckless."

"Patience, my man, patience. Good things come to those who wait."

"Unless they wait more than a week to pay off a bet," Tom said. "Then they get the shit pounded out of them across the street."

Joel laughed. Tom didn't have Adam Levy's biting wit, but he was definitely a funny guy. He thought about his old friend and what *he* might have done had he followed Joel into the mine and back to 1941.

There was no doubt about it. He would have definitely taken advantage of opportunities like this. The betting parties grew quiet in the third and fourth rounds as Conn, thirty-five pounds lighter, began to land punches and keep the champ at bay. But noise and tension returned in the fifth when Louis hit the light heavyweight challenger with thunderous body shots and left hooks to the jaw. Conn barely survived the round. He staggered to the wrong corner at the bell.

"Lucky son of a bitch," Private Ricky said.

Joel surveyed the room and saw that the dearth of takers to his bet had nothing to do with aversions to gambling. Piles of small bills and coins formed centerpieces at several tables, including the booth behind him, where four men in letterman sweaters tried to augment their summer income with pennies from heaven.

As the broadcast gave way to an advertisement, people crowded around Joel to see the whistler collect his cash. But rather than gloat at the conquered and run with his winnings, Joel attempted to draw others in. After stacking four new fives on top of his twenty, he slid out of his booth and spoke to anyone willing to listen.

"I can see from the money in this room that I'm among kindred spirits. So let's make this interesting," Joel said. He poured a third beer from a pitcher and sat on the edge of his table. "I have forty dollars here. I'll give it all to the first person who puts five on Louis to end this in the sixth. Heck, I'll even throw in another ten. That's five for fifty. Come on, gents. You can't get that kind of action in a cathouse!"

Several people rushed forward with fives, but Joel took the Lincoln from Private Ricky. Stung from defeat in the first bet, he relished a rematch.

"Don't think for a minute you're going to walk out of here with that pile, smart-ass," he said. "I'll stay here as long as it takes."

Ricky's civilian friends stood at his side and sneered at Joel, while the other private, named Lloyd, kept his seat and quietly assessed the competition. Sensing a trick, he studied Tom and looked for a clue but found none. The son of Melvin and Sandra Carter had his face in his hands.

* * * * *

Ricky did not win his bet – nor did his two slovenly dressed buddies in rounds seven and eight or four better-dressed football players in rounds nine through twelve. At the sound of each round-ending bell, Joel Smith, sports trivia extraordinaire from the age of jumbo screens and fantasy football, added cash to the pot, restated his terms, and scoured the Mad Dog for another sucker. They were as plentiful as P.T. Barnum quotes at a convention of used car salesmen.

To make the wagers as appealing as possible, and draw tens instead of fives, Joel threw in more of his own money and even some of Tom's. The recent graduate had gone from putting his face in his hands to putting his dollars on the table. By the time Round 12 had come to an end, the man with a plan had netted eighty bucks.

Conn too had exceeded expectations. Punching more and dancing less with each round, he had put Louis on the defensive. Repeated blows to the head had sent the champ to his corner where his trainer treated him to the reviving aroma of ammonia. The noise at the Polo Grounds and in the Mad Dog was deafening and decidedly in the favor of the challenger. Noting the shift in sentiment, Joel put a hundred dollars in his hand and held it up for the benefit of anyone with an open wallet and a useless mind.

"I have one more bet in me, people, one more," Joel shouted. "And this time I'm putting my dough on Louis. I'll put a hundred bucks against twenty that the champ ends this now, this round. Who wants to win their fall tuition?"

Tom's smirk vanished. He hastily slid out of the booth and pulled Joel aside.

"What the hell are you doing? You have these dopes on their heels," Tom said. "Don't blow it now by getting careless. Louis may not last another second."

"Where was that faith I saw a minute ago?" Joel asked. He smiled and put his arm around his skittish companion. "I said I'd show you a good time tonight – and I will."

Nearly a dozen sheep stepped toward the slaughter with twenties in their hands. Joel again evaluated the prospects and tried to determine who had families to feed and who did not. Once more, he went to the well.

"Much obliged, private. Good luck to you!"

By the time the thirteenth round began, more than thirty customers, brimming with alcohol-fueled cheer, crowded around the console near Joel and Tom's booth to take in two things: the final minutes of the best heavyweight fight in years and a potentially serious exchange of legal tender. Every punch and counter punch called on the radio whipped the listeners into a frenzy. One patron screamed hysterically and pounded the console with his fists, while several others paced frantically.

"I don't know if I can take this," Tom shouted into Joel's ear. "Even I don't throw this kind of money around. This is insane."

Sitting on the edge of his table with folded arms, Joel grinned at his fellow revelers like the Cheshire Cat, breaking eye contact only to periodically check the second hand of a clock above the bar. As it passed the two-minute mark, he gave Tom a pat on the shoulder and let history take its course.

Joe Louis, teetering on the brink of defeat just moments earlier, rebounded with crushing rights to his opponent's jaw and chin, putting a smile on his Mad Dog supporters and sending Private Ricky into shock.

"Conn is down! Conn is down! Conn is down!"

Joel emptied his beer, grabbed the cash, and motioned for Tom to follow him to their rivals' table, where he put a five spot next to an ashtray and smirked at the quartet. The civilians threw hostile glares, but Private Lloyd tipped his hat.

"Buy your friend a drink, gentleman," Joel said. "He shouldn't be alone tonight."

Joel guided Tom past several new admirers to the tavern door and the cool, clean air outside. When they descended the steps and reached the sidewalk, Joel pulled out his take for the night. He stuffed some bills in Tom's shirt pocket, a few more in his left hand, and the rest in his right.

"This is for the boat fuel I burned on my birthday, this is for graduating, and this is for being one hell of a good friend."

Joel shielded his eyes from a setting sun and peered southward down the Ave, where strolling couples and honking cars brought a Wednesday evening to life. Satisfied that the U-District had not yet rolled up its sidewalks, Joel ran a hand through his hair, put an arm around Tom, and grinned.

"My work here is done," Joel said. "Let's get some cigars."

31: SANDY AND MEL

Saturday, June 21, 1941

For the first time in weeks dinner at six was dinner for two. With Brenda babysitting and Tom and Joel returning from Westport, Sandy Carter had no one to cook for and no one to talk to, save the inattentive man hiding behind a newspaper at the other end of the table.

"When do you think the boys will get back?" Sandy asked, seeking both an answer and signs of intelligent life.

"It depends when they left," Mel Carter said. "It's only a three-hour drive, but the traffic can get thick on Saturdays. They'll get here."

"I know they'll get here. I just wanted to talk to you *before* they get here. I'm a little concerned."

Mel folded the paper and placed it to the side of an untouched plate of Salisbury steak, mashed potatoes, and sweet corn. Giving his wife his undivided attention, he took off his reading glasses and stared across the table.

"Concerned about what?"

"About the fact Joel hasn't received one letter from home – or anywhere else, for that matter – since he's been here. Don't you think that's odd?"

"I do. I've wondered about that myself. But that doesn't make it our concern."

"Perhaps you could talk to him and ask if anything is wrong at home. If Tom had gone away and I hadn't heard from him in three weeks, I'd be concerned."

"He's twenty-two years old, Sandra. I think he can manage his family. Unless he's running from the law or running from a wife, I don't think we should stick our noses in his business." Mel leaned back in his chair. "Do you want to send him packing?"

"Oh, no. I love having him here. He's a good influence on Tom and he's been very helpful around the house. He even picked up groceries for me on Tuesday. I just worry, that's all. Is he doing OK at the store?"

"He's doing more than OK. The kid is selling everything in sight and making new customers of everyone who walks through the door. Half the men who come in want to hire him and most of the women want to take him home. I've never seen anything like it."

"I know. He had the same effect on people at the party."

"So why don't you tell me what's really bothering you?"

Sandra took a deep breath, sipped her lemonade, and stared blankly at an antique oak hutch to her left. Filled with dishes and figurines, the massive china closet had been in her family for four generations. After several seconds of awkward silence, she got up from her chair, walked to Mel's side, and put a hand on his shoulder.

"There's something I want to show you."

* * * * *

A minute later Sandy returned to the dining room, sat down in a chair next to her husband, and placed a small, strange-looking object on top of the table. About five inches high, it featured a greenish screen, an array of white numbered-and-lettered buttons, and a stub-like projection on top that shot up from the dark blue case.

"What do you make of this?" Sandy asked.

Mel put on his glasses and closely scrutinized the item. He shook it, held it up to the lights of a chandelier, and then pressed it to his ear. None of the gestures yielded clues. Nor did punching the buttons or reading the lettering on the back.

"I don't know what to make of it. I've never seen anything like it in my life. Where did you find this?"

"It was under a cowboy hat in a cabinet in the trailer. I found it this morning when I went to change the sheets. What do you think it is?"

"Who knows? It looks like some sort of communication device, maybe a new kind of telephone. If it is, the manufacturers haven't let me in on it. It might even be a toy. Hell, I've seen odder things in department stores. I'm not sure. Either way, it's not ours and we should probably leave it alone."

Not satisfied with Mel's answer, Sandy picked up the item and examined it again. She considered raising more questions or even asking Joel himself when he got back but decided against it. She slipped the device into the pocket of her everyday dress.

"You're right," Sandy said. She forced a weak smile. "I'll put it back now. But if he doesn't get any mail or telephone calls in the next few days, will you at least talk to him?"

"I'll talk to him. I promise. Now, let's finish dinner."

Mel dug in. After drowning his potatoes in lumpy brown gravy, he cut his steak into bite-sized chunks and lifted the largest toward his mouth. But the moment he glanced across the table, he stopped his arm and lowered his fork. He stared at his plate, sighed, and then returned to his wife, as if finally validating her concerns and signaling his own about a stranger who had rapidly become an integral part of their lives.

32: JOEL

Tuesday, June 24, 1941

Joel did not struggle with where to go or whom to see. When Mel Carter said he could have Tuesdays off "from now until the end of time," he made a beeline for Klickitat Avenue. For someone seeking quality female company, the rustic rambler on the corner of Fifty-Sixth was a target-rich environment.

Joel knocked three times on the front door. When no one answered, he walked around the house. Once in back, he found not a flirtatious redhead or a dreamy blonde but rather a busy brunette. Virginia Gillette sat in a deck chair and made notations on typewritten papers. Wearing a blue blouse and white cotton shorts, she looked like a coed who had brought homework along on spring break.

"Greetings from the Kingdom of Carter," Joel said.

Ginny looked up and gave her caller a warm smile.

"Joel! What a pleasant surprise. What brings you here?"

The visitor shrugged.

"I don't know. Curiosity. Boredom. Lust. All three."

Ginny laughed.

"You should bottle that wit, Mr. Smith. It would sell in forty-eight states."

"I'll keep that in mind," Joel said. "I'm sorry if I interrupted anything. I just thought I'd drop by. I have the day off and wanted to visit with people who don't eat, sleep, and breathe couches and commissions. Did I come at a bad time?"

"No, not at all. Pull up a chair."

"OK. I will."

Joel grabbed the first chair he saw. He placed it at a respectful distance and sat down.

"You just missed the others," Ginny said. She managed a cigarette in one hand and a red pencil in the other. "So it looks like you're stuck with little old me."

"No problem," Joel said. "What are the others doing?"

"Grace and Katie are working at the library. Linda is attending a class."

"And you?"

"I'm putting together an article for the *Sun*. It's a mess, and it's due tomorrow."

"What's it about?" Joel asked.

"Local efforts to fight polio and the disease's impact on families in Seattle."

"It sounds weighty. Do you like writing about 'weighty' things?"

"As a matter of fact, I do. I like writing about things that have relevance to the lives of average people. Public health is my passion," Ginny said as she tapped ashes into a tray. "We could achieve so much if we could only educate the public about the importance of hygiene and healthy living. Do you agree?"

"Yes."

Ginny smiled at Joel.

"Just 'yes'? What happened to 'yes, ma'am'? Have you lost your twang?"

"Yes, ma'am. I left it in Westport," Joel said.

This gig is so over.

Ginny chuckled.

"You know, Joel, the reason I haven't pressed you for better answers is because I like you. I also like what you've done for Tom. He told me about your fun the other day."

"He did?"

"Oh, yes," Ginny said. "It was a lovely gesture, one that made a big impression. But it doesn't explain who you are or why you are here. Care to tell me?"

Joel wanted to tell her. He wanted to tell her everything, but he knew he couldn't. There was no way he could possibly explain magic mines and time travel without inviting skepticism, ridicule, and phone calls to mental health authorities.

"Not now," Joel said. "My story's complicated."

"I have time."

"It's very complicated."

"Fair enough," Ginny said as she returned to her papers. "I won't pry. But you should know that a lot of people are asking questions about you, including every member of this household."

"Are they good questions?"

"Well, let's see. Katie wants to know if you dress yourself, and just yesterday Linda asked if you had a girl back home. I said I didn't think so. She's quite fond of you."

"I gathered that from the kiss she blew me."

Ginny laughed.

"What about Grace?" Joel asked.

"She thinks you have a nice smile," Ginny said.

"Is that so? What can you tell me about her?"

"She's engaged. That's all you need to know."

"I can see this is going to be fun," Joel said. He pulled his chair closer. "Let's talk about something else then. Tell me about you and Tom. How did you meet? What do you think of him? Are things serious?"

"You ask a lot of questions."

"Isn't that how a good reporter gets answers?"

"Touché," Ginny said. She put her pencil down. "OK. I'll tell you. Tom and I have actually known each other for quite a while. Linda introduced us when he was a sophomore and I was a freshman. He and Paul were roommates at the time. I thought he was kind of a playboy. I still do. He spends far too much time drinking and gambling and playing with his toys and not enough time on important matters."

"Such as?"

"Such as his future. I know he's capable of running his father's store – and running it well – but he has the potential to do so much more."

"So what brought you together?" Joel asked.

"A spin on the water. Tom took Linda, Grace, Paul, and me out in his powerboat in April. We spent a whole day on the lake and had a wonderful time. When Tom and I discovered we had a few things in common, we decided to go out again. We've been dating ever since."

"And how are things now?"

"We're still finding our way. I rarely invest much time or effort in men, but I've made an exception with Tom," Ginny said. "He's a good man, with a heart of gold, and I'm lucky to have him. May I ask why this interests you?"

Because if you marry him, I might go poof!

"I'm curious, that's all," Joel said. "I know you mean a lot to him, and now that I'm running in his pack, I want to know the pack."

Joel watched Ginny chuckle and lean back in her chair. She no doubt knew that he was full of it but probably didn't care.

"We're all pretty tame," Ginny said. "You can take my word on that."

"Even Linda?" Joel asked.

"Even Linda."

Ginny added another paper to her stack, set the stack aside, and turned her attention to the smoldering tobacco product in her hand. She snuffed out the butt in the ashtray, looked under her chair, and retrieved her purse. She pulled a small package from inside the purse, tapped out another cigarette, and lit up.

Joel laughed and shook his head.

"Why do you smoke?" he asked.

"Because, Mr. Smith, I enjoy it."

"That's a good reason," Joel said matter-of-factly. "Of course, enjoying something alone isn't sufficient reason to do it. I personally would enjoy riding a motorcycle naked through Pike Place Market while shouting, 'The South will rise again!' But I have no immediate plans to do so."

"Perhaps you should reconsider," Ginny said. "I could arrange coverage by the *Sun*."

"No, thanks."

"Besides, does it really matter if I smoke?"

"Of course it does," Joel said. "Those things will kill you."

"Says who?"

"The surgeon general."

"Don't know him."

Joel grinned. If it wasn't obvious before, it was now. Ginny Gillette had come this way out of the box. Feeling like a person taking care of an aging parent, Joel leaned forward, gently pulled the cigarette from Grandma's mouth, and put it out.

"Why did you do that?" Ginny asked.

"Let's just say I have a vested interest in your health," Joel replied.

Ginny smiled and folded her arms.

"I can see we're going to get along famously."

33: JOEL

Friday, June 27, 1941

June 27, 1941, was a date that lived in infamy, at least in the meticulously maintained sales books of Carter's Furniture and Appliance. Joel sold sixteen mattress sets – five in his first hour. He even persuaded Doris Delamarter to dig out her checkbook after she bounced a few times on ventilating cushions. She bought a single bed for her guest room, in addition to two pillows and a lamp.

"What a crazy day," Tom said. He loosened his tie and plopped on a recently purchased blue corduroy settee. "I think I pushed a dozen couches out the door."

"People will buy anything if they think they're getting a deal," Joel said.

As he leaned on a nearby post, Joel Smith, sales wunderkind, wondered how many flat screens, laptops, and cell phones he could have moved were he not stuck in the age of radios, coffee percolators, and R2-D2 washing machines. He figured a lot. Consumers in the digital age were just as gullible and had a lot more credit.

By a quarter to five, customer traffic had dwindled to a trickle. In fact, it had nearly disappeared. Except for a young couple playing a Tommy Dorsey record on a phonograph, a fortyish woman examining a hutch, and an old man letting his cares drift away in a French club chair, the store was patron free.

Joel considered trying to sell the hutch but opted to stay put. If the lady really wanted to buy it, she would let someone know. The others, he concluded, were just passing time.

Tom stared blankly into space, as if taking stock of his day. A few seconds later, he looked at Joel with more focused eyes.

"Have you given any thought to my proposal?" Tom asked.

"I have," Joel said.

"And?"

"And let's wait until after Labor Day and find a place close to the campus. I want to build up a little capital first and get some decent furniture," Joel said. He sat on an ottoman in front of Tom and re-rolled the sleeves of his white dress shirt. "Besides, I've developed an addiction to your mother's cooking. I'm not ready to give that up just yet."

"OK. I just thought you might be getting tired of the trailer."

"I am. But I can be patient. Remember where I was sleeping a few weeks ago."

Tom laughed.

"How could I forget?"

Joel knew that Tom was eager for change. He had heard his friend moan about his situation on more than one occasion.

When Tom began moving from the fraternity to his parents' house on Memorial Day, he had planned to stay a month at most. Twenty-two-year-old men with twenty-one-year-old girlfriends did not reside with Mom and Dad – unless they lived in Appalachia or Greenwich Village. When Joel came along, the desire to move out became even stronger. Tom wanted his privacy, to be sure. But he also looked forward to sharing a house or an apartment with the "most entertaining man in the Evergreen State."

Joel let his eyes drift to the front of the store, where the record-playing couple and the hutch-touching woman headed for the door and a last-minute customer rushed in. She walked toward the sales team of Carter and Smith as the man in the chair snored.

"I think it's time to wake Rip Van Winkle and help your dad close up," Joel said.

"You go ahead," Tom said. "My knees are locked in place."

"Then maybe it's time to *unlock* them," the late arrival said as she reached the settee. "A gentleman would already be on his feet – and a true gentleman would have straightened his tie and combed his hair in anticipation of his one true love."

Tom turned to face Ginny Gillette.

"You mean my boat?"

Ginny laughed.

"That's pretty funny, handsome."

"Hi, Ginny," Joel said.

"Hello," Ginny replied as Joel started to stand. "And don't even think about getting up on my behalf. I was just teasing. You two look as though you've spent a day with a hundred customers or half a day with Doris."

"Both, actually," Tom said.

"Well, I have just the thing for you."

Ginny rummaged through the black hole that was her purse for nearly a minute before retrieving four colorful tickets. She handed them to Tom.

"These were a gift from my editor. He loved my piece on polio. In fact, he wants to run it above the fold in the city section on Sunday."

"Congratulations," Joel said. "I'm confused though. I thought that story was a mess."

"It was. But I interviewed two delightfully quotable sources after I spoke to you and pulled everything together Tuesday night. I'm pleased with how the article turned out."

"I'm proud of you," Tom said. "You'll be running the paper in no time."

"I doubt it. But I *am* making progress. I've been assigned two more stories for July," Ginny said. She turned her head. "And rest assured, Joel, they're very 'weighty.'"

Joel smiled.

"I wish I could take that comment back."

"There's no need to take anything back. You meant well," Ginny said. "In any case, I didn't come here seeking an apology. I came here seeking company at a baseball game. Unless you two are doing something else tomorrow night, let's plan on seeing some balls and strikes. San Francisco is in town."

"There are four tickets, dear," Tom said. "Who gets the other one?"

"That's for me to know and you to find out."

Ginny took the tickets out of Tom's hand and kissed the top of his head.

"Why don't you stop by the house at five? That will give us a chance to visit before the game begins. Nice to see you, Joel."

Ginny clutched her purse and started for the door, but she didn't get fifteen feet before the peanut gallery began to throw peanuts.

"You know, Ginny, Tom asked a good question. It might be nice to know who I'll be sitting next to tomorrow night – for three hours, maybe more – with mustard breath."

Ginny stopped, turned around, and grinned.

"Well, now, aren't we impatient? Bye, boys."

Ginny strutted toward the exit. As she passed the armchairs, she waved the tickets high over her head and woke Rip Van Winkle with a shout.

"Linda!"

34: JOEL AND GRACE

Saturday, June 28, 1941

The Boys of Baltic Avenue arrived fashionably late after their most adventurous member had turned a fifteen-block jaunt into a thirty-mile thrill ride.

Joel had insisted on driving Tom's graduation present at disturbingly high speeds through northeast Seattle. Tom, surprisingly, had agreed to let him.

Joel did not care that he had a driver's license that expired in 2002 or a collision policy from a company created in 1973. He had sought fun and found it in spades.

When Joel reached the corner of Fifty-Sixth and Klickitat, he whipped the metallic blue Plymouth Special Deluxe convertible to the curb, honked three times, and turned off the engine. Tom released his tight grip on the passenger door.

"Next time I'll stick to the roller coaster," Tom said. He laughed nervously. "Where did you learn to drive like that?"

"On Forest Service roads," Joel said.

Joel did not elaborate. He wasn't telling anyone he had rolled two vehicles and blown two transmissions as a permit-packing fifteen-year-old in 1993. He pulled the keys from the ignition and offered them to his skittish partner.

"Your keys, sire."

"You sure you don't want to drive to the stadium?" Tom asked.

"I'm sure."

Joel hopped out of the car, walked around the vehicle to the passenger side, and joined Tom on the sidewalk. The friends ran combs through their hair and then started toward the house. They didn't make it ten feet before Ginny rushed out to meet them.

Wearing a crisp white blouse, a knit sweater, and a dark blue skirt that showcased her slender form, Ginny looked ready for a night on the town. She offered her callers a thin smile that quickly became a frown.

"We have a bit of a problem," Ginny said to Tom. "Linda is sick, really sick. She has been vomiting all day and can't get out of bed. I think she has the flu."

"I'm sorry to hear that," Tom said. "Can we go another time?"

"We can't with my tickets. They're good only for tonight."

"What's Katie doing? Maybe she'll go. Let's ask."

"I already have. She said she has other plans."

Following the exchange from a few feet away, Joel processed the information and pondered the dire situation. Linda was out and Katie was out.

Well, hell's bells, Monty. What's behind Door Number Three?

"How about Grace?" Tom asked.

"I'm glad you inquired. She has agreed to help out. She'll be our pinch hitter tonight," Ginny said. She turned to Joel. "Provided that's all right with you, of course."

Joel looked at Ginny like she had just asked the dumbest question in history. He tightened the reins of the wild horses attempting to pull his indifferent expression into a mile-wide grin.

"Are you sure it's no bother?" Joel asked.

He didn't like hiding his enthusiasm. He felt as genuine as Eddie Haskell telling Mrs. Cleaver he was sorry that "Theodore" couldn't join "Wallace" and him at a game, but he didn't care. He would give his left steely for an evening with Blondie.

"I'm as sure of that as I'm sure it's no bother to you," Ginny said.

Ginny gave Joel a knowing smile. She was no doubt as skilled at reading him now as when he was eleven and had lied about tracking mud across her living room carpet.

"Your pinch hitter meets my approval," Joel said.

"I thought she would. We'll just be a minute."

Ginny ran inside. When she returned a moment later, she brought a friend who had lost no luster in fourteen days. Wearing a green summer dress and a wide-brimmed hat, Grace Vandenberg looked more like a well-prepared starter than a last-minute substitute.

"Hello, Joel," Grace said.

"Hi, Grace."

"It looks like we have a foursome after all," Tom said in an excited voice. He led the others to his glistening coupe, opened the passenger door, and flipped the front seat forward. "I like the idea of couples seating tonight. After you, my friends."

116

Joel helped Grace into the Plymouth. After he joined her in back, he pulled the front passenger seat into the upright position, allowing Ginny to enter the car.

Tom closed Ginny's door, scurried to his side of the vehicle, and quickly found his place behind the steering wheel. After starting the engine, he adjusted the rear-view mirror, activated the convertible's top, and grinned.

"Here's the situation, ladies," Tom said. "We have twenty-five minutes to make a thirty-minute drive. Fortunately for us, Joel showed me some tricks today."

"Tricks?" Ginny asked.

"He means efficiency measures," Joel said.

Tom looked ahead and pulled away from the curb.

"Hold on to your hats!"

* * * * *

Thanks to "efficiency measures" and a few helpful traffic lights on Rainier Avenue, Tom reached the stadium in twenty-two minutes.

Ten minutes later, the two couples found their seats twelve rows up behind the first base dugout. Though they brought light jackets, they did not need them for the first pitch. There was no wind, rain, or chilly air to spoil the evening. Conditions inside the three-year-old ballpark were nearly perfect for watching Class AA baseball.

"This is the life!" Tom said as he hoisted a beer. He had purchased four drinks and four hot dogs from a roving vendor. "The weather is great, the beer is cold, the crowd is festive, and we're sitting with the most alluring women in Seattle."

"I'll drink to that," Joel said.

The friends reached across their female companions to clink paper cups.

"You two are insufferable," Ginny said. "But you can talk that way all night."

Grace smiled but said nothing. She had said little on the drive to the stadium, but Joel did not interpret that as lack of interest. She had gently stared at him from start to finish, as if studying and evaluating something different and appealing.

"Do you like baseball?" Grace asked.

"Of course," Joel said. "I played three years in high school and see at least thirty Mariners games a year. Or at least I used to. We used to have season tickets."

"Who are the Mariners?"

117

"Probably some rookie-league team in Helena," Tom said. He finished his hot dog and looked at Joel. "They do play ball out there, don't they?"

"In between rodeos and summer blizzards," Joel said. He wondered how many more gaffes he'd have to explain before the evening was done.

Joel sipped his beer and returned his attention to Grace, hoping she was the kind who let sleeping dogs lie. She wasn't. She quickly hit him with another question.

"Did you participate in many activities in high school?"

"I did," Joel replied. "I played sports, took French and Spanish, and started a history club. You know, the usual cowboy stuff. No calf roping though."

Grace set her drink to the side and turned to face Joel.

"Parlez-vous français?" she asked.

"Oui," Joel answered.

"Then please show us what you've learned. Say something in French."

"Vous avez des jolis yeux bleus."

Grace smiled.

"Yes, Mr. Smith, my eyes are blue and some think they are pretty. Thank you for the compliment. But I suspect you can do better."

"Oh, I can!"

Joel massaged his temples for a few seconds, as if retrieving an assignment from third-year French, and then dropped his hands to his lap. He faced his peers.

"La dame au jolis yeux bleus est plus chaude que Veronica Lake."

Ginny grinned and Grace blushed.

"What did he say?" Tom asked Ginny. "What did he say?"

"Well, Tom, to put a fine point on things, our multilingual friend thinks the lady with the pretty blue eyes is 'hotter' than Veronica Lake."

"I know all the swear words too," Joel said. "But I'll save them for later."

Tom roared with laughter.

"I *have* to spend more time with this guy! I didn't learn anything like that in high school. I can't even count in German, much less swear."

Tom leaned to his side and addressed the woman two seats down.

"And he does have a point, Grace. You make Veronica Lake look like a barmaid."

The blonde smiled and shook her head.

"Thank you, both of you, for that kind assessment," Grace said. "But I was hoping for something else. It's been a while since I've had the chance to practice my French. Tell me something interesting, Joel. Tell me something about Montana."

"OK. Let me think," Joel said. He rubbed his chin. "How about this? Les rivières de Montana sont pleines de truites."

118

"J'en ai entendu," Grace replied. "So I've heard. The rivers are full of trout. Have you ever caught one of these fish?"

"I have. My grandparents took me fishing on the Madison River every year when I was a kid. We always caught our limit," Joel said truthfully. He spoke to Grace but gazed at Ginny. "I loved those trips. I loved sleeping under the stars. I loved spending time with *them*. The trips were the highlight of my summer."

"That's sweet," Grace said.

Joel let his mind drift. He *did* miss the campouts, just as he missed his grandmother and the man she had yet to meet. He knew he could reminisce all night, but he saw no point in doing so. His memories belonged to another life, one he couldn't have back. Gathering himself, he returned to 1941, Grace, and their favorite Romance language.

"How did you learn French?" Joel asked.

"My mother taught me," Grace said. "She was my primary teacher. I also took a semester in high school. I know just enough to get into trouble."

"You know much more than that. Trust me."

"Merci."

Joel settled into his seat and thought about the woman to his left. Grace Vandenberg wasn't just a looker. She was a thinker – and probably as smart as a whip.

Joel laughed to himself. He would stand in line to hear her speak, in any language, seven days a week, so long as she didn't ask questions about him. He saw nothing to gain by discussing his past, so he steered the conversation in a different direction.

"What about you, Grace?" Joel asked. "Did you do a lot in high school?"

As soon as Joel uttered the words, a pall settled over Row 12. Grace turned pale. Tom and Ginny looked away. The only thing missing was the sound of crickets. Joel knew he had stepped in something, but he didn't know what. He waited for someone to speak.

He didn't wait long. Ginny broke the silence a few seconds later. She grabbed Grace's hand, gave it a gentle squeeze, and then spoke to the man with the questions.

"Grace did quite a bit, actually, but she was too busy earning a full-ride scholarship to participate in activities. She got straight A's at Westlake High. Did she tell you that?"

"No. She didn't," Joel said. He gazed beyond the outfield fence, where hundreds of freeloading fans watched the game from Tightwad Hill, and slowly digested what Ginny had said. He turned to Grace. "Westlake, huh? I passed the school my first day here. How did you like going there?"

"It was all right," Grace answered in a weak voice. "I went there only a few months and didn't have the opportunity to do much except graduate."

119

"I see. Well, there's nothing wrong with winning a scholarship."

Joel closed his eyes and tried to guess how often he had passed the photo of the Class of 1938 in four years at WHS. He could not believe that he and Grace had attended the same school. The coincidence left him excited, numb, and strangely uncomfortable. Sensing that high school was not Grace's favorite topic, he moved on.

"Would you like something more to eat?" Joel asked.

"I think I would," Grace said.

"Then let's get it. Let's go for a walk."

* * * * *

Joel took his time guiding Grace from the right side of the stadium to the left. After buying two boxes of caramel corn, he gave her a tour of the concourse, the team museum, and an outer walkway that divided the box seats from the cheap seats. He provided running commentary the entire time.

"You know a lot about this place for someone who's never been here," Grace said.

"That's because baseball stadiums are all the same," Joel replied. "It doesn't matter if they're big or small, fancy or plain, or host major league teams or minor league teams. The trappings are all the same. So are the people who attend the games."

Grace stopped at a wide spot on the walkway, put a hand on the thick steel railing, and turned her head. She stared at Joel.

"Is that so?"

"It is," Joel said.

He looked at her face and chuckled.

"You don't believe me."

"I most certainly do not," Grace said.

"OK. Then let me elaborate."

Joel put a hand on Grace's shoulder and directed her attention to a pair of middle-aged men in gray suits a few rows behind home plate. The men took turns speaking, nodding, and moving their hands around.

"You see those two? I'll bet you anything they're talking dollars and cents instead of balls and strikes," Joel said. "They're here to conduct business because ballparks are the best business venues around. Don't get me wrong. They'll stand at the right times and cheer along with everyone else. They might even say disparaging things about the other team, but in between pitches, they'll trade stock tips and negotiate deals."

"Are you sure about that?" Grace asked. "Are you sure they aren't talking about their wives or children or perhaps their summer vacations?"

"I am," Joel insisted. "I'm positive. They're talking business. That's why they left their wives at home. The wives would only screw things up."

"Screw things up?"

"In a manner of speaking," Joel said. "The wives would mean well, of course, but it wouldn't be long before they would insist that their husbands invest in modern art or skin creams or some other nutty . . ."

Joel stopped when he glanced at Grace. He needed only to see her folded arms and white-hot glare to realize he had overstepped. He wasn't talking to Adam at a bachelor party. He backtracked quickly.

"You're mostly right though," Joel said. "Most people here don't discuss business. They talk about personal matters. Baseball is great family therapy. In fact, if you're looking for a real domestic situation, you need only to look up there."

Joel casually pointed to a party of four about ten rows up. An unsmiling man in his thirties, his frowning wife, and their twin sons, who appeared to be no more than six, followed the action on the field with varying degrees of interest.

"I know they are just sitting and staring now, but that family is easy to figure out," Joel said. "The boys are having fun. This is their first baseball game and everything is exciting and interesting because it is new. They have never seen this many people in one place and have never heard this much noise. They are happy because their usual routine on a Saturday night is a bath, a story, and a quick trip to bed. Who wants that?"

Grace smiled.

"How about the parents? Have you figured them out?"

"Of course," Joel said. "The man is *not* happy. He wanted take his sons to the game by himself. He wanted a boys' night out, but he didn't get it. The missus took issue with his recent behavior and insisted on coming along to punish him. They haven't resolved their differences, as you can see, and will continue to ignore each other at least until the seventh inning. Then the boys will fall asleep, Mom and Dad will pull them close, and they will realize that the poker game last night and the unpainted kitchen are pretty unimportant in the grand scheme of things."

"And you know all this simply by looking at them?"

"I do," Joel said. "The same thing is going on right now at a thousand other games in a thousand other towns. It's what baseball is all about."

* * * * *

Grace wondered if there were enough dump trucks in Seattle to carry Joel's social observations to the proper destination, but she made no attempt to disrupt his discourse or counter his commentary. She loved listening to his baloney.

121

When they reached the edge of the bleachers on the third-base line ten minutes later, they put their hands on the railing and gazed at the fans on Tightwad Hill. Some sat on lawn chairs. Others rested on blankets. A few stood or walked around. All enjoyed minor league baseball for free.

"What a bunch of cheapskates," Joel said.

"That's rather harsh. Maybe they don't have enough money to see the game."

"That's not the point, Grace. Baseball is a business that depends on ticket-paying customers. If everyone sat out there, the team would go bankrupt and no one could watch any game. They are undermining the franchise. The police ought to hose down the lot of them or at least make them buy a few bags of popcorn."

Grace sighed, shook her head, and then looked at the hill, where four teenagers ran toward a foul ball that had landed in a bush. Two fought for the ball until one finally claimed it and held it high over his head.

"You have to admit they are clever," Grace said. "They get most of the foul balls and home runs. All they have to do is wait."

"Have *you* ever gotten a foul ball?" Joel asked.

"No."

"I think I can change that, but we may have to stay here a while."

Grace shook her head.

"No. Let's go."

Grace wanted to return to their seats and their friends. Though she didn't mind listening to more of Joel's blather, or even watching the game, she wanted to do so while sitting down. She was tired of standing.

Joel compromised and talked her into staying an inning. He said it would only be a matter of time before a right-handed batter put a ball within their reach.

He was right. A few minutes later, a San Francisco slugger sent a hanging curve high over their heads. The deep fly sailed past the foul pole, struck a rock, and rolled into the parking lot. Within seconds Joel went through the railing, down the bleachers, over the fence, and out of the stadium.

"What are you doing?" Grace asked.

"I'm getting you a souvenir!" Joel shouted.

Two boys and a girl from Tightwad Hill also saw the ball and got the jump on Joel, but the time traveler made the most of a superior vantage point. He saw where the ball had rolled and headed straight for a shiny black sedan. In no time he pulled the object from behind a front tire, held it up, and smiled at Grace.

Apparently not content to win graciously, Joel waved the booty at his juvenile competitors and strutted like a bandleader as he returned to the stadium. When he reached the fence, he looked up at Grace and tossed the ball into her hands.

"For you, my lady."

Grace put the ball in her purse and then watched Joel attempt to scale an eight-foot fence. The spectacle proved more entertaining than the game.

For nearly a minute Joel paced frantically along the smooth-sided barrier. He searched for handgrips and footholds but found slick, useless steel. The useful stuff was on the other side. When he threw his hands up, Grace laughed.

Serves you right.

Just as Grace began to feel sorry for her hero and dig out his ticket, she glanced toward the knoll and saw the three ball-chasing kids bicker among themselves. The boys yelled at each other for losing the prize and at the younger girl for getting in their way. Unable to fend for herself, she began to cry and drifted away.

Grace stared at the girl for a moment and then raced down the bleachers to a spot closest to the outer wall. She called out to the youth. Dressed in denim overalls, the girl turned around and walked toward the well-dressed woman until she was within voice range. Grace dug the ball out of her purse and tossed it near the child's feet.

"Take it, dear," Grace said. "You deserve it. And don't let the others get to you. Boys can be dreadful at times."

The freckle-faced redhead hesitated for a moment, as if suspecting a trick, and then stepped tentatively toward the offering. When Grace smiled, the girl picked up the ball, flashed a toothless grin, and ran to her mother screaming about her new find.

* * * * *

Grace waved at the girl and then hurried back up the bleachers to Joel's departure point. When she arrived, she found him in the custody of a burly man in a security vest. Neither party appeared particularly happy. The security man spoke first.

"This guy says he's with you."

Grace walked up to Joel, gave him a close inspection, and wrinkled her nose a few times, as if offended by an odor. She smiled and turned to the authority figure.

"He is clearly mistaken," Grace said. "This man is obviously a cheapskate trying to undermine the franchise. You should hose him off and wash him of his sins."

Joel stared at Grace with wide eyes.

Are you freaking kidding me?

123

Joel started to speak but stopped when he saw more trouble approach. A tall Seattle policeman, wielding a baton, arrived on the scene just as the inning ended. The cop wore the face of a man who had not had his dinner.

"What's going on here?"

"I just nabbed a gate-crasher. He scaled the fence," the security man said. "You can even see the crate he used to climb over the top."

"I have a ticket, Officer. I have every right to be here," Joel protested. "I jumped out only to get my friend a foul ball. Tell him, Grace."

"Well?" the policeman asked. "Is that true?"

"I'm not entirely sure," Grace said. She shrugged. "It all happened so fast. One minute he was standing beside me. The next he was looking under parked cars. He said this place was good for business."

Joel sank.

The cop looked at Joel.

"Is that so?"

"No. It's *not* so," Joel said. "I did nothing but chase a ball into the lot. As God is my witness, that's all I did."

"It doesn't matter," the security man said. "You don't have a ticket. No ticket, no admission. You're going back out."

"You want some help?" the policeman asked.

The security man shook his head.

"I think I can handle him."

"Suit yourself."

The security man grabbed Joel by the elbow and ushered him forward.

"Let's go, buddy."

As the policeman departed and returned to his post near the home team's dugout, the security man slowly guided Joel through a crowded walkway toward the grandstand and the first available exit. Grace, smiling at the accused, followed closely behind.

Joel glanced over his shoulder at the blonde. He couldn't believe she had abandoned him like a feral dog. He had risked his neck to get that ball. Talk about ingratitude. He remembered something Adam had told him their freshman year.

Trust no woman.

But as the security man and Joel approached the exit, Grace put her hand in her purse and retrieved two slips of paper Ginny had given her at the gate. She rushed forward.

"Excuse me, sir," Grace said. "It seems I've made a terrible mistake. I have his ticket right here. I found it in my purse. I'll gladly claim him, if it's all the same to you."

Grace smiled and batted her lashes. She gave the man the stubs.

He examined them for a second, scowled, and handed them back.

"You're on the wrong side of the stadium. I suggest you return to your seats."

"We will, sir," Grace said. "Thank you."

The security man shook his head, released Joel, and walked away.

Joel stared hard at Grace.

"Why did you do that?" he asked. "I could have gone to jail."

"I thought your attitude needed a tune-up," Grace said. "Cheapskates are people too. They just have fewer pennies in their pockets."

The comment broke Joel like a twig. He looked at Grace and saw a disarming smile and gently scolding eyes. How could he get mad at that? How could anyone?

* * * * *

By the time Joel and Grace returned to their seats, the third inning had become the fifth, Seattle had taken a three-to-one lead, and Grace was smiling and laughing.

"I almost sent for security," Tom said. "Where did you go?"

Joel grinned.

"We went to chase foul balls, visit with law enforcement, and greet the tightwads on Tightwad Hill. They're still pretty tight."

"I'll bet they are," Tom said. He put his arm around Ginny. "You two need to stick around for a while. This *is* a double date, after all."

Tom turned his attention to the game as if nothing had happened. He seemed oblivious to the daisy-cutter he had dropped in Row 12.

Joel pondered Tom's choice of words. Was this, in fact, a date? He considered the question and its two possible answers. Then he looked at Grace and Ginny and saw they were likely doing the same. They offered knowing smiles but did not speak.

No one, it seemed, wanted to address such a delicate matter on what was supposed to be a simple night at the ballpark. Joel looked at Tom and changed the subject.

"Did you know the ponies ran today?" Joel asked. "It was the best opening day ever at Longacres. Some horse named Over Drive broke the track record for six furlongs."

"Did I know? Did I know? Do fish have lips? Of course I knew," Tom said. "If it weren't for this game and this gorgeous dame next to me, I would have been all over it. You and I are playing the ponies the next chance we get. I'm serious. I won't take 'no' for an answer."

"You won't get a 'no' from me."

"Good. Then it's set."

Joel settled into his seat just as San Francisco came to life. The visitors tied the score with two runs in the sixth and later surged ahead five to three. Seattle tallied two in the bottom of the ninth to force an extra inning.

Joel watched the game with indifference. He paid less attention to the action on the field than to a report by the public address announcer that Joe DiMaggio had extended his hitting streak to forty games with a double and a single against Philadelphia.

"Do you think he'll get to fifty?" Tom asked.

"I know he will," Joel replied. "In fact, he'll get to fifty-six."

"Fifty-six? Isn't that a bit optimistic?" Ginny asked. "He still has a long way to go. No one has reached fifty games – and only a few have made it to forty."

"OK. I'll put my money where my mouth is," Joel said. "Tom, do you know a bookie who can handle something like this?"

Joel regretted asking the question when he saw Tom blush. He suspected that even compulsive gamblers liked to maintain a modicum of innocence around those who did not share their lofty opinion of high-stakes betting.

"I think I could find one," Tom said.

"I thought so," Joel said. He pulled two twenty-dollar bills from his wallet, leaned to his left, and handed the bills to Tom. "Put the first one on DiMaggio to reach fifty-six – not fifty or fifty-five or fifty-seven but fifty-six. Put the other on Ted Williams to bat .406 for the season. This is going to be a good year for baseball."

Grace stared at Joel and smiled.

"You seem rather confident," she said. "Did you consult a crystal ball today?"

"No," Joel said. "Just my intuition."

And a very good memory.

* * * * *

Seattle won seven to six in ten innings. Its star first baseman doubled off the wall in left field to bring in two runs and send six thousand fans home smiling.

Joel smiled for another reason. On the trip back to the university district, he locked eyes with Grace for forty delightfully long minutes. Heavy traffic, red lights, and a conspicuous absence of efficiency measures nearly doubled the length of the drive home. No one in the Plymouth complained.

When Tom finally stopped in front of the house on Klickitat Avenue, he walked around to the passenger side, let Ginny out, and escorted her to the door. He kissed his girl good night, promised to call her the next day, and returned to the car.

Joel found his closing act a bit more challenging. He helped Grace out of the back seat and walked her to the house but froze when they arrived. He had never had to search for words to end a date – or at least what Tom Carter had called a date.

Ginny made the search easier. Standing inside the partially opened door, with her hand on the knob, she told her friend and sorority sister that it was time to come in.

Joel knew then that he didn't have the luxury of time. The right words would have to wait for another day, if there was another day.

"Good night, Grace. I enjoyed tonight," Joel said.

"I did too," Grace replied, eyes fixed on his. "Have a safe drive back. Good night."

35: GRACE AND JOEL

Tuesday, July 1, 1941

Grace looked at the stacks of paper and wondered if she would ever finish. Since eight that morning she had meticulously filed hundreds of three-by-five-inch cards into narrow wooden drawers, so that faculty, students, and staff might find new authors, subjects, and titles without blowing a fuse. By eleven thirty her mind had turned to mush.

"Machines will someday make that easier."

Grace smiled but did not lift her eyes from her tedious work or budge from her chair at a small wooden table. She recognized the mischievous voice.

"Have you come here to harass me, Mr. Smith?"

"Not at all," Joel said. "I'm seeking reference assistance."

"Then why don't you speak to the reference librarians?"

"Because they're mean and old and ugly and say 'shush' a lot."

"They do not!" Grace said. She lowered her voice. "They are all very pleasant – and some are young and pretty."

"OK. I won't argue."

Joel pulled up a seat opposite the disagreeable file clerk and visually inspected the small, stuffy room, which architects had placed in a windowless corner of the main library. Two other girls filed cards at a larger table a few feet away, but no Dickensian authority figures roamed the workhouse to keep the coeds in line or inhibit the time traveler's private pursuit of a public employee.

"That doesn't look like fun," Joel said with a playful grin. He lifted a title card from the top of a stack and inspected it for typos. "Do you ever shuffle the deck to make things interesting or bundle the cards with chewing gum?"

"I do not," Grace said matter-of-factly.

She continued to work.

"That's good," Joel said. "You're a consummate professional."

Joel grabbed another card, held it up to the light, and shook his head.

"I don't think we can accept this one, Grace. It spells Smith with a 'y' and an 'e.' I don't spell it that way."

"Perhaps you should," Grace said.

"Maybe I should. But if I took that name, I'd have to order a stiff upper lip to go with it. That might make eating difficult."

"You'd manage."

Joel returned the card to the stack, sat up straight, and put his hands together on top of the table. Realizing that the needle on Grace's annoyance meter was drifting into the red zone, he ditched the smirk and the attitude.

"I thought you worked in the rare books section. That's what Ginny said."

"I usually do. But the librarians needed help here this week, so I volunteered. There aren't many students around during the summer months," Grace said. She pulled more cards from a pile. "Why aren't *you* working today? Did Carter's run out of furniture?"

"No," Joel said. "The old man just decided to give me a weekday off. Business is slow on Tuesdays, so today was the obvious choice."

"And so you came here to watch me sort slips of paper."

"I came here to thank you for Saturday. I had a great time."

"I did too."

Grace took a breath, pushed the cards away, and looked at Joel. She knew he had come to the library to do more than thank her for an enjoyable evening. But she didn't know how to handle his visit any more than she knew how to handle the conflicting thoughts bouncing in her head.

"When do you get off?" Joel asked.

"I can leave at four, but I may stay later."

"Great. Maybe I can come back."

"I don't think that's a good idea," Grace said.

"Why?"

"Because I'm engaged to be married, and I don't think my fiancé would appreciate me spending time with another man – even as friends," Grace said in a hushed tone.

Grace patted herself for showing backbone and doing what she knew was right. But she immediately softened when she saw the disappointment and hurt on Joel's face.

"Don't get me wrong. I'm flattered by the attention. I really am. But I don't think we should spend more time together. Can you understand?"

"I just want to go for a walk," Joel said. "Is that asking too much?"

Yes, it is. I find you more than a little distracting, and the last thing I need now is a reason to do something stupid.

Grace put a hand to her forehead and glanced at her coworkers. Both, thankfully, kept to themselves, or at least did a good job of masking their interest in her affairs.

Grace looked at Joel and studied his face. Solemn, focused, and sincere, it was different than the one he had brought into the room. Joel Smith was no flirt with too much time on his hands. He was a serious suitor. A simple brush-off would not do.

"No. I suppose not," Grace said. "I get a break in twenty minutes. We can walk then."

* * * * *

When Grace got off at noon, she took the initiative and led Joel south toward the water. She wanted peace, privacy, and as much distance on the education building, where Linda McEwan had two classes, as time allowed.

"I'm sorry I was such a bear at the library," Grace said. "I want to be your friend, but I don't know how to do so without upsetting a lot of people."

"I'm the one who should apologize. I had no right to put you on the spot."

Grace relaxed and started to view Joel with more compassion and less suspicion. He was no longer a cowboy or a salesman or a baseball fan full of bravado but rather a sincere and probably lonely young man who just wanted someone to talk to.

"Then let me put *you* on the spot. Are you ever going to give us more than your name, rank, and serial number? Ginny said she tried to learn more the other day and did not get far."

"I want to tell you more and someday I will, but I can't now. My situation is more complicated than you could possibly imagine. Just know that I'm not trying to pull some kind of stunt. My intentions are pure. I genuinely like everyone I've met here and want to continue to be a part of your lives."

Grace smiled.

"I like that."

"Like what?"

"That side of you. When I met you at Tom's party, I thought you were just another of his shallow drinking and gambling buddies. I see I misjudged you."

"That's OK. I haven't exactly put on the same face every day. I haven't worn my cowboy hat since the day you saw me on the street."

"That was a sight I won't forget," Grace said with a giggle. "You did look good in it, though. You should wear it again sometime."

"For you, anything," Joel said.

Grace laughed to herself. He didn't let up.

She thought again about the wisdom of spending even an hour with him. This was different than filling in for a sick friend at a baseball game or speaking to him in the presence of others. This private stroll was undeniably optional and probably more than a little ill-advised. But the longer Grace Vandenberg walked and talked with the loquacious Mr. Smith, the more she felt comfortable with her decision to leave the library. She enjoyed his company.

* * * * *

As they passed groves of cedar, pine, and larch, Joel couldn't help but notice how little the university had changed in six decades. The commercial strips were night and day different, of course, but the campus itself was much the way he had left it.

When they reached Pacific Street, Joel put his hand on Grace's back and gently steered her east – away from the blazing midday sun and toward the football stadium. He was in no hurry to double back toward the human race. He didn't know how many more walks he'd get with this enchanting woman and wanted to drag this one out as long as he could.

"Now that I've expended a million syllables not answering your questions, maybe you can do the same for me. What's your story?"

Grace stopped and stared at Joel with doleful eyes. He sensed immediately that she had a story she had told often and did not care to tell again.

"So you really don't know?"

"I know only that you're engaged and went to Westlake High. Straight-A student. Ginny said that anything else was none of my business."

Grace smiled.

"That sounds like something she would say."

They continued walking.

"Well, my story, as you put it, is pretty short. My parents were missionaries. I was born in Minnesota, but I don't remember it. We never lived in one place for more than three years, except for the six in Africa. When I was fourteen, we moved from the Philippines to a village just outside Nanking, China. I liked it there. So did my father, even though he didn't convert a soul – or at least none I knew about," Grace said with a sad, sweet laugh no doubt rooted in a sad, sweet memory.

Guessing what was coming, Joel kept his questions in check. He wanted to learn more, but he did not want to interrupt a narrative that was likely as therapeutic for the teller as it was informative to the listener.

"We stayed nearly three years. Dad preached, Mom taught school, and I attended that school when I wasn't running around getting into trouble."

"I can't imagine you getting into trouble."

"Not your kind of trouble, that's for sure," Grace said. "But I wasn't a saint. One morning I said I was too sick to go to church. But instead of staying in bed, I played with several kids from the village. We had a big mud fight. I ruined a set of clothes and some new shoes. Dad grounded me for a month. Nothing but school and church."

"Let me guess. You left when the Japanese came in."

"We left in late November, when Westerners could still get out. Dad wanted to go to the safety zone in the city and stick it out, but my mother convinced him to leave. She was always the sensible one. So we fled to Shanghai and took the first boat out."

"How did you end up in Seattle?"

"My aunt, my mom's sister, lives here. We arrived just before Christmas and planned to stay until I finished school in June and Dad could get another assignment."

Grace paused and looked at a deer that stepped tentatively between two trees. She turned away and continued walking.

"You don't have to tell me the rest if you don't want to," Joel said.

Grace didn't reply immediately. She instead picked up a pine cone on the path and held it to her nose before placing it at the base of a large tree. She returned to Joel, hesitated for a moment, and then looked at him with moist eyes.

"On New Year's Eve 1937, a drunk driver ran a stoplight and struck my parents as they walked across an intersection. Mom died instantly. Dad lived another day, just long enough to say goodbye. I stayed with my aunt until I came here. You can probably figure out the rest."

Joel closed his eyes and sighed.

"Oh, Grace, I am so sorry."

Joel felt embarrassed, guilty, and angry. Since meeting Grace at the party, he had considered only his interests. Now those interests seemed trivial, shallow, and extraordinarily selfish. He booted a rock on the path.

"I feel stupid now, really stupid," Joel said. "The last thing you need is some dolt hitting on you and making you uncomfortable. If there is anything I can do, just let me know."

Grace lifted her head and gazed at Joel for several seconds, as if considering the possibilities of his offer. She took a breath and offered a weak smile.

"There is something."

"What? Just name it," Joel said. "I'll do anything – even take a hike."

Grace took his hand.

"Take me to a movie."

36: JOEL AND GRACE

Saturday, July 5, 1941

Joel and Grace's second non-date date in seven days began with a low-profile rendezvous on the corner of East Fifty-Second Street and University Way. She had insisted on meeting at a neutral location to avoid the appearance of impropriety. The two would arrive at the theater as friends, depart as friends, and keep danger at a safe distance.

Like moths to a flamethrower, Joel thought.

"Thank you for doing this," Grace said. "Paul rarely takes me to movies. He prefers dinners and parties, and the girls are usually too busy to go out."

"I can't think of anything I'd rather do," Joel said, still grateful she had not applied the coup de Grace when she'd had the chance.

When they reached the Phoenician, a Prohibition-era colossus that occupied nearly an entire block on the Ave, they joined a line that stretched to the corner of Forty-Seventh. From that vantage point, they could see *Road to Zanzibar* emblazoned on the side of a splashy marquee and touch a wrought-iron-and-oak bench that had served Joel well on the second of June.

"Do you remember this bench?" Grace asked.

"I remember who I saw while sitting on it," Joel said.

Joel grinned. He remembered everything about that night, both good and bad – the fatigue, the hunger, the sadness, the thrill of seeing an angel in white, and his fortuitous encounter with his new best friend.

"I wasn't sure what to make of you," Grace said. "You looked so sad."

"I was," Joel said. "But I found a cure."

Grace smiled.

"I can see that."

As they moved up the line, they passed dozens of burned paper shards that had blown across the street and gathered in the gutters. Empty matchbooks and fireworks packages littered the sidewalk. Independence Day had left its mark.

"What did you do yesterday?" Joel asked.

"Katie and I visited my aunt Edith. She loves the Fourth, and I wanted to help her celebrate. We baked apple pies all day and saw the fireworks at the lake," Grace said. "She's a wonderful lady. I hope you can meet her someday."

"I'd like that."

"How did *you* spend the day?"

"I did the same thing – at least the fireworks part," Joel said. He laughed. "The only baking I did was on the top of Tom's boat. I'm still pretty sore in back."

Note to self: Invent sunscreen.

"You two have become good friends," Grace said.

Joel pondered the comment, as if it were some sort of revelation, and nodded. He had not thought much about the friendship and his immersion in all things Carter because they had seemed so seamless and natural.

"Amazing, isn't it? I didn't know Tom a month ago, and now I'm a member of his family," Joel said. "I owe a lot to him – to all of them."

"I do, too, and not simply because they have been so kind to me," Grace said.

"What do you mean?"

Grace glanced at Joel and smiled but did not answer for several seconds. She had done that often at the ballpark, driving him bananas. Joel laughed to himself. The habit was as annoying as hell but effective. Grace knew how to hold an audience.

"Do you remember Ginny telling you that I had won a full-ride scholarship?" Grace asked.

"I remember," Joel said.

"Well, she held back a few details."

"Such as?"

"Such as the fact that all of the regular full-ride scholarships at Westlake went to students who had attended the school four years. I wasn't eligible for any of them."

"So how did you get yours?"

Grace looked at the many others standing in line, as if making sure they weren't listening in on state secrets, before turning to Joel. He had already pulled up a chair.

"It started with the *Sun*," Grace said. "They ran a big article on my parents after they died and a follow-up on me after my aunt told them I had been unable to get a scholarship. She was a particularly large thorn in their side."

Joel laughed. He had to meet this aunt.

"I get it. The paper stirred up some guilt and passed around the plate."

"I'm sure that was their intention. It certainly was my aunt's," Grace said. "But they never had the chance to pass the plate very far."

"OK," Joel said. "Now you've lost me."

"The day after the *Sun* ran the story on me, a local businessman wrote a check for five thousand dollars and donated it anonymously to my scholarship fund."

"Anonymously?"

"Yes, anonymously. For three years I never knew who put me through college or even why," Grace said. "I knew only that some nice man had paid for my education. Then I overheard Tom talk about it one day. He had known all along. So had Ginny. They all had."

Grace looked Joel in the eyes.

"My benefactor was Melvin Carter."

* * * * *

As they moved toward the nearest of two box offices, Grace saw several familiar faces but none she knew by name. That changed when Paula Caldecott, a busybody senior and a fellow traveler in the School of Education, emerged from a crowd and tapped Grace on the shoulder.

"Hi, Grace. I haven't seen you in ages," Paula said. "Who's your friend?"

Grace's stomach dropped as she tried to remember whether Paula knew Paul. She had not seen her since they had taken a methodology course in March.

"This is Joel Smith," Grace said. "Joel, this is Paula Caldecott. We're classmates."

Joel extended a hand.

"Hi, Paula."

"It's nice to meet you, Joel."

Paula held Joel's hand for several seconds. She held his gaze for several more. But as soon as she turned to Grace, she got to business in rapid-fire fashion.

"What are you doing this summer? Working? Playing? Did you and Linda move into a house? I remember you talked about it. I haven't seen her in any of my classes. Is she attending summer school?"

Paula's words hit Grace like echoes in a box canyon. She heard the questions and knew the answers but couldn't decide which, if any, put her engagement in mortal danger and which did not. She proceeded cautiously.

"Yes, Linda's taking classes, and yes, we moved into a house, with two other girls," Grace said. "I think you know Ginny. I'm taking the summer off and working at the library."

"That's great. That's wonderful," Paula said. After a long, awkward pause, she smiled at Grace and pointed to Joel with her eyes. "So . . . is *he* the one? Rita Moran told me a week ago that you were engaged. If so, then you're a lucky duck."

"Joel is just a friend. Rita must have mistaken me for someone else."

"That's odd. She seemed sure. Oh well. Too bad for you," Paula said, raising her eyebrows twice. A man waved from the far ticket counter and called her name. "Well, I have to go. It was nice seeing you. Maybe we'll have some classes this fall. Bye."

Paula vanished into the throng and took with her, at least for the moment, the threat of discovery. But the meeting had left Grace shell-shocked. Standing under the bright bulbs and shiny underside of the marquee, she stared blankly at Joel as he stepped forward to purchase their tickets. She scolded herself for thinking she could pull this off. Did she seriously believe she could mingle with dozens of other students in a public place and *not* run into someone who knew her relationship status?

Grace tried to recall a worse decision in college and couldn't. Just standing next to Joel invited a truckload of trouble. Yet when he slipped his hand in hers and led her into the theater, she had no desire to let go of that hand. Indeed, she had never wanted to hold anything more.

* * * * *

Joel didn't need to be a mind reader to know what Grace was thinking. He had listened to every word of her exchange with Paula and had seen her go from cheerful to cheerless in less than a minute. She was obviously reeling from a close call.

He had wondered about the wisdom of meeting like this. He had nothing to lose by taking her to a movie. Grace had everything to lose. Yet for days he thought only of the upside. He looked forward to a night of promise.

When he looked at her face, however, he could see that the night had taken an unexpected turn, and that was a big-time problem. It was a problem because Joel Smith had every intention of taking his friendship with Grace Vandenberg to the next level.

Had she rebuffed him on Tuesday, he would have walked – and kept on walking. He had meant it when he had told her that he would leave her alone. He had no right to impose on someone who already had more than her share of troubles and obligations.

But she had *not* rebuffed him. She had instead opened a door that led to wondrous new possibilities. Joel had a precious second opportunity to grab and hold the interest of someone he had obsessed about all week. If he lost her now, to fear or doubt or anything else, he could forget about Chance Number Three.

Joel thought about that chance as he took her hand and guided her through glass doors to the lobby of a theater that was as much a throwback as its name. Everything about the Phoenician screamed yesteryear, from a sign that boasted admission for a quarter to the plush carpeting, chandeliers, and marble walls.

When they reached the large, circular concession stand, he saw prices he thought existed only on the History Channel. Sodas, popcorn, and candy bars ran a nickel to a dime and came in sizes aimed to please. Joel gave twenty cents to the candy-striped girl behind the counter, and she gave him two colas in glass bottles and a large bag of popcorn. He handed one of the bottles to Grace.

"Are you sure that's all you want?" Joel asked.

"I'm sure, for now," Grace said as she lowered her eyes.

Fully aware of their predicament, even inside the theater, Joel whisked Grace from Point A to Point B. He was thankful that he needed only to find the entrance to a single 1,250-seat auditorium and not ply a crowded multiplex to Screen 16. When they stepped inside the darkened room, an usher disguised as a bellhop led them by flashlight up steep stairs to two cushioned, secluded seats in the balcony.

Joel glanced at the far wall, where a newsreel on the Battle of Britain gave way to an animated short. Massive velvet curtains flanked an impossibly large screen. Still holding Grace's hand, Joel felt his date return to life. She sighed and visibly relaxed for the first time since her near-death encounter with an education major.

"I'm sorry for dragging you into this," Grace said. "I'm normally not this reckless, and I'm not sure I'm being fair to you. I don't want to create impressions I can't honor."

Joel released her hand, wedged the bag of popcorn in the unoccupied, flipped-up seat to his left, and gave his remorseful companion the attention she deserved.

"Nobody dragged me into anything," Joel said. "There's no place in the world I'd rather be right now than in this theater, with you, watching cartoons."

A bungalow on the Big Island, however, might run a close second.

Grace smiled weakly, took Joel's hand, and stared at the screen with glistening eyes. A moment later she dropped her head on his shoulder and whispered two words.

"Me too."

37: GINNY

Sunday, July 6, 1941

For the first time since hot weather had moved into their maritime community, the full crew of the *S.S. Klickitat* manned their stations. Linda McEwan and Katie Kobayashi, wearing white shorts and colored tops, read books and sat in chairs on the starboard side of the deck. Grace Vandenberg, wearing a peach playsuit, read a letter and sat on a towel on the port side. She had just set aside an impressive array of nail clippers, emery boards, and bottles of nail polish.

"Is that letter from Paul?" Virginia Gillette asked.

Wearing a knotted midriff top and a pleated skirt, the captain of the ship sat upright in a lawn chair and lit her third cigarette of the day. A second draft of her first weighty story of the month rested on a table at her side.

"Grace?" Ginny asked more forcefully. "Is that from Paul?"

"It is," Grace replied.

"How is he doing?"

"He's coping. He doesn't care for Boston's humidity or some of the people in his program, but he says he's learning a lot."

"When does Paul get out?" Ginny asked.

"He gets his leave in August," Grace said. "He doesn't know where the Navy will send him next, but he believes he's headed to Hawaii."

"Wouldn't that be something? I think I could live there."

Ginny glanced at Linda and saw her dive deeper into her book. She considered that a good thing. The all-seeing, all-knowing leader of the pack knew that their pleasant, sunny afternoon probably wouldn't remain pleasant and sunny for long.

"We missed you last night," Katie said to Grace. "How was the movie?"

"It was good," Grace replied.

"Did you go by yourself?"

"No. I did not."

"Oh," Katie said. "I see."

"Whom *did* you go with?" Linda asked in a sarcastically sweet voice. She lowered her book to her lap and looked at Grace.

"You know who I went with, Linda," Grace said.

"What do you mean?"

"I mean you were staring out your window when I got home."

"Oh," Linda said. "In that case, how was your date with Joel?"

"It wasn't a date."

"It sure looked like a date."

"Well, it wasn't," Grace said. "Joel and I went to the movie as friends."

Katie returned to her book, *For Whom the Bell Tolls*. It was clear she wanted no part of the worms she had released from a can.

"Does Paul know about your 'friend'?" Linda asked.

"That's really none of your business," Grace said.

"Really?"

"Really."

"Well, as Paul's sister, I think it *is* my business."

"Zip it, Linda," Ginny said.

Linda snapped her book shut, slipped on her sandals, and got up from her chair. The redhead glared at Grace and stomped into the house.

"Forget her," Ginny said. "She's just mad because Lee Sorenson stood her up last night. He was supposed to take Linda to dinner and a show, but he took Barbara Dixon instead. Bigger boobs and a better temperament win every time."

Katie giggled.

"Stick to Hemingway, Sunshine," Ginny said.

"I'm trying, but you two make it difficult," Katie replied.

Ginny smiled at Katie and turned to Grace.

"Did Paul write anything else of interest?"

"He said he misses Seattle, his college friends, and me, of course," Grace said. "But he didn't write much about his training. I don't think he's enjoying himself."

"May I read the letter?" Ginny asked.

"Be my guest. Paul didn't write all that much."

Grace handed the letter to Ginny. A moment later, she opened a bottle of nail polish and resumed the maintenance of her fingers and toes.

When Ginny finished the letter, she placed it with her papers, put out her cigarette, and leaned back in her chair. She tapped her fingers on the armrest, stared at some blouses and underwear hanging on a clothesline, and finally turned to her friend.

"Grace?" Ginny asked.

"Yes?"

"What are you doing?"

"I'm painting my nails," Grace said.

"Grace?"

"Yes?"

"What are you doing with Joel Smith?" Ginny asked.

Grace put down the polish but kept her eyes on her feet. Katie lowered her book and moved her eyes to her peers. Hemingway, it seemed, had nothing on this.

"I'm making a friend," Grace said.

"Grace?"

"Yes, Ginny?"

"Do I need to remind you that you are engaged?"

"No," Grace said. She lifted her head and stared into space. "You don't."

38: JOEL

Wednesday, July 9, 1941

Joel sat in the second-largest chair in the manager's office and admired the art in the room. Sales awards, trade association plaques, and photos of clients with big cars, big boats, and big fish hung on the yellow walls like paintings in a gallery. Joel did not see a college diploma, but then he did not expect to find one. He knew that Melvin Carter was a self-made man.

"You like my pictures?" Mel asked as he entered the room.

"I do," Joel said. He pointed to a fishing photo. "I especially like that one."

Mel took a seat behind his large mahogany desk.

"I thought you might. I caught that salmon in Ketchikan. Four of us went up for a week and caught our weight in kings."

Mel pushed some papers to one side of the desk, creating space for a manila folder and a cup of coffee. He turned off a small gooseneck lamp.

"Would you like anything to drink?" Mel asked. "Evelyn just made some coffee."

"No, thank you," Joel said.

The manager sipped his coffee, settled into his chair, and flipped a pencil between his fingers like a majorette working a baton. A moment later, he put down the pencil, leaned forward, and gazed at his star employee.

"How do you like working here?" Mel asked.

"I like it, sir. I like it a lot," Joel said.

"That's good. I thought you did, but it's always nice to hear it from the horse's mouth," Mel said. He got up, adjusted the window blinds, and then returned to his chair and the matter at hand. "Joel, the main reason I called you in today is to go over some sales figures from June."

"Are they good?"

"They're more than good. They're the best monthly numbers I've seen in fifteen years," Mel said. He opened the folder, retrieved a sheet, and pushed it forward. "Go ahead. Take a look."

Joel took the sheet and studied the bottom line.

"I see we sold a lot of mattresses last month."

"No, *you* sold a lot of mattresses last month," Mel said. "You also moved a lot of washers and sofas and dining room sets."

"It appears so."

"You're doing a bang-up job, son. People I haven't seen in years are coming into the store because they've heard about our hotshot salesman."

"That's good," Joel said.

"It *is* good. It's good for me and good for you."

Mel pulled two checks from the folder.

"I want you to know that success is rewarded here and that you've more than earned these checks," Mel said. He handed the slips to Joel. "The first is a bonus. I usually hand them out at Christmas, but I'm making an exception now because I think the situation calls for it. The second check is your pay for the past two weeks. Please note the higher compensation rate."

Joel took the checks and studied the numbers. He liked what he saw.

"This is very generous. I don't know what to say."

"You don't have to say a thing. You've earned every penny," Mel said. "I only hope I can do this more often. Tom tells me that you plan to get a place by Labor Day and that you intend to stick around a while. I hope that's true. I don't want you to leave."

"You needn't worry about that. I like living in Seattle and working for you," Joel said. "I couldn't ask for a better job given my circumstances."

"That's good. I'm glad to hear it."

Mel smiled and nodded. He seemed pleased but also preoccupied. He fidgeted in his chair and played again with the pencil before returning his attention to Joel.

"Speaking of your circumstances, there is another matter I'd like to discuss," Mel said. "It's more personal in nature, so I hope you don't mind."

"I don't see why I should," Joel said. "Fire away."

"Mrs. Carter and I have noticed that you haven't received any mail or telephone calls from Montana or anywhere else. Is everything all right with your family?"

Joel settled into his chair. He had long expected the question and had rehearsed his reply many times over the past month. But he took his time delivering it.

"The truth is, Mr. Carter, that I didn't leave home on the best of terms. My father and I had a falling out, and I caught the first train out of town. My family knows I'm in Seattle and that I'm safe but not much more. I'd like to keep it that way – at least for now."

"I see," Mel said. "Well, that explains a lot."

"I hope that's not a problem," Joel said.

"It's not a problem at all. Just let me know if there's anything I can do. I would be happy to help. I know these family spats can be difficult."

"I appreciate that, sir. Will that be all?"

Mel picked up his pencil and gave it one last twirl as he looked around the room. When he looked again at Joel, he did so with serious eyes.

"There is one more thing," Mel said.

"Oh?" Joel asked.

Mel nodded.

"I feel awkward bringing it up, because it's really none of my business. But I consider you family – and I try to steer family in a positive direction when I think they are headed for trouble."

"You think I'm headed for trouble?"

"I do," Mel said.

"OK."

"I understand you've taken a liking to the Vandenberg girl."

Joel pondered the understatement of the century and wondered why his supervisor, of all people, cared about his social life. But he figured that Melvin Carter had his best interests in mind, so he didn't rush to defend a friendship that he himself had trouble explaining.

"Don't get me wrong," Mel said. "Grace is a lovely girl. I can see why you like her. But I believe she's engaged to Paul McEwan. And if there is one thing I've learned in fifty years, it's that the fastest way to get into trouble is to take something that doesn't belong to you."

"I understand," Joel said.

Mel folded his hands atop the desk.

"Just be careful, son. We all like you here and want you to be happy. Adjusting to a new town can be difficult enough without adding unnecessary complications."

"I agree. Thank you, sir. I appreciate the advice."

* * * * *

The sales phenom walked out of the office and thought about the surreal end to his otherwise pleasant and constructive chat with the boss. He really did appreciate Mel's advice, not to mention the hundred-dollar bonus and the pay raise, but he did not intend to walk away from his unnecessary complication. He intended to do just the opposite.

Joel, in fact, had walked *toward* his "complication" the previous day. He had visited the library just as Grace got off work and offered to walk her home.

Despite some reservations, Grace accepted Joel's offer. She left little doubt that she valued his company more than she feared discovery or the consequences of sending mixed messages.

Joel did not worry about mixed messages. He wanted to send a clear message and build on his momentum. If he had his way, Tuesdays with Grace would become a regular thing.

Joel walked to the end of a hallway, entered the showroom, and looked around for a potential sale. He took only five steps before Tom, walking briskly, caught him from behind and started a conversation in midstride.

"So did the old man lecture you about Grace?" Tom asked.

Joel shook his head.

"He didn't lecture me at all. He just gave me some friendly advice."

"I thought he might," Tom said. "He doesn't like interfering in other people's business, but he doesn't want you to screw up when you're doing so well. Neither do I."

"Let me guess," Joel said. "You have a solution in mind."

"As a matter of fact, I do."

Joel stopped and pivoted toward his friend.

"Care to elaborate?"

Tom smiled and threw his arm around Joel.

"I think it's time you gave Linda another look."

39: JOEL AND GINNY

Maple Valley, Washington – Saturday, July 12, 1941

The waltz proved difficult. Despite two private dance lessons in three days, Joel struggled with his footwork. He wondered how a linebacker who could run through a tire course without hitting rubber could not keep from tripping on a parquet floor.

"You dance divinely, Mr. Smith," Linda said.

Joel smiled.

"And you lie through your teeth, Miss McEwan."

Joel looked at his dance partner and admitted that the date designed to derail the Vandenberg Express was going far better than he could have imagined. Wearing a pink swing dress and a radiant smile, with a mood to match, Linda had brought her "A" game to the shores of Lake Wilderness, a recreation hot spot southeast of Seattle.

But then, from what Joel had heard, she had brought it all week, or at least the part of the week that followed his Wednesday night phone call asking her out. Though the double date had been Tom and Ginny's doing, the follow through had not. No one had had to twist his arm to ask out Linda McEwan or to take the date seriously.

The evening had started at five, when the Dynamic Duo pulled up to Coed Central and strutted to the door with orchids in hand. The flowers had been Joel's idea. Spotting a street vendor as he sped down Roosevelt Way at twice the posted limit, the designated driver had screeched to a stop for that little something extra.

For her part, Linda had left nothing to the last minute. She had spent most of the day preparing for the date, hitting a salon and three department stores between ten and two. Her effort had not gone unnoticed or unrewarded. When Tom had walked into the house and taken his first look at Ginny and Linda, he had asked, "Which one do I get?"

Katie too had joined in the fun. Like a mother sending a daughter to a prom, she had complimented Linda's appearance and snapped a dozen photographs with her Six-20 Brownie Junior before giving the camera to Joel. He had wanted to inspect the "relic" and take a photo of all four women.

Grace had pampered Linda in other ways, buying her breakfast and helping her select an appropriate outfit. The two had not exchanged more than pleasantries in six days but talked up a storm as Saturday night drew near. She had been far less talkative around Joel. When he had walked into the living room wearing a new gray suit, she had offered only a soft smile, a long gaze, and a simple hello.

Joel recalled the gaze as he and Linda retired to a leather love seat in the lounge of a cavernous lakeside lodge. Nearly a dozen sofas and recliners sat atop a polished hardwood floor and formed a tight barrier around a Tabriz rug and a river-rock fireplace.

What a change, Joel thought. Six weeks after riding the rails with Boxcar Charlie and digging through discards outside a grocery store, he had found contentment. He had wonderful new friends, an increasingly lucrative job, his arm around one beautiful woman, and his mind on another. Raised a Presbyterian, he wondered whether the denomination had any breakaway sects that smiled on multiple marriages.

"Having fun, you two?" Tom asked as he and Ginny plopped onto a facing sofa.

"Loads," Joel answered. "Though I wish I knew what I was doing out there."

"You'll get the hang of it," Ginny said. "Dancing is not as easy as it looks."

"I'm working with him," Linda said. "He's coming along."

Minutes later the band, which had covered Glenn Miller, Benny Goodman, and Tommy Dorsey expertly for ninety minutes, took a breather, sending more than a hundred smartly-dressed couples from the floor to the lounge, two exits, and the lake.

"Anyone want to get some air?" Ginny asked. Wearing a white hat and floral print dress that fell to her knees, she looked every bit the equal of her peers.

"I'm game," Tom said.

Linda didn't say a word but appeared receptive to Ginny's suggestion. She gazed at Joel for several seconds, seized his hand, and gently smiled.

Joel didn't budge. Tired and sore from falling on the floor, he wanted nothing more than a few more minutes on the comfortable couch. But even he could take a hint.

"Air sounds good."

* * * * *

Stepping out onto an elevated cedar deck that encircled the log-sided hall, the four worked their way through a small crowd to a quiet corner. In the distance, a lone canoeist plied the glassy water as a waning moon rose above an irregular horizon of treetops and hills.

Ginny reached in her purse, pulled out a pack, and lit her first smoke since dinner. She leaned on the railing and assessed the lake like it was a painting in progress, something she had already decided to purchase at more than the asking price.

"Beautiful, isn't it?" Ginny asked.

"It's the best," Joel said. He looked at her, shook his head, and chuckled. "I see my health talk the other day crashed and burned."

"Keep trying. I never tire of a good argument."

"Forget it, pal," Tom said. He grinned. "You have as much chance of getting Ginny to give up her vices as you do with me and mine. Speaking of sinful behavior, I put some cash on DiMaggio and Williams this morning, just like you asked. I got fifty-to-one odds on Joe and a hundred to one on Ted."

"Good man," Joel said.

"I guess you can afford to lose forty bucks after that bonus," Tom replied. "I'm off to the bar. Does anyone want a drink?"

"I'll have a scotch and water," Ginny said.

"Make that two," Joel added.

"How about you, Linda?"

"Nothing tonight, Tom. Thanks."

Ginny turned away from the lake toward a sight she thought she would never see: Linda refusing a drink. She smiled at her friend and congratulated herself for pushing the evening on Tom, who had wanted to go to the track or a game. She still had the touch.

When Tom returned, he distributed the cocktails and joined Ginny along the railing. Joel picked up his glass with his right hand because Linda had his left. She would not let go of him the rest of the night.

"This has been fun, kids," Tom said. "What do you say we all do something next Saturday? I could even go for a movie."

"I'd like that," Ginny said. "Just as long as you don't drag me to one of those awful Westerns. I'd rather watch dogs procreate than put up with another ambush at the pass."

Tom laughed.

"How about you two?"

Linda looked at Joel and nodded.

"Yeah," Joel said. "I'd like that."

147

"OK, then. It's a done deal. I'll never pass up an opportunity to drive my wheels around town with two lovely ladies."

Hearing the music start, Ginny dropped her cigarette to the deck and snuffed it out with a heel. She clutched her purse with one hand and Tom's arm with the other.

"Looks like the pipes are back in action," Ginny said. "Shall we go in?"

Joel gazed at Linda for several seconds, as if weighing all the possible answers to a very simple question, and smiled fondly at his date. Linda responded in kind and tightened her hold on his hand.

"You two go ahead," Joel said. He looked at Ginny and then at Tom. "I kind of like the fresh air. I think we'll stay out here for a while."

* * * * *

When most on the deck returned to the dance hall, Joel led Linda down a series of steps to a well-manicured lawn that ran thirty yards to the lake. Four deck lights provided strollers with enough illumination to walk to the water without falling in.

"You like the outdoors, don't you?" Linda asked.

"I do."

"I overheard you talk with Tom at dinner. I don't think I've ever known a person who gets excited about glaciers and igneous rocks."

"They're pretty hot stuff. That's why I keep all my geology magazines in brown paper wrappers under the bed."

Linda smiled.

"You're funny – and pretty learned for someone who never attended college. Have you ever thought of going to school or doing something besides selling furniture?"

"You mean like joining the circus or working as a cabana boy? Yeah, I've thought about it. But there's something about ventilating mattresses that keeps me grounded."

"I see why Ginny likes you."

"She does?"

"Oh, yes. She said just yesterday that 'Joel Smith is the only man I've ever met who can make me laugh and think at the same time.'"

Joel grinned.

Wait till she meets Grandpa.

For the next fifteen minutes, Joel and Linda stood at the edge of the water, arm in arm, and watched dusk turn into night. Neither said more than a few words, but neither had to. Their silence was a source of comfort, not discontent.

The tranquility was broken a moment later, when two couples noisily emerged from the hall. One walked to a shiny black Ford parked near the front of a dirt lot. The other stayed on the deck and propped open an exit, allowing the upbeat sound of "In the Mood" by Glenn Miller to drift across the lawn and drown out a cricket philharmonic.

"You sure you don't want to dance?" Linda asked.

"I'm sure – and not just because I don't want to fall on my face. I'd rather stay out here with you."

"Really?"

"Really," Joel said. He took Linda's hands and looked her in the eyes. "Why would you think otherwise?"

"Well, if you must know, I wasn't sure you even wanted to go out. I didn't exactly make the best impression at Tom's party. I had a little too much celebration," Linda said as she avoided Joel's gaze. "And I've noticed you've become rather sweet on Grace."

Joel took a breath.

"To be honest, I *wasn't* sure about going out tonight – not at first. But I'm glad we did. I'm really glad. You've been great, Linda. I couldn't have asked for a better date," Joel said. "As for Grace, I do like her. I like all of you. But I'm here now with you – not with Grace or Katie, but with you. That's what matters."

Joel meant it, too. His feelings for Grace had not ebbed a bit, but for the first time in weeks he began to ask serious questions – questions he should have asked at the start. Did he and Grace actually have something? Or was he just a fool holding Paul McEwan's jacket until he returned on leave?

And what about his so-called consolation prize? She had no restrictions and came exactly as advertised – smart, pretty, honest, flawed, and unabashedly interested in the new kid in town. If nothing else, Linda deserved a fair shake and an open mind. The old saying about a bird in the hand began to gnaw.

Joel considered another thing as well. It felt good having a woman in his arms and in his life. It had been two months since he had enjoyed a similar moment with Jana, two months and fifty-nine years. Life as a monk was getting old.

"Are you OK?" Linda asked. She looked at him with soft, expressive eyes, eyes any man could get used to. "You look kind of lost."

Joel smiled and pulled her closer.

"I was," he said, "but I'm not anymore."

Joel put a hand to Linda's face and took a long look at his Second Impression. He kissed her and, for a few splendid minutes, forgot why he was lost in the first place.

40: JOEL

Seattle, Washington – Tuesday, July 15, 1941

hree days after taking an evening stroll with Linda McEwan, Joel readied himself for an afternoon stroll with her would-be sister-in-law. This time, however, Tuesday with Grace was Tuesday with Grace and Katie.

"It looks like you have two dates today," Grace said as she stood with Joel and Katie outside the university library. "We rarely get off at the same time, but we did today. I hope you don't mind."

"Of course I don't mind," Joel replied.

"Thanks, Joel," Katie said. "I'll try to behave myself."

Joel laughed.

"Where would you ladies like to walk?"

"Where do you normally go?" Katie asked.

"I normally go south and west and then north," Joel said as if he had done that ten times instead of one. "That way I get to see the best of the campus."

"Then let's go north and east and then south," Katie said. "I'd like to see the worst."

Joel chuckled and shook his head.

Katherine Kobayashi did not let up. For the next twenty minutes she kept Joel in stitches from one end of the campus to the other with self-deprecating jokes, witty asides, and humorous anecdotes about her unusual college experience.

Joel asked himself why he had not spent more time with her. Then he looked at Grace and answered his own question.

"When did you two meet?" Joel asked.

"We met our freshman year at the library. Both of us worked in the circulation department," Katie said. "Grace checked out books, and I made sure she did it right."

Grace smiled but did not speak.

"When I learned she had lived in Asia, I made an effort to get to know her better. I knew we would have a lot to talk about," Katie said. "My parents came to this country from Yokohama."

"I see," Joel said.

"One day I asked Grace to attend a Hasu Club meeting with me and speak to the group about her experiences. Hasu means lotus in Japanese."

"Did she come?"

"She did," Katie said. "She did a wonderful job too. We loved her speech so much that we asked her to join."

Joel eyed Grace and wondered why she had not yet jumped in. This was her story too. He figured that she was more than content to let Katie tell the tale. Why take the time to talk about your past when a colorful interpreter could do it for you?

"Did Grace join the club?" Joel asked.

"She did!" Katie said. "She became very popular, too, in part because she brought us a special gift once a month."

"What was that?"

"Gingersnap cookies."

Joel laughed. He did not need to ask why others liked this pint-sized comic. She was a gem no jeweler could improve.

When Joel asked Katie about her background, she gave him her resume. The oldest daughter of a fish market owner, she had graduated fifth in her class at Multnomah High School in Portland and ventured north in search of change. The English major hoped to find work as a translator or a Japanese instructor when she left the university in June.

As the trio reached Forty-Fifth Street and turned west, not east, at Grace's request, Joel looked at Katie and thought about the fate that awaited her. More than four hundred Japanese American students had been forced to leave the university after Pearl Harbor and live in internment camps. Joel was certain Katie would be among them.

"Katie, do you mind if I ask you a serious question?" Joel asked.

"That depends. If you want to know how many boyfriends I've had, the answer is yes," Katie said. "Otherwise, I don't mind."

Joel smiled. She didn't miss a beat.

"OK. I'll stay away from boyfriend questions," Joel said. "I just want to know if you're concerned about what's going on in the Pacific."

Katie slowed to a stop and tucked away her infectious smile. She looked at Joel like a mother about to explain a complicated and sensitive subject to a child.

"I'm very concerned," Katie said. "I have relatives in Japan who would like to come to America but can't, and I worry about what might happen to them should our countries go to war. My family and I would be vulnerable. It's something I think about every day."

"I didn't mean to upset you," Joel said. "I'm just curious."

"You could never upset me. You're a good man. Others, though, are not so good. I fear a war would bring out the worst in people. That's why I hope the differences between America and Japan can be resolved peacefully."

With anyone else, Joel would have brought up Japan's "peaceful" occupation of Manchuria. But he did not want to pick a fight with a girl who was no doubt deeply torn by events over which she had no control. He imagined that Grace and Katie had probably had more than a few delicate discussions about the Rape of Nanking.

Joel turned to other topics as the three resumed their stroll. He talked about work and food until it became clear that his chat with Katie and Grace was really a chat with Katie.

Grace had not uttered more than a few words since leaving the library. Nor had she appeared all that interested in her friends' conversation. She seemed lost and dispirited.

When the trio reached the entrance to a drugstore, Katie stopped abruptly and peered into a window as if looking for someone or something. She turned to face the others.

"Well, this is my stop," Katie said.

"Your stop?" Joel asked. "I thought I was walking you home."

"Not today. I need to buy a magazine."

"Do you want us to wait?"

"No," Katie said. "I'll be a while – maybe an hour."

"You'll need an hour to buy a magazine?"

"Yes. There are many magazines in there. You two run along."

Embarrassed by his slow grasp of the obvious, Joel smiled and tried to contain the blush that swept across his face. He put a hand on Katie's shoulder.

"OK then," Joel said. "Pick a winner."

"I will," Katie replied. "Can we do this again sometime?"

"Of course. Count on it."

Katie searched her purse methodically for several seconds. She finally found some dollars she probably would not need and a key she probably would. She walked a few steps to a glass door and turned to face Grace.

"I'll see you at the house," Katie said.

Grace nodded but did not speak, just as she had not spoken during most of the long get-acquainted session between her talkative friends. She instead gazed at Katie, smiled wistfully, and mouthed words that Joel had hoped to hear: "Thank you."

When the third wheel rolled into the drugstore, Joel guided Grace to the end of the block. From there, they began a long, slow walk to the rambler.

"That's quite a friend you have there," Joel said.

"Katie and Ginny are the sisters I never had – the *siblings* I never had," Grace replied.

Joel tried to relate to her situation but could not. Somewhere in Seattle, albeit in a decidedly inconvenient parallel universe, he had a father, a mother, a sister, and a brother.

Grace had nothing except an aunt she seldom saw and a past she wished to bury. Was it any wonder she cherished her friends? Was it any wonder she clung to *him*?

They hurried across a busy intersection and then slowed their pace to a stroll. At five o'clock the streets and sidewalks were clogged with people coming and going, but Joel and Grace – friends, moviegoers, and hand holders – kept to themselves.

"You looked nice Saturday night," Grace said.

"You look nice every night," Joel replied.

Grace blushed but kept her eyes forward. She continued down the sidewalk with the stride of a woman who would not be distracted by flattery.

"Linda said you dance well for a beginner," Grace said.

Joel picked up her matter-of-fact tone and tried to lighten the mood. If compliments wouldn't cut it, perhaps humor would.

"She's being kind," Joel said.

"Was dinner nice?" Grace asked.

"I kept it down."

"How about the band?"

"They missed a note."

"The lake?"

"No fishing allowed."

And so it began. For thirty minutes, the two went back and forth. Grace asked pointless questions about a dance she missed. Joel gave pointless answers.

The exchange, at least in Joel's mind, did nothing to bring the participants together. It did much to exacerbate their differences.

"What about you and Katie?" Joel asked in an attempt to change the subject. "How did you spend the evening?"

"We bought some wine and played jazz on Ginny's phonograph," Grace said.

"What did you listen to?"

"Billie Holiday, Duke Ellington, and Louis Armstrong."

"That's good stuff. I'm envious."

Joel didn't expand on his "envy." He saw no point in making a case that couldn't be made. Even a night at home with Billie Holiday, Duke Ellington, and Louis Armstrong was no match for a night at the lake with Number One.

Joel knew that Grace wanted to talk about Linda, but he was determined not to be the first to bring her up. Nor was he sure he even *wanted* to talk about her. He'd had a great time with the redhead and didn't want to compound his many lies with more. So he did the next best thing and tried to engage Grace in small talk.

"How are things at the library?" Joel asked.

"Fine," Grace said.

"And at the house?"

"Swell."

Joel looked at Grace and saw tight lips and focused eyes. She was clearly irritated and annoyed, but he didn't know why. If she wanted to discuss something else, including the red-haired, green-eyed elephant in the room, now was her chance.

"Grace?" Joel asked.

"Yes."

"Are you upset with me?"

"No," Grace said.

"I thought you wanted to talk."

"I do."

The friends walked several more blocks in uncomfortable silence. Joel noticed that Grace would not even look at him. Was she frustrated? Upset? Scared? He did not know.

Joel wanted to talk more – he *needed* to talk more – but he had run out of things to say. As they approached a corner, two blocks from the house, where they usually parted, he used the opportunity to ask a question that had been on his mind.

"Have you heard from Paul?" Joel asked.

"I have," Grace said.

"How is he doing?"

"I don't want to talk about him."

"How come?"

"Because I don't!" Grace snapped. She stopped on the sidewalk and finally turned toward Joel. "I don't want to talk about Paul or jazz or the library or how I look today or any day. I want to know if you had a good time. I want to know if you like Linda."

154

Joel looked at Grace's face and saw frustration, anger, and fear. He realized then that he was more than just a passing fancy to her. He was much more.

But that made her outrage all the more difficult to digest. No matter what she felt for him, she wore the ring of another man. Joel did not like that at all. Nor did he care about sneaking around. Seeing an opportunity to clear the air, he pressed ahead with the kind of candor that would make their relationship or break it.

"To tell you the truth, Grace, I do like her, and I did have a good time. I had a terrific time. Linda was damn near perfect," Joel said. "She was charming, gracious, and affectionate. She didn't even drink. She wanted to make a good impression on me, and she sure as hell succeeded."

Joel's reply left Grace reeling. She doubled over like she had been punched in the gut and turned away when tears filled her eyes.

Joel didn't regret letting her have it. He knew his words would shock. He *wanted* them to shock. They were the method to his madness. As Grace started to walk away, he grabbed her hand and yanked her back.

"I'm not finished!" Joel said. "Everything I said was true. I do like Linda. I did have a good time. But I'd rather go on one walk with you than a thousand dates with her."

Joel pulled Grace in and kissed her like he would never see her again. She threw her arms over his shoulders and responded in kind.

Grace buried herself in the embrace of a man who was still very much a stranger and begged him to never let her go. But when she peered past him and saw three college-age women walking up the street, she shook her head and pushed herself free.

"I can't do this," Grace said. "I'm sorry. I can't."

Grace turned and ran. She ran away from Joel and away from the women. She ran back to the house on Klickitat Avenue and the safe, predictable, comfortable life she had known before a lonely cowboy from Montana had tipped his hat.

Joel tried to process what had happened but could not. There was plenty of good and bad in the exchange with Grace, and he wasn't sure which of the two had the upper hand. Her kiss had been the stuff of dreams and her plea for him to hold her music to his ears.

Yet when Joel thought again about what had transpired and the effect he had already had on others, he did not hear a symphony. He did not hear bells or whistles or even fireworks. Instead, he heard something ominous, something he had vowed to avoid and could not invite: the distant but unmistakable sound of thunder.

41: GINNY

T he view from the front seat of the Plymouth was postcard perfect. Beyond and below the pine-covered bluff, sailboats plied Puget Sound like skaters performing figure eights on a sheet of liquid gold. Along the horizon, an egg-yolk sun dropped below jagged, shadowy peaks and painted the summer sky fifty different shades of orange, red, and yellow. Tom Carter had driven to Magnolia, a bucolic district that residents shared with Fort Lawton, because it was the one of the few places in Seattle a couple could see a sunset like this. He put his right arm around Ginny, loosened a new tie he had worn at dinner, and turned on the car radio.

"Does it get better than this?" Tom asked.

"Only in dreams," Ginny replied.

Though the two shared the viewpoint with four other couples parked in the lot, they might as well have been alone. The bluff top was windless, bug-less, and quiet, save the soothing sound of a clarinet in Jimmy Dorsey's "Maria Elena."

"This song reminds me of the dance. That was a nice evening, Tom."

"I had a good time. So did our companions, from what I heard."

"Do you think it's going to work, Linda and Joel?"

"We'll know by Saturday. We're still on for a movie, no?"

"We're on. Linda would never forgive me if I backed out now, though I think she's more than capable of flying solo with the cowboy. She's definitely hooked."

"You're right about that," Tom said with a laugh. "But I'm not sure *Joel* is hooked. He could have asked Linda out again, but he hasn't. He stayed home tonight and helped Dad work on some cabinets. I think he's still got a thing for Blondie."

Ginny poured two flutes of champagne from a bottle between her feet and handed one to the man leaning back in his seat. Staring lazily at the darkening sky and wearing a ridiculously wide grin, he was the picture of contentment. She envied his ability to set aside his cares, both great and small, so quickly and easily.

"I worry about Grace. Something happened on Tuesday that put her in the dumps. She ran in the house crying and went straight to her room. She wouldn't talk about it at dinner and hasn't said much since."

"Give her some slack. She'll be better when Paul gets back."

"You really think so?"

"No," he laughed. "I just said that to get your mind on me."

Ginny smiled and kissed him on the cheek.

"You're incorrigible."

For another fifty minutes, the odd couple that had defied the odds for three and a half months held each other and enjoyed the kind of scenery that moved poets. They put work, friends, and a troubled world aside and talked of better things, including a future together. Though both spoke of days and weeks, rather than months and years, neither seemed threatened by commitment. Indeed, for two who had traveled alone for most of their twenty-plus years, the concept had wondrous appeal.

As the music turned to news at the top of the hour, Ginny lowered the volume and reached for the champagne. The bubbly was her idea, as was dinner on the pier. She had wanted to take Tom out earlier, in celebration of his graduation, but had found his dance card increasingly crowded with the arrival of his new best buddy. So she took advantage of a Thursday night that had unexpectedly opened up the day before.

Tom was about to get out of the car and stretch when he heard a few words on the radio that caught his attention. He reached across the dash and increased the volume.

"The Clipper hit hard grounders to third in the first and seventh innings, but Cleveland's Ken Keltner denied him each time. The Yankees won four to three. Repeating tonight's top story, Joe DiMaggio's hitting streak has come to an end at fifty-six."

Tom turned down the radio, took the bottle, and poured himself a second. Ginny turned off the radio, took the bottle back, and poured herself a third. They looked at each other, smiled, and toasted their amazing new friend.

Joel Smith had just won a thousand dollars.

42: JOEL

Sunday, July 20, 1941

The theater was dark – and that was a problem. Without the bellhop usher to lead the way, Joel found navigating the recesses of the Phoenician more difficult this time than the last. The hired help had apparently taken a potty break. Even so, Joel managed to locate his date with two colas in hand. He spoke to her when he arrived.

"I brought you something to drink."

He gave up one of the bottles and found a seat.

For the next three minutes, Joel sat in his chair, looked up at the screen, and let his mind wander. He couldn't help but think of the last time he had visited the theater – with another woman, under different circumstances. It hadn't been that long ago, but it seemed like an eternity. He felt awkward sitting next to this girl, though he was strangely at peace.

"Thanks for coming," Grace said.

Joel smiled.

"You wrote 'urgent' on the note you left at Carter's. I respond to emergencies."

Joel had not known what to expect when he had entered the Phoenician at twelve thirty, only hours after escorting Linda McEwan into the same theater. Grace had not provided any clues. She had simply asked him to meet her in the back row of the balcony during the first show of the double feature.

"Thanks, anyway," Grace said.

Joel glanced at his "date" and did not know whether to laugh or give her a hug. She was at once pathetic and adorable. Sitting prim and proper in a yellow dress she had no doubt worn to church, Grace stared at the screen through white plastic sunglasses.

"You can probably remove those now," Joel said.

Grace lowered her head, took off the glasses, and looked at Joel for the first time.

"I should glue them to my face. I've disappointed so many."

"By many, do you mean you, yourself, and you?"

"Yes," Grace said.

"You haven't disappointed me."

Joel put his arm around Grace and moved her way, partly to get comfortable for a potentially long sit and partly to provide the reassurance she appeared to need. He relaxed and returned his attention to the first of two movies he had seen the night before.

"Do you know what you've gotten yourself into?"

"A terrible mess, that's what," Grace said.

Joel laughed.

"No. I mean the movies today."

"Are they bad? I hope so. Then I can watch them as penance."

"They're not bad," Joel said, "but their titles are choice. I assume you read the marquee."

Grace blushed and held back a smile.

"I did."

In the first half of the matinee, actress Deanna Durbin starred in *Nice Girl?* In the second, Ronald Reagan and Lionel Barrymore supported Wallace Beery in *The Bad Man*. If God was sending a message, He wasn't being subtle.

Grace and Joel mostly ignored the movies and discussed places they wanted to see and things they wanted to do. Grace talked about Switzerland, skiing, mountains, and snow. Before coming to Seattle, she had seen mostly jungles, savannas, and subtropical plains. Joel talked about Hawaii, the answer to every question. But for three hours, the two remained fixed to their seats, as if the Phoenician were the most appealing place on the planet.

Joel laughed to himself at the thought. For all practical purposes, it *was* the most appealing place. At this stage of their relationship, they didn't need ski slopes or beaches but rather time alone. Privacy was paradise – and few venues on a campus of ten thousand students offered more privacy than the balcony of a movie theater on a Sunday in July.

* * * * *

When the credits of the second film rolled up the screen, Joel and Grace spilled out of the theater and onto the Ave. More than a hundred people gathered under or near the massive marquee, but none were friends or acquaintances. For the first time in two weeks, the Clandestine Hand Holding Club of King County caught a break. The pair took a circuitous

159

route to Klickitat Avenue, making the most of an hour before dinner and warm, sunny weather. The streets were bare, quiet, and inviting.

"I'm sorry for running away from you the other day. Everything happened so fast and I just wasn't ready to deal with it. I'm still not sure I am. I'm very conflicted."

Joel put his hand around her waist and pulled her close but remained silent. He did not know what to say. He knew only that he could not stand to be away from her and did not want to lose the momentum from the past week. Unlike Tuesday's walk, Sunday's stroll was peaceful, relaxed, and subdued. Joel asked about Paul and got some answers. Grace asked about Linda and got many more.

Saturday's date had gone as well as the dance, starting with an afternoon in Tom's boat and concluding with dinner, two movies, and drinks at the Mad Dog. Linda had not held back this time, ordering two beers and two cocktails, but was otherwise her same captivating self. Joel had spent much of the night wondering what he had done to deserve attention and affection he now knew he could never return in equal measures.

When the strollers reached their all-too-familiar departure point, Joel led Grace away from the sidewalk to a large oak tree that shaded two Victorian houses. Both homes appeared unoccupied and no residents walked their street or worked their yards. Joel did not want to let her go, but he knew that even ten more minutes together was not an option. Grace had promised Katherine Kobayashi she would be back in time to enjoy an authentic Japanese dinner she had planned for her housemates.

Joel backed up against the tree, took Grace's hands, and pulled her in. He studied her face for a moment but didn't say a word. For the first time since he kissed Tara Schmidt behind the maintenance building of Madison Park Elementary School, he had butterflies in his stomach – big butterflies, like those of the late Mesozoic Era.

"I love you, Grace."

Grace smiled, put a hand to his cheek, and met his gaze. She appeared receptive to his message but unsure about how to respond.

"I know."

Joel glanced at the ground and then at the girl. Was this a rejection or a rain check? He tried to look cheerful but could not force what he did not feel.

"That's not quite the reaction I had hoped for," Joel said. "Have I blown it?"

Grace shook her head.

"No. You haven't."

Joel looked at Grace with puzzlement.

"What is it then?"

"I was just thinking," Grace said.

"About what?"

"About how far we've come in just a few weeks and how I've underestimated you. My engagement ring would have scared off most men, but not Joel Smith. You saw something you wanted and went after it. You do that with a lot of things."

"Is that bad?" Joel asked.

"It can be. But in this case, it wasn't. I'm glad you didn't give up on me."

Grace took Joel's hand and continued.

"I'm also thinking about decisions I have to make. Do you work on Saturday?"

"No. Why?"

"I'll tell you later," Grace said. "Just be on the corner of Baltic and Forty-Second at seven in the morning. Come alone and bring a jacket and a hat."

"Why?"

"No questions. Just be there."

Grace kissed Joel on the cheek and walked out of sight.

43: JOEL

Saturday, July 26, 1941

The early bird rose with the sun. Groggy and sore from a night on a non-ventilating trailer mattress, Joel rolled out of bed, took a shower, and ate a bowl of oatmeal over the kitchen sink before any of the Carters stirred like a mouse. Only Max, the family cat, noticed his stealthy exit from 4125 Baltic Avenue. The two-year-old Abyssinian followed him out the door.

Joel had not heard from Grace since Sunday, when he had bared his soul under an old oak tree and left with little more than a chicken peck and mixed messages. He did not know what this meeting was about or why it had to start so early.

Joel knew only that he had an appointment to keep and that he would not be late. He arrived at the rendezvous point thirty minutes before Grace drove up in the second most impressive vehicle he had seen that week. The vermillion red 1936 Ford Deluxe V-8 coupe with whitewall tires was as inviting as its driver.

"Sorry I'm late, but I had to fill the tank and had trouble finding gas. There aren't many stations open at this hour," Grace said. "I should have done it yesterday."

Joel peered through an open window at the woman behind the wheel and pondered her apology. He wondered if it was even possible to get angry with her, for tardiness, neglect, or any other misdemeanor.

Joel laughed to himself and decided it was not. He adjusted the cowboy hat on his head, opened the passenger door, and jumped in the car.

Wearing a white blouse, a green plaid skirt, and a sweater, Grace pulled away from the curb and sped down Baltic Avenue toward East Forty-Fifth Street. From there she headed west to Route 5 and then south on the highway at a speed of fifty miles per hour. When she left the city limits, she turned her attention to her captive.

"Should I roll up my window?" Grace asked. "I don't want your hat to blow away."

"Leave it down," Joel said.

Grace glanced at her passenger.

"I bet you're wondering what this is about."

"The thought never crossed my mind."

The driver smiled.

"I see you're not going to make this easy."

Grace fumbled with some buttons on the dash as she passed a slow-moving vehicle.

"My aunt would kill me if she knew I was driving my uncle's pride and joy out of the city with a strange young man at my side."

"Am I strange?" Joel asked.

"You're very strange, but that's part of your charm."

"I see."

Grace took a breath.

"In any case, I want you to know there's no reason to be alarmed. You're not being kidnapped, at least not in the formal sense. I just thought that, before I burn any bridges, I should get to know you better – away from the campus, away from the theater, and away from Seattle."

With those words, Joel sighed with relief. He never doubted that he had gained Grace's interest, but he knew he would have to do more than gain her interest to convince her to break off her engagement to a United States naval officer.

"Do you often kidnap strange young men and take them out of the city?"

"No," Grace said. "You're the first."

"That's good. You had me worried for a while," Joel said, silently conceding he could still succumb to the Stockholm syndrome. He zipped his cotton jacket and settled into his seat. "I like this car. Did you say it was your uncle's?"

Grace nodded.

"I did. He bought it five years ago, a month before he died. After he passed away, my aunt returned it to the dealership and tried to get a refund. She explained that she didn't drive and had no use for a vehicle, but she got nowhere with the dealer. He offered her only half of what the car was worth. So she held onto it."

"And then gave it to you?"

"No. She kept it. But she lets me drive it when I want. I used to come home a lot on weekends. Driving this thing was more convenient than the alternatives."

"You mean taking the bus and walking?" Joel asked.

"Hitching too."

"You used to hitch rides?"

"I still do on occasion."

"Grace, that's insane."

"Why?" Grace asked with a smile. She seemed pleased she had found a subject that interested and even irritated him. "Is it because I'm a poor, defenseless female?"

"Yes!" Joel said. "There are a lot of crazies out there who would love to do bad things to good people, particularly poor, defenseless – and very pretty, I might add – females like you."

"Have you ever hitched a ride?"

"Only once. I got stuck outside an abandoned mine."

"See? You survived," Grace said.

"I did. But the guy who gave me a lift was a Buick dealer, not an ax murderer."

"And you, of course, can tell the difference."

Joel sighed, shook his head, and smiled at the lovable, quick-witted woman at his side. He had clearly met his match. He stared ahead at a remarkably uncluttered highway and tried to figure out what Grace had up her sleeve.

"By the way, Miss Vandenberg, seeing as you're kidnapping me and all, don't you think you should tell me where we're headed?"

"I should, and I will," Grace said smugly. She pointed to the southern horizon. "We're going there."

"Where? Puyallup?"

"No. There," Grace said as she pointed again. "The mountain."

164

44: GRACE AND JOEL

Paradise, Washington

Grace nailed the target on her first throw. Standing on a trail high above Paradise Inn, she fired a snowball that struck him on the shoulder as he emerged from a grove of young pines.

"Ouch!" Joel cried.

"That's for scaring the forest creatures," Grace said. "There are restrooms, you know."

Joel ducked as another snowball raced toward his head.

"And that's for turning your back on me."

Joel retreated to a defensive position, formed three balls, and unleashed a barrage of his own. He hit the belligerent in each leg and the chest.

"You want more?" Joel asked.

"Yes!"

For the next fifteen minutes, Grace gave as well as she took. She hid behind rocks and threw what she could when she could and ran squealing from her defenses when the return fire from the bad man in the cowboy hat became a little too hot. The experience brought back pleasant memories of her seemingly distant youth – memories of hide-and-seek in the streets of Usumbura, of Tumbang Preso on the lawns of Luzon, and of mud fights along the Yangtze. But even in those special places, she could not experience the sheer joy of a snowball fight in July. Above six thousand feet in Mount Rainier National Park, she could.

Disappointed that the snowfields at Paradise, one of the snowiest places on earth, had succumbed to summer, Grace had insisted that Joel take her to higher ground. After a thirty-minute hike up a well-traveled path, she had found what she had come for.

"OK. That's enough. I give," Joel said when he realized his aim was no match for her limitless enthusiasm. "If I fight any longer, you'll put me in the hospital."

Emerging from two boulders and the high ground for the last time, Grace walked down a thin patch of snow and approached her prisoner with an ear-to-ear grin. She put her arms around Joel and kissed him on the cheek.

"Thank you," Grace said. "You made my day."

From the battleground on the edge of the snowline, they walked down the trail to Uncle George's favorite toy and retrieved a large wool blanket and a picnic basket. Joel had offered to buy their meals in the historic hotel, but Grace would have none of it.

"I invited you, remember?"

So they hiked from the mile-high lodge up a less-traveled path to a meadow with an unobstructed view of the 14,410-foot peak. After giving the site a quick inspection, they spread the blanket on a flat spot bordered by daisies, cinquefoil, lupine, and aster.

Grace pulled two sandwiches, cheese, grapes, and a pie from the basket and set out a lunch she had planned all week. When she and Joel finished eating, they broke out a buck-fifty bottle of table wine and enjoyed a cloudless summer afternoon and spectacular alpine scenery. Mount Rainier had never looked better.

"Are you having a good time?" Grace asked.

"Do you really need to ask? I'd have a good time watching you eat crackers," Joel said.

Grace laughed.

"I'm glad we came here. I needed this."

Joel took her hand and looked her in the eyes.

"No, Grace, *I* needed this. I wasn't sure where I stood after our walk on Sunday. I've never been in this situation. This is new ground for me."

Grace met his gaze. She liked hearing those words. She liked it a lot. Humility was good. But she would need to see a lot more before jumping aboard the Buckaroo Express.

"You don't have feelings for Linda?" Grace asked. "Or anyone else?"

"I like Linda. I had two nice dates with Linda," Joel said. "I've had girlfriends too – several, in fact – but none like you. You make me bat-shit crazy."

Grace smiled.

"There are shots for that, you know."

He laughed.

Joel revealed more over the next hour. He said he had been smitten since his night on the bench and had continually sought opportunities to see her. He shared his positive thoughts about their mutual friends, living in Seattle, and working at Carter's Furniture and Appliance. He did not share anything significant about his first twenty-one years, eleven months, and three weeks – an omission that did not go unnoticed.

Grace knew she would probably not get all the answers in one afternoon, but she had expected more – much more. As the day wore on, she became increasingly concerned that the answers might not come at all. She did not have the luxury of time. With Paul returning to Seattle in three weeks, the clock was running.

She was about to ask Joel about his family when three couples in sunglasses walked past the picnic site on the narrow trail. All appeared to be of college age. Grace felt a chill, not unlike the one that swept through her at the Phoenician when Paula Caldecott came a calling, but it quickly passed. They were 110 miles from the campus, not 110 feet. If there was one place in Washington where she could escape nosy neighbors and malicious whispers, it was this meadow.

When the hikers rounded a corner and dropped out of sight, Grace closed her eyes and said a silent prayer. She loaded several items in the basket, brushed a few crumbs off of her skirt, and raised another subject that was on her mind.

"I understand that congratulations are in order."

"What do you mean?"

"Ginny said you won a thousand dollars on Joe DiMaggio."

Joel laughed.

"Oh, that."

"Yes, that. Fifty-six is a rather unusual number on which to bet twenty dollars. Do you want to tell me how you knew his hitting streak would end there?"

"I didn't bribe any players, if that's what you mean."

Grace smiled sadly. She appreciated the deft way he handled the question but not his content-free reply. She suspected that there was a lot more behind his remarkable wagering success of the past five weeks and wanted candor. Secrets were not good. She picked up a bouquet of daisies and asters that Joel had illegally harvested near the lodge. She brought the flowers to her nose, inhaled, and stared wistfully at an affectionate couple sitting on a large log in the distance.

"I know you didn't. But that's not what troubles me. There is so much about you that I don't understand. There is so much about you I don't know."

"Do you need to know everything?"

She winced as she took in the words. It was clear now that the answers she needed would not come in a neatly wrapped package or come anytime soon. Joel Smith would not be a work in progress but rather a leap of faith.

Grace lifted her left hand a few inches off the blanket and rubbed the bottom of a shimmering gold band with her thumb. She studied the ring for nearly a minute, hoping to find wisdom in its shine. She remembered the night Paul had proposed, a night the world seemed blissfully free of complication. She dropped her hand and faced the enigmatic man at her side. It was decision time.

"Somewhere in Cambridge, Massachusetts, there is a man who means a lot to me. He is someone I have dated for several months, someone I love and respect, someone I have pledged to marry. He is a good man – a kind, honest, honorable man. He is training to defend our country, saving money for a house, and planning a future with me."

Grace took a breath.

"What am I doing here?"

* * * * *

The question hit Joel like a well-placed snowball from out of the blue, and it stung because the answer – for the past few hours, anyway – had seemed clear. Grace had cast her lot with him. But now he wasn't sure. Was this a date or an audition?

He replayed the day in his mind and realized that he should have seen it coming. Grace had asked the question a dozen different times a dozen different ways. She had sought answers and clarity and found neither. He had only himself to blame for that.

Joel understood her predicament. He had understood it from the start. Grace had a lot to lose. She had a ring on her finger and the promise of hearth and home. What sane woman traded love and security for a stranger who would not even come clean about his past?

Still, he found the question unsettling. They had made great strides in July, thanks in part to Grace's own initiatives. The movies had been her idea. So had many of the walks and most certainly this trip. The kiss and the theatrics after the date with Linda needed no explanation. Yet here she was questioning her own handiwork.

Joel looked at Grace and saw a woman on the other side of a divide, a woman waiting for a sign. Despite all the attention and affection she had shown him, she had not yet decided to cross over. Seeing what even a flicker of doubt could do to their suddenly tenuous relationship, he moved swiftly to put it out.

"What are you doing here?" Joel asked. "You're doing what you came here to do."

He removed the cowboy hat from his head, placed it gently on hers, and gave her a long, soft kiss and the affirmation she needed.

"You're burning bridges."

168

45: LINDA AND GRACE

Seattle, Washington – Sunday, July 27, 1941

The spider patiently awaited her prey. Curled in one corner of the sofa, Linda McEwan tightened the belt on her robe, placed a ceramic mug on an end table, and picked up a recent copy of the *Saturday Evening Post*. She had risen at seven – much earlier than usual – and made a pot of coffee before staking a position in the living room.

By half past eight two others had emerged from their rooms and found their way to the kitchen and a long counter that divided the house's eating and living spaces. Ginny Gillette had gone straight for the coffee and an open newspaper and Katherine Kobayashi straight for a frying pan, eggs, and a loaf of bread. When the small clock on the mantle chimed nine times, Katie walked into the living room with a cup of coffee and sat on the unoccupied end of the couch.

"You're up early," Katie said. "Did you have trouble sleeping last night?"

"I had a lot of trouble sleeping last night," Linda said. She sipped her coffee. "But I'm better now. There's nothing this stuff won't cure."

Katie smiled and picked up an issue of *LIFE* magazine that featured Rita Hayworth on the cover. Another sleepy Sunday morning on Klickitat Avenue was under way.

Ten minutes later the last inhabitant of the rental house walked up the stairs, went into the kitchen, and poured a glass of juice. Wearing a yellow dress and a white straw hat, she spoke briefly to the journalist in residence and then headed toward the door.

The spider intervened.

* * * * *

"You seem to be in a hurry, Grace. Don't you want any breakfast?"

"No," Grace said. "I'm not very hungry."

"Oh," Linda replied. She swung her legs over the front of the couch and put her magazine on the end table. "Did you have a nice day yesterday?"

"Yes, I did."

"That's good. I did too. I had a particularly nice evening – or at least an interesting evening. Do you know what I did last night?"

"No," Grace said.

"I went to the Mad Dog."

"That's nice. I hope you had a good time."

"I did, for a while. Then I bumped into someone," Linda said. "Do you know who I saw at the Mad Dog?"

Grace knew immediately that the conversation would not end well. She desperately wanted to complete her walk across the entry and race out the door, but she knew she could not. Linda had set up a morality play and would not be denied her morning entertainment.

"No. I don't," Grace said. "Who did you see?"

"Why, I saw Betty. You know Betty – Betty DeConcini, our sorority sister, the one who helped you celebrate your birthday and your engagement to my brother."

"Yes, Linda, I know Betty."

"Well, it seems Betty also had a nice day yesterday. She and Tony went hiking with four others at Mount Rainier," Linda said. She got off the sofa and walked to the middle of the living room. "And do you know who Betty saw picnicking in a field at Paradise?"

"I'm sure you'll tell me," Grace said.

"She saw none other than Grace Vandenberg. Only Grace wasn't alone. She was having a nice time with a tall, dark-haired man in a cowboy hat."

When Linda's voice took an edge, Ginny walked from the kitchen to the entry. She stopped a few feet behind Grace and leaned on a wall. Katie had long since put Rita Hayworth on a table. Like Ginny, she wore a look of concern.

"Let's see," Linda said. "He was a tall, dark-haired cowboy. That doesn't sound like Paul, does it?"

"No, it doesn't," Grace replied.

"You're damn right it doesn't."

Linda narrowed her eyes and folded her arms.

"How could you, Grace? How dare you! You're my friend. We're supposed to be sisters. Does that mean anything to you?"

Grace glanced at her interrogator but couldn't maintain eye contact. She had no answers to Linda's questions. The morning from hell was just part of the price she would pay for falling in love with two men.

"I'm sorry," Grace said. "Things just happened."

170

Linda exploded.

"Things just happened? Things just *happened?* Day trips to Mount Rainier don't just happen. Cuddles in the theater don't just happen. Long walks on Tuesdays don't just happen. You've been planning this all along, even after Joel and I went to the dance and then to the movie."

Linda stepped closer to Grace and put her hands on her hips.

"And that's just me," Linda said. "What about my *brother?* Have you given him a thought since he left? He's serving our country and trying to better himself, and here you are whoring around the state behind his back."

"That's enough," Ginny said.

Linda stiffened.

"I'm not done! You're engaged, Grace. Engaged! Do you know what that means? It means you don't go running off to the woods to play with someone else. It means you stay faithful to the one you're supposed to marry. Did you get a room too? I hope so. I'd hate to think you'd wreck a lot of lives for a kiss."

"I didn't mean to hurt anyone," Grace said as tears cascaded down her face.

"I'm sure you didn't," Linda said. She lowered her voice to a loud whisper. "But you *did* hurt people. You did. And nothing you say or do now can change that."

Locked in a daze, Grace stared at the door as she considered whether to stay or go. It took all of her strength just to remain on her feet.

"Well, what are you waiting for?" Linda asked. "Go to church. Say a prayer for my brother and maybe yourself. God may forgive you, but I never will."

Grace turned to face Ginny, then Katie, and finally Linda. The first two offered empathetic smiles, the latter a look of disgust. Seeing no option but to step forward, Grace walked out the door to the world beyond. She didn't return for a week.

46: GRACE

Grace fed a multitude with two loaves of bread. But she did not feel much like Jesus, and the gratitude and devotion of her followers, a dozen noisy mallards on the south shore of Green Lake, was fleeting. They scattered with the last crumb.

Turning away from the web-footed vultures, she removed her sweater and settled into a surprisingly comfortable wooden bench. She gazed at a designated swimming area fifty yards away, where two women tried to teach twenty kids the crawl stroke. Mesmerized by the sights and sounds of splashing, squealing children, she did not hear Seattle's most intrepid young reporter approach from behind.

"Katie said I could find you here," Ginny said. "Do you mind if I sit?"

"No," Grace replied. "Please do."

Grace acknowledged her visitor with a glance but turned away when Ginny took a seat. She wasn't yet sure she wanted to look anyone in the eyes, even her oldest and dearest friend, following her total humiliation six days earlier.

After walking out of Linda McEwan's kangaroo court, Grace had driven her uncle's Ford to a nearby Lutheran church and then to a Queen Anne-style mansion in Madison Park. When Edith Tomlinson saw her niece's red eyes, she made up a bed and fixed lunch but asked no questions. Virginia Gillette had no such reservations.

"Have you seen Joel this week?" Ginny asked.

"We went for a walk on Tuesday, and he stopped by the library yesterday to bring me a sandwich, but that's it," Grace said. "He said he'd call today about a movie tonight, but he's not pushing. He's giving me room to sort things out."

"Is there still anything to sort out?"

"No. Not really. That's the one thing I'm sure of."

Ginny put an arm around Grace. In the distance quacking ducks competed with splashing swimmers, piercing the perfection of an otherwise tranquil Saturday morning.

"Ginny?" Grace asked.

"Yes?"

"Do you think I'm an evil person?"

"Heavens, no!" Ginny said. She laughed and hugged Grace tightly. "You're a woman in love, though sometimes the two are one and the same."

"Do you think I'm wrong?"

"Now, that's a different question. I don't have a clear answer for you. We all have to decide what's best for us, particularly on matters as important as marriage. I like Paul, and I think he would make you very happy. But I know why you love Joel. He's like an ice cream sundae you get for lunch every day. What you have to decide is whether you want a sundae seven days a week or something a little healthier."

"Your advice is not very helpful," Grace said with a hint of a smile. "You know how much I like ice cream."

"Oh, Grace, you are so precious! I've missed you. Katie has too."

"But not Linda."

"No. Not Linda," Ginny said. "She left on Thursday and moved into an apartment with one of her education friends. She said she'll remain active in the sorority, but I don't think we'll hear much more from her."

"What about our bills?" Grace asked.

"I'll pick up Linda's share – for the rest of the year, if necessary," Ginny said. "It's worth it to me to have you and Katie around. I couldn't ask for better housemates."

"Thanks."

"Trust me, Grace, the money is no problem."

"I mean thanks for coming out here," Grace said. "I know this is a busy time for you and that you have better things to do than manage my disaster of a social life."

"That's what friends are for."

Grace squeezed Ginny's hand and gazed again at the lake. Several outdoorsmen in rowboats and sailboats plied the waters nearby, including a flirty lad in a dinghy who had waved several times at the occupants of the bench.

"Is something wrong?" Ginny asked.

"No," Grace said. "I'm just thinking. I still have unfinished business. Paul knows nothing about any of this. It's not fair to keep him in the dark. I need to write him before he gets his leave in a couple of weeks. He'll be here August 16."

Ginny smiled sadly and gave Grace a gentle hug. She took a breath and turned to face her friend.

"I don't think a full rundown of the particulars will be necessary."

"Why is that?" Grace asked.

"I'm afraid Linda has beat you to it."

47: GRACE

Saturday, August 16, 1941

The café overlooked the Hiram M. Chittenden Locks, a component of a canal that linked the saltwater of Puget Sound with the freshwater of Lake Washington. Grace picked the restaurant because she knew Paul liked its sandwiches. She picked *a* restaurant because she wanted to meet him on neutral ground.

Arriving a few minutes late in a blue cotton dress, Grace walked through the café proper to French doors that led to a sunny patio in back. She moved quickly toward a uniformed naval officer seated at a far table. Except for a waitress wiping a table and an older couple enjoying coffee and newspapers, Grace Vandenberg and Paul McEwan had the dining area to themselves.

Paul stood up when Grace approached. He gave her a warm hug and a kiss.

"You look stunning," Paul said. "I've missed you."

"I've missed you too," Grace said with less enthusiasm.

Grace smiled and tried to look happy. She thought a happy face was the least she could give her fiancé after eight weeks apart.

Grace realized that maintaining that face would be difficult. By the time the waitress brought lunch to her table fifteen minutes later, she concluded it would be impossible.

"I got your letters," Paul said. He pulled two envelopes out of his jacket pocket. "I also got one from Linda. Care to tell me what's going on?"

Grace sighed.

"I've fallen in love with another man."

"So it appears," Paul said.

He paused before continuing.

"I'd like an explanation, Grace. I'd like to know what some guy who jumped off a train two months ago has over me. Is he better than me?"

"No," Grace said. "He's *not* better. He's just different, that's all. He interests me. I can't explain my change of heart. I know only that it has nothing to do with you."

"The hell it doesn't!" Paul snapped. "When I left Seattle, I thought we had an understanding, a commitment, a future. You took my ring. You said you loved me. Now you're telling me it's over because some slick-talking salesman 'interests' you? What do you really know about this guy?"

"I know enough. I know he loves me and truly wants what's best for me. He has given me all the time I need to think this through. I also know he's a gentleman with a keen intellect and a wonderful sense of humor, just like the man in front of me."

Paul scowled, shook his head, and looked away, toward the locks, where vessels of all shapes and sizes came and went with each rise and drop of the water level. He pushed aside his roast-beef sandwich and tapped his fingers on the tabletop.

Desiring to keep the conversation civil, Grace nudged it in a different direction. She asked Paul about his training at Harvard and his next assignment. He answered her questions but seemed distracted and annoyed.

"I get out of Boston in another six weeks. Then I'm off to San Diego for a month and Ford Island for a year. I'll help manage the supply depots at Pearl Harbor."

"I'm proud of you," Grace said. "I always have been. I want you to know that."

"Then let me make you prouder. Give me another shot," Paul said. He clasped her hands and pulled them across the table. "Let me be the husband you know I can be. We can still have a great life, Grace, if only you'll give us the chance."

Paul repeated the pitch in various ways over the next ten minutes. When the hard sell didn't work, he tried the soft. When that failed, he appealed to logic.

For a moment, Grace considered his offer. Sticking with Paul made sense. She would have security for life, the respect of her peers, and total devotion from a man who would make not only a good husband but also a good father. Grace would not, however, have the one thing she desired most. She would not have the man she loved.

Grace slid her engagement ring off her finger, placed it in Paul's palm, and closed his hand. She touched his face lightly and looked at him like a friend and not a lover.

"Are you going to be all right?" Grace asked.

"I'll be fine," Paul said. "I'm tough."

"OK."

Grace put two dollars next to her untouched salad, gathered her purse, and got up from her chair. She walked around the table and kissed Paul on the cheek.

"Goodbye, Paul."

Grace walked past the puzzled waitress and the suddenly interested elderly couple to a latched gate that led to the parking lot. She glanced back at her one-time fiancé and saw a man with his face in his hands. She opened the gate and left to the sound of sobs.

48: JOEL

Tuesday, August 19, 1941

The knock on the door stirred Joel from his best sleep in days and his best dream since Jana and Smiling Sarah had fought over his beach towel on Maui. Had he slept in and missed work? Had he missed something else? Joel peered out a window. Thankfully, he did not see Mel Carter tapping a foot impatiently. Nor did he see Sandy Carter with a basket of laundry or Tom Carter with a mischievous grin. Instead, he saw someone he had not seen in three weeks – someone who had once spanked him for feeding her prized apple butter to his dog.

Joel threw on some clothes and glanced at a wind-up alarm clock as he rushed to the door. He saw, much to his chagrin, that it was already nine fifteen.

"Ginny," Joel said as he opened the door.

"I'm sorry to bother you," Ginny said. "I know this is your day off. But I wanted to talk to you and knew I could probably catch you here."

"Come on in."

Joel welcomed Ginny into his castle. Dressed in a blue two-piece suit, she looked like a million bucks – a woman out to conquer the world. She stood out from the trailer trash wearing ratty shorts, a wife-beater undershirt, and a hairy face better suited for the Woodland Park Zoo.

Ginny took a seat at the small dining table as Joel put on a button-down shirt, ran a comb through his hair, and tried to elevate his appearance by one social level – if not two – in front of a mirror. She visually inspected the trailer and smiled at the sight of a hooded sweatshirt draped over a cushion.

"I see your taste in clothing runs toward the progressive," Ginny said. "I'm guessing that 'Candy' is something I wouldn't find at the five-and-dime."

Joel cringed. He grabbed the shirt and tossed it on the floor.

"That's just something I bought last year to keep warm on a camping trip. I didn't pay much attention to the graphic on the front."

"Obviously."

"Can I get you anything?" Joel asked. "I can run in the house and make some coffee."

"Thanks for the offer, but I think I'll pass. I've had plenty of coffee already and have to be at the *Sun* by eleven. I just wanted to see how you're doing. I haven't seen much of you lately and decided it was time for a visit."

Ginny retrieved some cigarettes from her purse but put them back when Joel tilted his head and raised a brow. She smiled and looked at her host with apparent amusement as he took a seat at the table.

"Do you like living in a trailer?" Ginny asked.

"I do, as a matter of fact. I have almost everything I need in here and the run of the house when I want food or a shower or a washing machine."

"Tom said that you two will move into an apartment after Labor Day."

"That's the plan."

Ginny lifted her bottom off the bench, straightened her skirt, and settled into her seat. She twitched her nose at the not-so-faint aroma of perspiration and dirty socks and cracked the window at her side.

"Sorry for the mess and the smell," Joel said. "I don't entertain much."

"That's all right. I didn't come here to talk about your housekeeping."

Joel grinned.

"That's a relief."

Ginny smiled again, took a breath, and then looked at Joel with serious eyes.

"I do, however, want to talk about Grace," Ginny said. "I want to discuss a few things before you see her on your walk today."

"Is she OK? I haven't spoken to her since Sunday."

"She's fine. She's still a little rattled from her meeting with Paul, but she's fine. I'm sure she gave you the highlights. She returned his ring. They're finished," Ginny said. "I can't say I agree with what's she's done, but I know she hasn't had any second thoughts."

"Oh."

"Joel, I came here because I care about Grace deeply. I don't want to see her get hurt. She may not have parents to look out for her anymore, but she does have a protective sister. She made a very big decision on Saturday, and I want to make sure that it doesn't come back to haunt her."

"I love her," Joel said. "You do know that."

"I do. I can't blame you either. Grace is the nicest person I have ever known, one of the smartest, and by far the most beautiful. I often joke that her parents rolled a seven on conception night. You can't buy those looks in a salon. It's a shame they can't see her now. I'd love to have a daughter like Grace someday."

Give yourself time.

Joel began to speak but paused to accommodate a noisy garbage truck that had stopped in the alley to pick up his weekly discards. He looked at the sweatshirt on the floor, laughed to himself, and wondered how Candy in Chains had made the cut.

"I feel bad about all this," Joel said. "I've been a bull in a china shop since coming here. But I couldn't let her go. I had to fight for her. Can you understand?"

"I can. But now that you've won Grace, you should know more about her."

"Have I missed something?"

"I doubt you've missed anything vitally important," Ginny said. "Grace is mostly as she appears: kind, moody, unpredictable, and more than a little naïve. But she has been through a lot, more than some people in a lifetime, and I don't know how much she has shared with you. She can be fiercely guarded about her past."

"I know how her parents died," Joel said.

"I know. But I doubt you know the whole story."

Joel looked at his guest with renewed interest.

"Continue."

"The Vandenbergs didn't just go out for a stroll that night. Grace sent them out. She had an upset stomach and insisted that someone get something for it. According to her aunt, she threw quite a fit. Her parents did not have driver's licenses, so they walked a few blocks to a place that was still open. The drunk driver struck them as they returned from the store. In Grace's mind, she sent her mother and her father to their deaths."

Joel closed his eyes and put a hand to his forehead. So much made sense now.

"As you can imagine, Grace was a mess," Ginny said. "When I first met her, as her roommate in the freshman dorm, she could barely function. She was utterly consumed by grief and guilt. At least once a week, she'd cry herself to sleep or call out for her mother in the middle of the night. And even when she didn't, she'd get up early in the morning, eat breakfast alone, and hole up with books the rest of the day. This went on for months. Grace kept to herself most of the time, even around me. I don't think she went to a single dance or party until late in the spring."

"Did Grace open up when she joined the sorority?" Joel asked.

"She did, a little. The sisters forced her to have fun. You can't remain a hermit for long in a place like Kappa Delta Alpha."

"She's not that way now."

"No. She's not," Ginny said. "She began to change our sophomore year. She had a boyfriend who had a great sense of humor and lavished a lot of attention on her."

"So what happened to him?"

"He ran off with a girl who lavished more attention on him."

Joel suddenly felt anger toward anyone who had wronged Grace Vandenberg.

"I'll bet that messed her up," Joel said.

"It did, for a few months. Paul helped her come out of her shell. Then you came along and really did wonders. Despite what you may think, you have had a positive influence on my friend. She's a different person now."

"How so?"

"She's happy. She's strong. She's confident," Ginny said. "She's doing things she would have never done even a year ago, like hauling you off to Mount Rainier. When I heard about that, I had to throw out everything I thought I knew about Grace. There is no way the girl I've known for three years would have pulled a stunt like that. But she did."

Joel smiled.

"Yeah, she did."

Ginny put a hand on Joel's forearm and looked him in the eyes.

"That's the point, though, and something you should remember if you want a happy future with her. Grace may never be someone you can read or understand. She may never be someone *anyone* can understand. But she will always be worth the effort and the wait. Beneath that delicate exterior is a strong, resolute woman who does nothing halfway. Never take her for granted and never underestimate her. She will amaze."

"I hear you," Joel said, impressed as much with the messenger as the message.

"Good. That brings me to another thing I want to talk about."

"What's that?"

"Labor Day weekend," Ginny said. "Tom and I have access to my family's beach house on the Oregon coast. My cousin in Seaside said she would clean the place up and have it ready for us the first day."

"That's nice. Have a great time."

"You don't understand. We want you and Grace to come with us. We think it would be a wonderful opportunity for you two to get to know each other, away from the campus."

"I don't know," Joel said. "We're not exactly at that stage in our relationship, if that's what you call a ballgame, four movies, eight walks, and a mystery date."

"Joel, I'm not suggesting anything more than a weekend at the coast."

"You don't have to twist my arm. I just don't want to put Grace in a spot where she feels pressure to do something she doesn't want to do. She's had a rough month."

"I agree," Ginny said. "That's why I made the same offer to her this morning."

"You did?" Joel asked.

"I did."

"What did she say?"

"She didn't say a thing," Ginny said.

"Nothing?"

"Nothing."

Ginny smiled.

"She just walked to her room and started packing."

49: JOEL

Seaside, Oregon – Saturday, August 30, 1941

He executed the spins like a pro, as well as the tosses and the footwork, and hit the floor for every song from "Sing, Sing, Sing" to "Boogie Woogie Bugle Boy." By the time Joel finished his eighth consecutive dance at the Bigelow, he was a swinging machine with an adrenaline rush, a weary partner, and a growing number of fans, including his twenty-one-year-old grandmother.

"When did our Renaissance man become Fred Astaire?" Ginny asked.

She smiled and tapped her cigarette over a tray.

"This month," Joel said as he caught his breath. "Zelda does wonders."

"I'll say."

Zelda Zubiria needed no introduction at their table for four. The owner, operator, and head instructor at the oldest and most prominent dance studio in north Seattle had turned hundreds of dead hoofers into ducky shincrackers.

Humbled by his showing at Lake Wilderness, Joel had taken corrective action and hired Zelda herself four days a week. Joe DiMaggio was the gift that kept giving.

"Fred Astaire or not, he's exhausting," Grace said. She smiled as she pulled up a seat. "You two should have warned me."

"Warned you?" Tom asked. "He was a klutz with Linda."

The mere mention of the jilted redhead brought Joel back to July and the lake. He had not seen Linda since their night at the movies six weeks earlier, but he still felt bad about how things had turned out. Linda deserved better and hopefully would find better.

Joel gave the past another moment of thought and then turned his attention to the present. He looked at Grace with curious eyes.

"Did you have fun today?" Joel asked.

"I had fun. You know I had fun," Grace said. She squeezed his hand on top of the table. "And I want to have *more* fun tomorrow."

Joel smiled as he thought of how she had started the day. Grace had not wasted a minute in the pursuit of pleasure. When the four friends reached their destination at noon, after a five-hour drive, Grace had jumped out of the car, run to the beach, and splashed up a storm in knee-high surf. No one had needed to ask why. Except on a trip to the Philippine Sea on her twelfth birthday, Grace had never played in the ocean.

She had also never seen a house quite like the one near Tillamook Head. With a crow's nest loft, a soapstone fireplace, a modern kitchen, a wraparound deck, and views of the Pacific on three sides, the place exceeded even Joel's expectations. It had two bedrooms, which Ginny quickly designated "the boys' room" and "the girls' room."

Carol Morgan had greeted the travelers at twelve thirty with groceries, firewood, and a bottle of homemade raspberry wine. Ginny's cousin, a perky twenty-five-year-old mother of two, asked a dozen questions of Tom, Joel, and Grace before nonchalantly advising Ginny to behave herself, turning over the keys, and returning to her home in town.

Two of the visitors then put their stamp on the day. At Tom's insistence, the four ate lunch at the Cranky Crab. At Grace's, they spent the rest of the afternoon beachcombing and riding the Ferris wheel, carousel, and bumper cars. Joel and Ginny gladly yielded the balance of their time and agendas to their enthusiastic companion.

As he sat across from Grace at their small round table, Joel thought about how strange and wonderful it was to see the world through her eyes. Until stumbling back in time, he had never known life without computers, jetliners, cable television, and modern medicine. Grace, on the other hand, had not known indoor plumbing until her seventeenth year. She had done without comforts her three affluent friends took for granted, yet she had arguably lived a richer life. Joel smiled as he watched her adjust a purple swing dress she had donned for the first time in months and play with a beaded bracelet he had won by throwing softballs at weighted bottles.

"I see you like your trinket," Joel said.

"I do," Grace said. "I love it, in fact. I shall wear it proudly as a reminder of the effort required to obtain it."

"That's killing with kindness, pal," Tom said with a hearty laugh. He lit a cigar and leaned back. "What did you spend on that? Five bucks? You threw twenty pitches."

Joel chuckled.

"Try thirty."

"Don't let Tom tease you," Ginny said. "You did a nice thing."

Joel grinned and then took a stogie from his colleague. He wondered how many minutes would elapse before his tobacco-loving granny lit into him about hypocrisy.

Ginny said nothing. Instead she smiled and studied him – not like a member of a long-lost tribe but rather like a long-lost family member she was just beginning to understand.

"So what's the deal with the house?" Joel asked Ginny. "Does your cousin own it – or is it a family-owned toy that gets passed around twice a month?"

"My parents built it ten years ago. They own it and come here about every other weekend in the summer. They would be here now if not for a wedding today in Portland. You'll meet them on Monday. We're having lunch in Forest Grove."

"Where does Carol fit in?"

"She and Eddie maintain the place. They live just up the street with their girls. We'll be there for breakfast tomorrow," Ginny said. "They're our chaperones, by the way."

"And I must say they're doing a mighty fine job," Tom said.

The girls laughed.

"How do you put up with him?" Joel asked.

"I don't," Ginny said. "I work with him. I believe men are creatures to be managed – not endured – and I think I've managed him nicely."

"Well put, sweetie," Tom said.

"Now, if you gentlemen will excuse us, I think Grace and I will run to the ladies' room before that line around the corner gets longer."

"Bon voyage," Joel said.

A moment after the women departed, Tom tapped a few ashes in the tray and settled into his chair. He looked at his friend, nodded, and smiled.

"You look happy."

"I am," Joel said.

"That's because you have a good woman."

Joel laughed.

"You're one to talk."

"Yes, I am. Ginny is a good woman. She's been good for *me*," Tom said. He blew a smoke ring at the ceiling. "So have you. I'm glad you could join us this weekend. I admit I wasn't sure Grace would be up for the trip. She was a sight after her spat with Linda. But it's obvious she's happy to be here and even happier to be Tonto to the Lone Ranger."

"I'm not complaining," Joel said.

Tom took a moment to observe others in the building as they walked across the floor, sat on benches, or passed though doors to the concession area. As he did, he smiled less and appeared to become more reflective.

"Do you ever think about your future?" Tom asked.

Joel tilted his head.

"With Grace?"

"With Grace, Linda, Betty Grable, anyone," Tom said. "Who you're with is not my point. Do you ever think about *where* you'll be in a year?"

"I do, sometimes, but I don't obsess over it."

"I wish I could think that way."

"What do you mean?" Joel asked.

"Look around."

Joel did as instructed and saw scores of people in the Bigelow, a skating rink turned dance hall that had hosted the likes of Benny Goodman, Harry James, Duke Ellington, and Les Hite. Most of the patrons dressed well. All behaved well. None seemed relevant to the conversation.

"OK. I looked," Joel said. "Do you have a point?"

"How many uniforms do you see?"

Joel paused and scanned the room again.

"I see twenty, maybe twenty-five. It looks like most are enlisted men."

"Exactly," Tom said. "And how many uniforms did you see at Lake Wilderness?"

"Maybe a third that many."

"Change is coming, buddy, and it's coming fast."

Joel leaned forward.

"Have you heard anything from the draft board?"

"No. But I will. I have a low number – and it's coming up. I have a feeling I won't be selling furniture in six months," Tom said. He pushed his cigar into the tray, watched an Army lieutenant walk by, and returned to Joel. "What about you? What's your number?"

Joel scrambled to discuss a matter that was on the mind of virtually every young American man. He'd had three months to work up a story and pick a high draft number, but he had let the matter slide. Remembering something he had read about Ted Williams, he offered an answer.

"It's 648."

"You have a while then," Tom said. "But they'll come for you, too, just as surely as they've come for some of my friends. Hell, they even drafted two football players. I hate having the war hang over our heads. I hate it. You can't make plans. You can't do shit. You can't believe what you read in the papers. Sometimes I just want to say 'to heck with it' and live for the moment."

"I know what you mean."

Joel, of course, knew nothing of the sort. Focused initially on economic survival and then on wooing Grace Vandenberg, he had not given much thought to what he would do after Pearl Harbor. Would he enlist? Was not enlisting even an option? He tried to picture a future with Grace, post-December 7, but each time he did, that picture turned into a blurry mess brought on by three hundred fighters and bombers coming to a Sunday this fall.

As the band started back up with another swing hit, Joel took in the ballroom and saw more than forty happy couples return to the floor. Even more came in from outside and reclaimed unoccupied tables. Most of the military had hung around.

Joel looked over his shoulder at the restrooms and saw a line that now worked its way toward the entrance. Ginny and Grace had barely moved in the queue but appeared no worse for wear. They smiled and waved at the man from Montana.

Finally, Joel turned to Tom. He saw that he was no longer the cocky, cheerful chap who had strolled into the Bigelow with Ginny on his arm but rather someone else. Talk of the Selective Training and Service Act of 1940 had left him depressed and beaten.

For the first time in a long time, Joel had no answers for a friend in need. He had no suitable jokes or flippant advice. So he did the next best thing and commiserated. Lifting his glass, he gestured to Tom, then the girls, and finally the crowd beyond.

"Here's to us, to them, and to living for the moment."

50: GRACE AND JOEL

Sunday, August 31, 1941

The ocean proved as predictable as a late summer day in the Pacific Northwest. It churned, surged, and roared, and produced a cool breeze and thick mist that prompted jackets even at noon. But to Grace Vandenberg, child of the jungle, it was as strange and wondrous as snow.

"I could never tire of this place," Grace said. She held Joel's hand as they walked northward on the Promenade. "It's so different than any place I've known."

"Haven't you ever seen the Washington coast?" Joel asked. "I'd hate to think you've spent three years of college hiding behind books."

Grace smiled.

"I spent only one year hiding behind books. But I've spent three in the library, which is essentially the same thing. When I was a freshman, some girls from my dorm went to Ocean Shores, but I did not go. Ginny did, though."

"I remember that trip," Ginny said. She walked with Tom a few steps back. "We missed you."

Looking at Joel, Grace realized that she had missed a lot of things – dances, dates, football games, beach trips, and certainly new friendships. Her thirty-six months at the university were less a full educational experience than a frustrating, self-imposed exile. With this interesting, extroverted man at her side, she vowed to change in her senior year.

An hour later Joel bought her some salt-water taffy and led her to the historic Turnaround, where the west end of Broadway ran headlong into the Prom and gave pedestrians and motorists one of the best views on the Pacific coast. He put his arm around her as they gazed at the limitless water beyond.

"Do you miss it, living overseas and all?"

"I miss the simplicity. Life is so much more complicated here."

"What was it like in all those places?"

"For my parents, it was a lot of work. But for me, it was paradise. I never had a care. One of my earliest memories was riding an elephant in Ruanda-Urundi, in Africa. I must have been seven or eight. My father never had much time for what he called 'frivolous matters,' but he always had time for me. When I asked one day if I could ride an elephant, he made it happen later that week. We traveled several hours to reach a plantation run by the Belgians. He did all that for a ride that lasted only twenty or thirty minutes."

"You miss him."

"I miss both of them. My parents were my world. They poured everything they had into me, and into most of the people they knew. They were givers."

"What do you think they would have thought of me?"

Grace stepped out of his grasp and plopped on top of a concrete railing that ran the entire mile-and-a-half length of the Prom. Extending her arms along the barrier for balance, she answered Joel as if addressing an audience with prepared remarks.

"My mother would have loved you. I have no doubt. She liked people who were different, people who defied labels and prejudices. She liked learning from those who could teach her new skills and new ways to think. That's how she was able to adapt so well from place to place. She looked at each assignment as an adventure, not a burden."

"What about your father?"

Grace paused and flashed an impish grin.

"He would have had many questions. He was very protective."

"That doesn't sound like a ringing endorsement."

"My father was a very traditional man. He would not have approved of many of the things I've done this summer. He would not have approved of my breaking off an engagement for someone I've known a very short time. But I think he would have liked you. He would have appreciated your intelligence and how you care for me."

"I'll take that."

Grace hopped off the railing, put her arms around Joel's neck, and gave him a tender kiss. If she ever had any doubts about returning Paul's ring, they were gone, long gone. Locking arms with Joel, she turned toward Broadway and dozens of shoppers who lined both sides of the street. Tom and Ginny approached with bags in each hand.

"There you are," Tom said with his usual grin. "Are you two just going to watch the waves all day? How boring. There's some good stuff in the stores."

"What did you do? Buy a snow globe?" Joel asked.

189

"Nah. I got something better. You'll see."

Tom put a hand on his friend's shoulder.

"Say, buddy, do you have a moment?"

"Sure," Joel said. He looked at Grace. "I'll be right back."

* * * * *

Leaving Grace and Ginny at the Turnaround, Tom guided Joel a few yards down the Promenade to a bench that faced the beach. He put two bags on the bench and hemmed and hawed a bit before getting to the point.

"Are you two having a good time?" Tom asked.

"We are," Joel said. "What's going on?"

"Well, how would you like to have a good time a little longer?"

Joel raised a brow.

"What do you mean?"

"Ginny and I have been talking and, well, I think we need some alone time. We were thinking about heading back to the house."

Joel dropped his head and shook it.

"You need some 'alone' time?"

"That's right."

"Tom, do you know what you're doing?"

You want to make it with my grandma.

"Of course I know what I'm doing. I'm living for the here and now, just like we talked about last night. Or was that all just talk?"

"No," Joel said. "It wasn't just talk. But I didn't think you meant something like this."

"What did you think I meant? Emptying my wallet at the carousel?"

"Just be careful."

"What are you now? My mother?" Tom asked. He patted Joel on the back. "I'm not stupid, Joel. But I'm not passive either. I'm not going to wait for some draft board to determine how I spend the next few months. I'm going to take charge of my life, starting today."

"OK. You do that. We'll be fine. We'll meet you back at the house around six."

"Thanks."

When Tom and Joel returned to the Turnaround, they found two best friends staring at each other with expressionless faces. They were not speaking.

Ginny held Grace's hand but dropped it when she saw the young men approach. She walked over to Tom, took his hand, and looked at Joel and Grace.

"We'll see you back at the house," Ginny said.

Tom and Ginny turned their backs and joined the flow of tourist traffic moving south along the Prom. Hundreds now crowded the waterfront to milk the second-to-last afternoon of the last weekend of the official Oregon summer.

Grace walked to the railing and stared at the surf.

"So are they going to the boys' room or the girls' room?"

"Don't be too rough on them," Joel said. "This is a hard time for Tom."

Grace turned to face Joel.

"I'm not mad. Just a bit disappointed, that's all. I know Ginny's very independent, and I admire her for that. I just wish she would have picked a different weekend to express her independence."

Joel moved closer to her and put a hand on her waist. In the distance, a lone surfer on a long board tried to ride a modest ripple all the way to the beach.

"I know."

"Are you disappointed that I'm not as progressive?"

Joel took Grace's hands and then turned her toward him.

"No. I'm not. I love you and respect you for who you are."

"I'm not a prude, Joel. I'm just a little old-fashioned. I believe you should save yourself for some things. I hope you understand."

Joel smiled and embraced his old-fashioned girlfriend.

"I do," he said. "I do more than you could possibly know."

Feeling better, they marched arm in arm into the heart of Seaside for more taffy, bumper cars, and carousel rides. Joel won a teddy bear with ten throws instead of thirty.

When they returned to the house with their own purchases and prizes, they found Tom barbecuing steaks out back and Ginny preparing salads and desserts in the kitchen. Joel and Grace offered to help with dinner but were politely refused. So they looked at the ocean from the railing on the deck until Ginny called them into the dining room. Tom followed moments later with a plateful of beef. He took off a chef's apron, joined his girl at the head of a well-appointed table, and threw an arm over her shoulders. Ginny smiled as she addressed her slightly puzzled guests.

"The first thing I want to say is 'thank you.' I want to thank each of you for joining us here. You've made this trip complete. I've been to this house and to Seaside many times over the years but I can't remember a more enjoyable weekend. You've both been wonderful. I can't imagine better friends or better company."

Joel was tempted to join in with something nice, but he knew a rehearsed speech when he heard one. She obviously had more to say. So he let her continue.

"I also want to apologize for our hasty exit this afternoon. It was insensitive and rude. I normally have better manners. But Tom and I

191

needed some time alone. We needed to work out a few things before we returned to Seattle."

"Work out what?" Grace asked.

Ginny placed her newly adorned left hand on Tom's shoulder and beamed.

"Our wedding plans," she said.

51: JOEL

The bachelor pad was the undiscovered jewel of East Fifty-Second Street. The house had everything two young men could possibly want – a state-of-the-art kitchen, a full bathroom, a patio and a barbecue in back, and a large recreation room with a built-in wine rack, dartboard, and mahogany bar. Leather sofas and recliners sat atop a hardwood floor in the living room, while bedroom sets that had recently gained Doris Delamarter's seal of approval filled each of the two sleeping quarters.

Tom Carter had found the gem in a classified ad in late August and cut a deal with the owner to move in on October 1. Joel had purchased the furnishings on September 30, two days after winning two thousand dollars on Ted Williams. The Red Sox slugger had batted six for eight in a season-ending doubleheader to finish with a .406 average and deliver serious cash to a time traveler he would never meet.

"Are you sure you don't want to add a few lamps?" Mel Carter asked as he fell into a love seat that had once graced his showroom. "I also noticed that your dining room table is scratched in a few places. It may be time for an upgrade."

"I think I've already contributed nicely to your bottom line."

"That you have, Joel, and in more ways than one."

Joel smiled. He had made Melvin Carter a wealthier man, just as he had made his son a happier man. Despite some reservations, he had agreed to be Tom's housemate until June, when Ginny had scheduled the wedding of the century. The furniture was an early wedding present for a couple that would almost certainly never marry.

Tom's engagement to Virginia Gillette had taken nearly everyone by surprise, from Joel and Grace to the would-be bride's patrician family in Forest Grove, Oregon. When the two announced their plans to Ginny's parents on Labor Day, Victoria Gillette nearly fainted. Old money did not marry new. Good girls did not gamble on gamblers. Republicans resisted Democrats. Presbyterians did not mix with Methodists. The Carters proved more welcoming. They threw a reception for the couple the following weekend and offered to help Ginny prepare for an event nine months away.

Joel laughed to himself as he replayed the last five weeks in his mind. He had forgotten how crazy weddings once were, not only for those planning them but also for those who had to live with the consequences of a "socially unacceptable" union.

On October 4, however, he cared only about the socially acceptable gathering in the living room of his new digs and making his important guests comfortable. He stepped away from the love seat when he saw Sandy Carter approach with a small plate of food and moved to a spot in front of the fireplace. The heat took much of the chill off a cold, rainy night.

"Is there anything I can get you, Mrs. Carter?" Joel asked.

"I have plenty, Joel. Thank you for asking."

"How about the other lovely ladies in the room?"

"I'm fine," Grace said.

"Me too," Katie added.

Sitting with Ginny on the larger couch with plates on their laps, they worked on a light dinner of finger sandwiches, deviled eggs, apples, and cake. When Tom made the rounds with a bottle of champagne, all three held out glasses.

"Thank you for the furniture, Joel," Ginny said. "The pieces are beautiful, as well as comfortable. It was a generous gift."

"Don't mention it. It was the least I could do for you. Besides, I got an excellent price from a trusted retailer."

Mel smiled as he finished the last of his cake.

"Next time you bet on baseball, give me some warning," he said. "I'll set you up right."

"What are you going to do with the rest of your winnings?" Katie asked.

Invest in war bonds.

"I don't know. I might look at a car. I can't bum rides off this lug for the rest of my life. Or I might just sock the money in a bank. I haven't given the matter much thought."

In fact, Joel had given it a lot of thought. But he decided not to push his luck. Thankful that Katie, like most of the others, had not asked many questions about three astonishing sports bets in less than four months, he tried to limit discussion to what he would do with his new windfall and not how he had obtained it.

Allowing himself to relax for the first time all evening, Joel grabbed a glass of champagne, sat on the hearth, and quietly reflected on those who had gathered in his cozy living room. He thought about how each had influenced his life and how they had become not only his friends but also his family.

The Carters were easy to assess. When Joel glanced at the middle-aged couple on the settee, he saw his own parents – a man and a woman who occasionally bickered but who brought out the best in each other and those around them. He also saw in their faces the thin but clear line between a life of ease and life on the streets. Had he saved a poor or ungrateful man on June 2, rather than the son of a gracious and well-connected family, he might be diving in dumpsters. Their friendship and generosity defied value.

The same could be said of Tom Carter and Virginia Gillette, who had welcomed him into their tight circle of kindred spirits. Because of them, he had made a near seamless transition from one happy, comfortable world to another. He wanted very much to be a part of their lives for years to come but wondered whether he would have the opportunity. He hated knowing that his existence was probably tied to their fortunes.

Joel glanced at the couch and saw Katherine Kobayashi finish a piece of cake. He still did not know her well, but he knew enough to admire and respect her. He appreciated that she had accepted him unconditionally, at a time others had asked questions, and had exercised discretion when he had pursued the forbidden fruit. He also admired how she had stepped out of her own, largely segregated world to integrate into one that was about to slap her down. He wondered what would become of her next year when the passion and prejudices of her countrymen replaced empathy and reason.

Then there was the woman at the center of the storm, the one who made him think differently and act more responsibly, the one he could not live without. Grace Vandenberg had made September one of the best months of his life by performing a dozen little courtesies, like bringing him cookies after long days at work, taking him for spontaneous spins in Uncle George's pride and joy, and gently weeding his eclectic wardrobe of orange ties, oversized shirts, and mismatched socks. Every Wednesday morning she had left a thoughtful note on the door of the Airstream. Every Thursday night she had made him dinner.

Joel smiled when he thought about how some from his time might have viewed these decidedly domestic acts of kindness. Many would have dismissed Grace as a love-struck lightweight, a submissive and even obsessive throwback who had sacrificed her individuality on the altar of her man. But he knew better. Grace was laying the groundwork for what she hoped would be a long and happy relationship, a relationship that would include not only a successful marriage and children but also a teaching career and separate interests. She was tending to her investment. Having forfeited much, including several friendships, to bring him into her life, she

195

was not about to lose him through neglect. They had not spent a single day apart since returning from Seaside.

Joel knew, of course, that there was more to consider than whether they could make it work. Much more. He had influenced and altered lives he was never supposed to touch. He could not imagine life without Grace, but he wondered whether he had made the right decision in pursuing her and wondered how it would all play out. If their commitment to each other was crystal clear, the impact that a rapidly approaching December morning might have on their relationship was not. Things could get complicated very fast. Recognizing the futility of worrying and speculating about events he could not control, he pushed the thoughts aside. They could wait for another day.

His introspection, however, had not gone unnoticed. While he was studying his guests, one of his guests was studying *him*. Upon finishing her dinner, Grace got off the couch and walked to the fireplace. She sat next to her host and put a hand on his knee.

"You've been kind of quiet. Is something wrong?"

"No. I'm fine."

"It doesn't appear that way. I saw you staring at Tom and Ginny," Grace said. "You're thinking about them. You're thinking about all of us. Am I right?"

Joel considered the question but only after considering the questioner. In just a few weeks, Grace had become remarkably adept at deciphering his facial expressions and responding accordingly. Jana had possessed the same gift, but she had rarely put it to use. As preposterous as it sounded, Grace knew him better than he knew himself.

"You're right. I'm thinking about everyone in this room," Joel said. He sighed. "I'm thinking about how lucky I've been. Had I not bumped into Tom and met all of you, my life would be much different today. I think about that a lot."

Grace took his hand, squeezed it, and gave him a reassuring smile.

"We're not all that different, you and I. This is my family too."

The gesture snapped Joel out of his funk but not off the topic. He kissed her on the head and walked to a table in the back of the room and a half-empty bottle of champagne. He pulled it out of a bucket of ice and filled six flutes before returning to the warmth of the fireplace. After topping off his own glass, he turned to face his guests.

"Thank you all for coming to our housewarming. I feel a bit strange, given that this fine-looking couple over here will kick me out in a few months and put me back on the street," Joel said, drawing laughter. "But that's OK. I feel privileged just to be here. It feels good to be surrounded by people who care. If I haven't said it before, I'm saying it now. Thank you. Thank you for making me a part of your family and giving me a home."

Joel raised his glass in a toast and acknowledged the warm smiles in the room. He pondered the beauty of the moment and the unique opportunity it had given him to square his accounts. He loved these people, all of them, and he wanted to tell them.

He knew he might never have the chance to tell them again.

52: JOEL

Saturday, October 25, 1941

He was a ripple in a sea of humanity but not a lot more. Every time Stanford came to the line late in the second quarter and the noise in the stadium began to rise, Joel Smith stood up and threw his hands to the sky. But no one stood with him, at least in a fashion designed to achieve the desired result.

"What are you doing, passing gas?" Tom asked, laughing. "It will take more than that to disrupt their offense."

"I'm trying to start a wave. Come on. Help me out."

"Tom has a point," Ginny said. "You're just annoying the people behind us."

"I don't believe it. You two have a chance to be forty years ahead of your time, and you're sitting on your cans."

"I'll tell you what. I'll stand up the next series, but I'll do it only once," Tom said, smiling. "I have a professional reputation to uphold."

"Never mind."

Joel sat down and lamented the missed opportunity. Seated near the top of the north grandstands, he surveyed the horseshoe-shaped arena on the shore of the lake and looked for anything familiar. The capacity crowd of 43,000 was sufficiently noisy but surprisingly tame. Cheerful cheerleaders in knee-length skirts worked the student section with pompoms and megaphones, but none availed themselves to a body pass or flashed the flesh in ways that might trigger alumni coronaries. No one batted around a beach ball or held up derisive signs. Even the fraternity rows along the fifty-yard line seemed sedate.

"Does the band ever play 'Tequila'?" Joel asked, knowing that a stupid question was sometimes the best way to stir conversation.

"What?" Tom asked. He looked at his friend like he had arrived from another planet. "I think you had a little too much coffee this morning."

Ginny smiled at Joel and put a hand on his shoulder.

"*I'm* enjoying myself, if that's any consolation," Ginny said. "I love homecoming."

She did, too. For Virginia Gillette, the past week had meant more than a football game. It had meant academic receptions, a dedicated series of articles for the *Barker*, pep rallies, bonfires, and dances. It had meant spending quality time with her alumnus fiancé and pondering *her* post-graduate future. For Joel, homecoming had always meant frat parties, tailgaters, and a Saturday watching his school tee off on Cal or Oregon State.

"It is pretty nice," Joel said, returning to the action.

Joel saw Stanford line up in a T formation and wondered if it was only a matter of time before the Indians' all-American quarterback provided grist for history's highlight reel. He hadn't seen a Statue of Liberty play in ages or a flea flicker since Westlake stunned Tacoma Central in the quarterfinals his senior year. He marveled too at the uniforms, particularly the retro wool jerseys, skimpy pads, and bulky leather helmets that turned every player into an aviator. By halftime, more than half the gridders were caked with mud. It was football as it was meant to be.

"It's too bad Grace couldn't join us," Ginny said. "She needs to get out more. But she didn't have a choice. A lot of people called in sick at the library today."

Joel grinned as he took in the comment. He had called in sick from his work-study job at the recreation center on more than one football Saturday. It seemed that some things had not changed in fifty-nine years.

"Where's Katie?"

"She's here at the game. But she's spending the day with the Hasu Club. I think they're over by the visitors' end zone."

When the last whistle of the first half signaled intermission, Tom reached for his wallet, counted the bills, and asked if anyone wanted something to eat. Having skipped breakfast, he seemed eager to hit the concession stands.

"Just tell me what you want. I'll get it. There's no sense in all of us standing in line."

Ginny requested a drink but passed on any food. Joel declined both. He put on his jacket and said he had to run but insisted he would return before the end of the game.

"Where do you think you're going?" Tom asked. "It's only 13-0. We can come back and win this thing. Have some faith, buddy."

"I have a lot of faith," Joel said. "I just want to stretch my legs and check out the sights. It's been a while since I've been a part of something like this."

"Suit yourself," Tom said. "I'm out."

When Thomas Carter reached the aisle and began to work his way down the steps to the exit, Joel turned to Ginny and gave her his program and a knowing glance.

"I'll try to be back," he said. "I mean it."

"I know you do," Ginny said with a smile. "Give our worker bee a hug."

53: GRACE AND JOEL

Grace looked at the book and shook her head. Five times she had tried to squeeze the oversized tome on Northwest plant species into its designated space. Five times she had failed. The crumbling volume, published during the McKinley administration, was too big for the shelf but apparently too valuable to be weeded.

She wondered – and not for the first time – why the library kept books that no one touched except spiders and mice. But she loved her work and so readily answered the call when Mrs. Lois Peabody, her supervisor in the rare books section of the library, had asked her to come in on a Saturday when two regulars had suddenly fallen ill with the flu.

Grace had reported at two, found a wooden cart full of books, and pushed it past the front desk to a door and a ramp that descended into a dark chamber. Open only to staff, the musty room was the final resting place for once prominent publications that time and even catalogers had forgotten. Senior staff called the storage area the library's soul. Students called it the Crypt.

Giving up on the book on plants, Grace glanced at the spine of another volume, flicked on a dim light in the stacks, and pushed the cart toward another shelf. She was about to put *The Minutes of the Privy Council of Scotland* in its rightful place when a sudden sound made her scream and drop the massive book on her foot.

"Boo!"

Joel popped his head through the space officially reserved for seventeenth century British documents and greeted the startled information specialist.

"Happy Halloween!"

"Don't ever do that again!" she snapped. "You scared me."

Grace watched a silly grin vanish from his face. Her flash of anger had apparently taken him as much by surprise as his unannounced visit had taken her.

"I'm sorry," a sorry-sounding Joel Smith said. "I couldn't resist."

"How did you get in here? Only library staff can enter this room."

Mr. Apologetic stepped out from behind the stacks and held out his hands. He addressed Grace only after she could see that he posed no threat to public safety.

"I walked in. I watched you push a cart through the door, and when Miss Pointy Nose left the desk, I seized the moment," Joel said.

Attired in a white, short-sleeved sweater and a crisp plaid skirt, the student worker stared at the roguish intruder. He sported an unshaven face and looked a lot like the varmint she had once seen on a bench. Grace wondered how many other unauthorized visitors had entered the Crypt on her watch.

"Well, you shouldn't have done that. It's against library rules."

Joel grinned.

"I'm sorry. Truly. Next time I'll make an appointment with Miss Pointy Nose."

"Peabody. Her name is Mrs. Peabody."

"Got it. Mrs. Peabody. I'll have my secretary call hers. There has to be at least one or two openings next week," Joel said. "Now, tell me, Grace, and be honest, what's a princess like you doing in a dungeon like this?"

Grace suppressed a smile. She was still a little angry with him but realized that she had no answer for a repentant young man who chummed the waters with flattery.

"I'm putting away rare and valuable books, so that less committed individuals can watch grown men in restrictive pants play in the mud for three hours."

* * * * *

Joel laughed at the slam and wondered what Grace would think of less worthy pursuits, like monster truck rallies, steel cage matches, tractor pulls, and mud wrestling. He knew the answer. She would want season tickets and front-row seats.

"Why aren't you at the game?" Grace asked. "I thought you liked football."

"I do," Joel said. "But I like rare books better."

"Well, I doubt you'll find anything of interest in here."

"That's rather presumptuous of you, Miss Vandenberg. Do you really know my tastes in literature? I'm serious. I'm a well-rounded individual."

Grateful that Grace's moment of anger had passed, Joel jumped on the opening she had offered him. He shifted the cart to get a better look at the titles.

"Do your tastes extend to the Privy Council of Scotland?" Grace asked.

"No. They don't. But I'm sure you have something I'd like."

Joel glanced at a nearby shelf and pulled a book with a nondescript cover. He quickly flipped to the first page of *Meandering Streams and Their Seasonal Impact on Vegetation in Coastal Lowlands*.

"I knew it! I've been searching for this for months. I'm impressed," Joel said. "You should keep this out front, though, and not in a cave."

Joel looked at Grace and then at a book she had retrieved from the cart.

"What's that?"

"It's a book," Grace said sheepishly.

Joel smiled and gently removed the book from Grace's hands. He looked at the title, *The Descent of Man, and Selection in Relation to Sex*, and nodded.

"Hmm. It appears that Darwin left us a gift. You know, Grace, I've given the descent of man and sex a lot of thought over the years. I believe the concepts are closely related. What say you?"

"I say you've been reading things you shouldn't."

"No. I've been reading only the good stuff, like this here. I think Darwin was on to something. But his research was incomplete. Sex can never be studied too extensively. I may have to pursue some field experiments this afternoon."

"Don't even think about it," Grace said.

Joel grinned and tried to step around the cart, but Grace pushed it in his path. He placed Darwin on top of the cart and ran around the lighted stacks in an attempt to flank his prey. But she had already moved to the other side.

"You're pretty quick for a librarian."

He pushed the cart forward, but she stopped it with her foot and shoved it back. So he ran around the darkened stacks and managed to grab her hand before she screamed loudly, broke free, and again barricaded herself behind the books that no one read.

"You stay right there, Mr. Smith. You have sin on your mind."

The two stared at each other and smiled – he scarily, she warily – for ten seconds before Miss Pointy Nose interrupted their cat-and-mouse moment.

"Is everything all right down there, Grace? I heard a scream."

"I'm fine, Mrs. Peabody. I thought I saw a mouse, but it was nothing."

"OK. I'm going to take a break now. I'd like you to come up and watch the desk."

"I'll be right there."

Joel put a hand to his chin, as if pondering something profound, and then turned his attention to Grace. He frowned and shook his head.

"You really ought to hire more security in this building. I'm serious. Any Johnny-come-lately could sneak down here and harass the help," Joel said. When he saw that his comment did not elicit a positive reaction, he threw up his hands and retreated toward an emergency exit. "I'll leave you alone now."

"You do that – and take a very cold shower when you get home," Grace said. "Or, better yet, stop by the police station and turn yourself in."

Joel laughed and continued toward a flight of stairs that led to a door with a push bar. When he reached the top, he heard a soft voice and looked back.

"Thank you for coming, Joel. Next time I'll go to the game."

Grace stepped around the cart and tiptoed over several books that had spilled onto the concrete floor, including a work on meandering streams that had meandered ten feet. She walked closer to the intruder and gave him the smile he had come for.

"Will I see you tonight?" Grace asked.

"You'll see me tonight."

"Joel?"

"Yeah?"

"I love you."

54: JOEL

Wednesday, November 12, 1941

When Joel returned to Fifty-Second Street from an unusually long day at work, he noticed two things: Tom slumped in a recliner and mail scattered on the wooden floor. Picking up the scraps of paper, he saw a flyer from a nearby market, a utility bill, a postcard from the alumni association, and an opened letter from a local draft board.

Joel sat on the couch, kicked off his shoes, and began reading the letter. Dated November 10, or two days earlier, it bore the official seal of the United States.

"I'll save you the trouble," Tom said matter-of-factly. He stared blankly out the living room window. "It's an order to report for induction. I have twelve days."

Joel examined the typed form letter and noted a date, November 24, and a place, the National Guard armory. The order instructed Tom to appear at eight o'clock.

From the armory, Tom would be transported to an induction station in Tacoma, examined and, "if accepted for training and service," be inducted into the Army. That branch of the service was circled in pen.

"It says here that you still have to pass a physical," Joel said.

"Yeah. I do. I have to be taller than Mickey Rooney, have half my teeth, and not have bad eyes, flat feet, or the clap," Tom replied bitterly. "I'll pass."

"Have you told Ginny or your folks?"

"I just called Ginny. I haven't talked to Mom or Dad. I'll tell them tonight. But they won't be surprised. They knew this was coming."

Joel placed the mail on top of the coffee table and settled into a corner of the couch. He tried to find comforting words but came up empty. He had never been in Tom's position or anything like it.

As a courtesy to his father, Joel had met with a representative of the Naval ROTC program his freshman year in college. But that was as close as he had ever come to the United States military. He had never served or been drafted, much less drafted against his will during a global conflagration.

"I'm really sorry, Tom. I wish I could help."

Joel pondered what the news meant for him as well. Unless Tom failed his physical, he would soon be without a housemate, a colleague, and a best friend – a friend who had taken him off the streets, found him a job, and introduced him to two women who were now the center of his life. He thought about Ginny, the wedding that would never happen, and how she would cope with a loss that was all but written in the stars.

"You know what really bothers me?" Tom asked. He looked at Joel. "I have no say in the matter. I'm as ready to defend this country as the next guy. But we're not at war, are we? It's not right, I tell you. It's not right."

"No," Joel said. "It's not."

Joel glanced at a chalet-style cuckoo clock on the mantle of the fireplace and noticed ornate hands in a straight vertical line. He got off the couch, slipped on his shoes, and walked over to his chum.

"You probably haven't had dinner, have you?" Joel asked.

"I haven't had lunch."

"Then let me take care of that. The steakhouse on Roosevelt Way doesn't require reservations. You and I are getting a serious meat fix tonight."

"Thanks, buddy," Tom said. He forced a small smile. "I could use that."

Tom got out of the recliner, retrieved his heavy coat, and stepped to the coffee table. He collected the draft letter, put it in his pocket, and turned to Joel. He placed a hand on his friend's shoulder.

"I guess I should look at the bright side," Tom said. "It's only a twelve-month enlistment. It'll be over in no time."

55: JOEL

Saturday, November 15, 1941

The line at the Phoenician didn't just wrap around the corner. It wrapped around the entire block. But Joel couldn't complain. He had a nice-looking woman on each arm and was about to do something none of his peers in 2000 had done – watch *Citizen Kane* in its first run.

"Thank you for taking me," Katie said.

Joel smiled at his bonus date and pulled her in close with his right arm. She had shivered more than once from the chill of an ice storm that had pelted them shortly after they had reached the theater and the monstrous line. But he suspected that even the storm was warmer than the frosty snub that had started her evening.

Stood up at the last minute by a junior varsity football player, Katie had been a tearful mess when Joel had come for Grace at six. Her previously enlightened suitor, a classmate in an English literature class, had called to say that dating a Japanese American girl was no longer something he was prepared to do in public.

"Don't mention it. I'm glad to have you along."

"I'm happy you're here too," Grace said with a sly smile. "Mr. Smith behaved rather poorly the other day and I fear I may require a chaperone."

Katie giggled.

The hour in line had given the three more than ample time to discuss the past week, Thanksgiving plans, and the pending departure of their friend. Though news of Tom's all but certain conscription into the armed forces surprised few, it still carried a punch.

Tom and Ginny had planned to attend the movie but opted out at the last minute, saying that they needed a weekend at the coast more than a Saturday at the flicks. Ginny had taken the news hard and had all but put her life on hold for the next two weeks.

"I keep thinking about Tom," Katie said, burrowing into Joel's side. "I know a lot of boys who have received their notices. Do you ever worry that you'll be next?"

Joel laughed to himself when he heard the question. This time he could honestly say he had given the matter serious thought. But he was no closer to providing an answer than when Tom had asked him essentially the same thing in Seaside.

"I do. But I try not to think about the draft. There's not a lot I can do about it."

"I'm concerned about Tom," Grace said. "Ginny said he is convinced we will be drawn into the war and that he will see combat by the summer. He is worried about how he will perform if he does. He's obsessed by it, in fact."

Joel flinched.

Make that two of us.

"I think he'll be OK," Katie said. "President Roosevelt has kept us at peace so far. I have faith he'll keep it that way."

Grace looked up at Joel, as if seeking clues to his views on the matter. But she did not expand on Katie's prediction or mention Tom's name the rest of the night. She instead tightened her hold on Joel's arm and turned to her friend.

"I hope you're right, Katie, for his sake and for ours."

* * * * *

When the movie ended three hours later, the trio headed not for the exits but rather the concession stand. The girls wanted drinks and Joel wanted change from a twenty. They requested both from a counter-wiping clerk as she shut down her shop. When the harried employee returned a moment later with two sodas and several bills, Joel heard a familiar voice.

"Well, now. It looks like we have a big spender."

Joel glanced at the other end of the counter and saw Mr. Congeniality, the white-trash bill collector who nearly beat Tom senseless that wild night outside the Mad Dog. At his side were two similar-sized friends from the trailer park.

"I'll bet you never thought you'd see me again."

"You're right," Joel said. "But then, I don't make prison visits."

Joel handed his dates their beverages and escorted them to the end of a line that slowly worked its way to the street. As he pressed forward, he noticed that the three men, dressed in work shirts and jeans, had not found a new distraction. They sneered and laughed at Katie. One man licked his lips.

Joel shook his head and pushed the punks out of his mind. He had far more pressing things to ponder, like his Army-bound friend and the gathering storm in the Pacific. Keeping his thoughts to himself, he guided Grace and Katie through the theater's entrance to the sidewalk.

The weather, mercifully, had improved during the show. The rain had stopped and the wind had subsided, leaving a cool but comfortable late fall evening behind. Buttoning their coats, the cinema-loving friends turned north and commenced a ten-block walk to Klickitat Avenue. They traveled three blocks before trouble announced itself with a shout.

"It's not fair, you know."

The bill collector had apparently tired of popcorn and peanuts.

"Keep going, Joel," Grace said in a firm voice.

"It's not fair, I tell you."

Joel stopped and turned to face the malcontent.

"What do you want?"

"Who said I want anything?"

The bill collector's companions, a pizza-faced brute named Rocky and a gap-toothed lout named Rex, stirred the pot. They laughed and leered.

"I'm just saying it's not fair. You have two dates – and we have none."

"Get lost," Joel said.

He put his arms around Grace and Katie and nudged them forward but not out of trouble. His decision to retreat only fed his antagonist's appetite for conflict.

"Two bits."

Once more, Joel stopped. Once again, Grace counseled restraint.

"Let it go," she said. "They're not worth it."

Joel took a breath and pushed his party northward. When they reached the end of the block, where the commercial zone met the residential, the fun resumed.

"I'll give you two bits for the Jap."

Joel stopped and pulled his arms from Grace and Katie.

"Ladies," he said. "I have to go."

With that, the linebacker, geology major, and furniture salesman left restraint behind. He let loose with a rage, charging the leader of the pack with an attack that surprised even the intended target. Like all good fighters, Joel got in the first good punch. His right hook to the bill collector's jaw sent him reeling into the base of a tree. He ignored the other two and hit his foe in the face and then in the stomach, unleashing all the frustrations of five months into one glorious display of violence.

This time, however, the accomplices did not flee but rather intervened and turned the tide. Seeing that their friend was about to get slaughtered, they attacked Joel from the sides and threw him to the cold wet grass.

When the ringleader regrouped, the three had their way and pummeled Joel repeatedly with blows to the face and chest.

Katie screamed and drew the attention of passers-by, while Grace yanked Rocky's hair and brought Joel needed relief. When the bully got up on a knee, turned on Grace, and tried to punch his way free, two men ran across the street to come to her aid.

The first responder pulled Grace out of harm's way and kept her attacker at bay. The second grabbed Rex by his collar, threw him to the curb, and kicked him twice in the side. A dozen others crowded around and gawked. When a policeman approached the scene a moment later and parked across the street, the three thugs scattered. But the damage had been done. Joel had a pulpy face and four badly bruised ribs. The gathering storm had come to the Ave.

56: EDITH, JOEL, AND GRACE

Thursday, November 20, 1941

Only one soul rattled in the mansion in Madison Park, but she knew how to cook. For the better part of two days, she had made bread, baked pies, sliced vegetables, and prepared a turkey for two guests, including one she had never met.

When the guests arrived at one, she took their coats and directed them to the living room. Bright sunlight streaming through a picture window and a roaring fire illuminated and warmed the antique-filled parlor.

"I'm so glad you could make it. You know how I hate dining alone," Edith Green Tomlinson said. "Were the roads bad?"

"They were icy in places but pretty good overall," Grace said. "We took our time."

The college senior embraced her sole remaining blood relative and then stepped back to make an introduction that was weeks overdue.

"Aunt Edith, this is my dear friend Joel Smith. Joel, this is my aunt."

"It's a pleasure to meet you, ma'am," Joel said as he extended a hand.

Edith shook the hand but quickly upgraded the greeting to an affectionate hug. She did not like stiff introductions, particularly to people who might become part of the family.

Still striking at forty-one, Edith had the regal look of a Nordic queen. Like her niece, she had a creamy complexion, crystal-blue eyes, and thick blond hair that had yet to see a touch of gray. Widowed for five years, she had survived, even thrived, by managing her late husband's real-estate holdings and by creating and selling landscape paintings that had become the talk of the city.

"Please make yourselves comfortable," Edith said with a West Country accent that had remained intact after two decades in the United States.

Edith retreated to the adjacent dining room while Joel and Grace sat on a sofa facing the fireplace. The hostess returned to the living room a few minutes later with a bottle of sherry. She poured three glasses and sat in an upholstered chair by the window.

"Grace tells me you grew up in England," Joel said.

"I was born and bred in Falmouth – in Cornwall – and came to Seattle with Grace's mother when we were eighteen. My father wanted us to pursue an education in America after the war. There was little for us in Britain, so Father put us on a boat shortly after the hostilities ceased. My uncle was a dean at the university."

"Did you go to school there?" Joel asked.

"I did. I enrolled at the first opportunity and eventually graduated with a degree in social work. Lucille was another matter. She met a young seminary student shortly after we arrived and ran off to Minnesota."

"You seem to have done well."

"My *husband* did well. He was a successful businessman. I met him the day I graduated, and we married the next year," Edith said. She topped off her glass and settled into her chair. "We had eleven years together before he died of a stroke."

"I'm sorry to hear that," Joel said.

"Thank you. It was difficult at first, but I managed. In any event, that is ancient history and more than enough about me. I would much rather talk about you. I don't receive many visitors, so forgive me if I seem inquisitive."

When Edith saw Joel glance at the corner of the room and smile, she immediately regretted playing the part of a lonely widow. He had no doubt seen the pipe and fedora resting on a small table and correctly concluded she wasn't quite as lonely as she made herself out to be. She kept his perceptiveness in mind over the next fifteen minutes as she listened to him recount his time in the city.

After pouring more wine for each of her guests, Edith turned toward Joel and finally brought up a subject that was no doubt on everyone's mind – the street fight. Though the bruises around Joel's eyes appeared to be fading and the cuts on his cheeks showed signs of healing, he still bore the marks of a serious beating.

"Thank you for protecting the girls the other night," Edith said. "I often worry about Grace's safety. It's nice to know someone is looking after her."

"I just did what anyone would have done," Joel said.

"Even so, you deserve to be thanked," Edith said. She brushed some lint off her dress. "Have the police found the men who harassed you?"

"Not yet," Grace said. "But they will. There were many witnesses."

"That's good. Acts like that should not go unpunished. In any case, I'm glad you are both all right. How are your ribs, Joel?"

"They're still sore – particularly on my left side – but they're getting better," Joel said. "As long as I don't play football this weekend, I'll be OK."

Edith flashed Grace a knowing smile. She could see why Grace had broken off her engagement and felt much better about a decision she had initially questioned.

"I'm happy to hear that. When Grace told me that you had been assaulted, I wasn't sure what to expect. She said you had been put in an ambulance and taken to the hospital."

"I went in for a routine exam," Joel said. "None of my cuts needed stitches, and none of my bones needed setting. The doctor looked me over and sent me home. If you really want to know who kept me intact, talk to Grace. From what I heard, she did a number on one of the men. She gave him the Custer treatment."

Edith looked at Grace with puzzled eyes.

"I grabbed his hair," Grace said. She blushed.

Edith laughed.

"I can just picture that. You can be very resourceful when you set your mind to something. Did you leave him with a scalp?"

"I think so," Grace said. "I hope so. But I don't know for sure. He wiggled a lot and screamed rather loudly."

Edith glanced at Joel as he smiled and shook his head. She could see from the sparkle in his eyes that he found Grace's empathy endearing. She had no doubt that his affection for Grace was as deep and genuine as it appeared.

"Well done, dear," Edith said as she turned back to Grace. "It appears that at least one unpleasant man in Seattle will not be bothering others anytime soon."

Edith got up from her chair.

"Now, if you two are ready to eat, please follow me to the table," she said. "We have a feast to enjoy."

* * * * *

Joel could not remember a better holiday meal.

Aunt Edith had topped even the most impressive efforts of Joel's mother and grandmothers. She had made everything from scratch and most things from memory.

Joel had loaded up on roasted turkey, chestnut stuffing, and candied yams, as well as mince pie, mashed turnips, and homemade biscuits with crabapple jelly. He thought of Norman Rockwell's *Freedom from Want* painting and wondered if others from this time ate that well. He concluded they probably did.

Joel also thought about how this Thanksgiving had differed from all the others. In the houses of Smith and Jorgenson, males made a seamless transition from apple pie and cheesecake to the Cowboys and the Lions. In the house of Edith Tomlinson, they went from dessert to the kitchen and tackled a stack of dirty dishes.

Shortly after putting the dishes away, Joel stepped out of the kitchen and into the living room. He took a seat and joined the hostess and her niece for coffee.

"Did you get enough to eat?" Edith asked.

Joel smiled.

"Trust me when I say that's a question you didn't need to ask."

Edith looked at Grace.

"I like him. You should bring him by more often."

"I would if I could," Grace said. "He always seems to be doing something. If he's not at the furniture store, he's running around town or getting into trouble with Tom Carter."

Edith turned to Joel.

"How *is* your friend?"

"He's holding up," Joel said. "But he's upset. He doesn't want to go into the Army."

"That seems to be a common sentiment," Edith replied. "The boy next door was just called up. He doesn't want to go either. These are such difficult times."

"They are."

"Do you think America will join the fight?"

Joel thought about the question and considered his reply. He wanted to tell Edith that the shit was about to hit the fan and that many more boys from her safe, comfortable neighborhood were about to be sent to unsafe, uncomfortable places.

He wanted to tell Grace that he knew what was coming and that it was time for them to escape to a place where they could ride out the ugliness and not think about Hitler or Tojo or catastrophic loss. But he knew things had already reached a point where even a prescient time traveler could do little more than make the best of a bad situation.

"I do," Joel said. "We can't hold out much longer. We'll be at war soon."

Joel hated dumping even that much pessimism on the others, but he was tired of hiding what he felt and what he knew. Edith did not appear to mind. She told Joel that she valued the opinions of those with a direct stake in a serious matter, and few Americans had a more direct stake in going to war than men subject to the draft.

Edith also said she enjoyed talking to people with different backgrounds. So for the next three hours, she inquired about Joel's. She

214

asked him about life in Montana, his job, and why he had never spent a day in college. She asked enough questions to fill a small book. Joel, for his part, did his best to answer them.

* * * * *

Grace listened to the stories almost as intently as her aunt. She had heard them often and never tired of them. But this time she paid less attention to what Joel said than to how he said it – and, with each passing hour, she noticed a change.

He spoke in low tones now and with little conviction. He rarely smiled or looked Edith in the eyes and answered her questions with minimal energy and noticeable economy, as if pushing out syllables were backbreaking work. Joel Smith was no longer the cocky, playful boy who had chased her around the Crypt or even the reasonably happy date she had brought to dinner but rather a hardened pessimist who had fallen into a funk that even fatigue could not explain.

Grace knew that Tom's draft status, the fight, and the daily barrage of depressing headlines had taken a toll, but she suspected that far more was in play. Each time Edith asked Joel about his goals or long-term plans he stopped talking or tried to change the subject. When he did discuss the future, he did so in terms of days and weeks rather than months and years. A condemned man exuded more optimism.

Deciding that Joel needed a change of scenery, Grace suggested that they see *Dumbo* that night at a theater downtown. The animated feature had opened to large crowds several days earlier and offered the kind of Disney escapism that might allow Joel to forget his troubles for a couple of hours. To her surprise, he agreed to go.

"Let's do it," Joel said with little enthusiasm. "But let's stop by my place first. I left my wallet behind and want to get some cash."

"OK," Grace said. "We can do that. I'll drive."

Aunt Edith did not let her visitors slip away without a proper send-off. She gave each a hug and an invitation to return at the earliest opportunity.

"Be sure to call me tomorrow," Edith said to Grace a moment later, after Joel had exited the residence. "I want to know how your friends are doing. Let me know if there is anything I can do for them."

"I will. Thank you for a wonderful dinner."

Edith guided Grace out the front door and into the blustery autumn night. She stopped at the edge of her covered wooden porch and glanced at the wet driveway and her late husband's coupe. Joel sat motionless in the passenger seat.

"Keep an eye on him, dear," Edith said. She put an arm around her niece. "There is something he's not telling us, something that's weighing heavily on his mind. He's a nice young man, but he is deeply troubled. He has something to work out, and I suspect it is something he'll have to resolve soon."

"I know," Grace said. "I see it too."

Grace stared blankly at the glistening vehicle and then at the ground before turning to her aunt. She took a breath.

"I'll be in touch."

57: JOEL AND GRACE

The drive to Fifty-Second Street was short and quiet but not uneventful. In three places along Fifteenth Avenue, a north-south arterial, Joel and Grace encountered flares, warning signs, and arm-waving policemen.

The storm that had rattled windows and garbage cans in Madison Park had sent power lines, branches, and debris into the streets elsewhere. When the travelers finally arrived at the bachelor pad, they found it dark. Though no trees or lines littered the pavement, no nearby streetlamps or houses emitted light.

"It looks like the power is out," Joel said.

He stepped out of Edith's Ford, escorted Grace to the door, and fumbled with some keys before finding one that opened the lock. Once inside, he led Grace to a switch near the dining table and flicked it. To his dismay, no lights came on.

Joel scanned his surroundings but saw little in the darkness. A waxing moon that pushed light through the kitchen window provided limited illumination.

"Do you have a candle?" Grace asked.

"I do," Joel said. "Ginny gave me one as a housewarming gift. Remember? I guess it's time I used it."

Joel stumbled his way into the kitchen, found some matches in the silverware drawer, and brought them back to the dining table. He struck a match and lit a stout white candle that sat in a clear glass holder. A soft glow quickly filled the room.

"That's better," Joel said. "Wait here while I get my wallet. It's in the bedroom, but I won't need the candle to find it."

When Joel disappeared around a corner, Grace walked through the residence – or at least the parts she could navigate by candlelight. She entered the kitchen, opened and closed a barren refrigerator, and took stock of a cluttered counter. She put two dirty dishes in a messy sink and an empty beer bottle in the trash.

From the kitchen she moved to the living room, where no newspapers littered the floor, no clothes lay on the furniture, and no artwork hung on the walls. Unopened letters covered the coffee table. Grace returned to the dining area just as Joel emerged from the hallway with a wallet in his hand.

"I found it on the floor by the bed," Joel said. He put the wallet in his pants pocket. "Are you ready to go?"

"No," Grace replied.

"No?"

"No."

Grace slowly but conspicuously stepped between Joel and the door. If nothing else, she succeeded in getting his attention.

"I thought you wanted to see a movie," Joel said.

"I do," Grace insisted. "But *Dumbo* can wait. You can't."

"What do you mean?"

"I mean I'm worried about you – very worried. You've been down in the dumps for days. What's bothering you? Is it Tom? The fight? Something else? Tell me."

Joel kicked himself for projecting gloom. He hated bringing others down, particularly people as important as Grace. He considered telling her the truth but decided against it. There was nothing he could say or do now to alter his circumstances.

"I wish I could, Grace. I really do. But I can't."

Grace stared glumly at the floor, like a student who had tried and failed to figure out the only question on a test – a test without an answer key. A moment later, she lifted her head, looked at Joel, and frowned.

"All right. I'll let it go for now, but I won't let it go forever," Grace said. "I want to be a part of you, Joel. I want you to trust me."

Joel looked at Grace, his amazing Grace, with weary eyes. He wondered what he had done to deserve the affection of such a remarkable woman. He let several seconds of awkward silence pass before he returned to the business at hand.

"We should go," Joel said. He took Grace's hand. "It may take a while to get to the theater. Are you ready to see *Dumbo*?"

"No," Grace answered.

"No again? You don't want to go out?"

Grace stiffened.

"No. I've changed my mind."

Grace released Joel's hand, walked to the kitchen counter, and turned on a Philco PT-87 portable radio, a gift from Melvin Carter and the only object in the house that ran on batteries. She moved the tuner until she found a station that played popular music. Glenn Miller's "Moonlight Serenade" streamed through the speaker.

"I would rather stay," Grace said. "I have all I need right here."

Grace put her purse on the table, kicked off her saddle shoes, and pulled Joel to an open space between the kitchen, the dining area, and the living room.

"I never got my slow dance in Seaside," she said. "I'd like to collect."

"OK."

Joel put an arm around Grace's waist, took her hand, and did something he couldn't do in July – lead a dance. When "Moonlight Serenade" gave way to more slow songs, he continued as before. When the radio played something up-tempo, he picked up the pace. When the station broke for commercials, he held Grace and moved as if the music had never stopped.

And so it went for more than two hours in the dark little house on Fifty-Second Street. Two kindred spirits, from different eras and backgrounds, danced, kissed, and held each other closely as a flickering candle cast shadows on a distant wall.

Joel did not want the evening to end. He did not want it to end at seven, when the music stopped for the news; at eight, when the lights came on and Grace casually walked across the room to turn them off; or at nine, when she lowered the volume of the radio, grabbed the candle on the table, and led him to a bedroom she had never seen.

Once inside, Grace closed the door behind them, put the candle on a dresser, and blew it out. Except for the dresser, the bed, and an unfinished nightstand, the room was bare. A sliver of moonlight streamed through a small window, allowing recognition of basic shapes and outlines but not much more.

Grace stared at Joel intently, threw her arms around his neck, and gave him a long, tender kiss. She sighed, withdrew her arms, and stepped back against the dimly lit wall. Maintaining eye contact, she slowly unzipped her blue gingham dress, loosened its hold on her slender form, and let it fall to the floor.

Joel looked at the lithe figure with awe and uncertainty. He had dreamed of this moment for weeks, even months, but he wasn't sure this was the time or the place to fulfill that dream. He feared that sympathy, not passion, had brought her to his room.

"We can't do this, Grace."

"Why not?" she asked.

"Because you're trying to make me feel better, that's why. I love you for that. I do. But this is not the answer," Joel said. "I know what this means to you. You told me yourself at the beach. You said you were saving yourself."

Grace took a breath and smiled sweetly. She gently pushed her dress aside with a foot and then stepped toward a man who was no more than a silhouette in the darkened room. She put an open hand to his solemn face.

"I did, and I have," Grace said. "I saved myself for you."

"But . . ."

"Hush."

Grace put two fingers to Joel's lips.

"No more talk. Not now."

She placed her arms on his shoulders.

"Not tonight."

58: TOM AND JOEL

Monday, November 24, 1941

Tom Carter could not remember a lonelier drive, despite the immediate or near immediate presence of his entire family and a dozen friends. He sat quietly in the back of his father's DeSoto sedan, behind his somber parents and beside his surprisingly supportive sister, who had extended her Thanksgiving break from UCLA by two days to see her brother off to the United States Army.

"Are you OK?" Brenda Carter asked.

She put a hand on her brother's knee.

"I'm as OK as I can be," Tom said. "But thanks for asking."

Tom smiled as he considered how far she had come in only a few years. She was no longer his scrawny and sometimes annoying kid sister but rather a grown woman who was no doubt turning heads in Westwood. On her own initiative, she had contacted many of his friends and urged them to take time from work and school to see him off. Brenda had also insisted that he ride with his family and not in the Plymouth with Ginny. She knew this was a particularly difficult time for their parents.

Not that Ginny was far behind. She rode with Joel and the rest of the Klickitat crew in the ragtop. Five fraternity brothers and four coworkers occupied two vehicles further back. For the first time in eight years, Melvin Carter had closed Carter's Furniture and Appliance on a non-holiday weekday. That alone, Tom thought, spoke volumes.

As the caravan passed through the only hometown he had ever known, Tom pondered the coming year. He lamented that a June wedding was no longer likely and wondered whether *any* wedding was likely. He and Ginny had had just eight months together. Could they survive a long separation? Probably, he reasoned. Ginny was equally committed to their future and not one to let any obstacle interfere with achieving a goal. If anyone could manage this kind of disruption, she could. But a year apart was still a year apart. A lot could happen in twelve months.

Tom thought of his father as well. He knew that this sudden turn of events had hit him hard and in ways most others could not see. The old man had great plans for his firstborn, plans to make him a full partner in an expanding enterprise, plans he would now have to shelve. Mel Carter would also have to confront fears he had talked about for years, fears of sending a son into combat. As an Army conscript in World War I, he had seen the worst fighting in the Battle of the Argonne Forest and had promised his children a more peaceful transition to adulthood.

The drive from Baltic Avenue to the National Guard armory downtown took only twenty minutes, the formalities inside just two hours. Tom walked to the back of a long line, presented his induction notice to the appropriate officials, and when finished headed outside to a large lawn in front, where he waited for his bus to Tacoma.

His entourage joined him in the mid-morning drizzle, along with other inductees and their families and friends. By noon more than a hundred had gathered on the green. Tom sent his fraternity pals away first and then his sales colleagues. Some tried to lighten his mood with jokes and memories, but most were uncharacteristically respectful. At least one had received his order to report and knew his turn would come soon enough.

From Grace and Katie, Tom proceeded to Brenda and finally to Joel. The man from Montana had worn his cowboy hat for the first time in weeks in an apparent attempt to get his friend's mind off the moment.

"That's exactly how I want to remember you – as a cowpoke who kicked some serious ass on my behalf," Tom said. "It's too bad I wasn't around to return the favor the other night. I would have enjoyed the payback."

"It's probably best you weren't there," Joel said. "Nothing good came out of that fight. But I don't think we'll be hearing from your betting buddy anytime soon. The bartender at the Mad Dog told me that I broke his jaw."

"Good job. Someone needed to shut his trap."

Both men laughed.

Joel smiled, put a hand on Tom's shoulder, and stared blankly toward the parking lot, as if revisiting the many laughs and experiences they had shared. A moment later he looked back at his friend, pulled a set of keys from a jacket pocket, and held them up.

"You still trust me with your car?"

"I do. Because I know you'll take care of it and I know you'll have fun with it," Tom said. "And if, by some miracle, they send me home tomorrow, I know I won't have to hunt you down to get it back."

"I'll have it washed and buffed if that happens."

The sound of an air brake shifted their attention to the next block, where the bus to Tacoma stopped for a sign.

"Well, I guess I should hurry up. I've got more important mugs than yours to see," Tom said with a laugh. He embraced his friend. "You're the best, Joel. I mean that. Take care of yourself and take care of my girls."

* * * * *

The cowboy gave as well as he got, giving Tom a firm hug before finally letting go. He paused to look at his pal. It was amazing how easy it was to like this guy.

Joel wasn't one to get caught up in the moment, in any moment, but this farewell hit him hard. He was not only saying goodbye to a dear friend but also allowing fate and history to take their course. For weeks he had considered pushing Tom into enlisting in the Coast Guard or even the Navy to shake things up. But he knew it wasn't his place to play God and knew that he had already overstepped his bounds with Grace. So he sent Tom on his way with the only words that made sense.

"Come back to us," Joel said. "Make your family proud. Don't be a hero."

Joel watched his housemate move down the line to his quiet father, tearful mother, and attentive fiancée, who straightened his collar, put a small photo in his hand, and followed him to the bus. Tom began speaking to Ginny when they reached the door.

Joel could not make out their conversation, but he saw the concern on her face. He thought of his Grandpa Joe and all the years he had seen him interact happily with his wife. He could not imagine anyone taking his place in the hierarchy of men in the life of Virginia Gillette. Yet as he watched Tom Carter say goodbye, he wasn't so sure. There had been someone else, before Joe Jorgenson, and he had been pretty damn important.

Minutes later the door closed and the bus, loaded with more than fifty inductees, slowly pulled away from the curb. Sitting in a window seat three rows back, Tom waved to his family, blew a kiss to Ginny, and gave Joel a half-hearted salute. His family and friends waved back. They never saw him again.

223

59: JOEL

Freeland, Washington – Sunday, November 30, 1941

Joel opened his eyes and stared at the ceiling. Though little light spilled through the crack in the curtains of the motel room, there was enough to make out water stains on the tiles, an overhead light hanging by a thread, and a small spider working its way toward the wall. The place was a dump. But Joel had wanted privacy and few places offered more than the Agate Inn on the southwest corner of Whidbey Island.

Groggy from a sleepless night, Joel threw on some jeans and a wool sweater and walked across the room. Parting the curtains slightly, he peered out the window and saw a bank of fog drift eastward over Admiralty Inlet. Dawn had come to Puget Sound.

Joel looked back at the bed and saw Grace pull a blanket over her shoulders and smile as she repositioned her face on a pillow. She was still asleep and very much lost in another place. He envied her ability to rest and dream and think about happy things. He tried to remember the last time he had seen something so beautiful.

They had come to the motel Friday night after work and school – at his suggestion – and checked in as Mr. and Mrs. Smith. Joel had loved the irony. By using his real name, rather than a plausible alias, he had needlessly invited additional scrutiny and judgment. But he no longer cared what strangers, like motel clerks, thought of his personal decisions. He cared only about escaping the lifeless house on Fifty-Second Street and spending more time with Number One.

The days following Tom's departure had been quiet and businesslike. The Army had taken Tom, of course, and already sent him to Fort Lewis for processing and basic training. Ginny had returned to her editing position at the *Barker*, Grace and Katie to their classes, and Joel to his job matching Seattle's most restless sleepers with Carter's most restful mattresses. But nothing was the same without the jovial joker who had held their little group together for almost six months.

Deciding to let Grace enjoy literally her last peaceful Sunday morning for the next four years, Joel put on his coat and quietly exited the room. He walked across a gravel parking lot to the motel's office, where he found the manager reading a weekend edition of the *Sun*. Joel poured himself a cup of coffee and sat at the lone table in the lobby.

"Can I have that when you're done?" Joel asked.

"You can have it now, if you want," the thin man in spectacles said. "I have to get back to work. Did you sleep well?"

"I did," Joel lied. "It's very quiet here."

"That's what we advertise."

Joel pictured his dilapidated room and juxtaposed that image with an ad he saw in a telephone book. He understood why the owners had promoted peace and quiet over cleanliness. He would have done the same. But he was in no mood to complain. He needed a mental break from the city and the Agate Inn had delivered. He took the *Sun* from the manager and returned to the table and his coffee. A moment later, he scanned the news of the day.

The headlines reflected the state of the world: TOKYO DEFIES U.S. ULTIMATUM, RED ARMY CAPTURES ROSTOV, BRITISH SINK EIGHT GERMAN SHIPS IN ARCTIC CONVOY. From other articles on the front page he learned that Navy had defeated Army, that Oregon State had won a trip to the Rose Bowl, and that Westlake had pounded Polk in the state semifinals. Joel laughed. Even in 1941, football held its own in the mainstream media.

From other pages he learned that ski conditions were improving across the state, that tuberculosis was on the rise, that an Idaho miner faced a bigamy charge, and that *A Yank in the R.A.F.* had been held over at a downtown theater. Another advertisement touted a "French permanent" for two and a half bucks.

Then Joel glanced at a small wire story that shook him to his core: SIX PLANETS TO ALIGN IN DECEMBER. He pushed his coffee aside and let his head fall to his hands. He did not need to read the article to know the details or what they meant to him. But he read it anyway. The story was the answer to a question that had dogged him for months.

WASHINGTON – Six planets, including the Earth, will fall into a rare alignment early next month in what scientists are calling a once-in-a-lifetime astronomical event.

Beginning late December 7 and continuing through most of the next day, the Earth and the moon will align with the sun and Mercury, Venus, Mars, Jupiter, and Saturn. Viewers in the Northern Hemisphere will be able to see at least part of the celestial arrangement both evenings with the aid of a telescope.

Last seen in 1882, the six-planet alignment will not occur again until May 2000, according to Dr. James Branson of the National Center for Physics and Astronomy.

Within seconds memories from a long ago May came flooding back – the cable news story at the Canary, the dusty tunnel, the glowing room, and the improbable journey through fifty-nine years. If Joel had any doubts that the places and events were tied to his predicament, they were gone. But questions remained. Did Colter Mine have a revolving door? And if it did, would it spin in seven days?

Joel tore the small article from the page, placed the newspaper on the table, and popped out of the office into the cold, misty air. Sunlight filtered through gray clouds to the east, bringing a badly needed glow to an otherwise dismal morning.

Walking westward toward a rocky, driftwood-strewn beach fifty yards away, Joel began a conversation with himself that would have seemed inconceivable even minutes earlier. He thought of Grace and Tom and a Japanese strike force that lurked in the North Pacific – and then of Jana and Adam and his family. He thought of all the things that tied him to two worlds and the likely opportunity that awaited him.

He had a chance to go home.

* * * * *

The question of whether to seize that chance was a no-brainer. Of course he would. He had nothing to lose – save a few dollars – by traveling to Montana and finding out whether the mine was a time machine full of promise or a dark hole full of rock and debris.

The question of whether to take Grace with him was another matter. That issue was filled with all sorts of complications – factors Joel had to consider.

Joel did not doubt that Grace would follow him. She would follow him to the ends of the earth. But did he have the right to take her there? Did he have the right to deprive Edith Tomlinson of a niece or Virginia Gillette and Katie Kobayashi of a friend or future children of a chance to exist? Grace had been prepared, after all, to marry someone else. Perhaps that was her destiny.

Joel considered her professional interests as well. Did he have the right to deny Grace the life she was meant to lead? Or deny countless students in the forties, fifties, and sixties an inspiring teacher? An instructor who might push their lives in important and even critical directions? He wondered if Grace had an Einstein or Edison or Salk in her future.

As he stepped on slick rocks, soft sand, and loose wood, Joel also asked hard questions of himself. Was this really about Grace? Or was it about his refusal to man up, like his grandfathers, father, and Tom Carter, and serve his nation when it needed him most?

The option to stay, of course, was always on the table and would become more than something to mull over if the mine turned out to be a simple hole in the ground. Joel would have to either serve or run and accept the consequences of his actions.

He could do what Patrick Smith had done on December 8, 1941, and enlist. But where would that lead? Would he storm the same beach in 1944 and take a bullet meant for someone else? Then there was Ginny. Could he really stick around and watch her life and his mother's unfold? Could he really watch his younger self grow up? Was that even possible?

Joel did not find life with Grace in the 1940s unappealing. He had come to appreciate the relative simplicity of the times. But if he stayed and served, there was no guarantee the two would have a long and happy life together. It was just as likely he would be killed in a firefight in Europe or the South Pacific and die for a cause whose outcome had already been decided.

He struggled with his thoughts as he walked along the shore. He had often found answers on long walks with Grace, but he wasn't finding them now. Knots and nausea gripped his otherwise strong stomach as he accessed the narrow path from the beach to the motel.

When he reached his room, he entered quietly, removed his coat, and sat at a table by the window. At nine o'clock, Joel found Grace exactly as he had left her – sleeping, smiling, and perfect. For another hour he studied her angelic face and considered all the questions and possibilities of the coming days. Each time he did, he came back to the same place – the unfamiliar ground of the honorable, the selfless, and the righteous.

In the end, he realized he didn't have a choice. The clarity that had eluded him on the walk and during the past several months suddenly pounded on his door. His course was clear.

I have to give you up.

60: JOEL

When Joel delivered the news to Mel Carter, he saw a grimace and then a nod. He knew the boss had already lost a good salesman, his son, to the Army, and did not want to lose a great one for any reason, particularly during the Christmas shopping season. But Joel also knew that Mel had promised to help bring the Smith family together in any way he could, making his leave request an academic exercise.

"If things go poorly, I'll be gone only a few days," Joel said, offering a line he had rehearsed all day. He straightened his posture on the living room couch and addressed his supervisor and adopted father figure as thoughtfully as he could. "But if they go well, I'll want to stay there for Christmas."

The furniture king settled into his reclining throne and put a hand to his chin. He said he was glad Joel had announced his plans at the house, after a satisfying roast-beef dinner, rather than at the store. He would have been less receptive to the news at a place that had struggled to meet the needs of two hundred consumers on an unusually busy Monday.

"I understand, son. Family is more important than work, particularly this time of year. The way I see it, you don't have a choice."

"Will you be able to hire extra help?"

"I think so. I put an ad in the paper last week and have already had several replies. There is no shortage of young men looking to make a buck. None have your ability, of course, but I don't think they'll need it. Not in December. Customers this time of year usually have their minds made up when they walk through the door and just need someone to fill out the paperwork."

"Well, like I said, if I come back early, I'll do what I can to help you out."

"I appreciate that."

Baltic Avenue had been the second stop on his farewell tour. He had informed Grace of his plans the day before, on their drive back from Whidbey Island. Like the Carters, she approved of his trip to Montana, even if it meant Christmas without him.

Joel hated deceiving people he cared about, but he did not know a better way to prepare them for what might be a permanent exit. If he did not return from Helena, they would understand. At least he hoped they would.

The plan he had sketched out was simple. He would work at Carter's through Friday, treat the girls to dinner and drinks that night, take a taxi to King Street Station Saturday morning, and catch the first train to Montana. He would enter the mine on Monday. If it sent him back to 2000, he would grab the first ride home. If it did not, he would return to Seattle, marry Grace, if she would have him, and enlist in the Navy.

Joel considered driving Tom's Plymouth to Helena, for the sheer experience and to eliminate the need for a cab on Monday morning, but he quickly dismissed the idea. Six hundred miles was a long drive on potentially icy roads and he did not want to create undue hardship on the Carters should he leave the car behind.

He also pondered flying. Though only fourteen years had passed since Charles Lindbergh had crossed the Atlantic, commercial aviation was as common as rain. A twenty-one-seat aircraft left Seattle for points east every night at eight forty. But the puddle-jumping flight did not arrive in Helena until well after one in the morning. A daytime train ride through the scenic Northwest had far more appeal. He would collect his thoughts in the comfort of a roomy sleeping car and save his third freight-hopping adventure for another day.

The only difficult task was deciding how to part with Grace. She deserved the truth, the complete and unvarnished truth. But he would not tell her the truth before he left and could not tell her afterward if the mine sent him home. So he resolved to write a long, meaningful letter and entrust it to Ginny, with the explicit instruction that she not give it to Grace before Christmas.

When the ornate moon-phase clock on the mantle chimed seven times, Joel got off the couch, walked to a corner of the living room, and lifted his jacket off an oak coat rack. He put it on, checked a pocket for his keys, and returned to face his hosts.

"I should probably get going. I told the girls I'd stop by tonight," Joel said. "Thank you for the dinner, Mrs. Carter. As usual, it was the best."

Sandra Carter acknowledged the compliment and smiled as she and Mel got out of their chairs and walked their visitor to the entry. She said she had missed cooking and caring for Joel, just as she no doubt missed cooking and caring for her grown children, who in September had left her with a conspicuously empty nest.

"You're always welcome here," Sandy said. "We've enjoyed being a part of your life, Joel. Have a safe trip to Montana."

Joel stepped forward and gave Sandy a long hug. When he finally pulled back, he noticed moisture in her eyes and wondered what had caused it. Did she know what he was about to do? Did she see what was coming?

She probably did, Joel thought. If there was one person in 1941 besides Grace who could read him like a book, it was this perceptive mother. Sandy could probably tell by Joel's body language alone that he wasn't saying so long. He was saying goodbye.

Joel zipped his coat, grabbed a plate of oatmeal cookies that Sandy had baked on Sunday, and turned to Mel. He offered a hand to the boss, who looked resigned.

"Can I count on you tomorrow?" Mel asked.

"You can. I'll report for work at eight, if not earlier," Joel said. He stepped toward the door and then stopped. "There is one more thing. What would you like me to do with the car? I won't need it after Friday."

"Leave it in your driveway," Mel said. "I have a spare key if I need to use it."

"All right," Joel said. He gazed at the Carters for a few awkward seconds. "Well, I guess this is it. If I get the chance, Mrs. Carter, I'll stop by before I leave. Knowing me, I'll probably bring some laundry."

Sandy brightened.

"If you do, I'll take care of it. It's no bother."

"Thanks," Joel said.

Sandy straightened the collar of Joel's jacket and then adjusted a rubber band that secured a sheet of wax paper to his plate. When he turned and started toward the door, she followed and spoke one last time.

"Joel?"

"Yes."

"Will you leave us an address?" Sandy asked.

Joel cringed. He *had* no Helena address, unless he counted the flophouse. He should have remembered that. Then again, it was hard to remember everything when you lived a lie. He wouldn't miss having to cover his tracks at every turn.

"I don't think that will be necessary. I don't plan to be gone long," Joel said. "If I stay more than a few days, I'll put something in the mail. I promise."

Joel meant it too. Where he would send that something, however, was a bit of a problem. Even the U.S. Postal Service did not deliver postcards to the past.

61: GINNY AND JOEL

Friday, December 5, 1941

The Mad Dog was as quiet as a graduate of obedience school. Ginny, in fact, had never seen the place so dead on a Friday night. But then, she had never seen the tavern compete with the Senior Ball, the biggest social event of the year. Hundreds of upperclassmen had already left the campus for the black-tie event at the Olympus Hotel.

"Thank you for doing this," Ginny said to Joel as they sat in a booth with Katie. "It seems as though every time I turn around, you're doing something nice for someone."

"You two deserve it," Joel replied. "I should have done this weeks ago. Then again, it's hard to beat tonight. Right?"

"Right," Katie said. "Who needs the ball, anyway?"

Ginny winced. She wanted to say, "I do," but held her tongue. She had thought of little else except the ball since reading a letter from Tom that morning. He had mentioned not only the dance but also how much he loved and missed her.

The letter should have made Ginny happy, but instead it made her angry. It reminded her of a wound that continued to fester. The Army had cheated her of a joyful senior year.

Katie had declined an invitation to attend the ball. She rebuffed a Japanese American friend late Thursday night when it became clear he was more interested in finding a dance partner than a girlfriend.

Grace had faced a different situation. When she had asked Joel to the dance on their drive back from Whidbey Island, he declined. He said he wanted to get a good night's sleep before taking the train to Montana Saturday morning.

Ginny wondered whether that slight had prompted Grace to respond in kind. Grace had accepted Joel's invitation to dinner but backed out at the eleventh hour to finish a collaborative academic project that apparently could not wait. When Ginny and Katie had left for the Mad Dog, Grace headed for an off-campus residence eight blocks away.

"When are you picking up Goldilocks?" Ginny asked.

"Eight o'clock," Joel said. He looked at Katie. "So I have two hours to spend with you lovely ladies. Have you figured out what you want to order?"

"I want the pork chops," Katie said.

Joel turned his head.

"Ginny?"

"I may try the fish," Ginny said. She grimaced and put a hand on her stomach. "Why don't you two go ahead and order? I have to go to the ladies' room and may be a while."

"No problem," Joel said. "Take your time."

Ginny slid out of the booth and walked slowly to the other side of the establishment, where ornate wreaths and strands of colorful lights adorned a wall and holiday music streamed out of a console radio. She said something to a waitress in a red fur-lined dress and a matching cap and then disappeared around a corner.

＊ ＊ ＊ ＊ ＊

"Ginny hasn't been the same since Tom boarded that bus," Katie said. "I've never seen her this way."

Joel slumped in his seat.

"I can only imagine how she's feeling," he said. "How is Grace doing?"

"She's doing great. She's been dancing in the clouds since Thanksgiving. You two must have had a terrific time that day."

"Yeah," Joel said. "We did."

Joel let his mind drift to an afternoon and an evening he would never forget.

"It's funny how things work out," Katie said.

"What do you mean?"

"I mean you and Grace. I never saw you coming together when we first met. You belonged to Linda then. She had all but ordered the monogrammed towels."

Joel laughed and shook his head. A moment later, he sighed, smiled, and looked at his friend with admiration.

"How come you didn't offer to take Linda's place at the baseball game the time she got sick?" Joel asked. "We would have had fun."

"Oh, I know! I wanted to go. I wanted to say yes to Ginny's invitation, but I decided it would be safer to say no. I knew Linda would get better soon – and I didn't want to stand in the way of that freight train. So I made up an excuse."

Katie's eyes lit up as she recalled her one opportunity to date Joel Smith. She said she regretted passing up the game, but not too much. She insisted she was happy with how things had turned out.

Katie spoke more about the good old days until Santa's Helper came to the table with a ticket pad in hand. She gave the waitress her order, waited for Joel to give two more, and then resumed the conversation in a more serious voice.

"You've made Grace very happy," Katie said. "When she returned from Whidbey Island, she told me she had stopped looking. She said she had found the man of her dreams. She loves you very much."

Joel cringed when he heard the words. He knew now that dumping Grace would leave serious scars. He revisited the seemingly impeccable logic that had driven him to this point and wondered if it was too late to reconsider at least one of his decisions.

Then he heard an exchange in an adjacent booth that made him think of something else – something far more pressing. Two male students debated the inevitability of war with Japan. Joel saw Katie frown when one of the men raised his voice.

"Don't let them get to you," Joel said. "They're just scared. Everyone's scared."

"I'm all right," Katie said. "I don't think anything could be worse than the other night. I really appreciate what you did for me. Not everyone would have done that."

Joel nodded but did not respond to the comment. He instead pulled a sealed envelope out of his jacket pocket and gave it to Katie. The envelope contained twenty-five one-hundred-dollar bills.

"I want you to hold this until I get back," Joel said.

"What is it?" Katie asked.

"I'd rather not say. Whatever you do, don't lose it. Keep it in a safe place. If I return next week, bring it to me. If I don't, keep it. I know you'll put it to good use."

"It's a mystery. I love it!"

Joel offered a sad smile. Solving mysteries would soon be the least of Katie Kobayashi's concerns. He wondered how she would cope with the coming changes.

Joel discussed lighter matters with Katie until the waitress returned to their booth. She put three dinners on the table and quickly left the scene. A moment later, the men in the other booth followed suit. Katie eyed the pair closely as they headed toward the door.

"I'm not sorry to see them go," Katie said.

"Neither am I," Joel replied. He fidgeted in his seat, sipped his beer, and then focused on his friend. "Katie, I want you to promise me something."

"What's that?"

"Don't lose your faith in humanity."

"I don't understand," Katie said. "Why would I do that?"

"Because sometimes stuff happens that can test that faith. Sometimes good people do bad things for reasons that don't make sense. But it doesn't mean you should give up on them. I want you to remember that in the years to come."

"You're scaring me. Can you tell me what this is about?"

"No. I can't," Joel answered. "I've said enough. Just remember what I said. OK?

"OK."

"Now let's talk about something else. I see Ginny coming."

* * * * *

Ginny smiled weakly at Joel as she walked to the booth and reclaimed her seat. She sipped a flat beer and stuck a fork in her rapidly cooling dinner.

"Thank you for ordering for me," Ginny said.

"You're welcome," Joel said. "Do you feel better?"

"My *stomach* feels better."

Joel caught the omission immediately. He reached across the table, put his hand on Ginny's, and held it for a moment.

"I know this is hard," Joel said. "I miss him too."

"It's so damn unfair," Ginny said as her eyes began to water. "We were just getting started. I'm so angry with myself for squandering the summer. I should have spent more time with Tom and less on my stories. They mean nothing to me now."

"I know."

Joel kept his eyes on Ginny's even as she conspicuously avoided his. It pained him to see her like this. He remembered all the times she had comforted him after he had scraped a knee or blown a game or flunked a test and wanted to pay her back in spades.

Joel wanted to say, "Yes, Virginia, there is a Santa Claus, and I'm pretty damn sure he'll put Tom in your stocking on Christmas Eve," but he doubted even that would help. He knew there was little he could do to lift her spirits at this point.

"You know, one of the reasons I wanted to eat here tonight is because this is where I met Tom," Joel said. "Of course, I was sleeping on the bench out front, and he was getting pummeled across the street, but that doesn't make this place any less special."

Ginny laughed through her tears.

234

"What am I going to do with you?" Ginny asked. She took a breath. "I can see why Tom didn't want to leave you. He so enjoys being your friend."

"Can you visit him at the base?"

"Not until he gets out of boot camp. He has seven more weeks. If I'm lucky, I'll get to see him when he boards another bus."

Ginny dried her eyes with a napkin and looked at Joel.

"I'm sorry to burden you with my troubles. We should be talking about you and your reunion with your family."

"That's OK."

"When do you leave tomorrow?" Ginny asked.

"Early," Joel said. "Very early."

"Are you excited?"

"I'm nervous."

"You've never told me much about your family," Ginny said. "Maybe now is a good time. I seem to have a lot of time on my hands."

Joel wanted to discuss something else but saw that he couldn't. Ginny and Katie had already gathered around the campfire. So Joel proceeded to talk about his fictional Montana past as his rapt listeners set aside their very real problems.

The conversation lasted an hour. When it finally sputtered to a stop, Ginny and Katie looked at Joel with eyes that revealed admiration, fascination, and affection.

"Have you told your family about Grace?" Katie asked.

"Yes," Joel lied. "They know all about her and want to meet her soon."

"It's too bad she can't go with you," Ginny said.

"Yeah. I know," Joel said. He looked at the clock on the wall and then at his friends. "It's ten till eight. I should go."

"Can I at least get a hug?" Katie asked.

"Of course."

Joel put two ten-dollar bills on the table and escorted Ginny and Katie to an empty lobby. He embraced each of the women and then retrieved an envelope from his jacket.

"This is a card for Grace," Joel said to Ginny. He handed her the card. "If I'm not back by Christmas, give it to her then – but not a day sooner. It's very important."

"I'll take care of it."

Ginny tucked the card in her purse. When she looked again at Joel, she saw a man with a frown on his face.

"Just how long will you be gone?" Ginny asked.

"I don't know," Joel replied. "I may be gone a few days – or several weeks."

"I *will* see you again, won't I?"

Joel laughed to himself as he thought of the question. His second go-around with Virginia Gillette had finally come full circle. He gave her another hug and smiled as he put a hand on the door and started to leave. For once, he could offer the truth.

"That's one thing I can definitely promise," Joel said. "You will see me again."

62: JOEL

Joel drove Tom Carter's Plymouth to a small green house on the Ave, knocked on the door, and called on Grace Vandenberg for the last time. Grace invited Joel into the house and introduced him to four studious coeds before putting on her coat, gathering some papers, and leading her boyfriend out the door. She appeared harried but happy and more than ready to start her Friday night.

"Have you had dinner?" Joel asked as he started the car.

"I have," Grace said.

"Then what would you like to do? Go to a movie? Get some drinks? Go back to my place?"

Grace smiled and raised an eyebrow.

"My, my. You're an eager boy."

Joel laughed. He didn't have his mind in the gutter, but his matter-of-fact question had implied just that. He was getting slow in his old age.

"Let's get a drink," Grace said. "There's a new place that opened on Forty-Fifth. I'd like to see it."

Five minutes later Joel pulled into the lot of a windowless establishment called The Dungeon and escorted Grace through the door. They passed two suits of armor, three coats of arms, and two wenches carrying beverages on their way to a dimly lit table. The only visible sops to the twentieth century were a lighted jukebox by the emergency door and a Christmas tree by the cash register.

"This place reminds me of your hideaway in the library," Joel said.

"I see no similarities," Grace sniffed. "But it is rather interesting."

When a wench with attitude came around with a pad and a pen, Joel ordered a beer he could not pronounce. Grace selected a red wine she had favored for months. Joel pondered what to say next when the server left the table. When she returned with the drinks and left again, he decided to start with something safe.

"Did you finish your project tonight?" Joel asked.

"We did," Grace said.

"Do you wish we had gone to the ball?"

"I do. But I understand why we didn't. You have a long trip tomorrow."

Grace placed her hands on Joel's and pulled them across the table.

"The dance is not important. I'll have other opportunities to get dressed up. The main thing is that we're here, together, tonight. You're all I need."

The words hit Joel hard as doubt filled his mind. Could he really do this? Was he honorable or just plain insane? Who walked away from this? He stared at Grace and – for a moment – considered laying it on the line. Screw the consequences. He wanted to tell her the truth and wanted to do it now, but he couldn't. Joel scanned the room and saw about twenty other people. Some engaged in lively conversations. Most seemed happy. All were completely oblivious to what awaited the nation in less than forty hours.

"What are your plans for tomorrow?" Joel asked.

"I'm going to spend most of the day with Aunt Edith. I need a break from school. Other than that, I'm not planning anything special," Grace said. She tightened her hold on Joel's hands. "I'm going to miss you."

Joel did not reply to the comment. He instead gathered his strength, took a breath, and changed the subject.

"Grace?"

"Yes, Joel."

"Do you believe in time travel?"

Grace spit out some wine and burst into laughter. She took a moment to mop up a mess on the table with a napkin before returning to Joel.

"I'm sorry," Grace said as she fought off a giggle. "I didn't mean to be rude. I guess I was expecting you to say something else."

Joel turned red and berated himself for misreading the moment. When he should have been quoting Barrett and Browning, he was channeling H.G. Wells.

"That's OK. Forget I asked," Joel said.

Grace put a hand on his arm.

"Don't feel bad. Time travel is a fascinating subject. It's just not one I've considered. I'm not sure what I believe. There is so much about physics and the universe I don't understand. I suppose anything is possible. Why do you ask?"

Because I'm about to dump you for a time machine, that's why.

"I read something in the paper the other day and wanted your opinion," Joel said.

"Well, now you have it! Would you like my opinion on anything else?" Grace asked. She smiled. "If I have any more of this wine, I may find I have a lot to say."

Joel frowned.

"What's the matter, Joel? You haven't been yourself for a long time," Grace said in a serious voice.

"I'm all right," Joel replied. "I'm just a little nervous about the trip."

"You'll be fine. I know you will. You'll mend fences with your family and be all the better for it. I really would like to meet them someday."

Joel nodded.

"I know."

Grace gazed at Joel for a moment and then reached down to get her purse. She poked around inside, pulled out a red envelope, and pushed it across the table.

"What's this?" Joel asked.

"It's your Christmas present," Grace said. "I was going to give it to you when you got back, but I just decided that now was as good a time as any."

Joel picked up the envelope, looked at Grace, and forced a smile. He wondered if it were possible for his messy exit to get any messier.

He opened the envelope and pulled out a homemade Christmas card, which featured a line drawing of a snow-covered cabin on the front. The card could have come straight from the presses of Currier and Ives, but it came from a source much closer to home. Edith Tomlinson had scribbled her name in a corner.

"I commissioned my aunt to draw this for the price of some cookies," Grace said. She grinned. "She held out for a dinner."

Joel opened the card and saw a stick figure skier on each of the inside panels. The one on the left wore a dress, the other a wide-brimmed hat. Both skied toward the center of the card and a handwritten message:

"My darling cowboy, I'm glad we're finally sliding in the same direction. Merry Christmas! Love, Grace."

"As you can see, I'm not much of an artist," Grace said with a laugh. "But as Ginny likes to say, it's the thought that counts."

"It's beautiful," Joel murmured.

Grace tilted her head and stared at Joel as if trying to will a more upbeat response. When she didn't get one, she took his hands and looked at him with softer eyes.

"The card is not your gift," Grace said. "It's a *preview* of your gift."

Joel scolded himself again, this time for dragging a black cloud over their table. The least he could do is put on a happy face and play the part of a grateful boyfriend – or even an interested boyfriend. Was that asking too much? He looked at Grace and smiled.

She brightened and proceeded with a thorough explanation.

"When you return from Montana, we're going skiing. I've reserved a cabin on Mount Hood for the last weekend in January," Grace said. "There's a new resort there called Timberline. I've saved enough money for lift tickets, gas, and all of our meals. I want you to teach me how to ski. Tom said you know how."

Joel did not respond right away. He paused for a moment to consider the gift and the giver. He had enough cash in his wallet alone to take Grace to Timberline for a month. But she did not even consider asking for help. She wanted to do this on her own. Her generosity and thoughtfulness knew no bounds.

Joel looked at Grace closely and admired the wonder before him. He wanted to remember this night and remember that face. He wanted to remember that for a few happy, incredible months, he had truly had it all.

"I *do* know how," Joel said. "I've skied since I was five. I would love to teach you."

Joel meant it too. He meant every word. He could not imagine anything more enjoyable than teaching the girl who loved snow to love snow as never before.

What Joel imagined now, of course, didn't matter. Nothing mattered. He was merely wasting words and wasting time – and time was running out.

"I thought you would," Grace said. "We'll have so much fun. I know we will."

"We will," Joel replied with manufactured cheer. "Thank you for the present, Grace. It's perfect. You're perfect. You're the best thing that's ever happened to me."

Grace let go of his hands, slipped on her coat, and grabbed her purse. She lifted her empty glass, clinked it to his, and flashed him her signature smile.

"To us, Mr. Smith," Grace said. "Now take me home."

* * * * *

At nine fifteen, Joel parked the Plymouth in front of the rambler on Klickitat Avenue, set the brake, and stared out the windshield. He said nothing for more than a minute as a light drizzle outside and the breaths of two people inside quickly fogged the glass.

"What are you thinking about?" Grace asked.

"I'm thinking about the good times I've had here," Joel said. "I'm thinking about Tom and Ginny and Katie and the Carters and even Linda. But mostly I'm thinking about you."

Grace kissed his cheek and rested her head on his shoulder.

"Don't ever leave me, Joel," she said. "I couldn't bear it. I love you."

240

Joel heard the words but did not react. He occupied another place – a place where reason trumped the heart and duty dispatched the soul.

He held Grace in his arms for thirty mostly silent minutes and thought about the past six months, people and places that mattered, and big questions that continued to defy answers. He thought about actions and consequences, his capacity to change, and the irrepressible power of fate.

When Joel finally concluded that it was all too much to absorb, he loosened his hold on Grace and withdrew his arms. The time had come to let go. Joel opened his door and walked around the back of the car to open Grace's. Taking her extended hand, he helped her out of the vehicle and escorted her up the walk to the top of the concrete steps and a lighted doorway. Rain continued to fall.

When they reached the door, Joel turned to Grace, offered a weak smile, and gave her a tender, affectionate hug. But he felt neither tenderness nor affection. He did not feel a thing. He had emotionally sedated himself in advance of the parting and simply went through the motions. Emotion was a luxury he could not afford.

"Good night," Joel said.

"Aren't you coming in?" Grace asked.

"No. I should go."

Joel looked at her face and saw wide eyes and a dropped jaw. He could see that his answer was not the one she had expected. She clearly had another nightcap in mind.

"It'll be all right," Grace said. "No one's inside. Ginny and Katie went to the late show tonight. They won't be back for at least another hour. Please come in."

"I have to go," Joel insisted.

Grace grabbed his hand as he started to leave and stopped him in his tracks. She gently pulled him back to the top step and stared at him with eyes that projected surprise, bewilderment, and hurt.

"Joel, I'm asking you to stay," Grace said. "I may not see you for weeks. Be with me. Please."

The ardent plea brought Joel out of a self-induced stupor. The emotions he had so carefully repressed began to surface. He gazed at Grace and fought back tears as the final, inevitable waves of guilt, regret, and doubt crested and crashed. Joel could not believe it had come to this, but it had. Overcoming one last temptation to change his mind, he took Grace's hands, kissed her softly, and stepped back.

"I love you, Grace. I will always love you," he said. "Never forget that."

Joel released her hands.

"Goodbye."

63: GRACE

G race needed a pen but couldn't find one. She couldn't find one in Uncle George's Ford, in her purse, or in any of the places she had looked in her house on Klickitat Avenue. Dressed in her Sunday finest, she had just returned from Madison Park. She was in a good mood after joining Aunt Edith for church, a walk, and a delicious brunch, but that mood was starting to sour.

Grace had work to do. She had a school assignment to finish and that assignment required a pen. No matter where she looked, she couldn't find one. She couldn't find her housemates either, even at eleven thirty. Katie's bed was rumpled but unoccupied; Ginny's hadn't been used. She had spent the night elsewhere.

Still needing a pen, Grace walked to Ginny's roll-top writing desk and opened the center drawer. She found the pen she sought, some paper she needed, and something she hadn't expected to see: an envelope with her name on it. Thick and rigid, the item bore no address or other names – just the word "Grace" in a man's handwriting.

Grace removed the envelope from the drawer and walked to the kitchen, where she poured herself a glass of juice and sat down at a small table. She held the item up to the light and debated whether to open it before finally succumbing to curiosity.

Breaking a light seal, she opened the off-white wrapper and pulled out a Christmas card, a handwritten letter, and a small brown envelope that protected something round and hard. On the cover of the card she saw a candle in a wreath. In the pages of the letter she found the musings of a man, a man she sorely missed and had thought about all weekend. She pushed aside her glass and began to read.

"Dearest Grace:

I can't imagine anything more difficult than writing this letter. Saying goodbye is never easy. Admitting to lies is even harder. But today I have to do both."

Grace settled into the vinyl-covered seat of the chrome diner chair and reread the first paragraph. Whatever this was, it was not a pleasant holiday greeting.

"For six months I have passed myself off as someone I am not. I have changed lives and altered events and made messes I cannot possibly clean up. I did so knowingly and willingly and with little regard for anyone but myself."

Katie Kobayashi entered the residence a moment later with a quart of milk, a block of cheese, and a carton of eggs. She said "good morning" and put the groceries in the refrigerator before approaching her housemate. She slowed to a stop when she glanced at Grace and an opened envelope bearing her name.

"You weren't supposed to see that before Christmas, Grace. Joel was very clear."

"Well, it seems he's clear about a lot of things."

Grace closed her eyes and tried to process the facts as Katie stepped forward and put a hand on her shoulder. Joel had left for good, he had lied, and he had used her friends to deliver a message he didn't have the courage to deliver himself. Taking a breath and bracing for more, she picked up the letter and continued reading.

"I'm not from Montana. I'm not even from this time. I'm from Seattle and a future so distant that I have yet to be born. I am the grandson of Virginia Gillette."

Grace dropped the letter and pushed the envelopes away as rage swept over her face. She had read enough. She couldn't believe that a man she had loved so purely and completely could abandon her so flippantly and cowardly.

The future? Oh, Mr. Smith, you are a clever one.

Grace shook off Katie's hand, picked up the juice glass, and threw it into the sink, where it shattered into dozens of pieces. She got out of her chair, slammed a cupboard door shut, and paced around the kitchen until she heard the phone ring.

"I'll get it," Katie said, turning away from the broken glass.

"No. I'll get it."

Grace ripped the handset off the black rotary-dial phone and shoved it to her face.

"Hello?"

243

"Grace? Is that you?"

"Yes, it is."

"Oh, thank God I caught you. Have you heard the news?" Edith Tomlinson asked in a voice that was both measured and filled with stress.

"What news?"

"You had better sit down, dear."

"What news?" Grace asked more forcefully.

"Turn on your radio," Edith said.

Grace pulled the handset from her face and turned to Katie. She pointed toward a radio at the end of the counter and snapped her fingers.

"Katie, turn on the radio."

"What station?" Katie asked.

"I don't know. Just turn it on."

Katie moved swiftly toward an appliance that had not been used in days. She plugged it in, pulled it forward, and turned a knob. Within seconds, the reason for the fuss became clear.

"According to administration sources, the Japanese attack on the Pacific fleet, based at Pearl Harbor, began at 1:25 p.m. Eastern Standard Time. Additional reports to our studios in New York indicate a coordinated air assault on Ford Island, Hickam Field, Wheeler Field, and other military installations on the principal island of Oahu."

"I'll call you back," Grace said into the mouthpiece.

She took a moment to digest the shocking turn of events. The news seemed almost surreal. She had lost the man of her dreams and a country at peace in a single weekend.

Grace looked for Katie and found her staring out a rain-splattered window in the darkened living room. She could only imagine what was swirling through her mind.

Grace turned down the volume of the radio, returned to the table, and tried to clear her head. She retrieved the letter and picked up where she had left off.

"I can't explain it. I don't expect you to believe it. But it's the truth. I entered a glowing room in a mine in 2000 and walked out in 1941. I knew war was coming, just as I knew about Conn and DiMaggio and Williams. I knew Tom would enter the Army. I know his fate. I know how the war will end and how the world will evolve."

Grace spread her arms across the table as rage gave way to confusion. She picked up the Christmas card, closely examined the image on the front, and brought a hand to her forehead. Of all the possible cards Joel could have chosen, he had selected one displaying a single candle – a vivid

244

reminder of their first night together. What was he trying to say? Grace felt dizzy and nauseous but pulled herself together and continued to read.

"On December 8, I entered the same mine and returned to my time. I wanted to take you. I agonized for days. I never wanted to leave you. But I knew I did not belong in your world, just as I knew you did not belong in mine."

Grace paused to consider Joel's story. If true, it would explain his winning bets. But it was just as likely that he had been very lucky. Predicting war required less imagination. Many had warned of conflict for months. The claim he was Ginny's grandson was novel but backed by no proof. Grace found it far easier to believe that Joel had left her for something else, or *someone* else, than to believe he had traveled fifty-nine years through a hole in the ground. As she resumed reading, her anger slowly returned.

"I'm sorry I lied to you. I'm sorry I left. I'm sorry I could not have been the man you wanted. You deserve better. Just know that my feelings for you are real and that I will never forget you. I will never stop loving you."

Grace put the letter down and looked at the radio. The reports were more frequent now, more detailed. She thought of Tom and Ginny and then Paul. He had been stationed at Ford Island. She worried about his safety and questioned how she could have traded such a fine, honorable man for a charlatan she barely knew. She also thought about Linda and wondered if it was too late to make amends and restore their friendship.

She was about to go to Katie and provide much-needed comfort when she spotted the small brown envelope on the table. She had not bothered to open it and considered tossing it in the trash. No trinket from Mr. Wonderful could possibly make up for his lies and abandonment. But she opened it anyway. She tore off the sealed end, turned the envelope upside down, and watched a small, strange-looking token drop to the table.

Grace picked up the item and saw it was a coin, a golden coin, an American dollar. The piece appeared freshly minted and bore the image of a stoic young woman with a sleeping infant strapped to her back. The woman was striking, angelic, the picture of innocence. But it was a number on the front of the coin that arrested Grace's attention. It was a date she had never seen. It was the year of the millennium, a year that Joel had mentioned in his letter, a year six decades away.

Grace grabbed the table and tried to steady herself as her head swam and her body went limp. She dropped her arm to her side and let the coin fall to the floor. She stared blankly out the kitchen window as the tears began to flow.

64: JOEL

Lewis and Clark County, Montana – Monday, December 8, 1941

The ride to the mine was a relatively quiet affair, which was just fine with Joel. After leaving Grace on her doorstep Friday night, he had not wanted to talk to anyone, whether train passengers or waitresses or hotel clerks or pedestrians asking if he had heard details about Imperial Japan's attack on U.S. military installations in Hawaii. He just wanted to go home and put an awful weekend behind him.

As the cab driver turned off the highway onto Gold Mine Road, however, Joel asked him to turn on the radio. President Franklin Delano Roosevelt's war address to the nation streamed through the rattling speakers. He figured he might as well get his last bit of history while the getting was good.

The driver, an older, less talkative version of Witty Pete, stared at him through the rear view mirror but did not say a thing. He did not ask him about the war or the speech or why a young man who should have been standing in a recruiting office was instead asking for a ride to an abandoned mine in sub-freezing weather.

He did, however, say it would cost extra to negotiate the goat trail. Joel did not mind. Unlike his last trip out, he had plenty of money and was more than happy to pay whatever it took to get to the mine. He gave the driver a ten-dollar tip and a twenty to wait near the entrance for thirty minutes.

At eleven twenty Joel stepped out of the cab and walked up a muddy road past Bonnie and Clyde's Ford and three structurally safe buildings to an unobstructed hole in Colter Mountain. Except for a few puddles in the lot and snow on the treetops, the scene looked virtually unchanged from the previous May.

Joel had considered wearing warm clothes but decided against it. He still did not understand the mechanics of this geologic wormhole and did not want to needlessly increase the odds of failure, whether that meant failing to return to the future or failing to return intact. So he wore the same clothes going in as he had coming out and purged images of *The Fly* and *The Philadelphia Experiment* from his mind. Candy in Chains and the cattleman crease cowboy hat would ride again.

For the same reason, Joel left behind virtually all of his personal belongings from 1941 – including the Christmas card from Grace – and did not bring a flashlight. He figured that his knowledge of the mine and the bright morning light would be enough to get him to the magic room – or at least close enough to crawl. He entered the adit at 11:25 a.m. Mountain Time, just as he had on May 29, 2000.

The precautions paid off – or at least did no harm. About halfway to his destination, Joel saw a faint blue light that he had feared existed only in his mind. When he reached the chamber, he saw another comforting sight. The flashlight he had abandoned lay exactly where he had dropped it. It threw light on an entrance with a low-hanging beam.

Joel picked up the flashlight. He directed its beam toward the back of the room and saw his favorite reptile. All was right with the universe.

Despite the presence of the snake, Joel walked a few feet into the chamber and placed his hands on the cold, shimmering rock. He figured any gesture that might improve his chances of getting home was worth the risk.

For five minutes Joel inspected the cavity, keeping a healthy distance from his venomous companion. The place was as mysterious and fascinating as ever. But a more thorough examination would have to wait for the next planetary alignment. Satisfied that he had gone through a sufficient number of motions, Joel saluted the rattler, ducked under the low-hanging beam, and exited the room.

Once in the main tunnel, Joel noticed two things he had not noticed before: dirt on his clothes and a dull ache in his head. He put his hands on his temples to stifle the pain but found that the pressure only made matters worse.

Since when did I get migraines?

Joel steadied himself, flipped the flashlight to its brightest setting, and proceeded through the adit. He walked just twenty feet before another shoe dropped. The room at his back with the soothing blue glow exploded in a violent spasm of blinding white light.

Joel fell to his knees, dropped his head, and covered his eyes. The flash exacerbated his headache tenfold and launched a galaxy of shooting stars. Then, just that fast, it was over. The painful white light disappeared, taking the soothing blue glow with it. The magic room lost its magic. Studio 54 went black.

Eager to escape the mayhem, Joel picked up his step. He wondered what the light show was about. Had he left his troubles behind or found new ones? Would he see 2000 at the end of the tunnel – or 1882? Just how precise was this time machine anyway?

Joel didn't wonder for long. As he drew closer to the outside world, he noticed that the light was brighter and the air was warmer. The rails and beams took on a familiar, weathered, abandoned appearance. So did the side passage. Even the bats assumed their usual posts.

When Joel reached the entrance, he saw a jagged breach in a boarded barrier. His handiwork had not been disturbed. Confirmation that he had returned to the right time and place came seconds later, when he passed through the narrow opening, stepped into the welcoming sunshine, and saw his best friend sitting on a boulder.

"Where the hell have you been?" Adam asked.

"How long have I been gone?"

"Thirty minutes, at least."

"Just thirty minutes?"

"Yeah. Which means you're twenty-five minutes late," Adam said. He climbed down from the rock. "What did you do? Take a power nap?"

Joel initially dismissed the flippant comment. Adam had a right to be pissed. But when he thought about the specific reference to sleep, he considered a possibility that now seemed as plausible as ever. What if his sojourn through 1941 had been nothing more than a crazy dream brought on by a bump on the head? Perhaps like Dorothy in *The Wizard of Oz* he had simply experienced some high-quality REM action.

"I was gone just thirty minutes?"

"That's what I said. Do you want a prize or something?"

Joel smiled. Adam had not lost his toxic tongue. He was still a smart-ass in a Red Sox jersey. But was everything else as it appeared?

Seeking definitive answers, Joel walked to the parking lot and looked for anything that might support the power nap theory or at least confirm that he had come back to the same planet. He recalled the fascist society that had greeted the returning time travelers in "A Sound of Thunder" and decided he could do without something like that.

When Joel reached his red Toyota, he found it as he had remembered it. Two mountain bikes hung on a black metal rack in back and partially obscured a "Visualize Whirled Peas" sticker on the bumper. He peered inside and saw a CD by R.E.M. protruding from the disc player and a copy of the Helena paper from May 29, 2000, lying on the dash. A Memorial Day tribute filled most of the front page. Nothing was written in German or Russian or some crazy language that might have evolved from a date with Grace Vandenberg.

He scanned the premises and saw more of what he expected to see. The buildings at the mine had broken windows and serious structural issues and the lot was empty. No rusting Ford sat among the weeds. Bonnie and Clyde's getaway car had gotten away.

There was every reason to believe that Adam's estimation was spot on, which cast serious doubt on what Joel had thought was a real experience. He could not have possibly crammed six months of 1940s living into thirty minutes. Grace, Ginny, Katie, Tom, and others had been nothing more than pleasant figments of his imagination. When the two piled into the SUV, Adam tapped anxiously on the glove box and checked his phone. It had run out of power. He whined about his sunglasses.

"Can we go to the Canary now?"

"Sure," Joel said. "Just let me get my bearings. I think we can go back and still be home by midnight. What time is it?"

"I don't know. My phone just died. It's probably close to noon."

Adam looked at Joel.

"Where's your watch?"

249

65: JOEL

Joel looked at his dinner and laughed. He loved fried chicken. He craved it, in fact, even though his mother had never put it on her table. She had never prepared it. She had never bought it – not in recent memory anyway. Cynthia Smith did not serve fried chicken.

Yet when her son came home for the first time since returning from Yellowstone, she did just that and in the process created a humorous scene. Instead of delectable wings, thighs, and drumsticks, Joel found Sunday supper at the Carters and déjà vu in a bucket.

"I hope you don't mind, honey," Cindy said as she hurriedly set the table. "Our tennis match with the Larsons ran long, and this was convenient. I'll do better tomorrow."

"It's no problem, Mom," Joel said. He laughed again. "I love this stuff. I eat it at school all the time. You should do this more often."

"I will if you come *home* more often."

Cindy gave Joel a scolding glance and removed his cowboy hat. She put his dinner-inappropriate souvenir on a coat hook and then joined her son and her husband at the table.

Fried chicken was not the only reminder of the trip that never happened. Furniture stores conjured images of ventilating mattresses. When Joel picked up a book, he thought of Grace and the Crypt. He associated Army recruiting advertisements with Tom.

Yet he no longer believed he had traveled back in time almost sixty years. The disappearance of his watch was a problem, to be sure. So was the presence of three crisp 1934-series hundred-dollar bills in his wallet. But to believe he had passed through a portal to his grandmother's time, spent six months building a new life, and then returned to the present while his friend twiddled his thumbs on a boulder was a bridge too far.

Joel Smith, man of science, subscribed to Occam's razor and therefore had a professional obligation to support the theory that made the fewest assumptions. And that theory was that he had taken one hell of a nap.

His skepticism had grown following a Tuesday visit to the yearbook section of the university library. Grace Vandenberg had not been pictured or listed among the 1938 graduates of Westlake High School or the 1942 graduates of the university. Joel could find no evidence that the blue-eyed blonde had ever walked the earth. Nor could he, with the same resources, prove the existence of their friends. Someone had removed several pages from the 1941 and 1942 university yearbooks, including the portraits of the seniors.

Joel planned to investigate the matter further, but he was in no hurry to do so. With each passing day, he thought more about graduating, finding a job, and getting his summer under way than about making sense of the past. By late Saturday afternoon, he thought only of his stomach. He glanced again at his dinner, inhaled its distinctive aroma, and dove in. He was glad to be home.

"Did you have a good trip, son?" Frank Smith asked.

"I did," Joel said.

"That's quite a hat you brought back. It reminds me of the one I wore the summer I worked on a ranch in Idaho."

Joel looked at Cindy, smiled, and then turned back to the graying but remarkably fit fifty-one-year-old to his right. His old man had his undivided attention.

"You worked on a ranch?" Joel asked.

"I did, for several months, before I joined the Navy, before I married your mother," Frank said. "It was hard work, but it was one of the best experiences of my life."

Joel laughed to himself. He hadn't lied. He was a rancher's son, after all.

"How come you never mentioned that before?"

"You never asked."

Cindy beamed.

"Grandma used to needle your father about that job. She said no daughter of hers was going to marry a cowboy. She meant it too."

"She didn't like cowboys?" Joel asked.

"Oh, I don't know about that. But she did like interrogating my boyfriends. Your father didn't meet her expectations for quite some time. Grandpa liked him though."

Frank sighed.

"Your mother was a tough bird."

Joel smiled and stirred the food on his plate. He loved learning little tidbits about his parents and the grandmother who was no longer around to defend herself.

"Are there any other sordid family secrets I should know before I graduate?"

"No," Cindy said. "I think that covers it. Your father gave up the life of a cowboy for the Navy. It's kind of a shame. He looked good in that hat."

Joel looked at his dad, who clearly wanted to steer the conversation in a different direction, and then at his mom, who clearly did not. Like many women, and all good wives, she knew how to keep her man on his toes. Just like Virginia Gillette Jorgenson – *and Grace Vandenberg.*

Joel was tempted to delve more into his father's wrangler past. He could picture Frank Smith working on a ranch. He could picture him enjoying it.

But Joel was far more interested in digging into the life of someone he had not seen in five years. Despite his conclusions about the mine and his real or imagined journey to 1941, he had thought a lot about his grandmother in the past few days and had many new questions about her. Ginny's apparent distaste for cowboys only fueled the fire.

"Mom, did Grandma leave any personal things behind when she died?" Joel asked.

Cindy turned her head.

"Like what?"

"You know, the usual stuff – pictures, letters, scrapbooks, things like that."

"She did. I haven't gone through all of it. But I know there's a large box in the attic full of keepsakes from her college days, including dozens of photographs."

Joel swallowed hard, lowered a drumstick to his plate, and stared blankly into space. He suddenly had a lot more to chew on.

"Do you mind if I see it?"

"Of course not," Cindy said. "But don't you have to study for your finals?"

"I do. But I can get to that tomorrow."

Joel took a breath, pushed his plate away, and faced his mother.

"I'd really like to see that box."

* * * * *

Twenty minutes later Cindy Smith carried a sturdy cardboard container into the shrine of a bedroom that was her son's home away from home. Joel sat on his waterbed, surrounded by trophies, books, consumer electronics, and posters of rock bands, sports stars, and supermodels.

"This is all I could find, but it's everything," Cindy said. She eased the box onto the bed. "At least I *think* it's everything."

"Thanks, Mom," Joel said.

252

"Let me know if you need anything else."

"I will."

When his mother left the room, Joel opened the box and found things he expected to find. Ginny Gillette had saved a lot from her college career, including letters, photographs, programs, pressed flowers, newspaper articles, and what looked like the silver bar of an Army lieutenant.

Joel started with some letters and cards at the top of the heap. He read several dull notes from Ginny's parents from 1939 and 1940 and more lively correspondence from 1941, including a tersely worded message that mentioned a man named Tom. Victoria Gillette did not seem enthused about her daughter's new boyfriend and counseled "patience."

When the wellspring of letters ran dry, Joel moved on to the articles. He handled the brittle, yellowing clips, loosely arranged in a manila folder, with the care of a surgeon. He found one story about poverty on campus and another about the fight against polio.

Two more pieces examined the lives of Japanese students at the university. Near the end of the second story, Ginny quoted a senior named Katherine Kobayashi – the colorful, humorous, and opinionated president of the Hasu Club.

Joel pushed the box away as a knot formed in his stomach and a sinking feeling he thought he had left in a dusty mine came rushing back. Could he do this? Could he finish the box? He looked out his bedroom window at the leafy street beyond and decided he could.

The photographs provided no relief. Joel picked up one and saw Ginny with a sorority sister who looked like a date from his make-believe past. He wondered whether the girl with the engaging smile, freckles, and long hair had a first name that started with an L.

Another picture showed Ginny with a young man who had heretofore existed only in Joel's mind. The man was shorter than Joel and a few pounds heavier, but he was an otherwise nice-looking guy with a baby face, a strong jaw, and short hair that was parted to the side.

Several more photos followed, including one of Ginny with the same man at the ocean. Written on the back of that snapshot was the name Tom Carter.

But the worst was yet to come. As Joel dug through the dozens of prints, he came upon several of Virginia Gillette with a sunny blonde. He did not know whether her eyes were crystal blue or whether she was the daughter of missionaries or liked movies or holding hands, but he did know one thing. He had seen her before.

Joel delved deeper and found a composite photo of the Kappa Delta Alpha sorority from 1940-41. Pictured in the middle of the third row was the sunny blonde, a young woman named Grace Vandenberg. Additional photos showed the woman at play: "Grace in dorm room," "Grace and

Linda at Lake Union," "Grace at rush dinner," and "Grace and Paul at spring dance."

Joel gazed at two large posters on the far wall. Cindy Crawford looked better than ever. So did Naomi Campbell. As he eyed the posters, though, Joel thought not about models from the 1990s but rather a figment of his imagination from the 1940s – a beautiful, pleasing, and deserving figment he had left on a cold, wet doorstep.

He moved quickly to the smoking gun. At the bottom of a stack of photographs stuffed in an envelope was a snapshot that brought his world to a crashing halt: "Grace and Joel at Seaside." The college-age man in the picture had wavy dark-brown hair, chiseled features, and a boyish grin that Joel had often seen in a mirror.

Joel closed his eyes for a moment and leaned back on the bed's headboard as he tried to put down a fresh round of nausea. He spread his arms across the covers for balance as someone knocked on the door and slowly pushed it open.

Cindy stuck her head through the door and peeked inside.

"I'm sorry to bother you, honey, but I just heated up some apple crisp and wanted to know if you would like some. Your father and I are going to watch a movie."

Cindy opened the door wider and took a closer look at her son. She saw a young man with a pale face and blank eyes.

"Are you all right?"

Joel took a deep breath and turned to face his mother.

"No. I'm not all right. I feel sick to my stomach."

"Do you want me to get something?" Cindy asked.

Joel shook his head.

"I can manage for now," he said. "But I want you to stay."

"OK."

Cindy entered the room and walked to the waterbed. She sat on the hardwood frame, leaned toward Joel, and put a hand on his clammy forehead. She saw several photographs of Virginia Gillette scattered on top of the bed.

"Did you learn anything interesting about Grandma?"

Joel pondered the question and did not know whether to laugh or cry. He thought of the things he could tell his mother – and a lot of other people – if only he could retain his sanity.

"I did," Joel said. "She had quite a life."

Cindy smiled sweetly.

"Yes, she did."

"Did she ever say much about her college days?" Joel asked.

"No," Cindy said. "That was one thing she rarely talked about – at least to me. I think it had a lot to do with Tom Carter, her fiancé. I told you about him once. He died in the war."

"Yeah, I remember. But did she ever mention her friends or the things she did?"

"No. I asked her about them too. I asked her a lot of questions about college when I was a high school senior, but she would talk only about academics and the newspaper. She never discussed her sorority or her social life."

"Did you ever wonder why?" Joel asked.

"Of course. She was my mother. But there was no point in pestering her. I figured she had probably had a bad experience and did not want to talk about it. Who knows? But whatever the reason, I suspect it went beyond Tom Carter."

"Why do you say that?"

"Because she was tight-lipped about everyone, including her girlfriends," Cindy said. "Years ago, when you were just a baby, I saw a photo, like some of these here, at her house. She was sitting next to two girls her age. I'm sure it was from college. But when I asked her about the picture, she ripped it from my hands and said it was none of my business."

"She really said that?" Joel asked.

"She really said that."

Cindy examined the prints on the bed until she found one that apparently grabbed her interest. Undated and unmarked, it showed Katie, Ginny, and Grace sitting on lawn chairs on a deck behind a house that still stood on Klickitat Avenue. Cindy picked up the photo.

"This is the one. I remember the lawn chairs."

Cindy handed the picture to Joel.

"Do you know who the other girls are?" Joel asked.

"I'm almost certain the one on the left is Katherine Saito," Cindy said. "I met her at the funeral. She was an old friend of Grandma's and a very nice woman. I haven't seen her since, but she sends us a Christmas card every year. She lives in Portland."

Joel held the photo in front of him with both hands and ran his right index finger over each of the three smiling subjects. He let the digit linger over the blonde at right and then tossed the picture in the box.

"I miss her," Joel said.

Cindy sighed.

"I do too."

Cindy again put a hand to Joel's forehead, fluffed his pillow, and then slid off the edge of the bed. When she got to the door, she looked back at her child – the last to leave the nest – and asked if he wanted lemon-lime soda for his stomach.

"No. I'm good," Joel said. "I feel better now. Thanks."

Cindy nodded.

"OK. If you change your mind about the apple crisp, let me know."

Joel watched his mother give a reassuring smile as she closed the door. When he heard her reach the end of the hallway and start down a flight of creaky stairs, he pushed the photos and letters off his bed and did something he had not done in five years. He wept.

66: JOEL

Saturday, June 10, 2000

The stone had changed little since last he had seen it. The elements had marred its polished finish and dirt had collected in a few of its recessed letters, but the marble monument was as impressive as ever. A tiny American flag, stuck in the ground nearby, flapped in the gentle breeze. Put there by volunteers on Memorial Day, it was a reminder that Joseph Jorgenson had served proudly in the United States Marines.

But on the sunny spring day before he graduated from college, Joel Francis Smith focused on the other half of the marker, the one dedicated to Joe's wife, Cindy's mother, and a woman who had done two tours of duty in the life of a mixed-up man.

As Joel stood before the final resting place of Virginia Gillette Jorgenson, high on a hilltop in a leafy cemetery in Madison Park, he asked the questions that had to be asked. Had she known? Had this intelligent, resourceful woman put the pieces together? Had she figured out that her beloved grandson was the same young man who had abandoned her friend in 1941? Could she have set aside skepticism about time travel or reincarnation long enough to admit that the two Joel Smiths of her life were one and the same?

She had been seventy-five when she died of lung cancer but had kept her wits to the end. Surely she had noticed that the seventeen-year-old boy at her deathbed bore a striking resemblance to her one-time friend. It is also possible that Grace had removed all doubt by showing her his letter or revealing its contents. In that event, Ginny would have known the truth from the start. Whatever the case, she had kept her thoughts to herself. She had died a stranger even to her husband and three children.

Joel pulled a clean rag from the back pocket of his jeans and gently wiped the engraved portion of the three-foot-high gravestone. He thought about his mother's words at dinner the week before. Ginny Jorgenson clearly had no use for ranchers and cowboys, and Joel just as clearly understood why. He had let her down. He had let all of them down. He tried to convince himself he had bolted for the noblest of reasons – reasons that were not difficult to find. Who would not want to see his family again? What honorable person could interfere with the lives of people he was never supposed to meet?

Yet Joel knew that his decision to run was rooted in a whole lot more. He had not wanted to serve in World War II and possibly leave behind a widow and a fatherless child, just as he *had* wanted to return to the comforts of a familiar, modern age. He wondered how many lives he had altered, particularly for the worse. Staring again at the stone, he conceded that he had altered at least one. Whether he had changed more was an open question. After taking his last final exam the previous day, Joel had driven to the downtown public library and tried to learn more about his long-lost friends.

Some answers had come quickly and easily. Army Lieutenant Thomas Carter had indeed died in the sands of Tunisia but not before saving eight soldiers in his platoon from certain slaughter. The furniture salesman and playboy who had frequently and openly questioned his own courage had been awarded the Distinguished Service Cross, posthumously, for uncommon valor in the Battle of Kasserine Pass.

Paul McEwan had survived Pearl Harbor but not the war. He had died in early 1945 at a hospital in the Philippines after contracting malaria. From Paul's obituary and other records, Joel had learned that Linda McEwan Rogers had married a naval officer and settled in Bremerton. She had taught for forty years in the public schools there, retiring with great fanfare in 1982. According to a local newspaper article, she had twice been named the school district's educator of the year. She was presumably still alive.

So was Katherine Kobayashi Saito. Joel did not need to spend an afternoon in a library to learn her whereabouts. He had the Christmas card she had sent his parents six months earlier. Katie lived in Portland, Oregon, with her husband, Walter. She had four children, sixteen grandchildren, and a great-grandchild on the way.

Even before reading the card, Joel had decided to contact Katie soon. If there was one person in his former circle of friends still willing and able to receive him, it would be the woman to whom he had left twenty-five hundred dollars.

There would be no contacting Edith Green Tomlinson. She had died a childless widow in 1960. Joel had found her lengthy obituary in the *Sun*, but it left him with more questions than answers. Edith had been preceded in death by her husband, her parents, and a twin sister, and survived by a brother-in-law and "legions of fans in the Seattle arts community," but apparently by no one else. Grace had not been listed among the deceased or the survivors.

And so the mystery continued. Joel had found no evidence that Grace had graduated from Westlake High School or the university or had even attended a sorority reunion. She had not been listed in any directories or vital records indexes or made the newspaper, as far as he could tell, in any way, shape, or form.

He had recognized up front the limits of searching for a person who probably carried a married name and who may have even left the country. Grace herself had said she had been happier living overseas. He would not at all have been surprised to see her name on a roster of Peace Corps volunteers. But on June 9, 2000, her name could not be found in any public records. She existed only in photographs and memories.

Joel finished wiping the gravestone and straightened Joe Jorgenson's flag. It was the least he could do for a grandfather who had taught him to fish and appreciate the virtues of patience, humility, and tolerance.

He took one last look at Ginny's name and asked her for forgiveness. He knew it was probably an empty gesture. If there was an afterlife, Ginny was badgering reporters at the *Heaven Gazette* and not hanging around a slab of marble. But he asked anyway. If nothing else, Joel needed to hear himself say the words. He needed to run through this hoop and others to achieve the one thing that still eluded him. Closure.

67: JOEL

Monday, June 12, 2000

S he looked better than a soon-to-be-ex-girlfriend had the right to look. Fresh from her summer job as a lifeguard at Green Lake, Stanford Law-bound Jana Lamoreaux walked into the Mad Dog wearing a white tight-fitting blouse, a denim skirt, and sandals that accented legs that belonged on a billboard.

Joel had long appreciated her year-round features, like her long brown hair, amber eyes, and olive skin that would always play well with a jury. But for some reason, he thought they looked even better the day after they had graduated from college.

"Sorry I'm late," Jana said.

She slid into the unoccupied half of a secluded booth, grabbed the pitcher of India Pale Ale that Joel had ordered minutes earlier, and poured a perfect pint.

Joel marveled at the ease with which she handled suds. Jana could pour a gallon of beer into a teacup and not spill a drop or leave a head thicker than a quarter of an inch. Like Ginny Gillette, the former beauty queen was a girl who could play with the boys, on their turf, and not leave an ounce of her femininity on the sidelines.

Joel had picked the Mad Dog as the venue to discuss their future because it was comfortable, convenient, and symbolically important. It was where they had started.

They had met in the same booth in the spring of 1998 as sophomores with fake driver's licenses, obnoxious friends, and a desire to put recent, painful breakups behind them. Joel hadn't needed any coaxing to better acquaint himself with the vivacious history major. Jana was as beautiful then as she was now and shared a number of his interests, from football and fishing to the Gilded Age and the Enlightenment. Staring blankly at a poster on the wall, he drifted to better times and better places before she reeled him back to the here and now.

"How did your interview go this morning?" Jana asked.

"It went well, kick-ass well," Joel said. "But I won't get the job."

"Why?"

"They want someone with more experience."

"You're kidding. What do they call a summer internship?"

"A step in the right direction."

Joel loved the irony that had followed him through the entire interview process, which had run nearly three hours. In fact, he had thought of little else all day.

Granted, he did not have experience in the oil industry. He did not have much experience in *any* geology-related industry. But he did have knowledge that could turn the entire field on its head. Joel thought of the fun he could have had educating his interviewers about fluorescent rock chambers that sent young men hurtling to the age of Rosie the Riveter. Had he not wanted the job, he might have said something. He would have enjoyed the moment immensely.

Joel sipped his beer and surveyed the establishment. The Mad Dog was as old as the Canary in Helena and just as popular. But it had gone in a much different direction over the years. Whereas the Montana diner had embraced the past, the campus watering hole had charged into the future. Instead of Depression-era jukeboxes, brass cash registers, and celebrity photos, it boasted modern lighting, data ports, fifteen televisions, and sushi. Only its name and its exterior had not changed. Tom Carter would not have recognized the place.

"Do you have any more interviews lined up?" Jana asked.

Joel nodded.

"I have one with a natural gas outfit. It's in two weeks, which is probably a good thing. I figure I have a month before the commander sends me to a recruiter."

"Your dad never lets up, does he?"

Joel chuckled.

"I'd think less of him if he did. What about you?" Joel asked. "Do you have any glorious plans before the Farm gets its hooks into you?"

"My parents want to take me to France in August. They insist on rewarding me for graduating," Jana said. She paused. "I'll probably go."

Joel raised a brow.

"Probably?"

"OK. Duh! Of course, I'll go. Who turns down Paris, right?"

Jana laughed and then sighed.

"What I'm looking forward to most, though, is working another summer at the lake and spending more time with you."

261

Joel smiled sadly. She wasn't making this easy.

Jana gazed at Joel for several seconds and brightened.

"I've missed that."

"Missed what?"

"Your smile. I haven't seen it for a while. I thought you left it in Wyoming."

"It's that obvious, huh?"

"Joel, you haven't smiled in weeks. You haven't been the same since you got back, and you've been particularly quiet lately. Do you want to tell me what happened?"

Do you want all six months or Adam's condensed version?

"I've just been stressed about finals and the interview."

Joel kicked himself. His pathetic explanation was technically true, but it was about as complete as the face of the Great Sphinx. Would he fib his way through the twenty-first century too? Fortunately, Jana didn't seem to care.

"Well, maybe we can do something about that."

Joel topped off his glass and looked at Jana's earnest face. He could see wheels spinning behind her playful eyes and knew she had brought her own agenda to the pub.

"What do you have in mind?" Joel asked.

"I was thinking about a nice, long hike in the Olympics. Rachel and Adam are going backpacking this weekend at Sol Duc and want us to come along. It would just be for three days, but I think it would do you some good. It would do *us* some good."

Joel considered the message and the messenger. Jana had correctly sensed the drift in their relationship and wanted to right the ship. But he had asked her to the pub to increase the distance between them, not decrease it. As much as he wanted to go hiking and maintain some kind of continuity, he wanted to be fair to her.

Even so, he didn't want to needlessly burn any bridges. Joel laughed to himself. Just the thought of that metaphor took him to a sunny meadow on Mount Rainier and a rainy doorstep only seventeen days and a stone's throw away.

Joel looked at his smart, lovely, considerate girlfriend and wondered what the hell was wrong with him. What kind of man dumped Miss Mercer Island? The problem, he concluded, wasn't Jana Lamoreaux or stress or an aversion to hiking in national parks. The problem was poor timing. He had not gotten over Grace.

Joel also had other plans for the weekend. Even before interviewing for the oil company position, he had decided to take one last journey to purge his mind of unhelpful memories of a time and a place to which he could never return. Unlike decisions about his future with Jana, that was a matter that could not wait.

"The backpacking trip sounds like fun. It sounds like a *lot* of fun," Joel said. He took a breath. "But I think I'll take a rain check."

Jana slumped in her seat and pushed her glass aside as her infectious smile gave way to an uncommon frown. She turned away for a moment and then looked at Joel with tears in her eyes.

"We're not going to make it, are we?"

Joel sank when he saw the tears. He hated pushing her back. He hated causing her pain. Jana deserved better – a lot better – and would no doubt find it in Palo Alto.

"I don't know," Joel said. "I really don't. I just know I have a lot of thinking to do and need some time alone. I'm still looking for answers."

"OK," Jana said. She smiled sadly. "I hope you find them."

68: JOEL

Portland, Oregon – Saturday, June 17, 2000

The journey began with a last-second detour. Joel had not planned to visit Katie Kobayashi Saito on his way to the coast. He had not planned to visit her on his way back.

He had instead planned to clear his mind of complications and clutter and then write a long letter easing his way in. Time travelers did not reestablish contact with long-lost friends by suddenly showing up on their doorstep. But as he caught U.S. Highway 26 and slogged through traffic on the west end of Portland, Joel succumbed to temptation.

Why come all this way, he thought, just to put off the inevitable for another day? When he approached the exit at Cornelius Pass Road, he threw caution to the wind and turned north.

A few minutes later Joel drove his RAV4 up a crooked access road to a small collection of pricey properties overlooking the lush Tualatin Valley. He checked a few mailbox numbers and finally pulled into the brick U-shaped driveway of a Tudor estate.

Japanese maple trees, azalea bushes, and fountains in the spacious front yard gave the place an unmistakable tea-garden feel, as did ruler-straight rows of weeping cherry trees on two sides of the property. Joel checked the mailbox again to confirm that he had not entered one of Portland's botanical parks.

Katie Kobayashi, your ship has come in.

Joel walked past a Mercedes in the driveway to a short wrought-iron fence. He opened the gate and continued up a stone path to a tiered brick porch and an imposing oak door. The mat under his feet read: WELCOME TO THE SAITOS. He rapped on the door, but no one came to greet him. No one answered his second knock either – or a doorbell that sounded more like a wind chime than a ding-dong. Joel walked along the front of the house to a large bay window. He peered inside but saw nothing of interest.

So he proceeded to the side of the house, where he peeked over a six-foot cedar fence and scanned an empty yard. Still convinced that someone was home, Joel moved to unlatch the gate and give the premises a more thorough inspection. But when he heard a menacing growl, he stopped and then withdrew. He knew that even an enlightening meeting with Katie was not worth an unpleasant encounter with a Rottweiler.

"They're not home."

Joel turned and saw a thirtyish woman wearing pink sweats and a ponytail stride up the driveway. She had the friendly but guarded demeanor of a soccer mom.

Joel returned to the path and moved briskly toward the wrought-iron gate and the driveway. He met the woman in front of the Mercedes.

"They're not home, and they won't be home until Monday," Soccer Mom said. "I'm their neighbor. The Saitos asked me to watch their place this weekend. Can I help you?"

"I'm here to see Mrs. Saito," Joel said. "She was a good friend of my grandmother's. I have some personal matters I need to discuss with her."

The woman put an index finger to her chin and stared at Joel, as if trying to decide whether young men who looked like underwear models were the kind who cased houses. A moment later, she smiled and extended a hand.

"I'm Jennifer Swingley."

"Joel Smith."

"Do you know the Saitos?" Jennifer asked.

"I met Mrs. Saito years ago, but I've never met her husband. Like I said, she knew my grandmother. She died in 1995. Have the Saitos lived here long?"

"I think so. I've been here only three years, but I know that their house is the oldest on this street. I don't think anyone else has lived in it."

"You say they'll be back on Monday?" Joel asked.

Jennifer nodded.

"Katherine said noon at the latest."

Joel pondered his options. Though he had planned to return to Seattle on Sunday, he saw no harm in delaying his trip by a day.

"Would it be all right if I left a note with you?"

"Of course," Jennifer said. "Do you need a pen and paper?"

"No. I have both in my car. Hold on a moment."

Joel returned shortly with a note bearing his name, address, and two phone numbers. He handed it to the woman, who quickly looked it over.

"You live in Seattle?" Jennifer asked.

"I do."

"Are you sure Katherine will remember you?"

"She'll remember me," Joel said. "You can be sure of that."

Ninety minutes later Joel checked into a downtown Seaside motel and unloaded a small suitcase, a laptop computer, and a toiletry bag in a room he had reserved on Monday. The joint fell four stars shy of optimal. The carpet was stained, the curtains were torn, and the toilet ran slightly better than the bulky, dust-covered television. The only gym he could see was the one attached to a grade school across the street. But that was OK. Joel had come to exorcise ghosts, not exercise his body.

The town had added just three thousand residents since his last visit, in 1941, but looked much different. Many of the hotels and establishments he remembered had been torn down, remodeled, or reused for other purposes. Only the aquarium and a few businesses on Broadway had remained largely unchanged. After grabbing a quick lunch at a seafood grill two blocks from the beach, he took a cab to Tillamook Head and a house that still stood in his memory, if nowhere else. The lot near the towering bluff now sported a condominium complex and a craft shop, not the magnificent vacation home that had remained in Gillette family hands through the 1960s. But Joel could feel the vibes. He had been here before and did not need a deed or a key or a photograph to prove it.

Joel felt foolish snooping around the premises. No matter how hard he looked, he would not find Ginny tossing a salad in a kitchen or Tom barbecuing steaks on a deck in back. But he continued to check the place out until a groundskeeper gave him a funny look and started pressing buttons on a cell phone. Rather than wait to be asked to leave, Joel wandered to a path near the parking lot and followed it down two flights of cedar steps to an appealing stretch of sand. He didn't need permission to walk on *this* ground. Thanks to a tenacious and enlightened governor named Tom McCall, Oregon's beaches belonged to the public.

Though the temperature was cooler than the last time he had explored this shore, Joel was more than comfortable in jeans and a long-sleeved sweatshirt. When he reached the beach, he kicked off his flip-flops, threw them in his pack, and walked barefoot the rest of the way to the south end of the Promenade. Once on the concrete walk, he began a slow trek toward town and let the serious reminiscing begin.

There was a lot to think about. This was, after all, the place where Joel and Grace had gone from silly to serious and from friends to something much more. It was the place where he rediscovered someone he thought he knew and where their friends made a commitment that would change how all of them looked at a perilous world.

As Joel drew closer to the center of town, he thought of his long Promenade walks with Grace and the things they talked about. He thought of her disappointment with Ginny, her enthusiasm for the carnival rides, and the poignant descriptions of her parents. Most of all, he thought about how incredibly stupid he had been to throw it all away and not take her to a future where they both belonged.

When he reached the Turnaround, he dodged two inline skaters and walked out of traffic to the edge of the Prom. He could almost see Grace sitting on the railing telling him why her mother would have loved him and why her father might have liked him. But almost was not close enough. He could not touch the face of a daydream. When he leaned on the barrier and looked out at the sea, he saw the sea and only the sea – that vast, timeless, perfect symbol of constancy and emptiness. Moments later he looked at the moving sky and noticed change. The sun had emerged from a large bank of clouds, bringing welcome warmth to those in swimsuits, T-shirts, and shorts. Finding a short flight of steps, Joel accessed the beach and once again put his bare feet on the soft sand. He began another walk. Only this time he headed west, not north, and moved at a slower pace.

Ten minutes and two hundred yards later, Joel reached the waves at low tide and the end of his journey. He had hoped the water would be like this. He counted on it even. There was nothing like this kind of surf to bring about the finality he needed. Rolling up his jeans, Joel slowly waded into the Pacific. The foot-high water was cold, colder even than Puget Sound, but tolerable. Then again, he had not come to swim.

Turning northward, Joel followed the water's edge to a spot where a beach-ball-sized rock protruded from the sand. He stopped in front of the rock and let the salt water invigorate his feet before pulling a snapshot from his back pocket. Slightly torn on one side and badly faded, the photograph represented everything he had gained and lost in a year that still defied explanation. It was the sole surviving evidence that Joel had ever known and loved a daughter of missionaries; a girl who rode elephants in Africa, splashed mud in the Yangtze, and threw snowballs in July; a woman who loved movies, books, bumper cars, and jazz; a kind, brave, principled soul who had overcome the worst kind of adversity to inspire others and make an indelible impression on a frequently thoughtless, cavalier, and superficial young man.

Joel placed the photo in the water and let the surf do the rest. The picture bobbed, twisted, and curled before finally sinking from sight. Joel gave the image one last thought before turning his back on the ocean and starting for town. He had made his peace with God and the girl. It was time to move on.

69: JOEL

Seaside, Oregon

Joel wanted to go home. After symbolically burying six months that would never be recorded in a family history book, he did not want to hang around a town that reminded him of that time. He did not want to see the amusements or the attractions. He just wanted to climb into his car, race back to Seattle, and resume his life as a mixed-up, unemployed, heartbroken man. But he had already paid for his motel room and figured that was reason enough not to run from his problems. So he stayed.

When he returned to the motel, he asked the clerk for a restaurant recommendation. The rough-looking woman named Bette gave him three – four if you count the biker bar on the edge of Seaside that served "killer bacon burgers" but could get "a little raucous at times." Joel figured the bar was his kind of place and wrote down its address before heading off to his room.

He watched television for more than an hour, flipping between the third round of the U.S. Open, the Mariners-Twins game, and *Sci-Trek: Dinosaur Attack!* When he became bored with all three, he walked to his second-floor window and glanced at the street below. No matter where he looked, he saw people – people eating, shopping, driving, walking, and even sitting on a bench playing chess. Most probably did not know each other. Most probably did not care. But all no doubt had one thing in common. They were having more fun than Joel Smith.

When Joel saw a young couple walk by holding hands and laughing, he threw the TV remote across the room and said the hell with it. He was going to pack his bags, leave Seaside, and drive back to Seattle as fast as he could. He was going to call Jana, apologize profusely, and take her out on the town. He was going to make crazy love to her – and then plan the next day.

Joel was sick and tired of being sick and tired. He looked at the digital alarm clock, saw four thirty, and started grabbing toiletries and clothes. With any luck, he would be back in Seattle by nine. Then he glanced at the room phone and saw a blinking light.

* * * * *

A few minutes later, Joel examined a scrap of paper in the motel office. It bore a message that was as clear as it was mysterious: "Be at the Turnaround at five." There was no name or number or even a clue as to who might be stalking him on his weekend getaway.

Bette wasn't much help either. After apologizing for not informing Joel of the message when he had returned from the beach, she told him that another clerk had taken the information and was presently unavailable. Joel did not know whether the caller was male or female, young or old, or even sincere. For all he knew, Adam was paying him back for skipping the hiking trip.

In the end, it did not matter. Joel had an appointment and intended to keep it. He slipped the note into his wallet, walked to where Broadway met the sea, and waited.

For more than twenty minutes, Joel watched hundreds of people walk down the Prom. The waterfront was crowded, even for a Saturday afternoon, which made his guessing game all the more difficult. He had no idea who – or what – he was looking for, so he just leaned against the railing and continued his vigil.

Then at five after five, Joel looked north along the Promenade and saw a woman move slowly his way. He didn't recognize her at first, but he suspected she was someone he knew. When she drew near, he looked at her and smiled. It had been a long time since he had seen her beautiful face, but not so long that he had forgotten its distinctive features. Joel pushed himself away from the railing and addressed his stalker.

"Hi, Katie."

The newcomer smiled.

"I want more than that, young man."

Joel grinned, stepped forward, and gave her a warm embrace.

Katie appeared smaller than the perky coed from the past. She had a slight hunch and walked with a cane, but she seemed otherwise fit and sharp. It was clear from her greeting that her wit had not dulled since the Roosevelt Administration.

"You've grown," Katie said. "But you're just as handsome as the last time I saw you."

"You mean at the Mad Dog in forty-one?" Joel asked.

"No. I mean at your grandmother's funeral. I greeted you as I left the church. You stood next to your parents in the receiving line."

"I wish I could say I remember that, but I can't."

"That's all right," Katie said. "You met a lot of people that day."

Joel stepped back and took another look at his long-lost friend.

"How on earth did you know I was here?"

"I called your mother. I told her I wanted to send you a graduation present and needed an address. During our conversation, she said you planned to drive to Seaside this weekend. When I asked if I could give you the gift in person, she gave me the name of your motel."

Joel laughed.

"That's my mom, the protector of my privacy."

"I also spoke to my neighbor. She called me from Portland," Katie said. "It appears you visited my house this morning."

Joel sighed.

"I had to see you. I've been going insane the past few weeks. You were the only one I could talk to about 1941 without getting sent to a funny farm. Even then, I wasn't sure you wouldn't treat me like a loon. How did you learn the truth?"

Katie smiled sweetly.

"I read the letter you left for Grace. I read every word," Katie said. "Even so, I did not completely believe your story until the year you were born. When Ginny told me that your parents had named you Joel, then I believed."

Katie moved her head, as if looking for something, and then glanced at Joel.

"May I sit? I don't have much energy these days."

"Of course," Joel said. He escorted Katie to a nearby bench, sat at her side, and draped an arm over her shoulders. "Can I get you anything?"

"No. I'm fine," Katie replied. "I just need to sit."

"You read my letter?"

"I did. I read it right after Grace did, shortly after Pearl Harbor was attacked."

Joel looked away for a moment.

"I'm sorry I left like I did. I just knew I couldn't stay."

"I understood," Katie said. "Grace did too. She had difficulty at first believing the time-travel thing. That required quite a leap. But then there was Pearl Harbor and that coin. They gave your story the ring of truth."

"That means a lot to me to hear that," Joel said.

Katie patted his knee.

"I'm glad."

Joel smiled.

"So you came all the way from Portland just to give me a gift?"

"Of course not. I wanted to see you!" Katie said with a laugh. "I figured by now you would remember me and that you would not mind meeting in a venue like this. Seaside is such a beautiful place. I assume your family knows nothing of your experience."

"No one does," Joel said. "They would lock me up if I told them the truth."

Katie put her cane to the side and reached into her large purse. After digging around for a moment, she pulled out an envelope that contained a card and a snapshot.

"Happy graduation," Katie said.

Joel looked at the card, laughed, and then examined a picture he had taken in July 1941. In the photo, Ginny, Grace, Linda, and Katie, arm in arm, smiled for the photographer before Linda's date with Joel at Lake Wilderness. Joel took a deep breath and stared into the distance.

"I remember that day as if it were yesterday. I remember the people too. You were perfect – all of you. You were four gorgeous, happy, amazing women who brought joy to my life," Joel said. He kissed Katie on the cheek. "Thank you."

"You're welcome."

Joel took a moment to observe the flow of pedestrians. It had not diminished since he had walked to the Turnaround, but that was all right. As far as he was concerned, he and Katie had the world to themselves.

"Katie, what became of Grace?"

The old woman retrieved her cane, tapped it on the concrete, and then held it upright. She clearly was gathering strength for a difficult discussion.

"I knew you would ask. It is one reason I had to speak to you in person," Katie said as moisture filled her eyes. "I'm afraid there is not much to say. Grace left Seattle shortly after you did. She said nothing could ever be the same without you. So she left. She took your departure hard – very hard. I did not hear from her again for many years. She loved you, Joel. We all did."

"Is she still alive?" Joel asked.

"She is. But her situation now is not good. It's not good at all. But before I say more, I want to introduce you to my husband. He is back at the hotel," Katie said. "Come."

70: JOEL

The sitting room of the Oceanfront Inn was meant not for sitting but for gawking. The plush furniture, fountains, artwork, plants, and rugs were so over the top that Joel had to wonder why anyone went outside. According to a plaque on the wall, most of the furnishings had belonged to a turn-of-the-last-century railroad baron. But Joel saw at least a few pieces that could have come directly from Carter's Furniture and Appliance. Clinging tightly to Joel's left arm, Katie guided her friend to a silk-upholstered sofa. She sat down, settled into one end of the couch, and retrieved a cell phone from her spacious purse. A moment later, she pressed a few buttons and began a short conversation.

"We're here . . ."

Joel sat down and, for the next few minutes, looked at the figure in the flowered dress. When he did, he saw two different women: the talkative, witty college girl he had known in 1941 and a dignified matron no doubt forged by a lifetime of challenges. He suspected that Katie had faced some tough times after Pearl Harbor, but he was just as certain she had overcome whatever history and misguided people had thrown her way.

Joel started to ask Katie a question but stopped when he saw someone open the door to the lobby and walk into the sitting room. He knew even before Katie smiled that the person was her spouse. Joel got up, helped Katie to her feet, and escorted her to the middle of the room, where they met the man who had built the impressive house on Portland's west side.

Katie jumped right in.

"Joel Smith, this is my husband, Walter Saito. Walter, this is Joel."

The men shook hands.

"It's a pleasure to meet you," Walter said. "Katherine has told me much about you."

"I'll bet she has," Joel replied. "It's a pleasure to meet you too."

The three walked to the couch and a facing armchair in the back of the room. Joel and Katie sat on the sofa. Walter took the chair.

Joel studied the man who had married Katie Kobayashi. No more than five feet seven, he had thinning hair, discolored skin, and the slow gait of a typical octogenarian. Though he was casually attired in cream-colored slacks and a green polo shirt bearing the name of a Portland country club, he projected class. Joel could plainly see that Walter Saito was a man of substance.

"I met Walter at Camp Minidoka, Idaho, in 1942," Katie said. "Our families were interned there during the war."

"I'm so sorry," Joel said. "I can't imagine what that was like."

"There is no need to apologize. You did not put us there. But you did help us rebuild our lives when we got out."

Katie turned toward her husband and gave him a knowing nod. She watched intently as Walter pulled an envelope from his back pocket and handed it to Joel.

"What is this?" Joel asked.

"This is your real graduation present," Katie said.

Joel opened the envelope and saw a check, made out in his name, for ten thousand dollars. He frowned, shook his head, and then looked at the elderly couple.

"I can't take this. This is a ridiculous sum."

"It's a pittance. I can never repay what you did for me, for both of us."

"I gave you some cash, Katie, that's all."

"To you, it may have been nothing. But to me, it was everything," Katie said. "After the war, I used the money to put Walter through law school. When he got out, he represented many Japanese who had lost their homes and businesses – including my parents. We created a foundation that still helps Nisei and Sansei, the children and grandchildren of those who came to this country. We've done much good with very little."

Joel smiled, threw an arm over Katie's shoulders, and pulled her in. He felt a lot less like a failure than he had a few hours earlier.

"I'm glad I could help."

"It wasn't just the money either," Katie said.

"What do you mean?"

"You gave me advice. You told me to keep my faith in humanity and never give up on those who might injure me through ignorance. I was very bitter when I entered the camp. I was angry with people I did not know. But I remembered your words and channeled that anger in a positive direction."

When Joel heard the testimonial, he wanted to put Katherine Kobayashi Saito in a box and take her home to Frank and Cindy. He wanted to show his parents that his greatest accomplishment in life had not been graduating from college but rather influencing a giant of a woman.

"You're incredible," Joel said.

"Perhaps," Katie said. "But I am a woman with regrets, many regrets. I cried the day Grace left Seattle. I had grown so fond of both of you and, just like that, you were gone. I questioned whether I could have done more to keep you together. I blamed myself for adding to your troubles. There is so much I wanted for you. It saddened me greatly that you were not able to grow old together and experience the treasures of married life."

"I wanted those things too," Joel said. "Believe me. But I think I did the right thing."

"I know you did. You thought of others before yourself."

Joel hugged Katie again. When he released her, he looked at Walter in a way that suggested both had done right by befriending this woman. Then he sighed and mentally prepared himself for a subject that was surely on all of their minds.

"Katie, tell me about Grace."

The old woman lifted her head, stared briefly at a painting on a wall, and then turned to face Joel. She offered a thin smile that revealed not joy but deep sadness.

"As I said, it was years before I saw her again. She contacted me out of the blue. She wasn't what I had expected," Katie said. "We did not have as much in common as we had in college, but we still had a bond. She was troubled and frightened but had the same spirit I had always admired."

"Did she speak of me?" Joel asked.

"Of course. She spoke of little else. She never married, you know. She never came close. You were the love of her life."

Joel closed his eyes and took a breath. This was the other side of the ledger. All the good he had done in the past could not erase his failings.

He remembered his first day in 1941, the walk down Gold Mine Road, and his vow not to disrupt the lives of others. He wondered if it were even possible to screw up the life of Grace Vandenberg any more than he had done in only six months. The bull in the china shop had broken a lot of dishes.

"You said she was still alive," Joel said. "Where is she? I want to see her again."

"And so you shall," Katie said.

She looked at her husband.

"Walter, please bring her in."

The old man got out of his chair, hesitated, and stared at his wife, as if to ask, "Do you really want to do this?" Seeing no change in her expression, he walked to the entrance, opened the door, and disappeared from sight.

"She's here?" Joel asked.

"She's here," Katie said. "But before you see her, I want you to open your mind. I want you to remember her as she was in college, when we were all at our best. She may not be what you expect. Nineteen forty-one was a long time ago."

Joel got off the couch and extended an arm to Katie, who had already collected her cane and her purse. He helped her up and then escorted her to the open space in the sitting room, where they stood on a large oriental rug and waited.

When Walter returned a minute later, he had a woman on his arm. He guided her slowly through the arched doorway and toward the center of the room, but he stopped when she pulled up, released his arm, and fixed her eyes on the others fifteen feet away.

Following several seconds of awkward silence, Katie stepped away from Joel and gave him some space. She looked at Grace and then at Joel and spoke.

"I believe you two know each other."

For a moment Joel could do nothing but stare. He instantly recognized the wistful eyes and a tentative smile that would stand out from Astoria. He also recognized a blue gingham dress he had last seen on a memorable night in a dark little house that no longer existed. But nothing else matched his expectations.

Katie, now beaming with a look that screamed "payback," had painted a grotesquely misleading picture. The woman standing before Joel did not appear physically frail or emotionally broken. She was radiant, fit, and breathtaking. She was twenty-one years old.

"It's you," Joel said.

"It's me," Grace replied.

Joel looked at the Vision of Forty-Seventh Street with shock and awe. Even dressed modestly with tears streaming down her face, she could not have looked more beautiful. Joel gazed at her a little longer – long enough to truly make sense of what he saw. Somehow, someway, she had made it.

When Grace raced forward, Joel rushed to meet her. He gave her the hug and kiss he should have delivered that rainy night, the hug and kiss that should have preceded a run to Montana and a shared future that was always in the stars. He pulled back, shook his head, and repeated the greeting.

"I'm so sorry, Grace. I can't even find the words."

"Then don't," Grace said as she wiped her eyes. "Don't apologize. I understand why you left. Just tell me I haven't made a mistake. Tell me you love me."

Joel smiled broadly and laughed to himself. Even now, after all he had done, she gave him the benefit of the doubt.

"Are you kidding? I love you so much it hurts. I've thought of nothing else since I left. I've been miserable," Joel said. He clasped her hands. "It's really you."

"It's really me," Grace said.

"But how?"

"I opened your card on December 7 and flew to Helena that night with money Katie gave me. I said goodbye to Aunt Edith and Ginny and left. Your letter was like a road map."

Joel looked at her face – her smiling, tearful, honest face – and tried to read more, but he could not. There was something missing, something that did not make sense.

"But it's not possible," Joel said. "It's not. Even if you left in time, you could not have known where to go. I never named the mine. There must be hundreds in Montana."

"There are *thousands*," Grace said. "But there was only one Buick dealer in Helena. He remembered you and where he'd picked you up. He was very helpful."

Joel smiled at Grace and then at Katie. He thought of her Oscar-worthy setup of this incredible scene and wondered what he could ever do to repay *her*. Then he thought of the other woman who was surely in the room, the one who had a stake in all of their lives, the one he should have heeded in the first place.

"Beneath that delicate exterior is a strong, resolute woman who does nothing halfway. Never take her for granted and never underestimate her. She will amaze."

Grace pulled her hands from Joel's and then put them on his face. She met his eyes, smiled, and gave him a tender kiss that brought a different kind of closure.

"You left me some crumbs," she said, "and I picked them up."

Made in the USA
Las Vegas, NV
28 December 2020